PRIZE STORIES 1955

The O. Henry Awards

PRIZE STORIES 1955: *The O. Henry Awards*

Selected and Edited by

PAUL ENGLE *and* HANSFORD MARTIN

Doubleday & Company, Inc., Garden City, N.Y., 1955

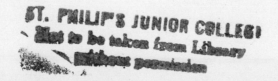

SC
P961
1955

Library of Congress Catalog Card Number 21-9372

8868

PUBLISHER'S NOTE

The present volume is the thirty-fifth in the O. Henry Memorial Award series, and the second to be edited by Paul Engle and Hansford Martin. No collections appeared in 1952 and 1953, when the continuity of the series was interrupted by the death of Herschel Brickell, who had been its editor for ten years.

In 1918 the Society of Arts and Sciences met to vote upon a monument to the American master of the short story, O. Henry. They decided that this memorial should be in the form of two prizes for the best short stories published by American authors in American magazines during the year 1919. Originally thought of as just these two prizes for a single year, the memorial promptly became an annual anthology of the best American short stories. With the exception of the two years mentioned above, it has been published by Doubleday & Company continuously ever since. Blanche Colton Williams, one of the founders of the awards, was editor from 1919 to 1932; Harry Hansen took over from 1933 to 1940; and Herschel Brickell edited the collection from 1941 to 1951.

The stories chosen for this volume were published in the period from August 1953 to July 1954 and subsequent volumes will also cover the period from August through July. A list of the magazines consulted appears at the back of the book. The choice of stories and the selection of prize winners is exclusively the responsibility of the editors.

CONTENTS

After the three prize stories the order is alphabetical by author

INTRODUCTION, 9

In the Zoo, Jean Stafford, First Prize, 15
THE NEW YORKER

A Circle in the Fire, Flannery O'Connor, Second Prize, 35
KENYON REVIEW

The Tiger, Frederick Buechner, Third Prize, 53
THE NEW YORKER

The Unpopular Passenger, Robert Bingham, 62
THE REPORTER

A Christmas Carillon, Hortense Calisher, 68
HARPER'S MAGAZINE

The Inland Years, R. V. Cassill, 85
WESTERN REVIEW

The Five-Forty-Eight, John Cheever, 103
THE NEW YORKER

Miss Cudahy of Stowes Landing, George P. Elliott, 117
HUDSON REVIEW

The Operator, Elizabeth Enright, 141
HARPER'S MAGAZINE

Man of Distinction, Mary Dewees Fowler, 155
ACCENT

Twilight in Southern California, Daniel Fuchs, 173
THE NEW YORKER

Joshua, Shirley Ann Grau, 190
THE NEW YORKER

The Green Fly, John Graves, 215
TOWN & COUNTRY

The Presence of Grace, J. F. Powers, 226
ACCENT

The Shirts off Their Backs, William Henry Shultz, 248
ESQUIRE

The Wanton Troopers, Max Steele, 262
HARPER'S MAGAZINE

The City of the Living, Wallace Stegner, 278
MADEMOISELLE

The Indomitable Blue, Ira Wolfert, 291
ESQUIRE

MAGAZINES CONSULTED, 312

INTRODUCTION

First prize for the best short story: To Jean Stafford, for "In the Zoo," published in *The New Yorker*.

Second prize: To Flannery O'Connor, for "A Circle in the Fire," published in *Kenyon Review*.

Third prize: To Frederick Buechner, for "The Tiger," published in *The New Yorker*.

Only a few writers have Jean Stafford's vision: to see childhood not in the tradition of Wordsworthian, or Tarkingtonian, splendor, but in the equally valid sense of a trap, from which one escapes by the fortunate accident of growing. And few have her ease of prose, her warm comic insight, and her generous care for all manner of people.

There is probably no young writer today who is creating a more important body of fiction than Flannery O'Connor. "A Circle in the Fire" is a perfection of the two tendencies in all her writing: the exposition of evil and the celebration of justice. It has that clarity which comes with the writer able to stand close enough to the story's characters to catch the full fleshy tissue of their particular predicament, and yet maintain a distance sufficient to realize the generally human in the specific incident. The reader who seeks the quick juicy thrill of emotional identification will not always find it. But what he will find, chastened by the cold honest tang of the author's special humor, is the flawed surface and the troubled depth of real people.

There is depth, too, beneath the humor of Frederick Buechner's "The Tiger." This addled hero has caught in his own confused way the feeling for one of America's lost paradises, an age which combined horseplay with genuine gaiety of spirit. "The Tiger" is an expression of what F. Scott Fitzgerald defined as "romantic readiness . . . an infinite capacity for hope." In this story the hope still lives below its joke and under the grotesque skin of the tiger.

THE SHORT-STORY SCENE

In 1895 *Collier's* serialized *The Turn of the Screw* by Henry James. The editors guess that no magazine would serialize it today. The publishing situation for the short story is changing rapidly, and the editors wish to discuss it briefly here.

The disappearance of such small but hopeful publications as *Furioso, The Hopkins Review,* and *New Story* proves a plain fact: the United States, in this crucial time of its cultural maturing, has no national literary magazine, in which the finest writing of our many talents can be widely circulated, the creative balancing the critical, and the short story not creeping shyly in between articles on the appalling political scene today. We need such a magazine desperately, and wish that one of the great foundations, which do so much that is useful for the survival of the race in terms of better sanitation in primitive countries, would devote the relatively small amount of money it would take to enhance the chances of literature surviving in this country. It is all very well to urge the brave writer to take his chances in the market place, but there is a limit to the beatings even his thick skull can take.

A close reading of American magazines in the past year shows clearly that short-story publishing has diminished. When daily reality is so dramatic, how can imaginary tales compete with the factual article? People quite properly want to know what they can about the astonishing plight they are in, and articles (which are expertly done) seem to offer solid truth, in contrast to the slippery fancies of fiction. When the evening newspaper pours the icy water of the world's reality down the reader's back, why should he not warm himself with dependable articles by those who know a little more about the nature of fire than he does?

But the American short story goes right on its brilliant and energetic way. Even if the "popular" magazines seem to be turning more strongly toward the more popular (with occasional but untypical exceptions), good things do turn up in them. And although the "literary" journals seem far less interested in imaginative writing than in critical, they do publish stories of genuine talent and often by the young writer.

A few statistics (just to imitate the article itself) may help to explain the position of the short story lately. *Harper's Bazaar* and *Mademoiselle* have for a long time printed excellent stories, their literary fashion being as alert and handsome as their clothing fashions. But in the first six months of 1954, *Harper's Bazaar* published six stories by European authors and only three by American. *Mademoiselle* continued its admirable story contest for college women, but from September of 1953 through July of 1954 it published only ten stories (two issues did not have a single story, although it was triumphant to print Dylan Thomas' verse play, *Under Milk Wood*). Of these ten, five were by Americans and five by foreign writers. This is not to argue for choosing short stories on a narrowly national basis. Editors must print the best stories where they find them, and we are all enriched by reading the work of our contemporaries abroad. But as the total number of stories in magazines of quality decreases, so does the number by Americans, and thus the number available for inclusion in this volume.

The literary quarterlies, such as the *Kenyon Review*, with rare exceptions, publish only one or two stories an issue. A recent number of *The Sewanee Review* contained one hundred and sixty-one pages of criticism and only twenty-nine of fiction, in a single story. This tremendous excess of criticism over the creative seems a great pity, and not at all the way to encourage those new writers who alone, ultimately, will make criticism possible.

The editors can always count on finding a good crop of fine stories in *Harper's Magazine*, and yet this admirable publication is also printing fewer stories. Its issue for May 1954 contained five major articles, seven pieces on travel, and one short story.

A further curious truth is that popular magazines are much more daring in their articles than in their fiction. Although they will print substantial studies of such subjects as homosexuality or juvenile delinquency, in their fiction they largely stick to obvious situation and type character. We ask these magazines two questions: Won't you print more stories that examine the human situation as seriously as your articles do? Will the same mind among your readers be equally interested in the excellent articles on human problems and in the superficial stories of quick sentiment?

This split has also invaded such wide-selling men's magazines as *Argosy, Adventure, Blue Book,* in which stories are often of a surprising literacy, as far as style is concerned, and of an intricate accuracy about the construction of Boulder Dams, the operation of Fiat motors, the navigation of atomic submarines. But the emotional framework in which stereotyped characters move is often as morally simple and as predictable as the gentler stories of the ladies' magazines. The brothers are sisters under the skin.

The plight even of the popular writer is worse. *Today's Woman,* which printed a fine level of stories, is no longer published. *Collier's,* where one looked for interesting examples, now issued but twice monthly, has followed the trend of featuring factual and pictorial articles and de-emphasizing fiction. The changed policy and status of these two magazines alone means that in a single year at least a hundred less short stories appeared.

The New Yorker goes on printing, in the midst of many stories of a very similar air, many which are witty and wise and moving. As our selection of five stories (two of them prize winners) from *The New Yorker* indicates, we respect its continuing publication of short stories of quality in abundance.

The proportion of stories about childhood remains high. It may be that reality seems more fixed and certain in childhood than in the naughty and explosive adult world.

We hope that this book shows that, no matter what the difficulties and however varying the market, even when he is kicked in the teeth, The Writer can still bite.

We wish to thank the following for helping us with this volume: Donald Justice, Jane Cooper, Henri Coulette, Robert Robertson, and Cynthia Pickard.

Paul Engle
Hansford Martin

PRIZE STORIES 1955

The O. Henry Awards

JEAN STAFFORD *rose to immediate literary prominence with the publication of her first novel,* Boston Adventure, *in 1944. Two others,* The Mountain Lion *and* The Catherine Wheel, *followed in 1947 and 1950. Her stories have appeared regularly in* The New Yorker *and similar magazines, and a collection,* Children Are Bored on Sundays, *was published in 1953. Born in 1915, in Covina, California, she was educated at the University of California and the University of Heidelberg. She has received two Guggenheims, in 1945 and 1948, and a grant from the National Institute of Arts and Letters. She is working on a new novel for her publishers, Harcourt, Brace & Co.*

IN THE ZOO

FROM THE NEW YORKER

Keening harshly in his senility, the blind polar bear slowly and ceaselessly shakes his head in the stark heat of the July and mountain noon. His open eyes are blue. No one stops to look at him; an old farmer, in passing, sums up the old bear's situation by observing, with a ruthless chuckle, that he is a "back number." Patient and despairing, he sits on his yellowed haunches on the central rock of his pool, his huge toy paws wearing short boots of mud.

The grizzlies to the right of him, a conventional family of father and mother and two spring cubs, alternately play the clown and sleep. There is a blustery, scoundrelly, half-likable bravado in the manner of the black bear on the polar's left; his name, according to the legend on his cage, is Clancy, and he is a rough-and-tumble, brawling blowhard, thundering continually as he paces back and forth, or pauses to face his audience of children and mothers and release from his great, gray-tongued mouth a perfectly Vesuvian roar. If he were to be reincarnated in human form, he would be a man of action, possibly a football coach, probably a politician. One expects to see his black hat hanging from a branch of one of his trees; at any moment he will light a cigar.

The polar bear's next-door neighbors are not the only ones who offer so sharp and sad a contrast to him. Across a reach of scrappy grass and litter is the convocation of conceited monkeys, burrowing into each other's necks and chests for fleas, picking their noses with their long, black, finicky fingers, swinging by their gifted tails on the flying trapeze, screaming bloody murder. Even when they mourn— one would think the male orangutan was on the very brink of suicide —they are comedians; they only fake depression, for they are firmly secure in their rambunctious tribalism and in their appalling insight and contempt. Their flibbertigibbet gambolling is a sham, and, stealthily and shiftily, they are really watching the pitiful polar bear ("Back number," they quote the farmer. "That's *his* number all right," they snigger), and the windy black bear ("Life of the party. Gasbag. Low I.Q.," they note scornfully on his dossier), and the stupid, bourgeois grizzlies ("It's feed the face and hit the sack for them," the monkeys say). And they are watching my sister and me, two middle-aged women, as we sit on a bench between the exhibits, eating popcorn, growing thirsty. We are thoughtful.

A chance remark of Daisy's a few minutes before has turned us to memory and meditation. "I don't know why," she said, "but that poor blind bear reminds me of Mr. Murphy." The name "Mr. Murphy" at once returned us both to childhood, and we were floated far and fast, our later lives diminished. So now we eat our popcorn in silence with the ritualistic appetite of childhood, which has little to do with hunger; it is not so much food as a sacrament, and in tribute to our sisterliness and our friendliness I break the silence to say that this is the best popcorn I have ever eaten in my life. The extravagance of my statement instantly makes me feel self-indulgent, and for some time I uneasily avoid looking at the blind bear. My sister does not agree or disagree; she simply says that popcorn is the only food she has ever really liked. For a long time, then, we eat without a word, but I know, because I know her well and know her similarity to me, that Daisy is thinking what I am thinking; both of us are mournfully remembering Mr. Murphy, who, at one time in our lives, was our only friend.

This zoo is in Denver, a city that means nothing to my sister and me except as a place to take or meet trains. Daisy lives two hundred miles farther west, and it is her custom, when my every-other-year visit with her is over, to come across the mountains to see me off on my eastbound train. We know almost no one here, and because our stays are short, we have never bothered to learn the town in more than the most desultory way. We know the Burlington uptown office and the respectable hotels, a restaurant or two, the Union Station, and, beginning today, the zoo in the city park.

But since the moment that Daisy named Mr. Murphy by name our situation in Denver has been only corporeal; our minds and our hearts are in Adams, fifty miles north, and we are seeing, under the white sun at its pitiless meridian, the streets of that ugly town, its parks and trees and bridges, the bandstand in its dreary park, the roads that lead away from it, west to the mountains and east to the plains, its mongrel and multitudinous churches, its high school shaped like a loaf of bread, the campus of its college, an oasis of which we had no experience except to walk through it now and then, eying the woodbine on the impressive buildings. These things are engraved forever on our minds with a legibility so insistent that you have only to say the name of the town aloud to us to rip the rinds from our nerves and leave us exposed in terror and humiliation.

We have supposed in later years that Adams was not so bad as all that, and we know that we magnified its ugliness because we looked upon it as the extension of the possessive, unloving, scornful, complacent foster mother, Mrs. Placer, to whom, at the death of our parents within a month of each other, we were sent like Dickensian grotesqueries—cowardly, weak-stomached, given to tears, backward in school. Daisy was ten and I was eight when, unaccompanied, we made the long trip from Marblehead to our benefactress, whom we had never seen and, indeed, never heard of until the pastor of our church came to tell us of the arrangement our father had made on his deathbed, seconded by our mother on hers. This man, whose name and face I have forgotten and whose parting speeches to us I have not forgiven, tried to dry our tears with talk of Indians and of buffaloes; he spoke, however, at much greater length, and in preaching cadences, of the Christian goodness of Mrs. Placer. She was, he said, childless and fond of children, and for many years she had been a widow, after the lingering demise of her tubercular husband, for whose sake she had moved to the Rocky Mountains. For his support and costly medical care, she had run a boarding house, and after his death, since he had left her nothing, she was obliged to continue running it. She had been a girlhood friend of our paternal grandmother, and our father, in the absence of responsible relatives, had made her the beneficiary of his life insurance on the condition that she lodge and rear us. The pastor, with a frankness remarkable considering that he was talking to children, explained to us that our father had left little more than a drop in the bucket for our care, and he enjoined us to give Mrs. Placer, in return for her hospitality and sacrifice, courteous help and eternal thanks. "Sacrifice" was a word we were never allowed to forget.

And thus it was, in grief for our parents, that we came cringing to the dry Western town and to the house where Mrs. Placer lived, a house in which the square, uncushioned furniture was cruel and the pictures on the walls were either dour or dire and the lodgers, who lived in the upper floors among shadowy wardrobes and chiffoniers, had come through the years to resemble their landlady in appearance as well as in deportment.

After their ugly-colored evening meal, Gran—as she bade us call her—and her paying guests would sit, rangy and acquiline, rocking on the front porch on spring and summer and autumn nights, tasting their delicious grievances: those slights delivered by ungrateful sons and daughters, those impudences committed by trolley-car conductors and uppity salesgirls in the ready-to-wear, all those slurs and calculated elbow-jostlings that were their daily crucifixion and their staff of life. We little girls, washing the dishes in the cavernous kitchen, listened to their even, martyred voices, fixed like leeches to their solitary subject and their solitary creed—that life was essentially a matter of being done in, let down, and swindled.

At regular intervals, Mrs. Placer, chairwoman of the victims, would say, "Of course, I don't care; I just have to laugh," and then would tell a shocking tale of an intricate piece of skulduggery perpetrated against her by someone she did not even know. Sometimes, with her avid, partial jury sitting there on the porch behind the bitter hopvines in the heady mountain air, the cases she tried involved Daisy and me, and, listening, we travailed, hugging each other, whispering, "I wish she wouldn't! Oh, how did she find out?" How *did* she? Certainly we never told her when we were snubbed or chosen last on teams, never admitted to a teacher's scolding or to the hoots of laughter that greeted us when we bit on silly, unfair jokes. But she knew. She knew about the slumber parties we were not invited to, the beefsteak fries at which we were pointedly left out; she knew that the singing teacher had said in so many words that I could not carry a tune in a basket and that the sewing superintendent had said that Daisy's fingers were all thumbs. With our teeth chattering in the cold of our isolation, we would hear her protestant, litigious voice defending our right to be orphans, paupers, wholly dependent on her —except for the really ridiculous pittance from our father's life insurance—when it was all she could do to make ends meet. She did not care, but she had to laugh that people in general were so small-minded that they looked down on fatherless, motherless waifs like us and, by association, looked down on her. It seemed funny to her that people gave her no credit for taking on these sickly youngsters who were not even kin but only the grandchildren of a friend.

If a child with braces on her teeth came to play with us, she was, according to Gran, slyly lording it over us because our teeth were crooked, but there was no money to have them straightened. And what could be the meaning of our being asked to come for supper at the doctor's house? Were the doctor and his la-di-da New York wife and those pert girls with their solid-gold barrettes and their Shetland pony going to shame her poor darlings? Or shame their poor Gran by making them sorry to come home to the plain but honest life that was all she could provide for them?

There was no stratum of society not reeking with the effluvium of fraud and pettifoggery. And the school system was almost the worst of all: if we could not understand fractions, was that not our teacher's fault? And therefore what right had she to give us F? It was as plain as a pikestaff to Gran that the teacher was only covering up her own inability to teach. It was unlikely, too—highly unlikely— that it was by accident that time and time again the free medical clinic was closed for the day just as our names were about to be called out, so that nothing was done about our bad tonsils, which meant that we were repeatedly sick in the winter, with Gran fetching and carrying for us, climbing those stairs a jillion times a day with her game leg and her heart that was none too strong.

Steeped in these mists of accusation and hidden plots and double meanings, Daisy and I grew up like worms. I think no one could have withstood the atmosphere in that house where everyone trod on eggs that a little bird had told them were bad. They spied on one another, whispered behind doors, conjectured, drew parallels beginning "With all due respect . . ." or "It is a matter of indifference to *me* but . . ." The vigilantes patrolled our town by day, and by night returned to lay their goodies at their priestess's feet and wait for her oracular interpretation of the innards of the butcher, the baker, the candlestick maker, the soda jerk's girl, and the barber's unnatural deaf white cat.

Consequently, Daisy and I also became suspicious. But it was suspicion of ourselves that made us mope and weep and grimace with self-judgment. Why were we not happy when Gran had sacrificed herself to the bone for us? Why did we not cut dead the paper boy who had called her a filthy name? Why did we persist in our willful friendliness with the grocer who had tried, unsuccessfully, to overcharge her on a case of pork and beans?

Our friendships were nervous and surreptitious; we sneaked and lied, and as our hungers sharpened, our debasement deepened; we were pitied; we were shifty-eyed, always on the lookout for Mrs. Placer or one of her tattletale lodgers; we were hypocrites.

Nevertheless, one thin filament of instinct survived, and Daisy and I in time found asylum in a small menagerie down by the railroad tracks. It belonged to a gentle alcoholic ne'er-do-well, who did nothing all day long but drink bathtub gin in rickeys and play solitaire and smile to himself and talk to his animals. He had a little, stunted red vixen and a deodorized skunk, a parrot from Tahiti that spoke Parisian French, a woebegone coyote, and two capuchin monkeys, so serious and humanized, so small and sad and sweet, and so religious-looking with their tonsured heads that it was impossible not to think their gibberish was really an ordered language with a grammar that someday some philologist would understand.

Gran knew about our visits to Mr. Murphy and she did not object, for it gave her keen pleasure to excoriate him when we came home. His vice was not a matter of guesswork; it was an established fact that he was half-seas over from dawn till midnight. "With the black Irish," said Gran, "the taste for drink is taken in with the mother's milk and is never mastered. Oh, I know all about those promises to join the temperance movement and not to touch another drop. The way to Hell is paved with good intentions."

We were still little girls when we discovered Mr. Murphy, before the shattering disease of adolescence was to make our bones and brains ache even more painfully than before, and we loved him and we hoped to marry him when we grew up. We loved him, and we loved his monkeys to exactly the same degree and in exactly the same way; they were husbands and fathers and brothers, these three little, ugly, dark, secret men who minded their own business and let us mind ours. If we stuck our fingers through the bars of the cage, the monkeys would sometimes take them in their tight, tiny hands and look into our faces with a tentative, somehow absent-minded sorrow, as if they terribly regretted that they could not place us but were glad to see us all the same. Mr. Murphy, playing a solitaire game of cards called "once in a blue moon" on a kitchen table in his back yard beside the pens, would occasionally look up and blink his beautiful blue eyes and say, "You're peaches to make over my wee friends. I love you for it." There was nothing demanding in his voice, and nothing sticky; on his lips the word "love" was jocose and forthright, it had no strings attached. We would sit on either side of him and watch him regiment his ranks of cards and stop to drink as deeply as if he were dying of thirst and wave to his animals and say to them, "Yes, lads, you're dandies."

Because Mr. Murphy was as reserved with us as the capuchins were, as courteously noncommittal, we were surprised one spring day when he told us that he had a present for us, which he hoped Mrs. Placer would let us keep; it was a puppy, for whom the owner had asked him to find a home—half collie and half Labrador retriever, blue-blooded on both sides.

"You might tell Mrs. Placer—" he said, smiling at the name, for Gran was famous in the town. "You might tell Mrs. Placer," said Mr. Murphy, "that this lad will make a fine watchdog. She'll never have to fear for her spoons again. Or her honor." The last he said to himself, not laughing but tucking his chin into his collar; lines sprang to the corners of his eyes. He would not let us see the dog, whom we could hear yipping and squealing inside his shanty, for he said that our disappointment would weigh on his conscience if we lost our hearts to the fellow and then could not have him for our own.

That evening at supper, we told Gran about Mr. Murphy's present. A dog? In the first place, why a dog? Was it possible that the news had reached Mr. Murphy's ears that Gran had just this very day finished planting her spring garden, the very thing that a rampageous dog would have in his mind to destroy? What sex was it? A male! Females, she had heard, were more trustworthy; males roved and came home smelling of skunk; such a consideration as this, of course, would not have crossed Mr. Murphy's fuddled mind. Was this young male dog housebroken? We had not asked? That was the limit!

Gran appealed to her followers, too raptly fascinated by Mr. Murphy's machinations to eat their Harvard beets. "Am I being farfetched or does it strike you as decidedly queer that Mr. Murphy is trying to fob off on my little girls a young cur that has not been trained?" she asked them. "If it were housebroken, he would have said so, so I feel it is safe to assume that it is not. Perhaps cannot *be* housebroken. I've heard of such cases."

The fantasy spun on, richly and rapidly, with all the skilled helping hands at work at once. The dog was tangibly in the room with us, shedding his hair, biting his fleas, shaking rain off himself to splatter the walls, dragging some dreadful carcass across the floor, chewing up slippers, knocking over chairs with his tail, gobbling the chops from the platter, barking, biting, fathering, fighting, smelling to high heaven of carrion, staining the rug with his muddy feet, scratching the floor with his claws. He developed rabies; he bit a child, two children! Three! Everyone in town! And Gran and her poor darlings went to jail for harboring this murderous, odoriferous, drunk, Roman Catholic dog.

And yet, astoundingly enough, she came around to agreeing to let us have the dog. It was, as Mr. Murphy had predicted, the word "watchdog" that deflected the course of the trial. The moment Daisy uttered it, Gran halted, marshalling her reverse march; while she rallied and tacked and reconnoitred, she sent us to the kitchen for the dessert. And by the time this course was under way, the uses of a dog, the enormous potentialities for investigation and law enforcement in a dog trained by Mrs. Placer, were being minutely and passionately scrutinized by the eight upright bloodhounds sitting at the table wolfing their brown Betty as if it were fresh-killed rabbit. The dog now sat at attention beside his mistress, fiercely alert, ears cocked, nose aquiver, the protector of widows, of orphans, of lonely people who had no homes. He made short shrift of burglars, homicidal maniacs, Peeping Toms, gypsies, bogus missionaries, Fuller Brush men with a risqué spiel. He went to the store and brought back groceries, retrieved the evening paper from the awkward place the boy had meanly thrown it, rescued cripples from burning houses, saved children from drowning, heeled at command, begged, lay down, stood up, sat, jumped through a hoop, ratted.

Both times—when he was a ruffian of the blackest delinquency and then a pillar of society—he was full-grown in his prefiguration, and when Laddy appeared on the following day, small, unsteady, and whimpering lonesomely, Gran and her lodgers were taken aback; his infant, clumsy paws embarrassed them, his melting eyes were unapropos. But it could never be said of Mrs. Placer, as Mrs. Placer her own self said, that she was a woman who went back on her word, and her darlings were going to have their dog, soft-headed and feckless as he might be. All the first night, in his carton in the kitchen, he wailed for his mother, and in the morning, it was true, he had made a shambles of the room—fouled the floor, and pulled off the tablecloth together with a ketchup bottle, so that thick gore lay everywhere. At breakfast, the lodgers confessed they had had a most amusing night, for it had actually been funny the way the dog had been determined not to let anyone get a wink of sleep. After that first night, Laddy slept in our room, receiving from us, all through our delighted, sleepless nights, pats and embraces and kisses and whispers. He was our baby, our best friend, the smartest, prettiest, nicest dog in the entire wide world. Our soft and rapid blandishments excited him to yelp at us in pleased bewilderment, and then we would playfully grasp his muzzle, so that he would snarl, deep in his throat like an adult dog, and shake his head violently, and, when we freed him, nip us smartly with great good will.

He was an intelligent and genial dog and we trained him quickly. He steered clear of Gran's radishes and lettuce after she had several times given him a brisk comeuppance with a strap across the rump, and he soon left off chewing shoes and the laundry on the line, and he outgrew his babyish whining. He grew like a weed; he lost his spherical softness, and his coat, which had been sooty fluff, came in stiff and rusty black; his nose grew aristocratically long, and his clever, pointed ears stood at attention. He was all bronzy, lustrous black except for an Elizabethan ruff of white and a tip of white at the end of his perky tail. No one could deny that he was exceptionally handsome and that he had, as well, great personal charm and style. He escorted Daisy and me to school in the morning, laughing interiorly out of the enormous pleasure of his life as he gracefully cantered ahead of us, distracted occasionally by his private interest in smells or unfamiliar beings in the grass but, on the whole, engrossed in his role of chaperon. He made friends easily with other dogs, and sometimes he went for a long hunting weekend into the mountains with a huge and bossy old red hound named Mess, who had been on the county most of his life and had made a good thing of it, particularly at the fire station.

It was after one of these three-day excursions into the high country that Gran took Laddy in hand. He had come back spent and filthy, his coat a mass of cockleburs and ticks, his eyes bloodshot, loud

râles in his chest; for half a day he lay motionless before the front
door like someone in a hangover, his groaning eyes explicitly saying
"Oh, for God's sake, leave me be" when we offered him food or
bowls of water. Gran was disapproving, then affronted, and finally
furious. Not, of course, with Laddy, since all inmates of her house
enjoyed immunity, but with Mess, whose caddish character, together
with that of his nominal masters, the firemen, she examined closely
under a strong light, with an air of detachment, with her not caring
but her having, all the same, to laugh. A lodger who occupied the
back west room had something to say about the fire chief and his
nocturnal visits to a certain house occupied by a certain group of
young women, too near the same age to be sisters and too old to be
the daughters of the woman who claimed to be their mother. What
a story! The exophthalmic librarian—she lived in one of the front
rooms—had some interesting insinuations to make about the deputy
marshal, who had borrowed, significantly, she thought, a book on
hypnotism. She also knew—she was, of course, in a most useful
position in the town, and from her authoritative pen in the middle
of the library her mammiform and azure eyes and her eager ears
missed nothing—that the fire chief's wife was not as scrupulous as
she might be when she was keeping score on bridge night at the
Sorosis.

There was little at the moment that Mrs. Placer and her disciples
could do to save the souls of the Fire Department and their families,
and therefore save the town from holocaust (a very timid boarder—
a Mr. Beaver, a newcomer who was not to linger long—had sniffed
throughout this recitative as if he were smelling burning flesh), but
at least the unwholesome bond between Mess and Laddy could and
would be severed once and for all. Gran looked across the porch at
Laddy, who lay stretched at full length in the darkest corner, shuddering and baying abortively in his throat as he chased jack rabbits in
his dreams, and she said, "A dog can have morals like a human."
With this declaration Laddy's randy, manly holidays were finished.
It may have been telepathy that woke him; he lifted his heavy head
from his paws, laboriously got up, hesitated for a moment, and then
padded languidly across the porch to Gran. He stood docilely beside
her chair, head down, tail drooping as if to say, "O.K., Mrs. Placer,
show me how and I'll walk the straight and narrow."

The very next day, Gran changed Laddy's name to Caesar, as being
more dignified, and a joke was made at the supper table that he had

come, seen, and conquered Mrs. Placer's heart—for within her circle, where the magnanimity she lavished upon her orphans was daily demonstrated, Mrs. Placer's heart was highly thought of. On that day also, although we did not know it yet, Laddy ceased to be our dog. Before many weeks passed, indeed, he ceased to be anyone we had ever known. A week or so after he became Caesar, he took up residence in her room, sleeping alongside her bed. She broke him of the habit of taking us to school (temptation to low living was rife along those streets; there was a chow—well, never mind) by the simple expedient of chaining him to a tree as soon as she got up in the morning. This discipline, together with the stamina-building cuffs she gave his sensitive ears from time to time, gradually but certainly remade his character. From a sanguine, affectionate, easygoing Gael (with the fits of melancholy that alternated with the larkiness), he turned into an overbearing, military, efficient, loud-voiced Teuton. His bark, once wide of range, narrowed to one dark, glottal tone.

Soon the paper boy flatly refused to serve our house after Caesar efficiently removed the bicycle clip from his pants leg; the skin was not broken, or even bruised, but it was a matter of principle with the boy. The milkman approached the back door in a seizure of shakes like St. Vitus's dance. The metermen, the coal men, and the garbage collector crossed themselves if they were Catholics and, if they were not, tried whistling in the dark. "Good boy, good Caesar," they carolled, and, unctuously lying, they said they knew his bark was worse than his bite, knowing full well that it was not, considering the very nasty nip, requiring stitches, he had given a representative of the Olson Rug Company, who had had the folly to pat him on the head. Caesar did not molest the lodgers, but he disdained them and he did not brook being personally addressed by anyone except Gran. One night, he wandered into the dining room, appearing to be in search of something he had mislaid, and, for some reason that no one was ever able to divine, suddenly stood stock-still and gave the easily upset Mr. Beaver a long and penetrating look. Mr. Beaver, trembling from head to toe, stammered, "Why—er, hello there, Caesar, old boy, old boy," and Caesar charged. For a moment, it was touch and go, but Gran saved Mr. Beaver, only to lose him an hour later when he departed, bag and baggage, for the Y.M.C.A. This rout and the consequent loss of revenue would more than likely have meant Caesar's downfall and his deportation to the pound if it had not been that a newly widowed druggist, very irascible and very much

Gran's style, had applied for a room in her house a week or so before, and now he moved in delightedly, as if he were coming home.

Finally, the police demanded that Caesar be muzzled and they warned that if he committed any major crime again—they cited the case of the Olson man—he would be shot on sight. Mrs. Placer, although she had no respect for the law, knowing as much as she did about its agents, obeyed. She obeyed, that is, in part; she put the muzzle on Caesar for a few hours a day, usually early in the morning when the traffic was light and before the deliveries had started, but the rest of the time his powerful jaws and dazzling white sabre teeth were free and snapping. There was between these two such preternatural rapport, such an impressive conjugation of suspicion, that he, sensing the approach of a policeman, could convey instantly to her the immediate necessity of clapping his nose cage on. And the policeman, sent out on the complaint of a terrorized neighbor, would be greeted by this law-abiding pair at the door.

Daisy and I wished we were dead. We were divided between hating Caesar and loving Laddy, and we could not give up the hope that something, someday, would change him back into the loving animal he had been before he was appointed vice-president of the Placerites. Now at the meetings after supper on the porch he took an active part, standing rigidly at Gran's side except when she sent him on an errand. He carried out these assignments not with the air of a servant but with that of an accomplice. "Get me the paper, Caesar," she would say to him, and he, dismayingly intelligent and a shade smart-alecky, would open the screen door by himself and in a minute come back with the *Bulletin*, from which Mrs. Placer would then read an item, like the Gospel of the day, and then read between the lines of it, scandalized.

In the deepening of our woe and our bereavement and humiliation, we mutely appealed to Mr. Murphy. We did not speak outright to him, for Mr. Murphy lived in a state of indirection, and often when he used the pronoun "I," he seemed to be speaking of someone standing a little to the left of him, but we went to see him and his animals each day during the sad summer, taking what comfort we could from the cozy, quiet indolence of his back yard, where small black eyes encountered ours politely and everyone was half asleep. When Mr. Murphy inquired about Laddy in his bland, inattentive way, looking for a stratagem whereby to shift the queen of hearts into position by the king, we would say, "Oh, he's fine," or "Laddy is a nifty dog." And Mr. Murphy, reverently slaking the thirst that was his talent and his concubine, would murmur, "I'm glad."

We wanted to tell him, we wanted his help, or at least his sympathy, but how could we cloud his sunny world? It was awful to see Mr. Murphy ruffled. Up in the calm clouds as he generally was, he could occasionally be brought to earth with a thud, as we had seen and heard one day. Not far from his house, there lived a bad, troublemaking boy of twelve, who was forever hanging over the fence trying to teach the parrot obscene words. He got nowhere, for she spoke no English and she would flabbergast him with her cold eye and sneer, "*Tant pis.*" One day, this boorish fellow went too far; he suddenly shot his head over the fence like a jack-in-the-box and aimed a water pistol at the skunk's face. Mr. Murphy leaped to his feet in a scarlet rage; he picked up a stone and threw it accurately, hitting the boy square in the back, so hard that he fell right down in a mud puddle and lay there kicking and squalling and, as it turned out, quite badly hurt. "If you ever come back here again, I'll kill you!" roared Mr. Murphy. I think he meant it, for I have seldom seen an anger so resolute, so brilliant, and so voluble. "How dared he!" he cried, scrambling into Mallow's cage to hug and pet and soothe her. "He must be absolutely mad! He must be the Devil!" He did not go back to his game after that but paced the yard, swearing a blue streak and only pausing to croon to his animals, now as frightened by him as they had been by the intruder, and to drink straight from the bottle, not bothering with fixings. We were fascinated by this unfamiliar side of Mr. Murphy, but we did not want to see it ever again, for his face had grown so dangerously purple and the veins of his forehead seemed ready to burst and his eyes looked scorched. He was the closest thing to a maniac we had ever seen. So we did not tell him about Laddy; what he did not know would not hurt him, although it was hurting us, throbbing in us like a great, bleating wound.

But eventually Mr. Murphy heard about our dog's conversion, one night at the pool hall, which he visited from time to time when he was seized with a rare but compelling garrulity, and the next afternoon when he asked us how Laddy was and we replied that he was fine, he tranquilly told us, as he deliberated whether to move the jack of clubs now or to bide his time, that we were sweet girls but we were lying in our teeth. He did not seem at all angry but only interested, and all the while he questioned us, he went on about his business with the gin and the hearts and spades and diamonds and clubs. It rarely happened that he won the particular game he was playing, but that day he did, and when he saw all the cards laid out in their ideal pattern, he leaned back, looking disappointed, and he said, "I'm damned." He then scooped up the cards, in a gesture unusually quick and tidy for him, stacked them together, and bound them with a rubber band. Then he began to tell us what he thought of Gran. He grew as loud and apoplectic as he had been that other time, and though he kept repeating that he knew *we* were innocent and he put not a shred of the blame on us, we were afraid he might suddenly change his mind, and, speechless, we cowered against the monkeys' cage. In dread, the monkeys clutched the fingers we offered to them and made soft, protesting noises, as if to say, "Oh, stop it, Murphy! Our nerves!"

As quickly as it had started, the tantrum ended. Mr. Murphy paled to his normal complexion and said calmly that the only practical thing was to go and have it out with Mrs. Placer. "At once," he added, although he said he bitterly feared that it was too late and there would be no exorcising the fiend from Laddy's misused spirit. And because he had given the dog to us and not to her, he required that we go along with him, stick up for our rights, stand on our mettle, get up our Irish, and give the old bitch something to put in her pipe and smoke.

Oh, it was hot that day! We walked in a kind of delirium through the simmer, where only the grasshoppers had the energy to move, and I remember wondering if ether smelled like the gin on Mr. Murphy's breath. Daisy and I, in one way or another, were going to have our gizzards cut out along with our hearts and our souls and our pride, and I wished I were as drunk as Mr. Murphy, who swam effortlessly through the heat, his lips parted comfortably, his eyes half closed. When we turned in to the path at Gran's house, my blood began to scald my veins. It was so futile and so dangerous and so absurd. Here we were on a high moral mission, two draggletailed, gumptionless little girls and a toper whom no one could take seriously, partly because he was little more than a gurgling bottle of booze and partly because of the clothes he wore. He was a sight, as he always was when he was out of his own yard. There, somehow, in the carefree disorder, his clothes did not look especially strange, but on the streets of the town, in the barbershop or the post office or on Gran's path, they were fantastic. He wore a pair of hound'stooth pants, old but maintaining a vehement pattern, and with them he wore a collarless blue flannelette shirt. His hat was the silliest of all, because it was a derby three sizes too big. And as if Shannon, too, was a part of his funny-paper costume, the elder capuchin rode on his shoulder, tightly embracing his thin red neck.

Gran and Caesar were standing side by side behind the screen door, looking as if they had been expecting us all along. For a moment, Gran and Mr. Murphy faced each other across the length of weedy brick between the gate and the front porch, and no one spoke. Gran took no notice at all of Daisy and me. She adjusted her eyeglasses, using both hands, and then looked down at Caesar and matter-of-factly asked, "Do you want out?"

Caesar flung himself full-length upon the screen and it sprang open like a jaw. I ran to meet and head him off, and Daisy threw a library book at his head, but he was on Mr. Murphy in one split second and had his monkey off his shoulder and had broken Shannon's neck in two shakes. He would have gone on nuzzling and mauling and growling over the corpse for hours if Gran had not marched out of the house and down the path and slapped him lightly on the flank and said, in a voice that could not have deceived an idiot, "Why, Caesar, you scamp! You've hurt Mr. Murphy's monkey! Aren't you ashamed!"

Hurt the monkey! In one final, apologetic shudder, the life was extinguished from the little fellow. Bloody and covered with slather, Shannon lay with his arms suppliantly stretched over his head, his leather fingers curled into loose, helpless fists. His hind legs and his tail lay limp and helter-skelter on the path. And Mr. Murphy, all of a sudden reeling drunk, burst into the kind of tears that Daisy and I knew well—the kind that time alone could stop. We stood aghast in the dark-red sunset, killed by our horror and our grief for Shannon and our unforgivable disgrace. We stood upright in a dead faint, and an eon passed before Mr. Murphy picked up Shannon's body and wove away, sobbing, "I don't believe it! I don't *believe* it!"

The very next day, again at morbid, heavy sunset, Caesar died in violent convulsions, knocking down two tall hollyhocks in his throes. Long after his heart had stopped, his right hind leg continued to jerk in aimless reflex. Madly methodical, Mr. Murphy had poisoned some meat for him, had thoroughly envenomed a whole pound of hamburger, and early in the morning, before sunup, when he must have been near collapse with his hangover, he had stolen up to Mrs.

Placer's house and put it by the kitchen door. He was so stealthy that Caesar never stirred in his fool's paradise there on the floor by Gran. We knew these to be the facts, for Mr. Murphy made no bones about them. Afterward, he had gone home and said a solemn Requiem for Shannon in so loud a voice that someone sent for the police, and they took him away in the Black Maria to sober him up on strong green tea. By the time he was in the lockup and had confessed what he had done, it was far too late, for Caesar had already gulped down the meat. He suffered an undreamed-of agony in Gran's flower garden, and Daisy and I, unable to bear the sight of it, hiked up to the red rocks and shook there, wretchedly ripping to shreds the sand lilies that grew in the cracks. Flight was the only thing we could think of, but where could we go? We stared west at the mountains and quailed at the look of the stern white glacier; we wildly scanned the prairies for escape. "If only we were something besides kids! Besides girls!" mourned Daisy. I could not speak at all; I huddled in a niche of the rocks and cried.

No one in town, except, of course, her lodgers, had the slightest sympathy for Gran. The townsfolk allowed that Mr. Murphy was a drunk and was fighting Irish, but he had a heart and this was something that could never be said of Mrs. Placer. The neighbor who had called the police when he was chanting the "Dies Irae" before breakfast in that deafening monotone had said, "The poor guy is having some kind of a spell, so don't be rough on him, hear?" Mr. Murphy became, in fact, a kind of hero; some people, stretching a point, said he was a saint for the way that every day and twice on Sunday he sang a memorial Mass over Shannon's grave, now marked with a chipped, cheap plaster figure of Saint Francis. He withdrew from the world more and more, seldom venturing into the streets at all, except when he went to the bootlegger to get a new bottle to snuggle into. All summer, all fall, we saw him as we passed by his yard, sitting at his dilapidated table, enfeebled with gin, graying, withering, turning his head ever and ever more slowly as he maneuvered the protocol of the kings and the queens and the knaves. Daisy and I could never stop to visit him again.

It went on like this, year after year. Daisy and I lived in a mesh of lies and evasions, baffled and mean, like rats in a maze. When we were old enough for beaux, we connived like sluts to see them, but we would never admit to their existence until Gran caught us out by some trick. Like this one, for example: Once, at the end of a long interrogation, she said to me, "I'm more relieved than I can tell you that you *don't* have anything to do with Jimmy Gilmore, because I happen to know that he is after only one thing in a girl," and then, off guard in the loving memory ðf sitting in the movies the night before with Jimmy, not even holding hands, I defended him and defeated myself, and Gran, smiling with success, said, "I *thought* you knew him. It's a pretty safe rule of thumb that where there's smoke there's fire." That finished Jimmy and me, for afterward I was nervous with him and I confounded and alarmed and finally bored him by trying to convince him, although the subject had not come up, that I did not doubt his good intentions.

Daisy and I would come home from school, or, later, from our jobs, with a small triumph or an interesting piece of news, and if we forgot ourselves and, in our exuberance, told Gran, we were hustled into court at once for cross-examination. Once, I remember, while I was still in high school, I told her about getting a part in a play. How very nice for me, she said, if that kind of make-believe seemed to me worth while. But what was my role? An old woman! A widow woman believed to be a witch? She did not care a red cent, but she did have to laugh in view of the fact that Miss Eccles, in charge of dramatics, had almost run her down in her car. And I would forgive her, would I not, if she did not come to see the play, and would not think her eccentric for not wanting to see herself ridiculed in public?

My pleasure strangled, I crawled, joy-killed, to our third-floor room. The room was small and its monstrous furniture was too big and the rag rugs were repulsive, but it was bright. We would not hang a blind at the window, and on this day I stood there staring into the mountains that burned with the sun. I feared the mountains, but at times like this their massiveness consoled me; they, at least, could not be gossiped about.

Why did we stay until we were grown? Daisy and I ask ourselves this question as we sit here on the bench in the municipal zoo, reminded of Mr. Murphy by the polar bear, reminded by the monkeys not of Shannon but of Mrs. Placer's insatiable gossips at their postprandial feast.

"But how could we have left?" says Daisy, wringing her buttery hands. "It was the depression. We had no money. We had nowhere to go."

"All the same, we could have gone," I say, resentful still of the waste of all those years. "We could have come here and got jobs as waitresses. Or prostitutes, for that matter."

"I wouldn't have wanted to be a prostitute," says Daisy.

We agree that under the circumstances it would have been impossible for us to run away. The physical act would have been simple, for the city was not far and we could have stolen the bus fare or hitched a ride. Later, when we began to work as salesgirls in Kress's it would have been no trick at all to vanish one Saturday afternoon with our week's pay, without so much as going home to say good-bye. But it had been infinitely harder than that, for Gran, as we now see, held us trapped by our sense of guilt. We were vitiated, and we had no choice but to wait, flaccidly, for her to die.

You may be sure we did not unlearn those years as soon as we put her out of sight in the cemetery and sold her house for a song to the first boob who would buy it. Nor did we forget when we left the town for another one, where we had jobs at a dude camp—the town where Daisy now lives with a happy husband and two happy sons. The succubus did not relent for years, and I can still remember, in the beginning of our days at the Lazy S 3, overhearing an edgy millionaire say to his wife, naming my name, "That girl gives me the cold shivers. One would think she had just seen a murder." Well, I had. For years, whenever I woke in the night in fear or pain or loneliness, I would increase my suffering by the memory of Shannon, and my tears were as bitter as poor Mr. Murphy's.

We have never been back to Adams. But we see that house plainly, with the hopvines straggling over the porch. The windows are hung with the cheapest grade of marquisette, dipped into coffee to impart to it an unwilling color, neither white nor tan but individual and spitefully unattractive. We see the wicker rockers and the swing, and through the screen door we dimly make out the slightly veering corridor, along one wall of which stands a glass-doored bookcase; when we were children, it had contained not books but stale old cardboard boxes filled with such things as W.C.T.U. tracts and anti-cigarette literature and newspaper clippings related to sexual sin in the Christianized islands of the Pacific.

Even if we were able to close our minds' eyes to the past, Mr. Murphy would still be before us in the apotheosis of the polar bear. My pain becomes intolerable, and I am relieved when Daisy rescues us. "We've got to go," she says in a sudden panic. "I've got asthma coming on." We rush to the nearest exit of the city park and hail a cab, and, once inside it, Daisy gives herself an injection of adrenalin and then leans back. We are heartbroken and infuriated, and we cannot speak.

Two hours later, beside my train, we clutch each other as if we were drowning. We ought to go out to the nearest policeman and say, "We are not responsible women. You will have to take care of us because we cannot take care of ourselves." But gradually the storm begins to lull.

"You're sure you've got your ticket?" says Daisy. "You'll surely be able to get a roomette once you're on."

"I don't know about that," I say. "If there are any V.I.P.s on board, I won't have a chance. 'Spinsters and Orphans Last' is the motto of this line."

Daisy smiles. "I didn't care," she says, "but I had to laugh when I saw that woman nab the redcap you had signalled to. I had a good notion to give her a piece of my mind."

"It will be a miracle if I ever see my bags again," I say, mounting the steps of the train. "Do you suppose that blackguardly porter knows about the twenty-dollar gold piece in my little suitcase?"

"Anything's possible!" cries Daisy, and begins to laugh. She is so pretty, standing there in her bright-red linen suit and her black velvet hat. A solitary ray of sunshine comes through a broken pane in the domed vault of the train shed and lies on her shoulder like a silver arrow.

"So long, Daisy!" I call as the train begins to move.

She walks quickly along beside the train. "Watch out for pickpockets!" she calls.

"You, too!" My voice is thin and lost in the increasing noise of the speeding train wheels. "Goodbye, old dear!"

I go at once to the club car and I appropriate the writing table, to the vexation of a harried priest, who snatches up the telegraph pad and gives me a sharp look. I write Daisy approximately the same letter I always write her under this particular set of circumstances, the burden of which is that nothing for either of us can ever be as bad as the past before Gran mercifully died. In a postscript I add: "There is a Roman Catholic priest (that is to say, he is *dressed* like one) sitting behind me although all the chairs on the opposite side of the car are empty. I can only conclude that he is looking over my shoulder, and while I do not want to cause you any alarm, I think you would be advised to be on the lookout for any appearance of miraculous medals, scapulars, papist booklets, etc., in the shops in your town. It really makes me laugh to see the way he is pretending that all he wants is for me to finish this letter so that he can have the table."

I sign my name and address the envelope, and I give up my place to the priest, who smiles nicely at me, and then I move across the car to watch the fields as they slip by. They are alfalfa fields, but you can bet your bottom dollar that they are chockablock with marijuana.

I begin to laugh. The fit is silent but it is devastating; it surges and rattles in my rib cage, and I turn face to the window to avoid the narrow gaze of the Filipino bar boy. I must think of something sad to stop this unholy giggle, and I think of the polar bear. But even his bleak tragedy does not sober me. Wildly I fling open the newspaper I have brought and I pretend to be reading something screamingly funny. The words I see are in a Hollywood gossip column: "How a well-known starlet can get a divorce in Nevada without her crooner husband's consent, nobody knows. It won't be worth a plugged nickel here."

FLANNERY O'CONNOR *was educated in the parochial schools of Savannah, Georgia, Georgia State College for Women, and the State University of Iowa. Her first novel,* Wise Blood, *was published in 1952. Her stories have appeared in such magazines as* Harper's Bazaar *and the* Kenyon Review, *and one of them was included in* Prize Stories 1954: The O. Henry Awards. *She is at present compiling a collection of them to be published by Harcourt, Brace & Co. under the title* A Good Man Is Hard to Find. *She lives in Milledgeville, Georgia.*

A CIRCLE IN THE FIRE

FROM KENYON REVIEW

Sometimes the last line of trees was a solid grey blue wall a little darker than the sky but this afternoon it was almost black and behind it the sky was a livid glaring white. "You know that woman that had that baby in that iron lung?" Mrs. Pritchard said. She and the child's mother were underneath the window the child was looking down from. Mrs. Pritchard was leaning against the chimney, her arms folded on a shelf of stomach, one foot crossed and the toe pointed into the ground. She was a large woman with a small pointed face and steady ferreting eyes. Mrs. Cope was the opposite, very small and trim, with a large round face and black eyes that seemed to be enlarging all the time behind her thick glasses as if she were continually being astonished. She was squatting down pulling grass out of the border beds around the house. Both of them had on sunhats that had once been identical but Mrs. Pritchard's was faded and out of shape while Mrs. Cope's was still stiff and bright green.

"I read about her," she said.

"She was a Pritchard that married a Brookins and so's kin to me —about my seventh or eighth cousin by marriage."

"Well, well," Mrs. Cope muttered and threw a large clump of nut grass behind her. She worked at the weeds and nut grass as if they were an evil sent directly by the devil to destroy the place.

"Beinst she was kin to us, we gone to see the body," Mrs. Pritchard said. "Seen the little baby too."

Mrs. Cope didn't say anything. She was used to these calamitous stories; she said they wore her to a frazzle. Mrs. Pritchard would go thirty miles for the satisfaction of seeing someone laid away. Mrs. Cope always changed the subject to something cheerful but the child had observed that this only put Mrs. Pritchard in a bad humor.

The child thought the blank sky looked as if it were pushing against the fortress wall, trying to break through. The trees across the near field were a patchwork of grey and yellow greens. Mrs. Cope was always worrying about fires in her woods. When the nights were very windy, she would say to the child, "Oh Lord, do pray there won't be any fires, it's so windy," and the child would grunt from behind her book or not answer at all because she heard it so often. In the evenings in the summer when they sat on the porch, Mrs. Cope would say to the child who was reading fast to catch the last light, "Get up and look at the sunset, it's gorgeous. You ought to get up and look at it," and the child would scowl and not answer or glare up once across the lawn and two front pastures to the grey blue sentinel line of trees and then begin to read again with no change of expression, sometimes muttering for meanness, "It looks like a fire. You better get up and smell around and see if the woods ain't on fire."

"She had her arm around it in the coffin," Mrs. Pritchard went on, but her voice was drowned out by the sound of the tractor that the negro, Culver, was driving up the road from the barn. The wagon was attached and another negro was sitting in the back, bouncing, his feet jogging about a foot from the ground. The one on the tractor drove it past the gate that led into the field on the left.

Mrs. Cope turned her head and saw that he had not gone through the gate because he was too lazy to get off and open it. He was going the long way around at her expense. "Tell him to stop and come here!" she shouted.

Mrs. Pritchard heaved herself from the chimney and waved her arm in a fierce circle but he pretended not to hear. She stalked to the edge of the lawn and screamed, "Get off, I toljer! She wants you!"

He got off and started toward the chimney, pushing his head and shoulders forward at each step to give the appearance of hurrying. His head was thrust up to the top in a white cloth hat striated with different shades of sweat. The brim was down and hid all but the lower parts of his reddish eyes.

Mrs. Cope was on her knees, pointing the trowel into the ground. "Why aren't you going through the gate there?" she asked and waited, her eyes shut and her mouth stretched flat as if she were prepared for any ridiculous answer.

"Got to raise the blade on the mower if we do," he said and his gaze bore just to the left of her. Her negroes were as destructive and impersonal as the nut grass.

Her eyes, as she opened them, looked as if they would keep on enlarging until they turned her wrongsideout. "Raise it," she said and pointed across the road with the trowel.

He moved off.

"It's nothing to them," she said. "They don't have to pay for the gas. It's nothing to anybody but the one with the responsibility. I thank the Lord all these things don't come at once. They'd destroy me."

"Yeah, they would," Mrs. Pritchard shouted against the sound of the tractor. He opened the gate and raised the blade and drove through and down into the field; the noise diminished as the wagon disappeared. "I don't see myself how she had it *in* it," she went on in her normal voice.

Mrs. Cope was bent over, digging fiercely at the nut grass again. "We have a lot to be thankful for," she said. "Every day you should say a prayer of thanksgiving. Do you do that?"

"Yes'm," Mrs. Pritchard said. "See she was in it four months before she even got thataway. Look like to me if I was in one of them, I would leave off . . . how you reckon they . . ."

"Every day I say a prayer of thanksgiving," Mrs. Cope said. "Think of all we have. Lord," she said and sighed, "we have everything," and she looked around at her rich pastures and hills that were heavy with timber and shook her head as if it all might be a burden she was trying to shake off her back.

Mrs. Pritchard studied the woods. "All I got is four abscess teeth," she remarked.

"Well, be thankful you don't have five," Mrs. Cope snapped and threw back a clump of grass. "We might all be destroyed by a hurricane. I can always find something to be thankful for."

Mrs. Pritchard took up a hoe resting against the side of the house and struck lightly at a weed that had come up between two bricks in the chimney. "Yeah?" she said, her voice a little more nasal than usual with contempt.

"Why, think of all those poor Europeans," Mrs. Cope went on, "that they put in box cars like cattle and rode them to Siberia. Lord," she said, "we ought to spend half our time on our knees."

"I know if I was in an iron lung there would be some things I wouldn't do," Mrs. Pritchard said, scratching her bare ankle with the end of the hoe.

"Even that poor woman had plenty to be thankful for," Mrs. Cope said.

"She could be thankful she wasn't dead."

"Certainly," Mrs. Cope said, and then she pointed the trowel up at Mrs. Pritchard and said, "I have the best kept place in the county and do you know why? Because I work. I've had to work to save this place and work to keep it." She emphasized each word with the trowel. "I don't let anything get ahead of me and I'm not always looking for trouble. I take it as it comes."

"If it all come at oncet sometime," Mrs. Pritchard began.

"It doesn't all come at once," Mrs. Cope said sharply.

The child could see over to where the dirt road joined the highway. She saw a pick-up truck stop at the gate and let off three boys who started walking up the pink dirt road. They walked single-file, the middle one bent to the side carrying a black pig-shaped valise.

"Well, if it ever did," Mrs. Pritchard said, "it wouldn't be nothing you could do but fling your hands."

Mrs. Cope didn't even answer this. Mrs. Pritchard folded her arms and gazed down the road as if she could easily enough see all these fine hills flattened to nothing. She saw the three boys who had almost reached the front walk by now. "Lookit yonder," she said. "Who you reckon they are?"

Mrs. Cope leaned back and supported herself with one hand behind her and looked. The three came toward them but as if they were going to walk on through the side of the house. The one with the suitcase was in front now. Finally about four feet from her, he stopped and set it down. The three boys looked something alike except that the middle-sized one wore silver-rimmed spectacles and carried the suitcase. One of his eyes had a slight cast to it so that his gaze seemed to be coming from two directions at once as if it had them surrounded. He had on a sweat shirt with a faded destroyer printed on it but his chest was so hollow that the destroyer was broken in the middle and seemed on the point of going under. His hair was stuck to his forehead with sweat. He looked to be about thirteen. All three boys had white penetrating stares. "I don't reckon you remember me, Mrs. Cope," he said.

"Your face is certainly familiar," she said, scrutinizing him, "now let's see. . . ."

"My daddy used to work here," he hinted.

"Boyd?" she said. "Your father was Mr. Boyd and you're J.C.?"

"Nome, I'm Powell, the secont one, only I've growed some since then and my daddy he's daid now. Done died."

"Dead. Well I declare," Mrs. Cope said as if death were always an unusual thing. "What was Mr. Boyd's trouble?"

One of Powell's eyes seemed to be making a circle of the place, examining the house and the white water tower behind it and the chicken houses and the pastures that rolled away on either side until they met the first line of woods. The other eye looked at her. "Died in Florda," he said and began kicking the valise.

"Well, I declare," she murmured. After a second she said, "And how is your mother?"

"Mah'd again." He kept watching his foot kick the suitcase. The other two boys stared at her impatiently.

"And where do you all live now?" she asked.

"Atlanta," he said. "You know, out to one of them developments."

"Well, I see," she said, "I see." After a second she said it again. Finally she asked, "And who are these other boys?" and smiled at them.

"Garfield Smith him, and W. T. Harper him," he said, nodding his head backward first in the direction of the large boy and then the small one.

"How do you boys do?" Mrs. Cope said. "This is Mrs. Pritchard. Mr. and Mrs. Pritchard work here now."

They ignored Mrs. Pritchard, who watched them with steady beady eyes. The three seemed to hang there, waiting, watching Mrs. Cope.

"Well, well," she said, glancing at the suitcase, "it's nice of you to stop and see me. I think that was real sweet of you."

Powell's stare seemed to pinch her like a pair of tongs. "Come back to see how you was doing," he said hoarsely.

"Listen here," the smallest boy said, "all the time we been knowing him he's been telling us about this here place. Said it was everything

here. Said it was horses here. Said he had the best time of his entire
life right here on this here place. Talks about it all the time."

"Never shuts his trap about this place," the big boy grunted,
drawing his arm across his nose as if to muffle his words.

"Always talking about them horses he rid here," the small one
continued, "and said he would let us ride them too. Said it was one
name Gene."

Mrs. Cope was always afraid someone would get hurt on her place
and sue her for everything she had. "They aren't shod," she said
quickly. "There was one named Gene but he's dead now but I'm
afraid you boys can't ride the horses because they aren't shod and
they're in the pasture and I'm afraid you might get hurt. They're
dangerous," she said, speaking very fast.

The large boy sat down on the ground with a noise of disgust and
began to finger rocks out of his tennis shoe. The small one darted
looks here and there and Powell fixed her with his stare and didn't
say anything.

After a minute the little boy said, "Say, lady, you know what he
said one time? He said when he died he wanted to come here!"

For a second Mrs. Cope looked blank; then she blushed; then a
peculiar look of pain came over her face as she realized that these
children were hungry. They were staring because they were hungry!
She almost gasped in their faces, and then she asked them quickly
if they would have something to eat. They said they would but their
expressions, composed and unsatisfied, didn't lighten any. They
looked as if they were used to being hungry.

The child upstairs had grown red in the face with excitement. She
was kneeling down by the window so that only her eyes and forehead showed over the sill. Mrs. Cope told the boys to come around
on the other side of the house where the lawn chairs were and she
led the way and Mrs. Pritchard followed. The child moved from the
right bedroom across the hall and over into the left bedroom and
looked down on the other side of the house where there were three
white lawn chairs and a red hammock strung between two hazelnut
trees. She was a pale fat girl of twelve with a frowning squint and a
large mouth full of silver bands. She knelt down at the window.

The three boys came around the corner of the house and the large
one threw himself into the hammock and lit a stub of cigarette. The
small boy tumbled down on the grass next to the black suitcase and
rested his head on it and Powell sat down on the edge of one of

the chairs and looked as if he were trying to enclose the whole place in one encircling stare. The child heard her mother and Mrs. Pritchard in a muted conference in the kitchen. She got up and went out into the hall and leaned over the banisters.

Mrs. Cope's and Mrs. Pritchard's legs were facing each other in the back hall. "Those poor children are hungry," Mrs. Cope said in a dead voice.

"You seen that suitcase?" Mrs. Pritchard asked. "What if they intend to spend the night with you?"

Mrs. Cope gave a slight shriek. "I can't have three boys in here with only me and Sally Virginia," she said. "I'm sure they'll go when I feed them."

"I only know they got a suitcase," Mrs. Pritchard said.

The child hurried back to the window. The large boy was stretched out in the hammock with his wrists crossed under his head and the cigarette stub in the center of his mouth. He spit it out in an arc just as Mrs. Cope came around the corner of the house with a plate of crackers. She stopped instantly as if a snake had been slung in her path. "Ashfield!" she said, "please pick that up. I'm afraid of fires."

"Gawfield!" the little boy shouted indignantly, "Gawfield!"

The large boy raised himself without a word and lumbered for the butt. He picked it up and put it in his pocket and stood with his back to her, examining a tattooed heart on his forearm. Mrs. Pritchard came up holding three Coca-Colas by the necks in one hand and gave one to each of them.

"I remember everything about this place," Powell said, looking down the opening of his bottle.

"Where did you all go when you left here?" Mrs. Cope asked and put the plate of crackers on the arm of his chair.

He looked at it but didn't take one. He said, "I remember it was one name Gene and it was one name George. We gone to Florda and my daddy he, you know, died, and then we gone to my sister's and then my mother she, you know, mah'd, and we been there ever since."

"There are some crackers," Mrs. Cope said and sat down in the chair across from him.

"He don't like it in Atlanta," the little boy said, sitting up and reaching indifferently for a cracker. "He ain't ever satisfied with where he's at except this place here. Lemme tell you what he'll do, lady. We'll be playing ball, see, on this here place in this development we got to play ball on, see, and he'll quit playing and say, 'Goddam, it was a horse down there name Gene and if I had him here I'd bust this concrete to hell riding him!' "

"I'm sure Powell doesn't use words like that, do you, Powell?" Mrs. Cope said.

"No, mam," Powell said. His head was turned completely to the side as if he were listening for the horses in the field.

"I don't like them kind of crackers," the little boy said and returned his to the plate and got up.

Mrs. Cope shifted in her chair. "So you boys live in one of those nice new developments," she said.

"The only way you can tell your own is by smell," the small boy volunteered. "They're four stories high and there's ten of them, one behind the other. Let's go see them horses," he said.

Powell turned his pinching stare on Mrs. Cope. "We thought we would just spend the night in your barn," he said. "My uncle brought us this far on his pick-up truck and he's going to stop for us again in the morning."

There was a moment in which she didn't say a thing and the child in the window thought: she's going to fly out of that chair and hit the tree.

"Well, I'm afraid you can't do that," she said, getting up suddenly. "The barn's full of hay and I'm afraid of fire from your cigarettes."

"We won't smoke," he said.

"I'm afraid you can't spend the night there just the same," she repeated as if she were talking politely to a gangster.

"Well we can camp out in the woods then," the little boy said. "We brought our own blankets anyways. That's what we got in thatere suitcase. Come on."

"In the woods!" she said. "Oh no! The woods are very dry now, I can't have people smoking in my woods. You'll have to camp out in the field, in this field here next to the house, where there aren't any trees."

"Where she can keep her eye on you," the child said under her breath.

"Her woods," the large boy muttered and got out of the hammock.

"We'll sleep in the field," Powell said but not particularly as if he were talking to her. "This afternoon I'm going to show them about this place." The other two were already walking away and he got up and bounded after them and the two women sat with the black suit-case between them.

"Not no thank-you, not no nothing," Mrs. Pritchard remarked.

"They only played with what we gave them to eat," Mrs. Cope said in a hurt voice.

"Maybe they don't like soft drinks," Mrs. Pritchard muttered.

"They certainly *looked* hungry," Mrs. Cope said.

About sunset they appeared out of the woods, dirty and sweating, and came to the back porch and asked for water. They did not ask for food but Mrs. Cope could tell that they wanted it. "All I have is some cold guinea," she said. "Would you boys like some guinea and some sandwiches?"

"I wouldn't eat nothing bald-headed like a guinea," the little boy said. "I would eat a chicken or a turkey but not no guinea."

"Dogs wouldn't eat one of them," the large boy said. He had taken off his shirt and stuck it in the back of his trousers like a tail. Mrs. Cope carefully avoided looking at him. The little boy had a cut on his arm.

"You boys haven't been riding the horses when I asked you not to, have you?" she asked suspiciously and they all said, "No mam!" at once in loud enthusiastic voices like the Amens that are said in country churches.

She went into the house and made them sandwiches and, while she did it, she held a conversation with them from inside the kitchen, asking where they went to school and what their fathers did and how many brothers and sisters they had. They answered in short explosive sentences, pushing each other's shoulders and doubling up with laughter as if the questions had meanings that she didn't know about. "And does your mother work, Powell?" she called.

"She ast you does your mother work!" the little boy yelled. "His mind's affected by them horses he only looked at," he said. "His mother she works at a factory and leaves him home to mind the rest of them only he don't mind them much. Lemme tell you, lady, one time he locked his little brother in a box and set it on fire."

"I'm sure Powell wouldn't do a thing like that," she said, coming out with the plate of sandwiches and setting it down on the step. They emptied the plate at once and she picked it up and stood holding it, looking at the sun which was going down in front of them, almost on top of the tree line. It was swollen and flame-colored and hung in a net of ragged cloud as if it might burn through any second and fall into the woods. From the upstairs window the child saw her shiver and catch both arms to her sides. "We have so much to be thankful for," she said suddenly in a mournful marvelling tone. "Do you boys thank God every night for all He's done for you? Do you thank Him for everything?"

This put an instant hush over them. They bit into the sandwiches as if they had lost all taste for food.

"Do you?" she persisted.

They were as silent as thieves hiding. They chewed without a sound.

"Well, I know I do," she said at length and turned and went back in the house and the child watched their shoulders drop. The large one stretched his legs out as if he were releasing himself from a trap. The sun burned so fast that it seemed to be trying to set everything in sight on fire. The white water tower was glazed pink and the grass was an unnatural green as if it were turning to glass. The child suddenly stuck her head far out the window and said, "Uggggrhhh," in a loud voice, crossing her eyes and hanging her tongue out as far as possible as if she were going to vomit.

The large boy looked up and stared at her. "Jesus," he growled "another woman."

She dropped back from the window and stood with her back against the wall, squinting fiercely as if she had been slapped in the face and couldn't see who had done it. As soon as they left the steps, she came down into the kitchen where Mrs. Cope was washing the dishes. "If I had that big boy down I'd beat the daylight out of him," she said.

"You keep away from those boys," Mrs. Cope said, turning sharply. "Ladies don't beat the daylight out of people. You keep out of their way. They'll be gone in the morning."

But in the morning they were not gone.

When she went out on the porch after breakfast, they were standing around the back door, kicking the steps. They were smelling the bacon she had had for her breakfast. "Why, boys!" she said, "I thought you were going to meet your uncle." They had the same look of hardened hunger that had pained her yesterday but today she felt faintly provoked.

The big boy turned his back at once and the small one squatted down and began to scratch in the sand. "We ain't, though," Powell said.

The big boy turned his head just enough to take in a small section of her and said, "We ain't bothering nothing of yours."

He couldn't see the way her eyes enlarged but he could take note of the significant silence. After a minute she said in an altered voice, "Would you boys care for some breakfast?"

"We got plenty of our own food," the big boy said. "We don't want nothing of yours."

She kept her eyes on Powell. His thin white face seemed to confront but not actually to see her. "You boys know that I'm glad to have you," she said, "but I expect you to behave. I expect you to act like gentlemen."

They stood there, each looking in a different direction, as if they were waiting for her to leave. "After all," she said in a suddenly high voice, "this is my place."

The big boy made some ambiguous noise and they turned and walked off toward the barn, leaving her there with a shocked look as if she had had a searchlight thrown on her in the middle of the night.

In a little while Mrs. Pritchard came over and stood in the kitchen door with her cheek against the edge of it. "I reckon you know they rode them horses all yesterday afternoon," she said. "Stole a bridle out of the saddle room and rode bareback, because Hollis seen them. He runnum out the barn at nine o'clock last night and then he runnum out at ten and they was smoking both times and then he runnum out the milk room this morning and there was milk all over their mouths like they had been drinking out the cans."

"I cannot have this," Mrs. Cope said and stood at the sink with both fists knotted at her sides. "I cannot have this," and her expression was the same as when she tore at the nut grass.

"There ain't a thing you can do about it," Mrs. Pritchard said. "What I expect is you'll have them for a week or so until school begins. They just figure to have themselves a vacation in the country and there ain't nothing you can do but fold your hands."

"I do not fold my hands," Mrs. Cope said. "Tell Mr. Pritchard to put the horses up in the stalls."

"He's already did that. You take a boy thirteen year old is equal in meanness to a man twicet his age. It's no telling what he'll think up to do. You never know where he'll strike next. This morning

Hollis seen them behind the bull pen and that big one ast if it wasn't
some place they could wash at and Hollis said no it wasn't and that
you didn't want no boys dropping cigarette butts in your woods and
he said, 'She don't own them woods,' and Hollis said, 'She does too,'
and that there little one he said, 'Man, Gawd owns them woods and
her too,' and that there one with the glasses said, 'I reckon she owns
the sky over this place too,' and that there littlest one says, 'Owns the
sky and can't no airplane go over here without she says so,' and
then the big one says, 'I never seen a place with so many damn
women on it, how do you stand it here?' and Hollis said he had done
had enough of their big talk by then and he turned and walked off
without giving no reply one way or the other."

"I'm going out there and tell those boys they can get a ride away
from here on the milk truck," Mrs. Cope said and she went out the
back door, leaving Mrs. Pritchard and the child together in the
kitchen.

"Listen," the child said. "I could handle them quicker than that."

"Yeah?" Mrs. Pritchard murmured, giving her a long leering look,
"how'd you handle them?"

The child gripped both hands together and made a contorted face
as if she were strangling someone.

"They'd handle you," Mrs. Pritchard said with satisfaction.

The child retired to the upstairs window to get out of her way and
looked down where her mother was walking off from the three boys,
who were squatting under the water tower, eating something out of
a cracker box. She heard her come in the kitchen door and say,
"They say they'll go on the milk truck, and no wonder they aren't
hungry—they have that suitcase half full of food."

"Likely stole every bit of it too," Mrs. Pritchard said.

When the milk truck came, the three boys were nowhere in sight,
but as soon as it left without them their three faces appeared, looking out of the opening in the top of the calf barn. "Can you beat
this?" Mrs. Cope said, standing at one of the upstairs windows with
her hands on her hips. "It's not that I wouldn't be glad to have them
—it's their attitude."

"You never like nobody's attitude," the child said. "I'll go tell
them they got five minutes to leave here in."

"You are not to go anywhere near those boys, do you hear me?"
Mrs. Cope said.

"Why?" the child asked.

"I'm going out there and give them a piece of my mind," Mrs. Cope said.

The child took over the position in the window and in a few minutes she saw the stiff green hat catching the glint of the sun as her mother crossed the road toward the calf barn. The three faces immediately disappeared from the opening, and in a second the large boy dashed across the lot, followed an instant later by the other two. Mrs. Pritchard came out and the two women started for the grove of trees the boys had vanished into. Presently the two sunhats disappeared in the woods and the three boys came out at the left side of it and ambled across the field and into another patch of woods. By the time Mrs. Cope and Mrs. Pritchard reached the field, it was empty and there was nothing for them to do but come home again.

Mrs. Cope had not been inside long before Mrs. Pritchard came running toward the house, shouting something. "They've let out the bull!" she hollered, "let out the bull!" And in a second she was followed by the bull himself, ambling, black and leisurely, with four geese hissing at his heels. He was not mean until hurried and it took Mr. Pritchard and the two negroes a half hour to ease him back to his pen. While the men were engaged in this, the boys let the oil out of the three tractors and then disappeared again into the woods.

Two blue veins had come out on either side of Mrs. Cope's forehead and Mrs. Pritchard observed them with satisfaction. "Like I toljer," she said, "there ain't a thing you can do about it."

Mrs. Cope ate her dinner hastily, not conscious that she had her sunhat on. Every time she heard a noise, she jumped up. Mrs. Pritchard came over immediately after dinner and said, "Well, you want to know where they are now?" and smiled in an omniscient rewarded way.

"I want to know at once," Mrs. Cope said, coming to an almost military attention.

"Down to the road, throwing rocks at your mailbox," Mrs. Pritchard said, leaning comfortably in the door. "Done already about knocked it off its stand."

"Get in the car," Mrs. Cope said.

The child got in too and the three of them drove down the road to the gate. The boys were sitting on the embankment on the other side of the highway, aiming rocks across the road at the mailbox. Mrs. Cope stopped the car almost directly beneath them and looked up out of her window. The three of them stared at her as if they had never seen her before, the large boy with a sullen glare, the small one glint-eyed and unsmiling, and Powell with his two-sided glassed gaze hanging vacantly over the crippled destroyer on his shirt.

"Powell," she said, "I'm sure your mother would be ashamed of you," and she stopped and waited for this to make its effect. His face seemed to twist slightly but he continued to look through her at nothing in particular.

"Now I've put up with this as long as I can," she said. "I've tried to be nice to you boys. Haven't I been nice to you boys?"

They might have been three statues except that the big one, barely opening his mouth, said, "We're not even on your side the road, lady."

"There ain't a thing you can do about it," Mrs. Pritchard hissed loudly. The child was sitting on the back seat close to the side. She had a furious outraged look on her face but she kept her head drawn back from the window so that they couldn't see her.

Mrs. Cope spoke slowly, emphasizing every word. "I think I have been very nice to you boys. I've fed you twice. Now I'm going into town and if you're still here when I come back, I'll call the sheriff," and with this, she drove off. The child, turning quickly so that she could see out the back window, observed that they had not moved; they had not even turned their heads.

"You done angered them now," Mrs. Pritchard said, "and it ain't any telling what they'll do."

"They'll be gone when we get back," Mrs. Cope said.

Mrs. Pritchard could not stand an anticlimax. She required the taste of blood from time to time to keep her equilibrium. "I known a man oncet that his wife was poisoned by a child she had adopted out of pure kindness," she said. When they returned from town, the boys were not on the embankment and she said, "I would rather to see them than not to see them. When you see them you know what they're doing."

"Ridiculous," Mrs. Cope muttered. "I've scared them and they've gone and now we can forget them."

"I ain't forgetting them," Mrs. Pritchard said. "I wouldn't be none surprised if they didn't have a gun in that there suitcase."

Mrs. Cope prided herself on the way she handled the type of mind that Mrs. Pritchard had. When Mrs. Pritchard saw signs and omens, she exposed them calmly for the figments of imagination that they were, but this afternoon her nerves were taut and she said, "Now I've had about enough of this. Those boys are gone and that's that."

"Well, we'll wait and see," Mrs. Pritchard said.

Everything was quiet for the rest of the afternoon but at supper time Mrs. Pritchard came over to say that she had heard a high vicious laugh, full of calculated meanness, and she had heard it come three times, herself, distinctly.

"I haven't heard a thing," Mrs. Cope said.

"I look for them to strike just after dark," Mrs. Pritchard said.

That night Mrs. Cope and the child sat on the porch until nearly ten o'clock and nothing happened. The only sounds came from tree frogs and from one whippoorwill who called faster and faster from the same spot of darkness as if he had forgotten what the danger was but remembered the warning. "They've gone," Mrs. Cope said, "poor things," and she began to tell the child how much they had to be thankful for, for she said they might have had to live in a development themselves or they might have been negroes or they might have been in iron lungs or they might have been Europeans ridden in box cars like cattle, and she began a litany of her blessings, in a stricken voice, that the child, straining her attention for a sudden shriek in the dark, didn't listen to.

There was no sign of them the next morning either. The fortress line of trees was a hard granite blue, the wind had risen overnight and the sun had come up a pale gold. The season was changing. Even a small change in the weather made Mrs. Cope thankful, but when the seasons changed she seemed almost frightened at her good fortune in escaping whatever it was that pursued her. As she sometimes did when one thing was finished and another about to begin, she turned her attention to the child, who had put on a pair of overalls over her dress and had pulled a man's old felt hat down as far as it would go on her head and was arming herself with two pistols in a decorated holster that she had fastened around her waist. The hat was very tight and seemed to be squeezing the redness into her face. It came down almost to the tops of her glasses. Mrs. Cope watched her with a tragic look. "Why do you have to look like an idiot?" she asked. "Suppose company were to come? When are you going to grow up? What's going to become of you? I look at you and I want to cry! Sometimes you look like you might belong to Mrs. Pritchard!"

"Leave me be," the child said in a high irritated voice. "Leave me be. Just leave me be. I ain't you," and she went off to the woods as if she were stalking out an enemy, her head thrust forward and each hand gripped on a gun.

Mrs. Pritchard came over, sour-humored, because she didn't have anything calamitous to report. "I got the misery in my face today," she said, holding on to what she could salvage. "Theseyer teeth. They each one feel like an individual boil."

The child crashed through the woods, making the fallen leaves sound ominous under her feet. The sun had risen a little and was only a white hole like an opening for the wind to escape through in a sky a little darker than itself, and the tops of the trees were black against the glare. "I'm going to get you," she said. "I'm going to get you one by one and beat you black and blue. Line up. LINE UP!" she said and waved one of the pistols at a cluster of long bare-trunked pines, four times her height, as she passed them. She kept moving, muttering and growling to herself and occasionally hitting out with one of the guns at a branch that got in her way. From time to time she stopped to remove the thorn vine that caught at her skirt and she would say, "Leave me be, I told you. Leave me be," and give it a crack with the pistol and then stalk on.

Presently she sat down on a stump to cool off but she planted both feet carefully and firmly on the ground. She lifted them and put them down several times, grinding them fiercely into the dirt as if she were crushing something under her heels. Suddenly she heard a laugh.

She sat up, prickle-skinned. It came again. She heard the sound of splashing and she stood up, uncertain which way to run. She was not far from where this patch of woods ended and the back pasture began. She eased toward the pasture, careful not to make a sound, and coming suddenly to the edge of it, she saw the three boys, not twenty feet away, washing in the cow trough. Their clothes were piled against the black valise out of reach of the water that flowed over the side of the tank. The large boy was standing up and the small one was trying to climb onto his shoulders. Powell was sitting down looking straight ahead through glasses that were splashed with water. He was not paying any attention to the other two. The trees must have looked like green waterfalls through his wet glasses. The child stood partly hidden behind a pine trunk, the side of her face pressed into the bark.

"I wish I lived here!" the little boy shouted, balancing with his knees clutched around the big one's head.

"I'm goddam glad I don't," the big boy panted, and jumped up to dislodge him.

Powell sat without moving, without seeming to know that the other two were behind him, and looked straight ahead like a ghost sprung upright in his coffin. "If this place was not here any more," he said, "you would never have to think of it again."

"Listen," the big boy said, sitting down quietly in the water with the little one still moored to his shoulders, "it don't belong to nobody."

"It's ours," the little boy said.

The child behind the tree did not move.

Powell jumped out of the trough and began to run. He ran all the way around the field as if something were after him, and as he passed the tank coming back, the other two jumped out and raced with him, the sun glinting on their long wet bodies. The big one ran the fastest and was the leader. They dashed around the field twice and finally dropped down by their clothes and lay there with their ribs moving up and down. After a while, the big one said hoarsely, "Do you know what I would do with this place if I had the chance?"

"No, what?" the little boy said and sat up to give him his full attention.

"I'd build a big parking lot on it, or something," he muttered.

They began to dress. The sun made two white spots on Powell's glasses and blotted out his eyes. "I know what let's do," he said. He took something small from his pocket and showed it to them. For almost a minute they sat looking at what he had in his hand. Then without any more discussion, Powell picked up the suitcase and they got up and moved past the child and entered the woods not ten feet from where she was standing, slightly away from the tree now, with the imprint of the bark embossed red and white on the side of her face.

She watched with a dazed stare as they stopped and collected all the matches they had between them and began to set the brush on fire. They began to whoop and holler and beat their hands over their mouths and in a few seconds there was a narrow line of fire widening between her and them. While she stared, it reached up from the brush, snatching and biting at the lowest branches of the trees. The wind carried rags of it higher and the boys disappeared shrieking behind it.

She turned and tried to run across the field but her legs were too heavy and she stood there, weighted down with some new unplaced misery that she had never felt before. But finally she began to run.

Mrs. Cope and Mrs. Pritchard were in the field behind the barn when Mrs. Cope saw smoke rising from the woods across the pasture. She shrieked and Mrs. Pritchard pointed up the road to where the child came loping heavily, screaming, "Mama, Mama, they're going to build a parking lot here!"

Mrs. Cope began to scream for the negroes while Mrs. Pritchard, charged now, ran down the road shouting. Mr. Pritchard came out of the open end of the barn and the two negroes stopped filling the manure spreader in the lot and started toward Mrs. Cope with their shovels. "Hurry, hurry!" she shouted, "start throwing dirt on it!" They passed her almost without looking at her and headed off slowly across the field toward the smoke. She ran after them a little way, charging them like a fierce dog, shrilling, "Hurry, hurry, don't you see it! Don't you see it!"

"It'll be there when we git there," Culver said and they thrust their shoulders forward a little and went on at the same pace.

The child came to a stop beside her mother and stared up at her face as if she had never seen it before. It was the face of the new misery she felt, but on her mother it looked old and it looked as if it might have belonged to anybody, a negro or a European or to Powell himself. The child turned her head quickly, and past the negroes' ambling figures she could see the grey column of smoke rising and widening unchecked inside the granite line of trees. She stood taut, listening, and could just catch in the distance a few wild high shrieks of joy as if the prophets were dancing in the fiery furnace, in the circle the angel had cleared for them.

FREDERICK BUECHNER *was born in New York City in 1926. He was educated at Lawrenceville School and Princeton University, with two years in the Army intervening. After graduating from Princeton, he returned to Lawrenceville, where he was a member of the English faculty for five years, one of which he spent on leave of absence in Europe. Since then he has taught creative writing for one summer at New York University. His other literary work consists of two novels,* A Long Day's Dying (1950) *and* The Seasons' Difference (1952).

THE TIGER

FROM THE NEW YORKER

Even though I lived nearby, I hardly ever went back to football games. I had enjoyed them as an undergraduate—had enjoyed the fresh, cold weather of them, at least, and the ringing autumn skies, the popping up all around me of familiar faces and of faces I'd think at first I recognized but would discover to be somehow hilariously unfamiliar, and the band, the parading at the half, all the trappings. More than anything else, perhaps, I used to enjoy watching the girls with their pink cheeks and shiny hair, their pennants and chrysanthemums, sitting all bundled up in coats and blankets beside their beaux and absolutely in the dark, as far as I could tell, about what was happening on the little green oblong of field that lay, as if seen through the wrong end of a telescope, far below. Not that it mattered, of course, because they'd tip up their little chins and drink like birds from the boys' flasks and then jump around with such excitement that they had to grab hold of the boys' arms for support—just as if the whole thing made good sense.

Once in a while, I used to bring a girl down myself, but I was a handholder in those days, and that made it almost impossible to pay attention to anything but the hand I was trying to hold. I was also a cuticle chewer, and it took all my ingenuity to hold hands without letting the girl either see or feel the ragged ends of my fingers. I always thought that if I ever found a girl who had ragged fingers, too, I'd ask her to marry me, but I never found one. So I finally took to going by myself, pretty much, and enjoying the spectacle alone. Still, once I graduated and started working, I seldom went back. But then, one day this October, a group of my classmates who had come down for a kind of unofficial reunion asked me to be the tiger, and although I knew that they did it mostly as a joke, because there was no one much less likely for the job than I, for some reason or other I said that I would.

When we were in college ourselves, there was always a real tiger. They'd rent an old one from a zoo, bring it down in a truck, march it around and around the stadium, and then cart it back again in the truck. As I think about it now, that seems characteristic of the late twenties. They were always going to fantastic amounts of trouble for something that was often rather silly, especially if it was something connected with having a good time, in this case with a real tiger. Nowadays you don't take so much trouble, but all you end up with is a fake. At every game now, they just get somebody to run around dressed up in a tiger costume, and that's that. On this particular occasion, I was it.

Although drinking falls far short of explaining everything that happened that day, I won't pretend that I didn't do a certain amount of it before assuming my new role. My classmates and I met in a boathouse not far from the stadium. The cry was pretty generally "Let's get the old tiger clobbered," and they went about it the way a woman will sometimes try to coax her child to finish its supper, with "Now a bite for Grandpa. Now a bite for Agnes. Now a bite for Uncle George."

"Here's one for your treacherous yellow eyes," one of them would say, and fifths would be tipped all around. Then "Here's one for your wiggly tail," "Here's one for your fuzzy whiskers and the stripes down your back," "Here's one for your lonely, savage heart," and so forth.

This went on for a good hour before we were due at the game, and I'll say in my own defense that several of them were hit a lot harder than I was. In fact, when it came time to help me on with my costume, Fred Bobo and Percy Meeker, who had been the two brightest lights athletically our upper-class years, could hardly stand. It's a wonder they ever managed to get me into the thing at all. It was a loose-fitting affair that zipped up the belly, complete with

big, floppy paws to cover your hands and feet, a tail hanging down
behind, and a fairly elaborate tiger head that came down over your
face and fastened in front. Attached to the inside of one of the paws
was a string with which you could open and close the mouth, and
inside the other was a small battery with a button that you pressed
to blink the yellow bulbs of the eyes. You looked out through two
tiny holes in the chin. It was a cumbersome outfit, but they got me
into it all right, and after a little difficulty seeing where I was going
I finally caught the hang of it and was able to get along quite well.

It was a gorgeous day—hardly a cloud in the deep sky, the air as
cool as the ocean in early spring, and a dazzling sun. The crowd
was already exhilarated just by the splendor of the afternoon, and
before the kickoff I was definitely the center of attraction. I walked
out onto the field a little unsteadily, I'm afraid, but when I flashed
my eyes on and off for them, and then, opening my whiskered jaws
wide, clapped my paws at my own prowess, they roared with pleasure.
All sorts of tricks kept occurring to me, and even after play started,
I managed, at relatively quiet moments in the game, to catch their
eye. I got down on all fours and chased my tail like a kitten, or
pounced at bits of paper or pop bottles that had fallen from the
stands; I picked up my tail and, holding it delicately in one paw,
did a rather erratic waltz; or I just circled around the track waving
at the children and purposely getting in the way of the cheerleaders.

My classmates, who sat in one of the lower tiers near the fifty-
yard line, were especially vociferous in their acclaim and kept urging
me to reinforce myself from one of their bottles. Once or twice I did
—not nearly as often as they would have liked, of course, but enough
so that there seemed to be a marvellous golden mist over the whole
scene. Everything sparkled like morning dew in a garden, and my
feet were as light as in dreams. The game was an intricate pastoral
rite and I the high priest; the players charged and fell, fumbled and
kicked, at my whim, and when the stadium rose to its feet in excitement, it was rising for me, and I would bow or do a somersault
in acknowledgment. All in all, I was jubilant enough as it was, so
you can imagine the degree of my exultation when I discovered that,
in addition to ritual and priest, there was also a goddess.

Once, as a child, I thought I saw an angel sitting in a dogwood
tree and trying to get a splinter out of its foot; I have seen two queens
in my life and I suppose at least a dozen movie actresses; but never
was I so struck by the apparition of beauty as when I came across

this girl stifling a small yawn there in the autumn sun. She was sitting across the aisle from where my classmates were, and I stopped for a moment beside her and cocked my head over one shoulder, the way animals do when they hear a noise that puzzles them.

"Look at the lovely tiger," she said, in a soft, hoarse little voice to the boy at her side. She had curly black hair and blue eyes.

"Look at the lovely old drunk inside," the boy answered.

"Why, there's nothing inside," she said. "That's all solid tiger. That's a tiger through and through."

"That's a tiger so they say,
And when he goes to Heaven, he'll go the other way."

The boy sang abominably.

"That tiger will go to Heaven," she told him.

Absurd as it may sound, I had already fallen in love with her. I loved even the feather in the hat she wore thrust down somewhat too firmly on the back of her head. It was somehow the bravest feather I'd ever seen. The world might do the worst it knew how, but that skinny feather would always go on not giving an inch. You could destroy it, of course, but you could never scare it.

"Drop dead, tiger," the boy said. "You're blocking the view."

And then there was a long end run, and they were all on their feet yelling. When I reached the track, running down two steps at a time, I tripped on my tail and went sprawling on the gravel, but the heavy costume kept me from being hurt very much. I stayed on the ground just long enough to see that the girl was watching me; then I jumped up again and ran around toward the cheerleaders.

The score was tied by the last quarter, and nobody was paying much attention to me. I did the kitten business a few more times, and a waltz or two, just to keep warm as much as anything—it had clouded over and there was a bitter wind—but I don't believe that more than a handful of children noticed. Then one of our tackles was injured, there was a long time out, and I took the opportunity to wander out onto the field—to the enemy side, where the enemy quarterback was down on one knee tightening some tape around his ankle.

He turned when I growled behind him, and I can't remember ever seeing an uglier human face—two little bullet-hole eyes and a loose, heavy mouth. Fanning my nose with my left thumb, I started circling around and pretending to box with him, but he wouldn't get up; he just stayed there on one knee, looking at me and continuing to fix his tape. As soon as he finished, he sprang to his feet, and I thought he was going to play along with me until the whistle blew, but instead he gave me a hard push. I came at him again, but again he pushed me, even harder than before. "Scat, you damned fool!" he said.

I should have let him alone, of course, but, like the damned fool he'd called me, I went down on the ground and started pouncing at his feet. The next thing I knew, he'd given me a kick strong enough to knock the tiger head back over my ears. I lay there for a moment half stunned, and then I did a most unusual thing.

I tried to bite him. Understand, I couldn't use my tiger jaws, because the thing had been knocked almost off; I used my own. I opened my mouth wide and tried to get him on the ankle. But, luckily for me, he sidestepped, and then the whistle blew, so he didn't have time for a reprisal. He just gave a kind of hooting laugh and ran back into position, and I returned to our own side of the field.

There were only about ten minutes left to go, and the crowd was so wrapped up in the game that there didn't seem to be much point in trying to distract them, so I just climbed back into the stands and took a seat with my classmates. They passed the bottle to me, of course, but I refused. I had reached that point where you see everything you do as plainly and objectively as though it really weren't you doing it at all, and where, when you look at yourself in a mirror, you see a face that's actually not your face and can say to it, "Well, my friend, and just what do you think you're all about?" It was a point that fascinated me, and I didn't want to spoil it by having any more to drink. So I merely sat there beside Fred Bobo, with the tiger head between my knees, and let my thoughts run free.

My bout with the quarterback had been a fiasco, and his parting hoot still rang in my head. If I really had managed to bite him, his revenge would undoubtedly have been bloodcurdling, but I would have felt better, anyway. It was one thing for a tiger to pounce at bits of paper and waltz with his tail, but to let somebody treat him as I had been treated and escape unscarred was quite another. I couldn't help thinking how one of the old real ones would have reacted, and the contrast depressed me. Times had changed, I decided, and then I looked up at the enormous sky, all silvery gray now, with masses of slow clouds, and wondered about that change. The tackle who had been hurt before had gone back into the game. Now he was hurt again, and while he was being carried off I made an attempt at discussing the subject with Fred Bobo. But all he would say was, "That lad's got courage, all right, spelled 'g-u-t-s.' "

I think he must have said it four times, so I had to keep my ideas to myself. What they consisted of mainly was the feeling that since the time when we had been undergraduates ourselves, things had changed in a way of which the difference between me and the real tigers was a kind of brief equation. And although it had been a change in the general direction of sanity, probably—renting tigers from the zoo had been ridiculously troublesome and expensive—I decided that there wasn't one of us who wouldn't gladly have gone back. The twenties might have roared themselves into a genuine mess, but at least they had genuinely roared. The fifties were all dressed up to look like something that could roar, but nothing came out except a whimper—me. There was no use trying to explain all this to Fred Bobo, though. He was too busy spelling out the kind of courage the injured tackle had.

And then we won the game. In college football, it never makes much difference, because you can have just as good a time drowning your sorrow as whooping up your victory, but I register the fact because, of course, I went down again and tried to look like a tiger trying to look like the band leader who, with me imitating him from behind, led the band in the slow, sad college anthem while most of the undergraduates stormed out onto the field to protect the goalposts from being torn down by most of the other undergraduates. With the tiger head back on again, I blinked my eyes and waved my tail in time to the music, and everybody was delighted.

Everybody remained delighted for some time. They piled into the various clubs—the big, popular clubs and the small, ratty ones, the clubs traditionally for athletes and the literary ones, the social ones —all of which were, for once, really very much the same. In each of them, bottles multiplied like the loaves and fishes, and what had at the stadium been only so many gloves clutching so many fur collars about so many chilly throats turned out to be flesh-and-blood wives. The undergraduates' young ladies, who, unlike the wives, always manage even during the game to preserve their identities, became even more unmistakably young ladies as they took off their polo coats and blankets, shook the autumn out of their hair, and twittered on about how divine it all was—just *it*—and how divine it was all going to be.

The men, in other words, were playing a relatively minor role, but on this particular occasion I, at least, received considerable attention. As soon as we left the stadium, I had been all for going straight to the boathouse and changing back into my own clothes, but Percy Meeker said I could pick them up if I wanted to, but that it had taken him and Bobo hours to get me into the tiger thing and he'd be damned if I didn't keep it on till Monday morning, at least. So I arrived at the club in full regalia and, naturally, caused some little stir. Bobo kept coming up from behind, grabbing hold of my tail, and saying that I had to keep drinking until it was warm down to the tip; somebody's wife insisted that I come and be a rug in her husband's study once the football season was over. I did my best. With a glass of beer in one hand and my tiger head in the other, I tried to conduct myself with a dignity appropriate to my memory of the real and gallant old tigers they had used when I was in college. And then I saw the girl again.

She was sitting on an enormous, canvas-covered bass-fiddle case with an Army mackinaw thrown over her knees, and there was no one with her. I could hear her humming, a little off key, the song the band was playing in another room, and then she noticed me and stopped.

"Tiger, tiger, burning bright," she said as I crouched down by her. "Why are you wearing that sad little false face when you have such a lovely tiger face of your own?"

I told her that I would take it off in a second if she really wanted me to, but that there had been a certain amount of anti-tiger feeling going around lately and I would just as soon not be recognized right away.

"Well, there's a lot of anti-sad-little-false-face feeling going around, too," she said, "but I guess you know what you're doing. I've never known a tiger who didn't."

"Then you've known others?" I had not been aware of looking sad, but I tried to smile, although even before I started, I knew it wasn't going to work out very well.

"Not a single one," she said. "Tell me about them."

There are times, Heaven knows, when anything you say is bound to be the wrong thing, but there are also times—much less common, of course—when anything you say is bound to be right, and this was one of those. It's like when you're holding hands under the table with a girl. Almost anything you can think of to say is all right, because underneath the table your hands are together and that sets everything straight. She'd asked me to tell her about tigers, but I knew that whatever came into my head would be fine by her—even telling her about the time I thought I saw the angel in the dogwood tree. As things turned out, though, I didn't get a chance to say another word. Crouching there beside her in tiger fashion, I reached forward to touch her fingers with my floppy paw and, in so doing, lost my balance. By reaching out to steady myself, I tipped over a golf bag that was leaning against the wall beside us, and it, in turn, fell down on a flimsy table loaded with half-empty glasses. There was a ghastly clatter, and the next thing I knew, Fred Bobo, who probably thought that things were getting a little dull anyway, had rushed up from behind, grabbed hold of my tail, and given it a mighty tug.

"Why, it's not even warm halfway down!" he shouted, waving the black pompon at the tip toward the girl. "Feel it for yourself. Cold as a haddock! Maybe you thought you had yourself a tiger, young lady, but this is just an old fake. Why, you lousy fourflusher!" he continued, clapping me playfully across the back. "Just an old fake on the make. A tired old fake on the tired old make. What do you think of that?"

His eyes bulged his question at her—what did she think of that, of his irresistible eloquence, of me, of the whole fantastic day, perhaps? Heaven knows what. I knew only that what had begun with the toasting in the boathouse and a waltz beneath the sparkling autumn sky had ended precisely here, and my only reaction was an overwhelming desire to get away.

Looking back at it, I can't help feeling that there's something of the poet in Fred Bobo. His phrase about the old fake on the make pleased him as much as courage spelled "g-u-t-s," and as a result he forgot about me entirely in his eagerness to pass it on to Percy Meeker, who was in no condition to appreciate it, and I was able to get away without any trouble at all.

As for the girl, I could easily have said goodbye to her—could have tried matching Fred's wit with something of my own, an "Abyssinia" or an "Olive oil"—but actually I never gave her so much as a backward glance. And, of course, I never got a chance to tell her about tigers, as she had asked me to, either. If I had, it would probably have gone something like this: Tigers are wild-hearted creatures of great strength and dignity who are to be found in jungles or in zoos and nowhere else. There was a time when every once in a while you'd see one parading around, unhurried and in superb control, at a football game, but that was twenty-five years ago, so if you think you see one there nowadays, you can be sure it's only a fake.

To that extent, then—I would have wanted her to know—Fred Bobo spoke the truth. In other words, to put it as briefly and painlessly as possible, in the world we're pretty much stuck with there simply are no tigers any more.

ROBERT BINGHAM *was born in 1925 in Lima,
Ohio. After his graduation from Exeter in 1943
he saw combat as an infantry private in Europe. He
then attended Harvard, where he met Janet Mc-
Phedran. They were married in 1950 and now
live in New York City. Mr. Bingham is assistant
managing editor of* The Reporter *magazine and
most of his published writing has been of a jour-
nalistic nature. He is now at work on a novel.*

THE UNPOPULAR PASSENGER

FROM THE REPORTER

Snow was falling out of the dark into the tiny cones of light under
street lamps down below as the plane circled to land at Cleveland.
When the hostess saw that I was awake and that my safety belt was
already fastened, she smiled efficiently and moved on down the aisle,
waking the other passengers and asking them to fasten their safety
belts. I did not make the effort to return her smile but turned again
to look down on the miniature suburbs below.

The young soldier sitting next to me stretched awake and looked
out the window too. "Must be a late party at that house," he said
through a yawn. He pointed to where the lights were on in one
half of a brick two-family house on a street of unlighted but otherwise identical brick two-family houses. Or somebody dying, was my
first thought.

Being awake at three or four in the morning, sober and bored,
waiting only for a certain time to elapse or a certain distance to be
traveled, reminded me inevitably of my own days and nights as a
soldier, of an emptiness in which at last even the too familiar prospect of death loses its power to provoke emotion.

After hovering uncertainly in the air, the plane settled clumsily
on the ground, stumbled to a stop, and then waddled into the brightly
lighted area around the terminal building, wheezing and gasping.
"One hour and forty-five minutes late," declared a resonant bass voice
several seats behind me. "I told them we'd be there at a decent

hour, but at this rate we won't be there before dawn." Several other passengers glanced at their wrist watches.

Those of us who were getting off at Cleveland stood in the aisle, and while I waited behind a woman with yellowish-white hair who was pointing at things she wanted her husband to pass down from the luggage rack, I was pushed abruptly against my seat by a short, fat man wearing a broad-brimmed blue hat that fitted down very far on his head. He also pushed the woman in front of me, and with an exaggerated cry of alarm she let herself fall back into the seat from which she had just arisen. A thin fox scarf had fallen onto the floor and lay there staring up at its mistress with eyes of orange bead. The woman snatched the animal to her and shook it violently. "Really!" she said indignantly, glaring back down the aisle at her assailant, who by this time had forced his way through the other passengers to be the first one out of the plane when the door was opened. Then she glared at her husband, a small man with steel-rimmed glasses, who averted his eyes and reached for a patent-leather hatbox. "Really!" the woman said again, this time loud enough for everyone in the plane to hear. "Some people just have no consideration."

When I left the plane I found the man in the big hat blocking my way at the bottom of the portable stairway. He was breathing heavily. "Hey, there, Miss Hostess!" he shouted past me up at the door of the plane. "I got to make a phone call." He coughed and turned his head to spit. "So where's the phone?" His face was made up of four round and very nearly equal bulbs of flesh—a forehead, two cheeks, and a nose. Under this last bulb a large lower lip hung down, wet and open.

The hostess suggested that if he would follow the other passengers to the terminal building he would find public telephones in the lobby. After glancing suspiciously through the screen of soft, dry snow in the direction she had pointed, he wheeled himself around and trotted awkwardly away on his short legs.

"And not one word of thanks, you'll notice," said the woman with the yellowish-white hair, clutching the bright-eyed fox firmly about her throat.

Even though the short, fat man had run all the way, I got to the terminal building almost as soon as he did. "Hey, there, Johnny!" he shouted to a uniformed pilot. "I got to make a phone call." He snapped his plump fingers impatiently. Looking down on the man in the big hat, the pilot permitted his mustache to twitch several times before he jerked his thumb contemptuously over his shoulder and paraded away.

Just outside the only booth that was free, two men had set down their briefcases and were going through their pockets for change, but the man in the big hat dived right between them toward the booth. "Just a minute there, my friend," said one of the men, taking hold of the intruder's elbow. It was the same resonant bass voice I had heard on the plane.

"I got to make a phone call," said the man in the big hat, weaving himself free of the taller man's grip and working his way into the booth.

"Oh, you got to make a phone call, have you?" the man with the deep voice mimicked. "Well, listen, my friend, I got to make a phone call too, and I was here first."

The man in the big hat drew in his breath and seemed about to speak, but instead he broke the grip on his elbow with a sudden snap and slammed the collapsible door of the booth shut behind him.

His mouth held open as if in speechless amazement, the man with the deep voice turned to his companion for confirmation of what he had just seen.

"How come you let him get away with that?" said the other man, stuttering slightly. The man with the deep voice stared angrily into the booth but said nothing. The voice from the booth, alternately threatening and pleading, was loud but indistinct. He might have been speaking in a foreign language.

The snack bar and the magazine stand were boarded over for the night, and so I stood outside near the limousine that would take me to downtown Cleveland and waited for the baggage to be brought around. The night was cold: I felt the walls of my nostrils sticking together, and the snow groaned and complained under my feet. Both the lights and the sounds of the airport were dimmed by the thickly falling snow.

Out of the dark a crowd loomed up upon me. There were five passengers, a man in a leather jacket whom I took to be the driver of the limousine, and two porters pulling a baggage cart. The passengers were all talking to the whole crowd at the same time, as if they were old friends or relatives who had just met after a long separation instead of strangers who had arrived in a large city by chance on the same plane.

One of the passengers—it was the man with a slight stutter—said, "I still don't see why you let him get away with it." He held the right front door of the limousine so that his companion would have to sit in the middle.

"He knocked me down, I tell you," said the woman with the fox scarf.

"What do you mean, why did *I* let him get away with it?" said the man with the deep voice. "You were standing right there. Why didn't you do something?"

"Well, for one thing," said the other man sarcastically, "it was you that wanted to use the phone, not me."

"Oh, what's the use?" said the man with the deep voice, accepting the inside seat. "It never does any good with people like that. They never change."

"You're absolutely right," said the woman with the fox scarf, employing elaborate gestures to arrange herself in the middle of the back seat. Her husband got in next to her, and I, not noticing the folded jump seats, sat down on the other side of her. The soldier took the jump seat in front of her husband, and the other two men were in the front.

"I wonder what he was in such a hurry to get to that phone for," said the soldier. He spoke in a flat nasal drawl.

"Business," said the man with the deep voice. "With those people it's always business." He held up a gloved hand and rubbed his thumb and forefinger together.

"And then you never can tell," said the soldier. "He might have had something on his mind."

"And did you notice the way he treated that sweet little hostess?" the woman interrupted. "Did you notice, dear?" Her husband cleared his throat. "With those people it's always self, self, self," she went on. "They have no human consideration for anyone whatsoever."

"Oh, I knew one or two of them that was all right," said the soldier. The man with the deep voice hummed skeptically.

After watching the porters stow our luggage in the trunk, the driver had gone back to the terminal building, and for a while we awaited his return in silence. We felt rather than heard the heavy rhythm of the limousine's motor. Both men in the front seat were smoking cigars, and the soldier and the woman lighted cigarettes. The stale air nauseated me, and at last I lowered my window about five or six inches. The woman, who had been smoking rapidly and nervously, stiffened beside me. "The snow seems to be coming in the windows," she pronounced mincingly. She sucked in a mouthful of smoke and expelled it immediately with a small explosion. Both men in the front seat turned around and watched me as I cranked up the window. Since leaving the plane, the woman had drawn an incongruously wide line across her mouth with lipstick. In the pale green light that came to us filtered through snow from the terminal building her mouth looked purple. "Really!" she muttered.

The man with the deep voice kept turning around to stare back at the terminal building, and we waited in silence once more. Tired as I was, I did not even look forward to sleeping. For me the tedium was almost entirely devoid of interest, appetite, or emotion. It was meaningless time, empty time, and the only thing I felt at all was a weak hatred for the other passengers.

"I wonder what keeps us waiting so long," said the soldier.

"Can't somebody do something?" the woman demanded resentfully.

The man with the deep voice stubbed his cigar out in the ash tray and devoted himself for several minutes to staring back at the terminal building before he gave it up and lighted another cigar. "I never should have let him get away with it," he said softly. The motor was running all the time.

Finally there were voices, and we all looked to see who was coming. The driver was walking rapidly toward the limousine carrying a small aluminum suitcase, and trotting along beside him, looking up into his face earnestly, came the short, fat man in the big hat.

"So that's who kept us waiting so long," said the woman, settling back triumphantly. "So that's who it is," said the soldier. The man with the slight stutter grunted. "No human consideration for anyone else whatsoever," the woman reminded us.

After the trunk had been slammed shut behind us, the driver opened the door beside me, pulled up the second jump seat, and stood back to let the last passenger get in. But before the short, fat man got in, he examined the driver's face carefully. "And I could get a cab right away?" he asked.

"Yes, yes, you could get a cab right away," said the driver, his tone suggesting that he had already answered the same question many times.

The man who had delayed our departure peered into the dark limousine suspiciously before taking his place on the jump seat in front of me. Only the stutterer met the newcomer's eyes, and then he looked expectantly at his companion. But the man with the deep voice was staring straight through the windshield in front of him. Nobody said a word.

The driver got in and we started on our way, with one loose chain clanking tiresomely against a fender above the soft sound the tires made pressing down against the dry snow. The short, fat man sat sideways in his seat, his face almost pressed against the glass. At first I thought that he was merely watching the view, trying to get a glimpse through the windows of houses where for some reason there happened to be people still up at that late hour. But each time the limousine passed under a street lamp, as it did with rhythmic regularity, I could see that he was weeping, biting his large lower lip cruelly in an effort to control his trembling, contorted features.

HORTENSE CALISHER'S *first published story was included in* The O. Henry Awards *for 1949. It had appeared originally in* The New Yorker, *a magazine to which she has continued to contribute, as well as publishing in* Mademoiselle, Charm, *and others. A collection,* In the Absence of Angels, *was issued by Little, Brown & Co. in 1951. She was abroad on a Guggenheim Fellowship in 1952–53, and it was in London, during that time, that she wrote "A Christmas Carillon." A native of New York City, and a graduate of Barnard, after residence in upstate New York and the Middle West, she has been settled, for the last seven years, in the Hudson Valley with her husband and two children.*

A CHRISTMAS CARILLON

FROM HARPER'S MAGAZINE

About four weeks before Christmas, Grorley, in combined shame and panic, began to angle for an invitation to somewhere, anywhere, for Christmas Day. By this time, after six months of living alone in the little Waverly Place flat to which he had gone as soon as he and his wife had decided to separate, he had become all too well reacquainted with his own peculiar mechanism in regard to solitude. It was a mechanism that had its roots in the jumbled lack of privacy of an adolescence spent in the dark, four-room apartment to which his parents had removed themselves and three children after his father's bankruptcy in '29. Prior to that, Grorley's childhood had been what was now commonly referred to as Edwardian—in a house where servants and food smells kept their distance until needed, and there were no neurotic social concerns about the abundance of either—a house where there was always plush under the buttocks, a multiplicity of tureens and napery at table, lace on the pillow, and above all that general expectancy of creature comfort and spiritual order which novelists now relegated to the days before 1914.

That it had lasted considerably later, Grorley knew, since this had been the year of his own birth, but although he had been fifteen when they had moved, it was the substantial years before that had faded to fantasy. Even now, when he read or said the word "reality," his mind reverted to Sunday middays in the apartment house living room, where the smudgy daylight was always diluted by lamps, the cheaply stippled walls menaced the oversized furniture, and he, his father and brother and sister, each a claustrophobe island of irritation, were a constant menace to one another. Only his mother, struggling alone in the kitchen with the conventions of roast chicken and gravy, had perhaps achieved something of the solitude they all had craved. To Grorley even now, the smell of roasting fowl was the smell of a special kind of Sunday death.

Only once before now had he lived alone, and then too it had been in the Village, not far from where he presently was. After his graduation from City College he had worked a year, to save up for a master's in journalism, and then, salving his conscience with the thought that he had at least paid board at home for that period, he had left his family forever. The following year, dividing his time between small-time newspaper job and classes, living in his $27 per month place off Morton Street, he had savored all the wonders of the single doorkey opening on the quiet room, of the mulled book and the purring clock, of the smug decision not to answer the phone and let even the most delightful invader in. Now that he looked back on it, of course, he recalled that the room had rung pretty steadily with the voices of many such who had been admitted, but half the pleasure had been because it had been at his own behest. That had been a happy time, when he had been a gourmet of loneliness, prowling bachelor-style on the edge of society, dipping inward when he chose. Of all the habitations he had had since, that had been the one whose conformations he remembered best, down to the last, worn dimple of brick. When he had house-hunted, last June, he had returned instinctively to the neighborhood of that time. Only a practicality born of superstition had kept him from hunting up the very street, the very house.

He had had over two years of his freedom, although the last third of it had been rather obscured by his courtship of Eunice. Among the girl students of the Village there had been quite a few who, although they dressed like ballerinas and prattled of art like painters' mistresses, drew both their incomes and their morality from good, solid middle-class families back home. Eunice had been the prettiest and most sought after of these, and part of her attraction for some, and certainly for Grorley, had been that she seemed to be, quite honestly, one of those rare girls who were not particularly eager to marry and settle down. Grorley had been so entranced at finding like feelings in a girl—and in such a beautiful one—that he had quite forgotten that in coaxing her out of her "freedom" he was persuading himself out of his own.

He had not realized this with any force until the children came, two within the first four years of the marriage. Before that, in the first fusion of love, it had seemed to Grorley that two could indeed live more delightfully alone than one, and added to this had been that wonderful release from jealousy which requited love brings—half the great comfort of the loved one's presence being that, *ipso facto*, she is with no one else. During this period of happy, though enlarged privacy, Grorley confided to Eunice some, though not all, of his feelings about family life and solitude. He was, he told her, the kind of person who needed to be alone a great deal—although this of course excepted her. But they must never spend their Sundays and holidays frowsting in the house like the rest of the world, sitting there stuffed and droning, with murder in their hearts. They must always have plans laid well in advance, plans which would keep the two of them emotionally limber, so to speak, and *en plein air*. Since these plans were always pleasant—tickets to the Philharmonic, with after-theater suppers, hikes along the Palisades, fishing expeditions to little-known ponds back of the Westchester parkways, whose intricacies Grorley, out of a history of Sunday afternoons, knew as well as certain guides knew Boca Raton—Eunice was quite willing to accede. In time she grew very tactful, almost smug, over Grorley's little idiosyncrasy, and he sometimes heard her on the phone, fending people off. "Not Sunday. Gordon and I have a thing about holidays, you know." By this time, too, they had both decided that, although Grorley would keep his now very respectable desk job at the paper, his real destiny was to "write"; and to Eunice, who respected "imagination" as only the unimaginative can, Grorley's foible was the very proper defect of a noble intelligence.

But with the coming of the children, it was brought home to Grorley that he was face to face with one of those major rearrangements of existence for which mere tact would not suffice. Eunice, during her first pregnancy, was as natural and unassuming about it as a man could wish; she went on their Sunday sorties to the very last, and maintained their gallant privacy right up to the door of the delivery room. But the child of so natural a mother was bound to be natural too. It contracted odd fevers whenever it wished, and frequently on Sundays became passionately endeared to their most expensive sitter, or would have none at all, and in general permeated their lives as only the most powerfully frail of responsibilities can. And when the second one arrived, it did so, it seemed to Grorley, only to egg the other one on.

There came a morning, the Christmas morning of the fourth year, when Grorley, sitting in the odor of baked meat, first admitted that his hydra-headed privacy was no longer a privacy at all. He had created, he saw, his own monster; sex and the devil had had their sport with him, and he was, in a sense that no mere woman would understand, all too heavily "in the family way." Looking at Eunice, still neat, still very pretty, but with her lovely mouth pursed with maternity, her gaze sharp enough for *Kinder* and *Küche*, but abstract apparently for him, he saw that she had gone over to the enemy and was no longer his. Eunice had become "the family" too.

It was as a direct consequence of this that Grorley wrote the book which was his making. Right after that fatal morning, he had engaged a room in a cheap downtown hotel (he and Eunice were living out in Astoria at the time), with the intention, as he explained to Eunice, of writing there after he left the paper, and coming home weekends. He had also warned her that, because of the abrasive effects of family life, it would probably be quite some time before "the springs of reverie"—a phrase he had lifted from Ellen Glasgow —would start churning. His real intention was, of course, to prowl, and for some weeks thereafter he joined the company of those men who could be found, night after night, in places where they could enjoy the freedom of not having gone home where they belonged.

To his surprise, he found, all too quickly, that though his intentions were of the worst, he had somehow lost the moral force to pursue them. He had never been much for continuous strong drink, and that crude *savoir-faire* which was needed for the preliminaries to lechery seemed to have grown creaky with the years. He took to spending odd hours in the newspaper morgue, correlating, in a halfhearted way, certain current affairs that interested him. After some months, he suddenly realized that he had enough material for a book. It found a publisher almost immediately. Since he was much more a child of his period than he knew, he had hit upon exactly that note between disaffection and hope which met response in the breasts of those who regarded themselves as permanent political independents. His book was an instant success with those who thought of themselves as thinking for themselves (if they had only had time for it). Quick to capitalize upon this, Grorley's paper gave him a biweekly column, and he developed a considerable talent for telling men of good will, over Wednesday breakfast, the very thing they had been saying to one another at Tuesday night dinner.

Grorley spent the war years doing this, always careful to keep his column, like his readers, one step behind events. With certain minor changes, he kept, too, that scheme of life which had started him writing, changing only, with affluence, to a more comfortable hotel. In time also, that *savoir-faire* whose loss he had mourned returned to him, and his success at his profession erased any guilts he might otherwise have had—a wider experience, he told himself, being not only necessary to a man of his trade, but almost unavoidable in the practice of it. He often congratulated himself at having achieved, in a country which had almost completely domesticated the male, the perfect pattern for a man of temperament, and at times he became almost insufferable to some of his married men friends, when he dilated on the contrast between his "continental" way of life and their own. For by then, Grorley had reversed himself—it was his weekends and holidays that were now spent cozily *en famille*. It was pleasant, coming back to the house in Tarrytown on Friday evenings, coming back from the crusades, to find Eunice and the whole household decked out literally, and psychologically, for his return. One grew sentimentally fond of children whom one saw only under such conditions—Grorley's Saturdays were now spent, as he himself boasted, "on all fours," in the rejuvenating air of the skating rinks, the museums, the woods, and the zoos. Sundays and holidays he and Eunice often entertained their relatives, and if, as the turkey browned, he had a momentary twinge of his old *mal de famille*, he had but to remember that his hat was, after all, only hung in the hall.

It was only some years after the war that Eunice began to give trouble. Before that, their double ménage had not been particularly unusual—almost all the households of couples their age had been upset in one way or another, and theirs had been more stable than many. During the war years Eunice had had plenty of company for her midweek evenings, for all over America women had been managing bravely behind the scenes. But now that families had long since paired off again, Eunice showed a disquieting tendency to want to be out in front.

"No, you'll have to come home for good," she said to Grorley, at the end of their now frequent battles. "I'm tired of being a short-order wife."

"The trouble with you," said Grorley, "is that you've never adjusted to postwar conditions."

"That was your 1946 column," said Eunice. "If you must quote yourself, pick one a little more up-to-date." Removing a jewel-encrusted slipper-toe from the fender, she made a feverish circle of the room, the velvet panniers of her housegown swinging dramatically behind her. She was one of those women who used their charge accounts for retaliation. With each crisis in their deteriorating relationship, Grorley noted gloomily, Eunice's wardrobe had improved.

"Now that the children are getting on," he said, "you ought to have another interest. A hobby."

Eunice made a hissing sound. "1947!" she said.

In the weeks after, she made her position clear. Men, she told him, might have provided the interest he suggested, but when a woman had made a vocation of one, it was not easy to start making a hobby of several. It was hardly much use swishing out in clouds of Tabu at seven, if one had to be back to feel Georgie's forehead at eleven. Besides, at their age, the only odd men out were likely to be hypochondriacs, or bachelors still dreaming of their mothers, or very odd men indeed.

"All the others," she said nastily, "are already on somebody else's hearth rug. Or out making the rounds with you." Worst of all, she seemed to have lost her former reverence for Grorley's work. If he had been a novelist or a poet, she said (she even made use of the sticky word "creative"), there would have been more excuse for his need to go off into the silence. As it was, she saw no reason for his having to be so broody over analyzing the day's proceedings at the UN. If he wanted an office, that should take care of things very adequately. But if he did not wish to live *with* her, then he could not go on *living* with her. "Mentally," she said, "you're still in the Village. Maybe you better go back there."

Things were at this pass when Grorley's paper sent him to London, on an assignment that kept him there for several months. He was put up for membership in several exclusively masculine clubs, and in their leonine atmosphere his outraged vanity—("creative" indeed!) —swelled anew. Finally, regrettably near the end of his stay, he met up with a redheaded young woman named Vida, who worked for a junior magazine by day, wrote poetry by night, and had once been in America for three weeks. She and Grorley held hands over the mutual hazards of the "creative" life, and on her lips the word was like a caress. For a woman, too, she was remarkably perceptive about the possessiveness of other women. "Yes, quite," she had said. "Yes, quite."

When she and Grorley had made their final adieu in her Chelsea flat, she had held him, for just a minute, at arms' length. "I shall be thinking of you over there, in one of those ghastly, what do you call them, *living rooms*, of yours. Everybody matted together, and the floor all over children—like beetles. Poor dear. I should think those living rooms must be the curse of the American family. Poor, poor dear."

On his return home in June, Grorley and Eunice agreed on a six-months trial separation prior to a divorce. Eunice showed a rather unfeeling calm in the lawyer's office, immediately afterward popped the children in camp, and went off to the Gaspé with friends. Grorley took a sublet on the apartment in Waverly Place. It was furnished in a monastic modern admirably suited to the novel he intended to write, that he had promised Vida to write.

He had always liked summers in town, when the real *aficionados* of the city took over, and now this summer seemed to him intoxicating, flowing with the peppery currents of his youth. In the daytime his freedom slouched unshaven; in the evenings the streets echoed and banged with life, and the moon made a hot harlequinade of every alley. He revisited the San Remo, Julius', Chumley's, Jack Delaney's, and all the little Italian bars with backyard restaurants, his full heart and wallet carrying him quickly into the cameraderie of each. Occasionally he invited home some of the remarkables he met on his rounds—a young Italian bookie, a huge St. Bernard of a woman who drove a taxi and had once lived on a barge on the East River, an attenuated young couple from Chapel Hill, who were honeymooning at the New School. Now and then a few of his men friends from uptown joined him in a night out. A few of these, in turn, invited him home for the weekend, but although he kept sensibly silent on the subject of their fraternal jaunts, he detected some animus in the hospitality of their wives.

By October, Grorley was having a certain difficulty with his weekends. His list of bids to the country was momentarily exhausted, and his own ideas had begun to flag. The children, home from camp, had aged suddenly into the gang phase; they tore out to movies and jamborees of their own, were weanable from these only by what Grorley could scrape up in the way of rodeos and football games, and assumed, once the afternoon's treat was over, a faraway look of sufferance. Once or twice, when he took them home, he caught himself hoping that Eunice would ask him in for a drink, a chat that might conceivably lead to dinner, but she was always out, and Mrs. Lederer, the housekeeper, always pulled the children in as if they were packages whose delivery had been delayed, gave him a nasty nod, and shut the door.

For a few weekends he held himself to his desk, trying to work up a sense of dedication over the novel, but there was no doubt that it was going badly. Its best juice had been unwisely expended in long, analytic letters to Vida, and now, in her air-mail replies, which bounced steadily and enthusiastically over the Atlantic, it began to seem more her novel than his. The Sunday before Thanksgiving, he made himself embark on a ski-train to Pittsfield, working up a comforting sense of urgency over the early rising, the impedimenta to be checked. The crowd on the train was divided between a band of Swiss and German perfectionists who had no conversation, and a horde of young couples, rolling on the slopes like puppies, who had too much. Between them, Grorley's privacy was respected to the point of insult. When he returned that night, he tossed his gear into a corner, where it wilted damply on his landlord's blond rug, made himself a hot toddy—with a spasm of self-pity over his ability to do for himself—and sat down to face his fright. For years, his regular intervals at home had been like the chewed coffee bean that renewed the winetaster's palate. He had lost the background from which to rebel.

Thanksgiving Day was the worst. The day dawned oyster-pale and stayed that way. Grorley slept as late as he could, then went out for a walk. The streets were slack, without the twitch of crowds, and the houses had a tight look of inner concentration. He turned toward the streets which held only shops, and walked uptown as far as Rockefeller Center. The rink was open, with its usual cast of characters—

ricocheting children, a satiny, professional twirler from the Ice Show, and several solemn old men who skated upright in some Euclidian absorption of their own. Except for a few couples strolling along in the twin featurelessness of love, the crowd around the rink was type-cast too. Here, it told itself, it participated in life; here in this flying spectacle of flag and stone it could not possibly be alone. With set, shy smiles, it glanced sideways at its neighbors, rounded its shoulders to the wind, turned up its collar, and leaned closer to the musical bonfire of the square. Grorley straightened up, turned on his heel, smoothed down his collar, and walked rapidly toward Sixth Avenue. He filled himself full of ham and eggs in one of the quick-order places that had no season, taxied home, downed a drink, swallowed two Seconal tablets, and went to bed.

The next morning, seated at his desk, he took a relieved look at the street. People were hard at their normal grind again; for a while the vacuum was past. But Christmas was not going to catch him alone. With set teeth, he picked up the phone. At the end of the day he was quite heartened. Although he had not yet turned up an invitation for Christmas Day, he had netted himself a cocktail party, which might easily go on to dinner, for two days before, a bid to an egg-nog party on New Year's Day, and one weekend toward the middle of December. A lot of people did things impromptu. A phone call now and then would fix him up somehow.

But by Christmas week he was haggard. He had visualized himself as bidden to share, in a pleasantly avuncular capacity, some close friend's family gathering; he had seen himself as indolently and safely centered, but not anchored, in the bright poinsettia of their day. Apparently their vision of him was cast in a harsher mold; they returned his innuendoes with little more than a pointed sympathy. Only two propositions had turned up, one from a group of men, alone like himself for one reason or another, who were forming a party at an inn in the Poconos, and one from a waif-like spinster— "Last Christmas was my last one with dear mother"—who offered to cook dinner for him in her apartment. Shuddering, he turned down both of these. The last thing he wanted to do on that day was to ally himself with *waifs* of any description; on that day he very definitely wanted to be safely inside some cozy family cocoon, looking out at *them*.

Finally, the day before Christmas, he thought of the Meechers. Ted was that blue-ribbon bore, the successful account executive who believed in his slogans, and his wife, a former social worker, matched him in her own field. Out of Ted's sense of what was due his position in the agency, and Sybil's sense of duty to the world, they had created a model home in Chappaqua, equipped with four children, two Bedlingtons, a games room, and a part-time pony. Despite this, they were often hard up for guests, since most people could seldom be compelled twice to their table, where a guest was the focus of a constant stream of self-congratulation from either end. Moreover, Ted had wormed his way into more than one stag party at Grorley's, and could hardly refuse a touch. And their Christmas, whatever its other drawbacks, would be a four-color job, on the best stock.

But Ted's voice, plum-smooth when he took the phone from his secretary, turned reedy and doubtful when he heard Grorley's inquiry. "Uh-oh! 'Fraid that puts me on the spot, fella. Yeah. Kind of got it in the neck from Sybil, last time I came home from your place. Yeah. Had a real old-fashioned hassel. Guess I better not risk reminding her just yet. But, say! How about coming up here right now, for the office party?"

Grorley declined, and hung up. Off-campus boy this time of year, that's what I am, he thought. He looked at his mantelpiece crowded with its reminders—greetings from Grace and Bill, Jane and Tom, Peg and Jack, Etcetera and Mrs. Etcetera. On top of the pile was another air-mail from Vida, received that morning, picture enclosed. Sans the red in the hair, without the thrush tones of the assenting voice, she looked a little long in the teeth. Her hands and feet, he remembered, were always cold. Somehow or other, looking at the picture, he did not think that central heating would improve them. "The living room is the curse," she had said. That's it, he thought; that's it. And this, Vida, is the season of the living room.

He looked down into the street. The Village was all right for the summer, he thought. But now the periphery of the season had changed. In summer, the year spins on a youth-charged axis, and a man's muscles have a spurious oil. But this is the end toward which it spins. Only three hundred days to Christmas. Only a month—a week. And then, every year, the damned day itself, catching him with its holly claws, sounding its platitudes like carillons.

Down at the corner, carols bugled steamily from a mission soup-kitchen. There's no escape from it, he thought. Turn on the radio, and its alleluia licks you with tremolo tongue. In every store window flameth housegown, nuzzleth slipper. In all the streets the heavenly shops proclaim. The season has shifted inward, Grorley, and you're on the outside, looking in.

He moved toward the phone, grabbed it, and dialed the number before he remembered that you had to get the operator for Tarrytown. He replaced the receiver. Whatever he had to say, and he wasn't quite sure what, or how, it wasn't for the ears of the kids or the Lederer woman. He jammed on his hat. Better get there first, get inside the door.

Going up to Grand Central in the cab, he pressed his face against the glass. Everything had been taken care of weeks ago—the kids had been sent their two -wheelers, and he had mailed Eunice an extra-large check—one he hadn't sent through the lawyer. But at five o'clock Fifth Avenue still shone like an enormous blue sugarplum revolving in a tutti-frutti rain of light. Here was the season in all its questionable glory—the hallmarked joy of giving, the good will *diamanté*. But in the cosmetic air, people raised tinted faces, walked with levitated step.

In the train, he avoided the smoker, and chose an uncrowded car up front. At his station, he waited until all the gleaming car muzzles pointed at the train had picked up their loads and gone, then walked through the main street which led to his part of town. All was lit up here too, with a more intimate, household shine. He passed the pink damp of a butcher's, the bright fuzz of Woolworth's. "Sold out!" said a woman, emerging. " 'S try the A & P." He walked on, invisible, his face pressed to the shop window of the world.

At Schlumbohn's Credit Jewelry Corner he paused, feeling for the wallet filled with cash yesterday for the still not impossible yes over the phone. This was the sort of store that he and Eunice, people like them, never thought of entering. It sold watches pinned to cards, zircons, musical powder-boxes, bracelets clasped with fat ten-carat hearts, Rajah pearl necklaces and Truelove blue-white diamonds. Something for Everybody, it said. He opened the door.

Inside a magnetic salesgirl nipped him toward her like a pin. He had barely stuttered his wants before he acquired an Add-a-Pearl necklace for Sally, two Genuine Pinseal handbags for his mother-in-law and Mrs. Lederer, and a Stag-horn knife with three blades, a nailfile, and a corkscrew, for young George. He had left Eunice until last, but with each purchase, a shabby, telephoning day had dropped from him. Dizzy with participation, he surveyed the mottoed store.

"Something . . . something for the wife," he said.

"Our lovely Lifetime Watch, perhaps? Or Something in Silver, for the House?" The clerk tapped her teeth, gauging him.

He leaned closer, understanding suddenly why housewives, encysted in lonely houses, burbled confidences to the grocer, made an audience of the milkman. "We've had a—Little Tiff."

"Aw-w," said the clerk, adjusting her face. "Now . . . let me see. . . ." She kindled suddenly, raised a sibylline finger, beckoned him further down the counter, and drew out a tray of gold charms. Rummaging among them with a long, opalescent nail, she passed over minute cocktail shakers, bird cages, tennis rackets, a tiny scroll bearing the words, "If you can see this, you're too darn close," and seized a trinket she held up for view. A large gold shamrock, hung on a chain by a swivel through its middle, it bore the letter I on its upper leaf, on its nether one the letter U. She reversed it. L.O.V.E. was engraved across the diameter of the other side. The clerk spun it with her accomplished nail. "See?" she said. "Spin it! Spin it and it says I. L.O.V.E. U!"

"Hmmm . . . ," said Grorley, clearing his throat. "Well . . . guess you can't fob some women off with just a diamond bracelet." She tittered dutifully. But, as she handed it to him with his other packages, and closed the glass door behind him, he saw her shrug something, laughing, to another clerk. She had seen that he was not Schlumbohn's usual, after all. As he walked up his own street he felt that he was, after all, hardly anybody's usual, tonight. It was a pretty street, of no particular architectural striving. Not a competitive street, except sometimes, in summer, on the subject of gardens. And, of course, now. In every house the tree was up and lit, in the window nearest the passer-by. Here was his own, with the same blue lights that had lasted, with some tinkering on his part, year after year. Eunice must have had a man in to fix them.

He stopped on the path. A man in. She was pretty, scorned, and—he had cavalierly assumed—miserable. He had taken for granted that his family, in his absence, would have remained reasonably static. They always had. He'd been thinking of himself. Silently, he peeled off another layer of self-knowledge. He still was.

He walked up the steps wondering what kind of man might rise to be introduced, perhaps from his own armchair. One of her faded, footballish resurrections from Ohio State U., perhaps: Gordon, this is Jim Jerk, from home. Or would she hand it to him at once? Would it be: *Dear*, this is Gordon.

The door was unlocked. He closed it softly behind him, and stood listening. This was the unmistakable quiet of an empty house—as if the secret respiration of all objects in it had just stopped at his entrance. The only light downstairs was the glowing tree. He went up the stairs.

In the bedroom, the curtains were drawn, the night light on. The bed was piled with an abandoned muddle of silver wrappings, tissue paper, ribbons. He dropped the presents on the bed, tossed his hat after them, let his coat slip down on the familiar chair, and parted the curtains. It had a good view of the river, his house. He stood there, savoring it. He was still there when a car door slammed and the family came up the path. The Christmas Eve pantomime, of course, held every year at the village hall. Georgie had on one of those white burnooses they always draped the boys in, and Sally, in long dress and coned hat, seemed to be a medieval lady. He saw that this year she had the waist for it. Eunice and Mrs. Lederer walked behind them. He tapped on the glass.

They raised their faces in tableau. The children waved, cat-called, and disappeared through the downstairs door. Mrs. Lederer followed them. Below, Eunice stared upward, in the shine from the tree-window. Behind him, he heard that sound made only by children— the noise of bodies falling up a staircase. As they swarmed in on him, she disappeared.

"You shoulda been to the hall," said Georgie, seizing him. "Christmas at King Arthur's court. I was a knight."

"Was it corny!" said Sally, from a distance. She caught sight of herself in a pier glass. "I was Guinevere."

"Had to do some last-minute shopping," said Grorley.

"I saw my bike!" said Georgie. "It's in the cellar."

"Oh . . . Georgie!" said Sally.

"Well, I couldn't help seeing it."

"Over there are some Christmas Eve presents," said Grorley.

"Open now?" they said. He nodded. They fell upon them.

"Gee," said Georgie, looking down at the knife. "Is that neat!" From his tone it was clear that he, at least, was Schlumbohn's usual.

"Oh, Dad!" Sally had the necklace around her neck. She raised her arms artistically above her head, in the fifth position, minced forward, and placed their slender wreath around Grorley's neck. As she hung on him, sacklike, he felt that she saw them both a tender picture, in some lurking pier glass of her mind.

The door opened, and Eunice came in. She shut it behind her with a "not before the servants" air, and stood looking at him. Her face was blurred at the edges; she had not decked herself out for anybody. She looked the way a tired, pretty woman, of a certain age and responsibilities, might look at the hour before dinner, at the moment when age and prettiness tussle for her face, and age momentarily has won.

"Look what I got!" Georgie brandished the knife.

"And mine!" Sally undulated herself. "Mums! Doesn't it just *go!*" She stopped, looking from father to mother, her face hesitant, but shrewd.

"Open yours, Mums. Go on."

"Later," said Eunice. "Right now I think Mrs. Lederer wants you both to help with the chestnuts."

"No fair, no fair," said Georgie. "You saw ours."

"Do what your mother says," said Grorley. The paternal phrase, how it steadied him, was almost a hearthstone under his feet.

"Oh, well," said Eunice, wilting toward the children, as she invariably did when he was stern with them. Opening the package he indicated, she drew out the bauble. Georgie rushed to look at it, awarded it a quick, classifying disinterest, and returned to his knife.

"Oo—I know how to work those! Margie's sister has one," said Sally. She worked it. "If that isn't corny!" she gurgled. Eunice's head was bent over the gift. Sally straightened up, gave her and Grorley a swift, amending glance. "But cute!" she said. She flushed. Then, with one of the lightning changes that were the bane of her thirteen years, she began to cry. "Honestly, it's sweet!" she said.

Grorley looped an arm around her, gave her a squeeze and a kiss. "Now, shoo," he said. "Both of you."

When he turned back to the room, Eunice was looking out the window, chin up, her face not quite averted. Recognizing the posture, he quailed. It was the stance of the possessor of the stellar role— of the nightingale with her heart against the thorn. It was the stance of the woman who demands her scene.

He sighed, rat-tatted his fingers on the table top. "Well," he said. "Guess this is the season the corn grows tall."

A small movement of her shoulder. The back of her head to him. Now protocol demanded that he talk, into her silence, dredging his self-abasement until he hit upon some remark that made it possible for her to turn, to rend it, to show it up for the heartless,

illogical, tawdry remark that it was. He could repeat a list of the game
birds of North America, or a passage from the Congressional Record.
The effect would be the same.

"Go on," he said, "get it over with. I deserve it. I just want you to
know . . . mentally, I'm out of the Village."

She turned, head up, nostrils dilated. Her mouth opened. "Get it
ov—!" Breath failed her. But not for long.

Much later, they linked arms in front of the same window. Supper
had been eaten, the turkey had been trussed, the children at last
persuaded into their beds. That was the consolatory side of family
life, Grorley thought—the long, Olympian codas of the emotions
were cut short by the niggling detail. Women thought otherwise, of
course. In the past, he had himself.

Eunice began clearing off the bed. "What's in those two? Father's
and Mother's?"

"Oh, Lord. I forgot Father."

"Never mind. I'll look in the white elephant box." The household
phrase—how comfortably it rang. She looked up. "What's in these
then?"

"For Mother and Mrs. Lederer. Those leather satchel-things. Pinseal."

"Both the same, I'll bet."

He nodded.

Eunice began to laugh. "Oh, Lord. How they'll hate it." She
continued to laugh, fondly, until Grorley smirked response. This,
too, was familiar. Masculine gifts: the inappropriateness thereof.

But Eunice continued to laugh, steadily, hysterically, clutching her
stomach, collapsing into a chair. "It's that hat," she said. "It's that
s-specimen of a hat!"

Grorley's hat lay on the bed, where he had flung it. Brazenly dirty,
limp denizen of bars, it reared sideways on a crest of tissue paper,
one curling red whorl of ribbon around its crown. "L-like something
out of Hogarth," she said. "The R-rounder's Return."

Grorley forced a smile. "You can buy me another."

"Mmmm . . . for Christmas." She stopped laughing. "You know
. . . I think that's what convinced me—your coming back tonight.
Knowing you—that complex of yours. Suppose I felt if you meant
to stand us through the holidays, you meant to stand us for good."

Grorley coughed, bent to stuff some paper into the wastebasket. In fancy, he was stuffing in a picture too, portrait of Vida, woman of imagination, outdistanced forever by the value of a woman who had none.

Eunice yawned. "Oh . . . I forgot to turn out the tree."

"I'll go down."

"Here, take this along." She piled his arms with crushed paper. In grinning afterthought, she clapped the hat on his head.

He went to the kitchen and emptied his arms in the bin. The kitchen was in chaos, the cookery methods of *alt Wien* demanding that each meal rise like a phoenix, from a flaming muddle below-stairs. Tomorrow, as Mrs. Lederer mellowed with wine, they would hear once again of her grandfather's house, where the coffee was not even *roasted* until the guests' carriages appeared in the driveway.

In the dining room, the table was set in state, from damask to silver nut dishes. Father would sit there. He was teetotal, but anecdotalism signs no pledge. His jousts as purchasing agent for the city of his birth now left both narrator and listener with the impression that he had built it as well. They would hear from Mother too. It was unfortunate that her bit of glory—her father had once attended Grover Cleveland—should have crystallized itself in that one sentence so shifty for false teeth—"Yes, my father was a physician, you know."

Grorley sighed, and walked into the living room. He looked out, across the flowing blackness of the river. There to the south, some-where in that jittering corona of yellow lights, was the apartment. He shuddered pleasurably, thinking of all the waifs in the world to-night. His own safety was too new for altruism; it was only by a paring of luck as thin as this pane of glass that he was safely here—on the inside, looking out.

Behind him, the tree shone—that *trompe-l'oeil* triumphant—yearly symbol of how eternally people had to use the spurious to catch at the real. If there was an angel at the top, then this was the devil at its base—that, at this season, anybody who opened his eyes and ears too wide caught the poor fools, caught himself, hard at it. Home is where the heart . . . the best things in life are . . . spin it and it says I.L.O.V.E.U.

Grorley reached up absently, and took off his hat. This is middle age, he thought. Stand still and heard the sound of it, bonging like carillons, the gathering sound of all the platitudes, sternly coming true.

He looked down at the hat in his hand. It was an able hat; not every hat could cock a snook like that one. From now on, he'd need every ally he could muster. Holding it, he bent down, and switched off the tree. He was out of the living room and halfway up the stairs, still holding it, before he turned back. Now the house was entirely dark, but he needed no light other than the last red sputter of rebellion in his heart. He crept down, felt along the wall, clasped a remembered hook. Firmly, he hung his hat in the hall. Then he turned, and went back up the stairs.

R. V. CASSILL *grew up in Iowa and taught at the State University there after Army service in the South Pacific. He received his M.A. from the University of Iowa in 1947, and later taught in the Writers' Workshop there. Following a year in Paris on a Fulbright scholarship, he now lives in New York City. He has published a novel,* The Eagle on the Coin, *and many short stories.*

THE INLAND YEARS

FROM WESTERN REVIEW

"LAKE ARTHUR—ROUND AS THE WORLD" it said in the publicity folder we received from the Arthur Chamber of Commerce, and the folder contained a map which truly showed the lake like a blue globe in a green surrounding atmosphere of midwestern prairie. The town of Arthur sat on top of it like an exaggerated polar cap, and it was ringed with the traces of highways and the indication of beaches where summer cabins clustered like sham cities. But Ellen said in amusement, as she had ever since I first met her, "It's square as a bear."

Before her family dispersed when she was fifteen she had spent several summers at Lake Arthur with them, and of course from the time she and I began talking of the possibility, one of her motives for vacationing there was to make a non-sentimental pilgrimage— like going back armed and disinterested to see something you have loved and been deceived by.

In the time when we were first married, nine years ago, and were trying to give each other our childhoods for sympathy and safe-keeping, she had told me a lot of stories of Lake Arthur's summer Society, and her mothers' adventures and preoccupations with it. From Ellen's insistent presentation Lake Arthur had come to stand for a bogey of the past that we were fleeing together—a world without more roots than were required to make it viciously rigid, not particularly rich except on a midwestern scale but still wealthy enough to base its behavior and tastes on distinctions of ownership, outrageously provincial in its belief in its own cosmopolitanism, and as capable of dictating the path of error to those who fascinated themselves with it as the bigger Society that Edith Wharton wrote about. This last was classically demonstrated by the nonsensical marriage and divorce of Ellen's parents. So Lake Arthur, as Ellen used to speak of it, was a well-understood point of reference from which we could orient the departure of our lives.

Of course I had not the same personal recollections of it that Ellen had. When I was a child I saw pictures in the Sunday paper of people boating on Lake Arthur, the governor holding a pike and embracing a UP official from Omaha on the amusement pier at Arthur, this or that family breakfasting by the lakeside with their guests from Minneapolis. It hadn't made a great impression on me until I heard Ellen talk of it. Then I took over, perhaps with some sentiments of gratified snobbery, Ellen's resentments toward it.

I felt, though, that I knew Lake Arthur well enough so that for me as well as for Ellen going there would be a sort of return, however partial and qualified. She and I were much too poor to take better than a cabin on one of the newly built-up beaches where there was only marsh and forest the last time Ellen had seen it. That would be close enough to spy, from a removal of years and circumstances, at a landscape and a way of life which were reminiscent of "some baggage we checked somewhere."

Of course there were more definable reasons for choosing to go there. In anticipation we spoke of the coming week at the lake as our "bourgeois vacation" because it was to be the first in our nine years together when we were going to give up ambitious plans for trips and lie back resting in a lakeshore cottage. Some years when we had no money or I was in the Army there'd been no vacation at all, and again we'd made hectic and too extravagant trips to Mexico, Canada, and California in unreliable cars. This was our year to rest, and be damned to all that might be interesting and far off. Also we had no car to go junketing in. We were both thirty-one that year and in the spring we'd put all the money we could raise into a down payment on a house. I had a job on a home furnishing magazine which looked as though it would be the one to last unexcitingly forever, so buying a house had at least seemed justifiable.

For my part I was wonderfully content with our plan. I couldn't have faced the idea of traveling, which always manages to concentrate my interest in myself. For me it was a great thing to lapse entirely, so that what I saw could become more important than I, even if that was no more than the banal perimeter of the lake and the static weather of early August.

For the first couple of sunny days there I had an orgy of dissolving myself in favor of whatever I could see without rolling too energetically from a prone position on the beach or the pier. Such effort as I made was like taking a bit of plain bread and concentrating fully on how it tastes. I would squint over the lake and think, How round it is, and, because I wasn't in any competition to prove myself smart, could be pleased with such a perception. I got the same kick out of the straightness of the light rays that made the chiaroscuro of the diving tower at the end of the pier. With the little girls who went out to dive I could enjoy either the color of their legs and suits against the blue sky or their adolescent shapes without feeling the slightest interest in them as people. I watched the boats tick and sway against the pier and sometimes fixed in a dumb way on the pink house directly across from us on what was currently the "best" beach.

Built as it was down close to the water it looked like a tunnel mouth or a bomb shelter except for its vivid color. Really it was impossible not to look at it. It would seem to be in my eye, just as it was in the natural colors of the lake and woods, like a metallic grain, an annoyance, however beautifully modern it might be. Sometimes in utter childishness I would hold up my little finger to blot it out. It was an irritant that made me think—about bomb shelters and modern architecture and home furnishings and what they each cost—and my sun-softened body protested against thinking.

I made some querulous jokes about it to Ellen—this was her lake, how did she account for this monstrous piece of candy cluttering up the shoreline? All she knew about it was that it had been built since her time, as any jerk ought to know. "At least it's better than they used to build," she said. "We'll go across to Arthur one time and I'll show you the Swiss chalets and English half-timbered houses they threw up in the twenties." I began to argue that sometimes irrational structures like those fitted ideologically into a landscape— I may have said "timescape"—even though aesthetically they were grossly out of place.

"I don't know what you mean," she said shortly. I admitted I didn't either and said I certainly didn't intend to argue about it.

Ellen laughed. "Then the vacation is paying off already. Let's row over and see the pink house. Want to?"

The rowing put me in an odd state, seeming about to wake me up but never fully succeeding, as though I had been deeper immersed in sleepiness for the last few days—or maybe much longer—than I had realized. The afternoon wind on my chest and bare arms and the slap of waves on the boat bottom were so insidiously insistent on my relaxing into sleep that I had a period of silly panic in which I would keep glancing over my shoulder at Ellen to be reassured that she was actually there.

"You're huffing and puffing, old boy," she called. "We don't have to go this fast."

"Pretty big waves," I said. "I want to get in closer to shore." Frightened by something I couldn't name I was trying to cover it over with a more ordinary fear.

Ellen said, "Relax. If we swamp I'll hold you up. But this is nothing."

Idling to a stop forty yards out from the pink house, dropping the oars and turning to look squarely at it for the first time, I saw why it might have made me think of a tunnel entrance. The lower story was all open to the lake, an austere concrete cave overhung by a deck and the rooms of the second floor. I had not been able to make out these details of construction from my view on our beach, but I suppose they had registered and called up that particular comparison.

Everything about the house looked groomed, polished, stripped for action. A beautifully varnished speedboat hung on davits at the house corner which thrust a little way into the lake—it could have been the lifeboat hanging at a ship's side. There was no sign of any inhabitants. I assumed—projecting my own state, I suppose—that they were sleeping through this hot part of the afternoon.

I asked Ellen how she liked the house and she shook her head. "It's a machine for living. I'm not for it, are you?"

"It's very Walt Disney," I said. "I personally believe that the people who live here are all enchanted. Look, not a creature stirring. Want to land and look in?"

"Oh no. But let's drift here a minute. You tuckered yourself out with that speed coming over."

We bobbed there for a while without saying anything. After a while a dumb-looking boy in a sweat-shirt with the legend "Athletic Dept. U of Minn" appeared on the second-story deck and leaned on the rail, peering at us in the same dull way we peered at him. He had a drink in his hand from which he gulped occasionally, but he made no sign of recognizing us as human beings. It was like being with someone in a dream and feeling as though you knew him well and being at the same time unhappily doubtful that you would know him if you saw him again. The few yards of water that separated us from him might as well have been an ocean.

"Screech at him," I said to Ellen in a low voice. "See if he's real."

The boy up-ended his glass, worked for a while to get an ice cube into his mouth and pointed the glass at us. "Oo. Dayox oh eh."

Ellen said, "That's right, I remember now. He says there's rocks over there. Swing us with your left oar and then pull out farther. I thought I knew this place."

Once I had turned I kept going. We had seen the house and I felt enough anxiety, however unwarranted, about the crossing back to want to get it over with.

"You know about those rocks?" Ellen said. "There used to be three frame cottages up above them on the hill and that's the way I had them located. Well—those rocks were where the eighteen high school kids drowned once."

"Shipwreck?" I said brightly.

She began moving in the most oblique ways toward her story. It was perfectly simple in essence, but in her memory it was confused with a lot of recollections of the way the shoreline had looked to her when she had first heard it, what her father had said to her about it, and how, year after year when she returned to the lake, she had felt when she looked at or passed near that point. For her, clearly, this personal recall was of the same material as the incident itself.

"It was the whole senior class from Rhinebeck," she said finally. "Rhinebeck's a little town about fifty miles from here. There were eighteen in the class. I think it was eight girls and ten boys."

"No chaperone," I said. "That explains it all to me. Whew. These eighteen kids had the greatest orgy Rhinebeck ever produced, so they made a suicide pact and drowned themselves for shame the next day. Kids then weren't as nice and well brought up as they are now."

Our rowboat grounded gently just about this time, and that seemed to me a lucky termination for such a pointless argument. I hopped out briskly and tied up the boat. Ellen was looking back over the three miles of water to where the pink house squatted at the shore, frowning toward it as though it might be the memorial of those drowned kids she was remembering or imagining.

She said, "It was an accident and one of them wouldn't desert the others."

"Be realistic. Maybe some of them tried to get away and the others dragged them down."

"I don't know why you have to have it that way."

"I merely happen to think it could have happened that way."

"I suppose so," she answered sombrely.

Later that night we were wakened in our cabin by a rainstorm that beat loudly on the roof and blew in chilly drops at a couple of windows. I closed the windows and lay comfortably, feeling protected against the wide, noisy attack of the rain. I could smell our wet bathing suits in a far corner. The smell of drying wool and of dust enclosed me peacefully enough. I knew Ellen was awake but we did not speak for a long time. I thought she must have fallen asleep again when all at once she said, "There was a pair of twins on the Rhinebeck team. I remember them as plain. They were tall and shy and everybody that saw them play said they were the greatest ever. I guess that must have been the year. They'd come up here and rented a couple of cottages for their senior sneak day. As far as anyone knows they must have gone wading out on those rocks. Then one of them fell into deep water or got panicked and the others tried to help and the consequence was that every one of them got drowned."

I can't say what it was I didn't like about her telling that story. Perhaps part of it was a lack of satisfaction with its realism. As she told it, it didn't seem quite true. "Couldn't any of them swim?" I asked. "Surely one or two of them could have got out."

"I didn't know them personally. Maybe they couldn't swim," she said. "I think I'd seen some of the boys because Rhinebeck had a whiz of a basketball team and they used to come down to the state tournament nearly every year."

"Who saw all this to tell about it if everyone was drowned?" I demanded.

"I don't know," Ellen said doggedly. "That's the way it happened and there were people who knew."

The reason for my resentment of the story began to clear. In her tone I had heard something of her love for the lake, a new revelation of an attitude that seemed incongruous with the person I had felt sure of knowing, a revelation of something she had never wished to share with me, pretending to share everything. And yet, it was too silly to argue straightforwardly over her repetition of a story she once heard.

"Wasn't there a chaperone with them maybe?" I asked.

"I suppose so. Either they'd stayed overnight or were planning to stay overnight, so there must have been a chaperone. I had my little red coat with the rabbit muff. I thought how fine it would be if one of the twins noticed me. I was so little then that of course they wouldn't have. They seemed like real grown-ups to me, though they were probably only sixteen or seventeen."

"Were they in that bunch that drowned?"

"I think so."

"I never heard of an orgy involving twins. Must have been quite a gathering."

"Oh, funny," she said. "Go to sleep."

"Are you going to sleep?"

"I will pretty soon. You go ahead."

In the morning, well rested, I went with cane pole and sunglasses to fish from the pier. Arthur was the kind of lake where any dope or child could catch perch by dropping in a baited hook and where good fishermen, given luck and patience, could bring up some pretty fancy pike and lake trout. I only wanted to be idle and perhaps get enough perch for dinner.

The beach's population of adolescent girls was out in force by the time I took my station. I ought to mention that from the time of our arrival Ellen and I had been aware that there was no one else our age renting at this beach. There was one generation ranging up from about ten years older and another one ranging from sixteen down. This latter included an unaccountably large number of daughters fifteen or sixteen, probably spending the last vacation they would ever have in the bosom of their family. These girls were addicted to gum, fluty cries, fancy sunglasses, and to giving sultry glances to every passing male except their respective fathers. Impatiently they lay tanning, and sometimes, rolling over to expose another slope or muscle to the sun, they stared out with fierce virility at our little lake as though it should have been a thousand-mile stretch of sea. It was these teen-age girls who gave our beach its one quality beyond comfort and quiet and made it seem worthy of looking out on something broader than the 1950's and the mediocre tremor of inland waves.

Pretty frequently, in late morning or late afternoon, boys came in speedboats from other beaches to raid our beach for these girls. You'd hear sooner than see the speedboats. They would blast a high note out beyond the pier end and settle to a halt almost within the waves of their own wake while four or five boys in sweat-shirts and trunks studied the display of girls. The boat would creep in to be tied up at the pier with flourishes and self-conscious horseplay.

In the morning while I was fishing the boat came from the pink house. I recognized first the boy with the U of Minn shirt. There were three others and after tying up they strutted with more than the ordinary raiding party's arrogance among the blankets where the girls —and a few parents and wee ones—were whiling the morning away. While they went up the beach like a party of slavers a sort of hush ran along parallel with them the way it will when a visiting general passes groups of soldiers not yet at attention. It occurred to me that the mothers, fathers, and tots as well as the daughters were holding their breath and waiting for the choice to be made. There was a twitching of little tan thighs and shoulders and, I hope, a clenching of little jaws on the chewing gum.

I missed the actual selection because Ellen had come down from her housework in the cabin "to see what I was catching," and I turned my attention to chatting with her. Presently I heard the speedboat start and looked over her shoulder to see the boys.

When the aristocratic blatting of the motor died, the beach sounds dropped to normal, though they seemed clarified, as though the addition of an intense chemical precipitated out a certain former murkiness. A little kid was yelling, "Daddy, float over to me, over to me." The little boys playing shuffleboard on a floor among the trees resumed their clatter. I tried to communicate to Ellen the total impression this raid for girls had made on me. She snorted and accused me of exaggeration. "You make it sound like Pluto coming up to steal that girl, whatever her name was," she said.

"That's it," I said. "We won't have summer again until he brings her back."

She scratched my belly with her knuckles. "You big fake. Here you are broiling in the sun and still pretending it's not summer enough for you. Look"—I heard the motor noise grow as she pointed —"they're bringing them back already. It's just an innocent young people's way of getting together here. It's always been done that way, my lad. When we used to come up here there were motorboats too, and the boys bummed from one beach to another in them to get acquainted with the girls."

"I wouldn't let a daughter of mine go out in one of those hell boats. I'd sooner see her dead at my feet."

"It's probably just as well you haven't any daughters."

"All right," I said. "I'd let them go. They could do what they pleased."

"Look, there are your little girls back safe on dry land. Not hurt a bit and they've had fun."

"And the boys line them up for hanky-panky later when it's dark."

Ellen was sitting with her knees folded up to her chin and her arms locked around her knees. Above her knees she gave me a secretive, happy smile that clung a long time on her mouth. "You caught on. The girls will take the steamer over to the amusement pier tonight and the boys will meet them at the dock there and they'll go up for a dance at Roseland. At intermission they'll bum down the Midway and eat cotton candy or something else awful, pick up a kewpie doll, and get kissed a time or two on one of the benches at the dock while they're waiting for the last steamer to bring them home."

"Well, happy memories," I said. "After all these years I get confessions. Who was the man—boy?"

"Mmmm no one. None in particular. A kid named Charlie Fox one time. Someone—I can't remember his name—that I thought was the smoothest dancer."

"Did he have a speedboat?"

"I don't know. Listen, let's take the steamer over tonight. Will you?"

"It would be fun."

"Lots." She stood up suddenly and prepared to leave. "Catch fish," she said.

The steamer was the grandest relic left at Lake Arthur. I suppose it must have been about sixty feet in length and, put-putting solemnly around the shoreline as it did five times a day, it appeared to be almost as high as it was long. I'm not sure whether there was a lot of grillwork and gingerbread around the upper decks or if it merely gave that impression. It was completely white and against the color of the lake it always struck me as being phony and nice—the white and blue were just as starkly innocent as something you'd see on a postcard. For all its height the steamer had an absurdly shallow

draught and could pull into water you would not think deep enough
to float one of the speedboats. It stopped at any pier where someone
hailed it, chuffling and whistling and being a great delight to the
children as Ellen said it had been for as long as she could remember.

It was as much fun to ride as to watch. Our trip around to the
amusement pier at Arthur was probably the nicest hour of our vacation. Ellen had dressed for the occasion in a fresh and bellowy print
—one she'd debated bringing, since we'd been dead set on the principle that this trip was to be as uncomplicated as possible—and she
seemed to feel how pretty she looked. In the dusk she seemed suddenly shy and withdrawn from me, yet happier to be with me than
on any occasion I could remember of the recent past.

Mounting the steamer we leaned into the half-enclosed engine
room set slightly below the main deck to see the old machinery hiss
and slide like a dinosaur breathing. We read the 1897 in raised
letters on the steam cylinder and suddenly looked at each other as
though we'd shared an insight, but also as though neither of us
could say what it was.

We climbed to the top deck to sit alone while the steamer backed
away from our pier, and we remained alone up there until it had
made two more stops. Then a family of five came up and took
benches ahead of us.

I was surprised by how few lights seemed to border the lake as we
went around. Those few appeared weak and almost desperately isolated. It was then, I suppose, that transitional hour when most of
the vacationers were hanging on to the last of the day's outdoor
pleasures before going in to light their cottages and begin the evening.

Underneath us—it seemed very far down—the lake was a steady
and yielding blackness. Now and then a solid wave would collide
with the bow and split away hissing. I remembered being frightened
the day I had rowed Ellen across to see the pink house and I was
ashamed that I had permitted myself that fear.

Ellen touched me and said, "You know I'm happy," and I answered
that I was glad of that. For the time of the trip we seemed equal
to the cold neutrality of the lake, balanced, and owing it neither fear
nor gratitude for what it might be.

When we landed it was still not time to go dancing, so we turned
along the Midway, trying with a little too much eagerness to be
excited by the music from the merrygoround, the smells of popcorn,

and the thin crowd. After I'd tried the shooting gallery and Ellen had thrown hoops at a peg floating in a water barrel our good judgment suggested that we not spoil the evening ahead by trying to eat either cotton candy or any of the other confections available and there was nothing else to do. Ellen was sure that there were some bars up in the town, and we left the pier to find them.

The one we picked at random—choosing it with no special reason —was called the Orchid Room. It was small, which we could tell from outside, and expensively furnished, which we discovered with some uneasiness once we had entered. I was afraid the price of drinks would not suit us.

At that time we were the only customers, though there was a green-faced fat man on a raised platform between a piano and a Hammond organ and a middle-aged woman behind the bar. It was fairly dim in the room, but not so dim that we missed being impressed by the white orchids painted on all the walls.

As we sat down the fat man played a run on the Hammond and asked if there was anything we wanted specially to hear. Ellen said "These Foolish Things" would be fine. He shook his head comically and answered, "That one was before my time." Then he began slowly picking it out on the Hammond and presently was playing it confidently.

"How about the piano?" Ellen asked. "I'd rather hear it on the piano." Obediently he swung half around to face the other instrument. "The old songs are corniest, aren't they?" he said. He played marvelously well. We relaxed to listen while the little place began to fill with customers. Presently those who came in were moist with rain, and Ellen, noticing this, said, "Anyway we can't go to the dance until the rain's over. How about that old 'Running between the Raindrops,' Zach?"

"Zach"—because by now she had discovered who the piano player was and in the general fondness she was feeling for anything that echoed from her past she was insistently overusing his nickname. Sixteen years ago Zach Winthrop and his Rhythm Boys had been very popular in this part of the state, she explained to me. She thought it probable that once when she was at Roseland his boys had been playing there and she meant to ask him in some break between numbers if this might not be so.

But presently when she went to the toilet she found Mrs. Shaw and Mrs. Shaw kept us busy for the rest of the evening. Mrs. Shaw

—who had been Rita Chase before she married and had spent summers in the cottage next to the one occupied by Ellen's family—struck me as being drunk as a pig when she wobbled to our table with Ellen. However, she went by waves, apparently ready to pass out for a period, then, recovering herself, was remarkably, bitterly, and suspiciously sober, while we went more steadily downward.

"Well, murder, kid," Mrs. Shaw would say to Ellen, "we've certainly got to do something about this. You know I had no idea that you or any of that silly family of yours was in this part of the country any more. I really hadn't thought of you for years and then" —turning to lay her round, moist little hand on the back of mine— "I go in to daintily powder my nose and who says 'Hello, Rita' over the partition to me but silly little Ellen Park."

"This isn't home country any more," Ellen said. "Harvey and I are only . . ."

"What do you know about that?" Mrs. Shaw marveled. "That is, what do you *know?* Hey, Sally." She was calling to the woman behind the bar and beckoning her over. "Sally, guess what the rain druv in. It's stupid little Ellen Park that used to live next door here at the lake when I was fresh and young." She put her arm around Sally's hips and hugged her with an immoderate shiver. "You kids know who Sally *is,* I'll bet, don't you? Why you're sitting in her *intime* establishment. Sally, they never heard of Sally Racine."

"Of course we have. Hello, Sally," Ellen said. I rose and shook hands.

"Hi," Sally said. "Everybody having a good time?"

Mrs. Shaw wiggled her finger at me. "Who is Sally?" She tightened her hold on Sally and leaned in my direction. "You don't know, you silly ass. Well, you can just go over there and look." She flung her free hand toward a glassed display panel on the opposite wall. "Go on and learn something."

"Don't pay any attention to her," Sally said, breaking free.

Ellen prompted me nervously, "Miss Racine was a *Scandals* star."

"She was the goddamned White Orchid of 1921," Mrs. Shaw said. "Get over there and look at that picture." I did as I was told and found that the glass covered a two-page spread, in color, from a 1921 magazine. On one page was a picture of Sir Harry Lauder looking rosy-cheeked as a boy scout. The other page carried a full-length photo of Miss Sally Racine, the White Orchid. She too looked healthy and plump and, in her weird costume, about eleven feet tall. I stood for some time studying the pictures, trying to assemble an appropriate comment to carry back to the table.

Fortunately Sally had gone—to mix us drinks, as it turned out— and Mrs. Shaw was on another line by then. She was talking about Ellen's grandfather and then about Ellen's brother, who was killed on Saipan. She remembered his building a tree house down the bluff from the cottage and calling it the Park Hotel. She rubbed some tears away. "Then the silly little jerk got himself shot boom, boom in their silly war. Isn't that the way it goes, Elly? Tell me, isn't it?"

She went on, "I remember The Champ—I call my husband The Champ and God knows why—used to play catch or toss a football with him sometimes when he'd come around to pick me up for a date. Thought he was the swellest little guy in the world. He really did, Elly. When he heard about him getting shot he really took on. I can't remember all the things he said."

"What's your husband doing now?" Ellen said. "I remember him very well."

"He's doing all right," Mrs. Shaw said. She yelled for Sally. "Give us another round, Sally, and God bless us every one."

I protested against any more drinks, not very vigorously, I suppose. At any rate they paid no attention to me.

"What's become of that insane grandfather of yours that had the fish farm?" Mrs. Shaw demanded. "He must be dead."

"He wasn't insane," Ellen said laughing. "He was the smartest one of the Parks, anyway. You know there's a bronze plaque for him in the town hall here for what he did in conservation." Her glance flickered in my direction and she said, "I'll show you sometime if you're interested."

"Why sure," I said.

"He was really a professor, wasn't he?" Mrs. Shaw asked.

"Yeah. He taught at Creighton for just dozens of years before he started the laboratory here. How I loved that old man, Rita. You remember the way he and grandma were with each other? It was always 'my love this and my love that' with them." She coughed suddenly with laughter. "You know that old Hupmobile he drove for so long. He'd get it out to drive into town here, then the two of them would be standing by it and grandma would say, 'Darling, hadn't you better, if you want to, change your shoes before we go?' 'Well, honey,' he'd say and balk like a ten-year-old and sulk till she made him go neat up. They were so great. And I remember . . ."

I felt chilly and cheated and again commenced to argue that if Ellen and I were going to the dance at all we would have to leave soon or risk missing the last boat back to our beach. My argument wasn't solid. Then there was still plenty of time, of course. I became further irritated that the two of them could so easily refute me. "It wasn't entirely my idea to come to the dance," I pointed out.

"Relax then," Ellen said. "We'll finish this drink and by then you may be in a better mood for the dance."

Mrs. Shaw said grimly, "You're not going anywhere while we're having fun. If the boat's gone I'll drive you home. Where you staying, Elly?"

"Gorsky's Beach," I answered. "It's a long way around by road. We won't trouble you."

"Drink up and be quiet." She pinched the skin on the back of my hand with her red, dirty nails. "What are you doing around at Gorsky's? It's no fun clear over there."

"We can afford Gorsky's," I said. "We can't afford to have fun." In my agitation I had gulped my drink and was waving at Sally to bring us another one. I still didn't mean to get drunk that evening, but in some irrational way that felt like a revenge for the mesh of weakness and accident that had involved us with Mrs. Shaw I wanted to get just a little higher. There seemed to be something waiting to be said that would solve her—I remember thinking in those terms.

Ellen said, "We have fun in our own way, Rita. We enjoy quiet things. I read a lot and Harvey fishes. We row in the afternoons."

"Huh," Mrs. Shaw said, "that sounds dull as hell. What do you read? You mean he *fishes?*" She crawled half across the table to peer at me.

"He watches the little girls, too," Ellen said.

"Like your papa did."

"I don't either," I said. "I'm interested in people that's all."

The two of them laughed absurdly, as though they shared a vision of my motives so secret that I could never hope to guess it.

"He is interested in people," Ellen said. "He's gathering material for a play. He wrote a play once, right after the war, about his experiences on a Liberty ship."

Mrs. Shaw studied me with a momentarily sober and perfectly hard amusement. "I know that one. *Mr. Roberts.*"

"You've got it," I said.

"Well, he almost sold it," Ellen said. "I told him he should go on and revise it or write another one. That's been four or five years now."

"I didn't almost sell it."

"Anyway the people he showed it to thought it was very good. Of course *Mr. Roberts* had come out by then," Ellen said. I could see she was wobbling in her chair. I thought perhaps I ought to grab her arm and drag her out of the place—even give her a swift punch and carry her out, the way you do in rescuing someone from drowning. I let the moment of good intention pass and dissolve in sulkiness and resentment.

That my quiet Ellen was drunk is true and that fact explains exactly nothing. Of course the alcohol and our encounter with Mrs. Shaw were necessary to start her talking, but they merely released something which had a dynamic of its own and was in motion below a level that the alcohol could reach. For a little while longer it was not apparent that Ellen was pouring out a monologue. Mrs. Shaw interrupted with questions or irrelevant attempts to change the subject or turned frankly and drunkenly to start a separate conversation with me, and from time to time I made my own bitter additions.

But as an hour passed and another after that Ellen kept talking, piling up more and more of the whole story of her life. She kept smiling apologetically and abstractedly, and while she appeared to be watching Mrs. Shaw—she certainly wasn't telling it to me—perhaps she was looking past Mrs. Shaw too. It was, I suppose, like listening to a medium, though here it was Ellen talking through herself.

There was a long part of it which was given over to an account of her life with me. At some point she mentioned the way we'd married in haste in 1943 when I was being drafted into the Army and how that hectic time had been brightened by the promise of the life we'd begin when I got back. Then there was the leave spent together in San Francisco. She'd just heard of her brother's death, but we'd been able then to keep a good heart because the war's end was at least visible. Then came the year in the trailer while I was finishing college, the year I'd written my play and we'd talked of how great it would be to get out with jobs of our own and our own apartment. Then how I'd got involved with Larris in promoting his cartoon books and how we'd traveled all over the country on that scheme. How we'd saved money on different occasions to buy a house, had spent the money and started saving all over again.

She said at one point that now we were really about to begin some of the living that we'd postponed so long, but this observation was given in passing. There was no end. Her story kept lapping back over itself as though a while before she had passed over too quickly —or missed—a key episode on which all the rest could hang.

I don't know what the ugliest point of her monologue was, whether it was her pathetic eagerness to get it all spilled out, or Mrs. Shaw's drunken, uneven attention, or my own resentment of what the story implied. The details of the story were ordinary enough, yet among the three of us we managed to qualify them so it seemed to be an endless record of failure. The same incidents might have sounded different somewhere else. Yet I hated Ellen because I thought she was using an unbearably strict measure to account for our lives, a measure strict as the edge of a knife—and then offering this knife edge to Mrs. Shaw to use against us in whatever capricious, drunken way she wanted. I thought it was as though Ellen refused to judge Mrs. Shaw in some desperation to submit us two to judgment.

I remembered, without wanting to go there any more, the dance at Roseland. I imagined that the dumb-looking boy from the pink house would be there with one of the girls he had found that morning on our beach. Later they might go to the steamboat dock and kiss while they waited for the last boat. I was afraid that even if we went now, I couldn't stand seeing those kids.

I shook the table and said, "Let's get out of here." To Mrs. Shaw, "Come on, you said you'd drive us."

"Lay off, Harvey. We're having a good time, aren't we? There'll be a lot more interesting people in here before it closes. A lot more interesting than you two, I might add." She put the back of her hand beside her mouth and stage-whispered to me, "What's your wife telling me all this crap for?"

"So we've bored you," I said. "O.K. Take us home."

"Christ, if you've gotta go, call a taxi. What's the matter, can't you even afford a taxi?"

As a matter of fact and among other things, I was not sure that I could. After the first round I had paid for everything, including a pack of cigarettes for Mrs. Shaw. The drinks weren't cheap, and here I was left with less than two dollars.

"Never mind," Ellen said dreamily. "We'll take a taxi."

I said, "I'm not sure we have taxi fare. Get this old bag in motion. She's your friend, remember?"

"Sally," Mrs. Shaw yelled. "Sally." The music from the organ stopped and everyone was watching us. When Sally arrived Mrs. Shaw said, "What class of people you catering to these days? These two latched onto me and now they want me to drive them home. I'm afraid of them. Tell them to get out and leave me alone."

Sally winked at me to show she was not taking this quite seriously. She beckoned me to come with her to the bar. "Look, Rita's drunk," she said. I heard Mrs. Shaw wailing, "They get me off on a dark road and God knows what would happen to me."

"You don't want to ride with her anyway," Sally said. "I'll have a taxi here in a jiffy. You have money? Never mind, I'll fix it with the driver and get it from her tomorrow when she's cooled off."

"But she's a friend of my wife's," I said.

Sally, not bothering to try to understand that one, grinned wisely. "Rita's nobody's friend. You and your wife can wait in the entry if you want to."

While Ellen and I waited Mrs. Shaw came out to us. "You know how it is," she said. "If I left here now I'd be all sobered up before I got back, and my whole evening would be shot. Besides I'm afraid to drive that far by myself. I've only got this silly little Pontiac and I don't like the way it drives. You see how it is, Elly?"

"Sure, honey," Ellen said. "Stay and have a good time."

"Oka-a-ay," Mrs. Shaw said reluctantly, as though we were forcing her to an action she would undertake only because we wanted her to so badly.

"It was nice running into you," Ellen said. She was swaying and looking pale. I could not tell how sober she was.

I said to her, "You might at least get your fat buddy to kick in for cab fare. Or for one round of drinks, just as a sign of affection."

"You bet I will," Mrs. Shaw said uncertainly. "Wait, don't move. I must have left my purse at the table or I can borrow something from Sally. Don't go away. Wait. Wait now."

Who knows whether she came back with the money? The cab honked in a little while and Ellen and I went to it quickly, agreeing on that without having to speak to each other.

We sat on opposite sides of the seat. It was raining a little again, and the windshield wipers seemed to be cutting even pink slices of the neon lights from the bars bordering the road.

"You had nothing to gain by that last byplay," Ellen said.

"It did me good. Why take all that guff without answering?"

"You couldn't make allowances, could you?" She hiccuped gently. "Rita used to be such a quick, wonderful girl, I thought."

"You wanted to be like her when you grew up. I know."

"Yes I did. Yes. To hell with you."

"That's a good reason for telling her what a crumby life you've had with me."

"I didn't tell her that. I told her where we'd been and what we'd done, like . . . Don't quarrel with me any more, just for tonight, please. I'm too tired of it, and I don't know how much longer I can take it."

"So I'm always at you," I said. "I never give you a minute's peace. If you'd just realize sometimes that it hasn't been all roses for me either. Then, while I didn't spend my childhood in this paradise, I have my feelings about it, too. Why am I excluded? Why do you have to talk to a drunken pig like that instead of me?"

"Yes, why?"

"I give up," I said. "I merely thought we were going over to dance at Roseland. Just like old times. Was it my fault we never got there?"

"No. It wasn't your fault. You win the argument."

"At least you admit . . ."

"You always win your argument."

"Then what . . ." She interrupted me by turning abruptly against the side of the cab and crying, knowing that I knew my own answer, knew that she knew, knowing that neither of us could ever hide from the other again the commitment to betrayal that time had forced on us by the subtlest and most kindly-seeming frauds. I knew that it was nothing so easy as a particular or personal sin that she was accusing, and in the dark cab the longer I thought this over in silence the more it began to seem to me that she was weeping really for those children from Rhinebeck who had drowned once in the lake, holding each other's hand in a faithful line and never letting go.

JOHN CHEEVER *was born in Quincy, Massachusetts, in 1912 and attended Thayer Academy in Braintree. He first appeared in the* O. Henry *in 1941 with "I'm Going to Asia" and again in 1950 with "Vega." His stories have appeared in* The New Yorker, Harper's Bazaar, Mademoiselle, Collier's, The Atlantic Monthly, New Republic, *and others. He is the father of two children and has spent most of his time since leaving college in New York and Washington.*

THE FIVE-FORTY-EIGHT

FROM THE NEW YORKER

When Blake stepped out of the elevator, he saw her. A few people, mostly men waiting for girls, stood in the lobby watching the elevator doors. She was among them. As he saw her, her face took on a look of such loathing and purpose that he realized she had been waiting for him. He did not approach her. She had no legitimate business with him. They had nothing to say. He turned and walked toward the glass doors at the end of the lobby, feeling that faint guilt and bewilderment we experience when we by-pass some old friend or classmate who seems threadbare, or sick, or miserable in some other way. It was five-eighteen by the clock in the Western Union office. He could catch the express. As he waited his turn at the revolving doors, he saw that it was still raining. It had been raining all day, and he noticed now how much louder the rain made the noises of the street. Outside, he started walking briskly east toward Madison Avenue. Traffic was tied up, and horns were blowing urgently on a crosstown street in the distance. The sidewalk was crowded. He wondered what she had hoped to gain by a glimpse of him coming out of the office building at the end of the day. Then he wondered if she was following him.

Walking in the city, we seldom turn and look back. The habit restrained Blake. He listened for a minute—foolishly—as he walked, as if he could distinguish her footsteps from the worlds of sound in the city at the end of a rainy day. Then he noticed, ahead of him on the other side of the street, a break in the wall of buildings. Something had been torn down; something was being put up, but the steel structure had only just risen above the sidewalk fence and daylight poured through the gap. Blake stopped opposite here and looked into a store window. It was a decorator's or an auctioneer's. The window was arranged like a room in which people live and entertain their friends. There were cups on the coffee table, magazines to read, and flowers in the vases, but the flowers were dead and the cups were empty and the guests had not come. In the plate glass, Blake saw a clear reflection of himself and the crowds that were passing, like shadows, at his back. Then he saw her image— so cloes to him that it shocked him. She was standing only a foot or two behind him. He could have turned then and asked her what she wanted, but instead of recognizing her, he shied away abruptly from the reflection of her contorted face and went along the street. She might be meaning to do him harm—she might be meaning to kill him.

The suddenness with which he moved when he saw the reflection of her face tipped the water out of his hatbrim in such a way that some of it ran down his neck. It felt unpleasantly like the sweat of fear. Then the cold water falling into his face and onto his bare hands, the rancid smell of the wet gutters and pavings, the knowledge that his feet were beginning to get wet and that he might catch cold—all the common discomforts of walking in the rain—seemed to heighten the menace of his pursuer and to give him a morbid consciousness of his own physicalness and of the ease with which he could be hurt. He could see ahead of him the corner of Madison Avenue, where the lights were brighter. He felt that if he could get to Madison Avenue he would be all right. At the corner, there was a bakery shop with two entrances, and he went in by the door on the crosstown street, bought a coffee ring, like any other commuter, and went out the Madison Avenue door. As he started down Madison Avenue, he saw her waiting for him by a hut where newspapers were sold.

She was not clever. She would be easy to shake. He could get into a taxi by one door and leave by the other. He could speak to a policeman. He could run—although he was afraid that if he did run, it might precipitate the violence he now felt sure she had planned. He was approaching a part of the city that he knew well and where the maze of street-level and underground passages, elevator banks, and crowded lobbies made it easy for a man to lose a pursuer. The thought of this, and a whiff of sugary warmth from the coffee ring, cheered him. It was absurd to imagine being harmed on a crowded street. She was foolish, misled, lonely perhaps—that was all it could amount to. He was an insignificant man, and there was no point in anyone's following him from his office to the station. He knew no secrets of any consequence. The reports in his briefcase had no bearing on war, peace, the dope traffic, the hydrogen bomb, or any of the other international skulduggeries that he associated with pursuers, men in trench coats, and wet sidewalks. Then he saw ahead of him the door of a men's bar. Oh, it was so simple!

He ordered a Gibson and shouldered his way in between two other men at the bar, so that if she should be watching from the window she would lose sight of him. The place was crowded with commuters putting down a drink before the ride home. They had brought in on their clothes—on their shoes and umbrellas—the rancid smell of the wet dusk outside, but Blake began to relax as soon as he tasted his Gibson and looked around at the common, mostly not-young faces that surrounded him and that were worried, if they were worried at all, about tax rates and who would be put in charge of merchandising. He tried to remember her name—Miss Dent, Miss Bent, Miss Lent—and he was surprised to find that he could not remember it, although he was proud of the retentiveness and reach of his memory and it had only been six months ago.

Personnel had sent her up one afternoon—he was looking for a secretary. He saw a dark woman—in her twenties, perhaps—who was slender and shy. Her dress was simple, her figure was not much, one of her stockings was crooked, but her voice was soft and he had been willing to try her out. After she had been working for him a few days, she told him that she had been in the hospital for eight months and that it had been hard after this for her to find work, and she wanted to thank him for giving her a chance. Her hair was dark, her eyes were dark; she left with him a pleasant impression of darkness. As he got to know her better, he felt that she was oversensitive and, as a consequence, lonely. Once, when she was speaking to him of what she imagined his life to be—full of friendships, money, and a large and loving family—he had thought he recognized a peculiar feeling of deprivation. She seemed to imagine the lives of the rest of the world to be more brilliant than they were. Once, she had put a rose on his desk, and he had dropped it into the waste-basket. "I don't like roses," he told her.

She had been competent, punctual, and a good typist, and he had found only one thing in her that he could object to—her hand-writing. He could not associate the crudeness of her handwriting with her appearance. He would have expected her to write a rounded backhand, and in her writing there were intermittent traces of this, mixed with clumsy printing. Her writing gave him the feeling that she had been the victim of some inner—some emotional—conflict that had in its violence broken the continuity of the lines she was able to make on paper. When she had been working for him three weeks—no longer—they stayed late one night and he offered, after work, to buy her a drink. "If you really want a drink," she said, "I have some whiskey at my place."

She lived in a room that seemed to him like a closet. There were suit boxes and hatboxes piled in a corner, and although the room seemed hardly big enough to hold the bed, the dresser, and the chair he sat in, there was an upright piano against one wall, with a book of Beethoven sonatas on the rack. She gave him a drink and said that she was going to put on something more comfortable. He urged her to; that was, after all, what he had come for. If he had any qualms, they would have been practical. Her diffidence, the feeling of deprivation in her point of view, promised to protect him from any consequences. Most of the many women he had known had been picked for their lack of self-esteem.

When he put on his clothes again, an hour or so later, she was weeping. He felt too contented and warm and sleepy to worry much about her tears. As he was dressing, he noticed on the dresser a note she had written to a cleaning woman. The only light came from the bathroom—the door was ajar—and in this half light the hideously scrawled letters again seemed entirely wrong for her, and as if they must be the handwriting of some other and very gross woman. The next day, he did what he felt was the only sensible thing. When she was out for lunch, he called personnel and asked them to fire her. Then he took the afternoon off. A few days later, she came to the office, asking to see him. He told the switchboard girl not to let her in. He had not seen her again until this evening.

Blake drank a second Gibson and saw by the clock that he had missed the express. He would get the local—the five-forty-eight. When he left the bar the sky was still light; it was still raining.

He looked carefully up and down the street and saw that the poor woman had gone. Once or twice, he looked over his shoulder, walking to the station, but he seemed to be safe. He was still not quite himself, he realized, because he had left his coffee ring at the bar, and he was not a man who forgot things. This lapse of memory pained him.

He bought a paper. The local was only half full when he boarded it, and he got a seat on the river side and took off his raincoat. He was a slender man with brown hair—undistinguished in every way, unless you could have divined in his pallor or his gray eyes his unpleasant tastes. He dressed—like the rest of us—as if he admitted the existence of sumptuary laws. His raincoat was the pale, buff color of a mushroom. His hat was dark brown; so was his suit. Except for the few bright threads in his necktie, there was a scrupulous lack of color in his clothing that seemed protective.

He looked around the car for neighbors. Mrs. Compton was several seats in front of him, to the right. She smiled, but her smile was fleeting. It died swiftly and horribly. Mr. Watkins was directly in front of Blake. Mr. Watkins needed a haircut, and he had broken the sumptuary laws; he was wearing a corduroy jacket. He and Blake had quarrelled, so they did not speak.

The swift death of Mrs. Compton's smile did not affect Blake at all. The Comptons lived in the house next to the Blakes, and Mrs. Compton had never understood the importance of minding her own business. Louise Blake took her troubles to Mrs. Compton, Blake knew, and instead of discouraging her crying jags, Mrs. Compton had come to imagine herself a sort of confessor and had developed a lively curiosity about the Blakes' intimate affairs. She had probably been given an account of their most recent quarrel. Blake had come home one night, overworked and tired, and had found that Louise had done nothing about getting supper. The gin bottle was half emptied, and the first three glasses he took from the bar were smeared with lipstick grease. He had gone into the kitchen, followed by Louise, and he had pointed out to her that the date was the fifth. He had drawn a circle around the date on the kitchen calendar. "One week is the twelfth," he had said. "Two weeks will be the nineteenth." He drew a circle around the nineteenth. "I'm not going to speak to you for two weeks," he had said. "That will be the nineteenth." She had wept, she had protested, but it had been eight or ten years since she had been able to touch him with her entreaties.

Louise had got old. Now the lines in her face were incradicable, and when she clapped her glasses onto her nose to read the evening paper she looked to him like an unpleasant stranger. The physical charms that had been her only attraction were gone. It had been nine years since Blake had built a bookshelf in the doorway that connected their rooms and had fitted into the bookshelf wooden doors that could be locked, since he did not want the children to see his books. But their prolonged estrangement didn't seem remarkable to Blake. He had quarrelled with his wife, but so did every other man born of woman. It was human nature. In any place where you can hear their voices—a hotel courtyard, an air shaft, a street on a summer evening—you will hear harsh words.

The hard feeling between Blake and Mr. Watkins also had to do with Blake's family, but it was not as serious or as troublesome as what lay behind Mrs. Compton's fleeting smile. The Watkinses rented. Mr. Watkins broke the sumptuary laws day after day—he once went to the eight-fourteen in a pair of sandals—and he made his living as a commercial artist. Blake's oldest son—Charlie was fourteen—had made friends with the Watkins boy. He had spent a lot of time in the sloppy rented house where the Watkinses lived. The friendship had affected his manners and his neatness. Then he had begun to take some meals with the Watkinses, and to spend Saturday nights there. When he had moved most of his possessions over to the Watkinses' and had begun to spend more than half his nights there, Blake had been forced to act. He had spoken not to Charlie but to Mr. Watkins, and had, of necessity, said a number of things that must have sounded critical. Mr. Watkins' long and dirty hair and his corduroy jacket reassured Blake that he had been in the right.

But Mrs. Compton's dying smile and Mr. Watkins' dirty hair did not lessen the pleasure Blake took in settling himself in an uncomfortable seat on the five-forty-eight deep underground. The coach was old and smelled oddly like a bomb shelter in which whole families had spent the night. The light that spread from the ceiling down onto their heads and shoulders was dim. The filth on the window glass was streaked with rain from some other journey, and clouds of rank pipe and cigarette smoke had begun to rise from behind each newspaper, but it was a scene that meant to Blake that he was on a safe path, and after his brush with danger he even felt a little warmth toward Mrs. Compton and Mr. Watkins.

The train travelled up from underground into the weak daylight, and the slums and the city reminded Blake vaguely of the woman who had followed him. To avoid speculation or remorse about her, he turned his attention to the evening paper. Out of the corner of his eye he could see the landscape. It was industrial and, at that hour, sad. There were machine sheds and warehouses, and above these he saw a break in the clouds—a piece of yellow light. "Mr. Blake," someone said. He looked up. It was she. She was standing there holding one hand on the back of the seat to steady herself in the swaying coach. He remembered her name then—Miss Dent. "Hello, Miss Dent," he said.

"Do you mind if I sit here?"

"I guess not."

"Thank you. It's very kind of you. I don't like to inconvenience you like this. I don't want to . . ." He had been frightened when he looked up and saw her, but her timid voice rapidly reassured him. He shifted his hams—that futile and reflexive gesture of hospitality—and she sat down. She sighed. He smelled her wet clothing. She wore a formless black hat with a cheap crest stitched onto it. Her coat was thin cloth, he saw, and she wore gloves and carried a large pocketbook.

"Are you living out in this direction now, Miss Dent?"

"No."

She opened her purse and reached for her handkerchief. She had begun to cry. He turned his head to see if anyone in the car was looking, but no one was. He had sat beside a thousand passengers on the evening train. He had noticed their clothes, the holes in their gloves; and if they fell asleep and mumbled he had wondered what their worries were. He had classified almost all of them briefly before he buried his nose in the paper. He had marked them as rich, poor, brilliant or dull, neighbors or strangers, but no one of the thousands had ever wept. When she opened her purse, he remembered her perfume. It had clung to his skin the night he went to her place for a drink.

"I've been very sick," she said. "This is the first time I've been out of bed in two weeks. I've been terribly sick."

"I'm sorry that you've been sick, Miss Dent," he said in a voice loud enough to be heard by Mr. Watkins and Mrs. Compton. "Where are you working now?"

"What?"

"Where are you working now?"

"Oh don't make me laugh," she said softly.

"I don't understand."

"You poisoned their minds."

He straightened his back and braced his shoulders. These wrench-ing movements expressed a brief—and hopeless—longing to be in some other place. She meant trouble. He took a breath. He looked with deep feeling at the half-filled, half-lighted coach to affirm his sense of actuality, of a world in which was not very much bad trouble after all. He was conscious of her heavy breathing and the smell of her rain-soaked coat. The train stopped. A nun and a man in overalls got off. When it started again, Blake put on his hat and reached for his raincoat.

"Where are you going?" she said.

"I'm going up to the next car."

"Oh, no," she said. "No, no, no." She put her white face so close to his ear that he could feel her warm breath on his cheek. "Don't do that," she whispered. "Don't try and escape me. I have a pistol and I'll have to kill you and I don't want to. All I want to do is to talk with you. Don't move or I'll kill you. Don't, don't, don't!"

Blake sat back abruptly in his seat. If he had wanted to stand and shout for help, he would not have been able to. His tongue had swelled to twice its size, and when he tried to move it, it stuck horribly to the roof of his mouth. His legs were limp. All he could think of to do then was to wait for his heart to stop its hysterical beating, so that he could judge the extent of his danger. She was sitting a little sidewise, and in her pocketbook was the pistol, aimed at his belly.

"You understand me now, don't you?" she said. "You understand that I'm serious?" He tried to speak but he was still mute. He nodded his head. "Now we'll sit quietly for a little while," she said. "I got so excited that my thoughts are all confused. We'll sit quietly for a little while, until I can get my thoughts in order again."

Help would come, Blake thought. It was only a question of minutes. Someone, noticing the look on his face or her peculiar posture, would stop and interfere, and it would all be over. All he had to do was to wait until someone noticed his predicament. Out of the window he saw the river and the sky. The rain clouds were rolling down like a shutter, and while he watched, a streak of orange light on the horizon became brilliant. Its brilliance spread—he could see it move—across the waves until it raked the banks of the river with a dim firelight. Then it was put out. Help would come in a minute, he thought. Help would come before they stopped again; but the train stopped, there were some comings and goings, and Blake still lived on, at the mercy of the woman beside him. The possibility that help might not come was one that he could not face. The possibility that his predicament was not noticeable, that Mrs. Compton would guess that he was taking a poor relation out to dinner at Shady Hill, was something he would think about later. Then the saliva came back into his mouth and he was able to speak.

"Miss Dent?"

"Yes."

"What do you want?"

"I want to talk with you."

"You can come to my office."

"Oh, no. I went there every day for two weeks."

"You could make an appointment."

'No," she said. "I think we can talk here. I wrote you a letter but I've been too sick to go out and mail it. I've put down all my thoughts. I like to travel. I like trains. One of my troubles has always been that I could never afford to travel. I suppose you see this scenery every night and don't notice it any more, but it's nice for someone who's been in bed a long time. They say that He's not in the river and the hills but I think He is. 'Where shall wisdom be found,' it says. 'Where is the place of understanding? The depth saith it is not in me; the sea saith it is not with me. Destruction and death say we have heard the force with our ears.'

"Oh, I know what you're thinking," she said. "You're thinking that I'm crazy, and I have been very sick again but I'm going to be better. It's going to make me better to talk with you. I was in the hospital all the time before I came to work for you but they never tried to cure me, they only wanted to take away my self-respect. I haven't had any work now for three months. Even if I did have to kill you, they wouldn't be able to do anything to me except put me back in the hospital, so you see I'm not afraid. But let's sit quietly for a little while longer. I have to be calm."

The train continued its halting progress up the bank of the river, and Blake tried to force himself to make some plans for escape, but the immediate threat to his life made this difficult, and instead of planning sensibly, he thought of the many ways in which he could have avoided her in the first place. As soon as he had felt these regrets, he realized their futility. It was like regretting his lack of suspicion when she first mentioned her months in the hospital. It was like regretting his failure to have been warned by her shyness, her diffidence, and the handwriting that looked like the marks of a claw. There was no way now of rectifying his mistakes, and he felt —for perhaps the first time in his mature life—the full force of regret. Out of the window, he saw some men fishing on the nearly dark river, and then a ramshackle boat club that seemed to have been nailed together out of scraps of wood that had been washed up on the shore.

Mr. Watkins had fallen asleep. He was snoring. Mrs. Compton read her paper. The train creaked, slowed, and halted infirmly at another station. Blake could see the southbound platform, where a few passengers were waiting to go into the city. There was a workman with a lunch pail, a dressed-up woman, and a man with a suitcase. They stood apart from one another. Some advertisements were posted on the wall behind them. There was a picture of a couple drinking a toast in wine, a picture of a Cat's Paw rubber heel, and a picture of a Hawaiian dancer. Their cheerful intent seemed to go no farther than the puddles of water on the platform and to expire there. The platform and the people on it looked lonely. The train drew away from the station into the scattered lights of a slum and then into the darkness of the country and the river.

"I want you to read my letter before we get to Shady Hill," she said. "It's on the seat. Pick it up. I would have mailed it to you, but I've been too sick to go out. I haven't gone out for two weeks. I haven't had any work for three months. I haven't spoken to anybody but the landlady. Please read my letter."

He picked up the letter from the seat where she had put it. The cheap paper felt abhorrent and filthy to his fingers. It was folded and refolded. "Dear Husband," she had written, in that crazy, wandering hand, "they say that human love leads us to divine love, but is this true? I dream about you every night. I have such terrible desires. I have always had a gift for dreams. I dreamed on Tuesday of a volcano erupting with blood. When I was in the hospital they said they wanted to cure me but they only wanted to take away my self-respect. They only wanted me to dream about sewing and basket-work but I protected my gift for dreams. I'm clairvoyant. I can tell when the telephone is going to ring. I've never had a true friend in my whole life. . . ."

The train stopped again. There was another platform, another picture of the couple drinking a toast, the rubber heel, the Hawaiian dancer. Suddenly she pressed her face close to Blake's again and whispered in his ear. "I know what you're thinking. I can see it in your face. You're thinking you can get away from me in Shady Hill, aren't you? Oh, I've been planning this for weeks. It's all I've had to think about. I won't harm you if you'll let me talk. I've been thinking about devils. I mean if there are devils in the world, if there are people in the world who represent evil, is it our duty to exterminate them? I know that you always prey on weak people. I can tell. Oh, sometimes I think that I ought to kill you. Sometimes I think you're the only obstacle between me and my happiness. Sometimes . . ."

She touched Blake with the pistol. He felt the muzzle against his belly. The bullet, at that distance, would make a small hole where it entered, but it would rip out of his back a place as big as a soccer ball. He remembered the unburied dead he had seen in the war. The memory came in a rush: entrails, eyes, shattered bone, ordure, and other filth.

"All I've ever wanted in life is a little love," she said. She lightened the pressure of the gun. Mr. Watkins still slept. Mrs. Compton was sitting calmly with her hands folded in her lap. The coach rocked gently, and the coats and mushroom-colored raincoats that hung between the windows swayed a little as the car moved. Blake's elbow was on the window sill and his left shoe was on the guard above the steampipe. The car smelled like some dismal classroom. The passengers seemed asleep and apart, and Blake felt that he might never escape the smell of heat and wet clothing and the dimness of the light. He tried to summon the calculated self-deceptions with which he sometimes cheered himself, but he was left without any energy for hope or self-deception.

The conductor put his head in the door and said, "Shady Hill, next, Shady Hill."

"Now," she said. "Now you get out ahead of me."

Mr. Watkins waked suddenly, put on his coat and hat, and smiled at Mrs. Compton, who was gathering her parcels to her in a series of maternal gestures. They went to the door. Blake joined them, but neither of them spoke to him or seemed to notice the woman at his back. The conductor threw open the door, and Blake saw on the platform of the next car a few other neighbors who had missed the express, waiting patiently and tiredly in the wan light for their trip to end. He raised his head to see through the open door the abandoned mansion outside of town, a no-trespassing sign nailed to a tree, and then the oil tanks. The concrete abutments of the bridge passed, so close to the open door that he could have touched them. Then he saw the first of the lampposts on the northbound platform, the sign "SHADY HILL" in black and gold, and the little lawn and flower bed kept up by the Improvement Association, and then the cab stand and a corner of the old-fashioned depot. It was raining again; it was pouring. He could hear the splash of water and see the lights reflected in puddles and in the shining pavement, and the idle sound of splashing and dripping formed in his mind a conception of shelter, so light and strange that it seemed to belong to a time of his life that he could not remember.

He went down the steps with her at his back. A dozen or so cars were waiting by the station with their motors running. A few people got off from each of the other coaches; he recognized most of them, but none of them offered to give him a ride. They walked separately or in pairs—purposefully out of the rain to the shelter of the platform, where the car horns called to them. It was time to go home, time for a drink, time for love, time for supper, and he could see the lights on the hill—lights by which children were being bathed, meat cooked, dishes washed—shining in the rain. One by one, the cars picked up the heads of families, until there were only four left. Two of the stranded passengers drove off in the only taxi the village had. "I'm sorry, darling," a woman said tenderly to her husband when she drove up a few minutes later. "All our clocks are slow." The last man looked at his watch, looked at the rain, and then walked off into it, and Blake saw him go as if they had some reason to say goodbye—not as we say goodbye to friends after a party but as we say goodbye when we are faced with an inexorable and unwanted parting of the spirit and the heart. The man's footsteps sounded as he crossed the parking lot to the sidewalk and then they were lost. In the station, a telephone began to ring. The ringing was loud, plaintive, evenly spaced, and unanswered. Someone wanted to know about the next train to Albany, but Mr. Flannagan, the stationmaster, had gone home an hour ago. He had turned on all his lights before he went away. They burned in the empty waiting room. They burned, tin-shaded, at intervals up and down the platform and with the peculiar sadness of dim and purposeless light. They lighted the Hawaiian dancer, the couple drinking a toast, the rubber heel.

"I've never been here before," she said. "I thought it would look different. I didn't think it would look so shabby. Let's get out of the light. Go over there."

His legs felt sore. All his strength was gone. "Go on," she said.

North of the station there was a freight house and a coalyard and an inlet where the butcher and the baker and the man who ran the service station moored the dinghies from which they fished on Sundays, sunk now to the gunwales with the rain. As he walked toward the freight house, he saw a movement on the ground and heard a scraping sound, and then he saw a rat take its head out of a paper bag and regard him. The rat seized the bag in its teeth and dragged it into a culvert.

"Stop," she said. "Turn around. Oh, I ought to feel sorry for you. Look at your poor face. But you don't know what I've been through. I'm afraid to go out in the daylight. I'm afraid the blue sky will fall down on me. I'm like poor Chicken-Licken. I only feel like myself when it begins to get dark. But still and all I'm better than you. I still have good dreams sometimes. I dream about picnics and Heaven and the brotherhood of man, and about castles in the moonlight and a river with willow trees all along the edge of it and foreign cities, and after all I know more about love than you."

He heard from off the dark river the drone of an outboard motor, a sound that drew slowly behind it across the dark water such a burden of clear, sweet memories of gone summers and gone pleasures that it made his flesh crawl, and he thought of dark in the mountains and the children singing. "They never wanted to cure me," she said. "They . . ." The noise of a train coming down from the north drowned out her voice, but she went on talking. The noise filled his ears, and the windows where people ate, drank, slept, and read flew past. When the train had passed beyond the bridge the noise grew distant, and he heard her screaming at him, "*Kneel down!* Kneel down! Do what I say. *Kneel down!*"

He got to his knees. He bent his head. "There," she said. "You see, if you do what I say, I won't harm you, because I really don't want to harm you, I want to help you, but when I see your face it sometimes seems to me that I can't help you. Sometimes it seems to me that if I were good and loving and sane—oh, much better than

I am—sometimes it seems to me that if I were all these things and young and beautiful, too, and if I called to show you the right way, you wouldn't heed me. Oh, I'm better than you, I'm better than you, and I shouldn't waste my time or spoil my life like this. Put your face in the dirt. *Put your face in the dirt!* Do what I say. Put your face in the dirt."

He fell forward in the filth. The coal skinned his face. He stretched out on the ground, weeping. "Now I feel better," she said. "Now I can wash my hands of you, I can wash my hands of all this, because you see there is some kindness, some saneness in me that I can find again and use. I can wash my hands." Then he heard her footsteps go away from him, over the rubble. He heard the clearer and more distant sound they made on the hard surface of the platform. He heard them diminish. He raised his head. He saw her climb the stairs of the wooden footbridge and cross it and go down to the other platform, where her figure in the dim light looked small, common, and harmless. He raised himself out of the dust—warily at first, until he saw by her attitude, her looks, that she had forgotten him; that she had completed what she had wanted to do, and that he was safe. He got to his feet and picked up his hat from the ground where it had fallen and walked home.

GEORGE P. ELLIOTT *was born in Indiana in
1918. His family subsequently moved to California
and since 1937 he has lived in Berkeley, where
he obtained his M.A. in English from the University of California. For several years now he has
been teaching at St. Mary's College. Last year he
traveled to London, Paris and New York on a
Ford Foundation Fellowship, studying poetic
drama in contemporary staging.*

MISS CUDAHY OF STOWES LANDING

FROM HUDSON REVIEW

1

Bingham could not knock at a strange door without a sense of adventure; to greet, and win if he could, whatever smiling or screw-
eyed or blank stranger the door opened onto made his heart beat a
little faster, his breath come shorter. In the course of his duties
with the Superior Court, he met very few new people, most of whom
were lawyers or their secretaries; he liked the fact that in the manner
of their official dealings lawyers still wear wigs, but he made no
friends among them. He had a few acquaintances and family friends,
and another friend, a woman, whom he might have married several
years before but did not. Nearly every door he knocked at he had
knocked at a hundred times before, except for the doors of old houses,
which held his happiness.

Therefore, when one Saturday in early summer he knocked at
Miss Cudahy's house in Stowes Landing and no one answered, he
gratefully set about inspecting the exterior of the house with the
attention it deserved. The telephone operator—in one of these small
towns she is the central intelligence—had given him Miss Cudahy's
name and had volunteered him the information that she was old,
suffered from rheumatism, and was very much the lady. He could
see from the outside of the house that the operator had been right;
only a lady would befit this grandest house in town, only a lady would
have maintained it so handsomely against the sea-weather of Men-

docino, only a lady would have kept a marble bird-bath in the garden, a Latin sun-dial under that usually overcast sky, a bronze stark-naked well-patinaed faun in a Concord arbor.

For although he was not sure of the rose-window over the door, yet the dormer windows, the overhang, the complication of the roof, the five gables, these meant to him New England on a hostile coast. Stowes Landing had been built seventy years ago on the flats back from a 300-foot cliff, north above a logging stream; the meadows stretched freely back for a mile to the line of forest and descending hills; nothing protected the houses from the sea-breeze but a hedge for those that planted one: and yet Miss Cudahy's house stood two and a half stories tall and massive, like some determined New Englanders bunched together, suspicious and prepared, resisting whatever the Indians, Spaniards, Mexicans, Russians, Southerners, Middle Westerners, Chinese, Filipinos, Japanese, Africans, Italians, Armenians, of this dangerous land might have settled among themselves heathenishly to do. That was all right, what one expected, for 1880; but to find it so purely preserved, still yellow with green shutters, in these provinces of light stucco or stained wood, to be able to walk up to it behind its hedge in a legitimate because pure curiosity, that affected Bingham as strongly as some people are affected by shaking the hand that shook the hand of Lincoln. He was more excited, as he began his tour, than was altogether reasonable.

On the southern side of the house, the side where the hedge was only twenty feet tall, he found a grizzled little man leaning on the handle of a shovel. His stance and dull stare bespoke one who has worked hard and learned how to rest like a horse standing up; but there was no new-turned bed, no deep hole, only a small cleared space where he was probably going to plant a fuchsia, there being already sixty or seventy fuchsias about the garden.

"Hello," said Bingham. The man did not respond; people frequently didn't. "The lady of the house is not home."

"Happen Phoebe's out buying," he said in a British dialect so heavy Bingham could hardly understand him.

"I see. I hope you don't mind my looking around till she returns."

He had always made it a point not to start small talk in a situation like this; but that unresponsive gaze said to him, Birth marriage death may be sizable enough to talk about mister but they are none too large; the man rubbed his chin on the end of the handle.

"I'm only interested in the house," Bingham went on, embarrassed to be introducing a subject so fugitive. "Miss Cudahy—could you tell me . . ."

But he heard, for the second time, he realized, a sharp sound behind and above him, a sound as of a gem rapped against glass; when he felt the hairs stand up on the back of his hand, he knew that he was being watched from behind the curtains by the eyes of one who had heard but had not answered his knock at the door. He left his sentence to dangle as it would and went on with his inspection; the man began to dig.

In the rear, there was a pile of wood, far more orderly than most of the garden, a vegetable patch, and a clothesline. And in the corner beyond the clothesline, half hidden by an arc of delphiniums, there was a garden to itself, earth scratched and leveled, scarcely a dead petal on the blossoms, no rows but a wandering intermixed variety of plants and shrubs, steppingstones for paths; there were single roses and single geraniums, three tulips, Indian paintbrush and succulents from the sea-cliffs, most of them with small bright flowers, for June is spring in Mendocino, and a rolling fringe of yellow oxalis. He stood in a sort of wonder at the sweetness of that garden, at how dainty and feminine and itself it seemed down between the still too vigorous old huge house and the hedge which here was more than thirty feet in height. He wondered who Phoebe was.

That hedge; there were a number of such hedges along that part of the coast, but Miss Cudahy's was as dense and perfectly trimmed as any he had seen and was much the highest. These hedges were dark green and thick and not very noisy even in the wind, very dark green; they were kept trimmed smooth as moss, with rounded edges, and this one had ascents and dips in it for no reason that he could make out, at one point rose taller than the house; dark, impermeable cypress green, for though it kept out the wind it kept out everything else as well. He could not imagine how Chin-on-Shovel did the job of trimming, and he did not even want to imagine what it was like to live out a life with a prospect of grey skies, unkept fuchsias, and the dark of the green.

One at the front and the other at the rear, two arches ran through the hedge like the mouse-runs that pierced the vast walls of Muscovite palaces. Through the rear gate, as he was standing there, entered a young woman with a basket of groceries in one hand, a bonnet on her head—more a bonnet than a hat—and a spring to her step. "Hello," he said, but she did not look at him. He stepped forward between two delphiniums and called again. She stopped, her lips a little open with surprise, and looked at him with a directness, a lack of demure withdrawal, which rather surprised him. "Could you tell me, please," he began, but she turned from him and ran, quite ran, up the stairs and into the house. He could think of no better course than to wait for a few discreet minutes and go knock at the front door. This he did, though not without trepidation.

She answered, with lowered eyes. He apologized for having startled her, and handed her his card. Without a word she walked back into the house. She appeared, at closer sight, a plain young woman, her hair drawn severely back to a bun, her face devoid of make-up yet not sallow, her clothes undistinguished for their color or grace; yet there was a certain tone to her body that quite set her off from an ordinary maid or housekeeper, a vigor to her step and a flirt, a fillip perhaps, to her skirts when she turned, that charmed him. She returned and opened the door wide to him; he thanked her and stepped into the hall; she smiled, not just politely but as though she were suppressing some private amusement, and ushered him into the parlor.

There lay, swathed in pastel chiffons, a large old woman on a chaise-longue.

"Mr. Bingham!" she called forth like the captain of one brig to the captain of another. "Come in, sir. Sit down." And she made what seemed to be some sort of complicated hailing motions with her hands.

"Thank you, Miss Cudahy," he said, and sat in a pale-oak horse-hair chair near her. When he looked around, the girl had disappeared. "I'm afraid I rather startled Phoebe out in the garden a few minutes ago."

"Did you?" she cried. "She did not inform me of that. And how do you know her name?"

"Your gardener, I gathered it from him."

"Ah yes, of course." And he saw how, with a loll of her great head and a flick of her left hand, heavy with rings, she peered out between the curtains invisibly. Then she, with a suddenness that surprised him, turned back and said to him sharply, "You're from the FBI."

He had seen witnesses caught off-balance, and had pitied them for their slowness and dullness; but here he was thrown by an old woman's judo.

"Who, me?" he said. "Oh no, gracious no. I'm only . . ."

"Very well," she waved his stuttering aside. "One of the other investigators. Which?"

"No, I assure you, I am interested in old houses. I enjoy them very much, and I . . ."

"I see." She paused, the sort of pause that did not permit him to speak. He sat watching her fill a curved pipe with tobacco, tamp it expertly, and light up. "You may smoke," she said, and docilely he lit a cigarette. "You traced me through the California Historical Society."

"No," he said, "I am merely traveling, alone, along the Mendocino coast, looking for houses of the New England captains that settled here. And I found yours simply by driving down the street looking for it."

"How did you discover me behind this hedge?"

"By getting out of my automobile and looking through the gate."

"I see." She stared with a concentration as great as Phoebe's; it had an altogether different effect on him. "Well, you've seen the outside and you're in the parlor. What do you think?"

He began to exclaim over it, and rising asked her permission to investigate the parlor more closely.

"In good time," she said. "Sit down, Mr. Bingham. We will have tea."

She pulled a tasseled cord behind her head, and Phoebe appeared. She waved her hands at Phoebe with a mixture of fluttering and grace and indolence, and threw her head back onto the pillows. "Pardon me," she murmured; her mouth fell a little ajar. "One has to rest a good deal. More than one would have chosen."

He could look at her closely now. It was a heavy, pale, sensual face with dark pouches under the deep eyes; she was not so old as he had originally thought, not over sixty. Her arms were bare and fleshy; day was, he imagined, when those white arms had excited at least the admiration of men. He could see that one of her legs, extended on the chaise-longue, was bound in some sort of rubber legging reaching halfway down the calf; the other, foot on the floor, would have served well on a duke in the days of knee breeches. She breathed heavily, nearly wheezing. "Asthma," she muttered, "damned nuisance." He sat straight in his slick, hard chair.

At the sound of Phoebe with the tea-tray at the door, he turned in pleased expectation. "Don't bother to speak to her," said Miss

Cudahy scarcely moving her grey lips; he realized that she must have been watching him from under her lids. "Phoebe is deaf and dumb." He blushed, and did not know where to look.

2

He did not see them again for a month and would not have gone back at all, even to see the rest of the house, had it not been for the newel, which he had only glanced at as he had been leaving the house; there was not another in California to compare to it. The month was workaday and legal, marked only by his failure to persuade an owner in North Oakland not to redecorate a Victorian specimen with mourning veil eaves, and by a rather curious invitation to speak. He received a telephone call and then a visit from a cultivated, charming, shrewd little woman named Pickman-Ellsworth, who wanted him to speak to the Alameda Fuchsia Society about the use of fuchsias in New England. He had to explain to her that he knew little about the subject and nothing at first hand. She received his refusal without protest, yet she continued talking, about one thing and another; she said that she had read some of his articles in the magazine *Golden West*; she kept throwing him subjects, visibly trying to "draw him out." He did not quite understand her purpose. She had black, quick eyes and sat very erect in her chair. She spoke to her chauffeur, as she left, with precisely that combination of dryness, condescension, and politeness with which she had addressed Bingham.

The newel at the foot of the stairs drew him back, that exquisitely carved, white newel with its promise of fine interiors on the second floor; the fluted newel, and, he had to confess it to himself, a curiosity about Miss Cudahy's household stronger than his repugnance for her herself.

He opened the gate, went through the hedge tunnel and walked up the stairs to the porch without seeing the Englishman gardener. He knocked the grand knocker—Miss Cudahy had no doorbell, indeed he felt that the electric lights in the old gas fixtures had furthered progress enough for her—and he stood waiting for Phoebe to open to him. He had calculated to himself what expression and gesture would best let Phoebe know the friendliness and pity he felt for her, what smile would blend recognition and warmth and yet least intrude upon her intimacy: the deference of the superior to the afflicted seemed to Bingham one of the few courtesies surviving

from that high and better-mannered world lost to us to our diminution. This he had calculated—or, rather, had hoped to achieve—
but he reckoned without Phoebe. How could he have known her?
A glimpse of her, brown-dressed in the garden scurrying like a quail
for cover; as maid in the hall, eyes downcast, smiling; a tea through
which she had sat like a little girl, knees tightly pressed together,
watching with a twinkle in her eye everything they did. How could
he have known that the moment she opened the door now and saw
him her eyes would light up, her cheeks would flush rosy red, her
poor voice would crack a little, her hands would open out to him?
Open so warmly and impetuously that he, smiling, would clasp them
warmly in his, to the distress of all courtesy but to his most grateful
pleasure. He did not touch people with casual affection, but rather
shrank from it; he preferred words of congratulation to a slap on the
back, the smile of privacy to a cocktail-party kiss; fastidiousness en-
tails its dangers: he accepted them knowingly. But Phoebe's hands,
rough-skinned and strong with work yet smaller than his, feminine
in his, did not presume any intimacy or force any warmth of response: they extended him her words of greeting, inflection of her
pleasure, her affection even, yet with hand's immediacy, touch's
conviction. He smiled at her, foolish with sudden pleasure; his condescension snapped in her hands like a twig. He did not even feel
embarrassed. It was as though he had known her a long time.

She took his hat and coat—it was a windy afternoon—and when
she returned from hanging them up and found him admiring the
newel, she pointed out to him something he had not yet noticed,
the baseboard running along below the banisters, fretted beautifully
and out of pure exuberance, uselessly, obscurely. She clasped her
hands in pleasure at his pleasure. He started to his feet at Miss
Cudahy's large voice: "Mr. Bingham, is that you?" He pointed, and
Phoebe led him by the hand to the parlor door; as she opened the
door she let go his hand; after he had gone in she withdrew from
them like a maid.

"Mr. Bingham," said Miss Cudahy, frowning as he advanced,
"what delayed you in the hall?"

"The newel," he said. "And Phoebe drew my attention to the
fretted baseboard on the staircase."

"Did she?" said Miss Cudahy. "I hope you are well." And she
took his hand.

"Very well," he answered, and it was all he could do to outsqueeze the grey-faced, lame old woman. "I hope in turn that your health has improved."

"How could it?" she said; she lolled back and pulled the rope. "At my age, in a climate like this, with no one to talk to?"

"It is hard," he said; he could scarcely have said less.

"Do you know how hard?" she replied scornfully. Phoebe appeared and Miss Cudahy waved some message at her. "Mr. Bingham, are you intending to buy my house? What do you want of me?"

"Believe me, I am interested only in the beauty of your house. I study old houses as an avocation."

"Beauty comes high on the market these days," she said fixing him with her eye. "Some kinds of beauty. Does this kind?"

"No," he answered rather flatly. "It does not."

"Are you just here for the day again, Mr. Bingham?"

"No, I am spending part of my vacation exploring these parts."

"How much of it, do you think?"

"That depends on many considerations."

"One of which is me, I take it?"

"Indeed," he said in the manner of a gallant, "how could it be otherwise?"

"The *Golden West* said you were a lawyer."

"Not exactly a lawyer. I am in legal work."

"Not a lawyer but in legal work," she repeated. "Slippery."

"Miss Cudahy," he said, arising, with all the dignity he could muster, "I would very much appreciate your permission to explore the rest of this house. I will take no photographs of it, and write nothing about it for publication, without your signed permission." This was more than she had let him get out during his entire first visit; only his anger had broken him through her complex defense so that he could now confront her simply with what he wanted.

"Ho," she shouted, "I've offended you, have I? I offend people. It usually takes longer with others. You are different. Sit down, young man, you've seen only this room and the hall, and there's more here worth the seeing, you may be sure."

He sat down, gritting his teeth behind his smile. "The newel, Miss Cudahy, is worthy of McIntire himself."

"Yes," she said quizzically, "worthy of him. In the master bedroom"—she knew how to play her mouse—"on the second floor, Mr. Bingham, where I have not been for three years . . . My damned joints," she said banging the knee of her left leg. "In the master bedroom, when you get to it, you will notice the mantel. McIntire, is it? I must tell you about that some day."

"Why not tell me now?" he said with the last of his anger.

Phoebe came in bearing the tea things; neither of them turned towards her.

"Because, Mr. Bingham, it is not my pleasure."

They had tea.

3

For the twentieth time he looked at the note she had slipped into his hand: "Meet me outside the rear gate at 4:30." Already he had waited a quarter of an hour; a cold wind was blowing in from the sea; every fantasy of waiting afflicted him, wrong time, wrong place, accident, change of heart; he shivered back into his car. He did not happen to be looking when she came through the hedge and ran around the back of his car. Suddenly there she was, opening the door and slipping in beside him smiling. The ruefulness, the trace of anxiety, vanished from her face when she saw how gladly he forgave her, her forehead smoothed, she squeezed his arm. What could he do but take her hands in his? The good humor and affection of her smile became a sort of radiance which warmed him as he would not have believed possible three hours before.

What did she want? He started to draw out a pencil and paper, but she gently restrained his hands. With perfect good humor and seriousness, in a few quick gestures, she suggested driving somewhere, getting out, and walking. He started the car; she directed. On the cliff above a turbulent, rocky surf, she stopped them and led him down a path. He heard a bell buoy offshore busy in its melancholy; he had never stood close to rough weather on the sea before. Phoebe sprang up onto a rock beside him and leaned her hand on his shoulder; her hair glistened with blown spray, there were tiny drops on her eyelashes; she kept looking from the surf back at his face expectantly; he did not disappoint her for she clapped her hands and occasionally her voice emitted some of its pathetic, ugly symptoms of excitement. She led him to a sort of overhang where they could squat protected from the wind; he noticed that Phoebe's free hand pressed feelingly against the rock, and he imagined her delicate excitement from the waves' crashing on the outside of the rocks of their cave. He knew that later he would worry about the propriety of his behavior with Phoebe, wonder what he should have done instead, speculate on what she was thinking, what his actions meant to her; but for the time they huddled together there, his affection for her, pure and unamorous as though she were a child, dissolved all questions of motive, propriety, consequence, and left only a residue of unalloyed content. Squatting in a cold cave, with a view of lashing breakers under a heavy sky, damp, feet cold, holding hands with a deaf-mute girl he had met only once before, truly he thought himself seven sorts of fool, but he grinned at the thought.

She peered out of the cave at the sky, looked at him ruefully, and made some sign gestures; then, remembering he could not understand them, she put her hands gently on his arm, with a look of apology. Phoebe's gestures, the movements of her features, expressed, with the economy and delicacy of a trout swimming in a clear pool, a range of ideas and emotions as great as many a person can manage with words. Yet physically she was not delicate but rather blunt and unsymmetrical, not pretty but, as Bingham thought, one of the beautiful opposites of pretty. She taught him then and there in the cave a dozen ordinary words in sign language: I, you, car, home, day, like, go, sea, be together, mama, not, must. They laughed a great deal as his fingers blundered some sentences together: I you together like go sea. When he asked her how to say happy she showed him, and house, and door; but when he wrote love on the sand with a twig, she shook her head. She made the gestures of liking and being together, but pointed at love and looked at him reprovingly. He saw that she had more tact than he, and very likely more honesty. She told him then she had to go home to mama. Mama? he asked her, and she nodded. Who? he said with his lips. Miss Cudahy, she wrote on the sand, sprang up and ran off towards the path. For a few moments he watched her, incredulous and frustrated; he felt very fond of her. He watched her climb the path, not thinking, but only looking at the slight figure quick and graceful in its brown, practical, shapeless clothes, not feeling even, only wishing he knew her well. And just before he got up to follow her he remembered Miss Cudahy's hard look when Phoebe had spilled some tea on the table, and he shuddered to feel cold little feet creeping about his back as they would when, lying in bed on the way to sleep, he chanced to think about the latest advances in bomb-making.

Next morning, arriving just after the postman, he carried Miss Cudahy's mail up to the front door with him. He saw one from Mrs.

Pickman-Ellsworth. He was feeling grim when Phoebe let him into the parlor.

"Oh, ho," cried Miss Cudahy after the civilities; she waved an envelope at him. "Let's see what Nell has to say about you. Just step into the dining room till I call you, Mr. Bingham, if you don't mind. You'll find Phoebe polishing the silver."

He fumbled among his unsorted emotions, unable to find the one that would suit his response; what he did was simply to thank her and do what she said—after all, he reflected, he had not yet seen the dining room.

Phoebe did not stop polishing, but whenever, in his inspection of the room, he passed near her she would rub against him a little like a cat. Miss Cudahy shouted him back.

"She says you're respectable," she said, and puffed on her pipe a few times gazing at him. "Good reputation, good family. I want you to stay with me, Mr. Bingham, for as long as you're going to be in this vicinity. I like you. You may have the master bedroom; I'll tell you who it was made for, some day. Phoebe needs the society of a cultivated man. Poor creature. Do you like her?"

"Very much." But he did not want to talk about her to Miss Cudahy. "Thank you for the invitation. I do not want to intrude . . ."

"Nonsense, that's my concern, not yours. There are not many literate people hereabouts. Mrs. Townson in Mendocino City, the Chiverses in Fort Bragg, who else? You ask me why I continue to live in Stowes Landing. My answer to you is, I don't. I live in this house."

"You have good taste in houses."

"Because it is your taste? Well, I like to be flattered, Mr. Bingham, but don't try to flatter me about my knowledge of New England houses. Between us we could write a good book on the old houses of this county." She puffed reflectively, gazing at him. "Mine's the best of course. Think it over. You could live here while we were at it, of course. I want to look at my mail now. Would you be so good as to step into the garden and tell Japheth to spray the roses?"

He looked at the appointments of the parlor and hall with a new eye as he walked out: they were his to use, and she would tell him all she knew. On the front steps he imagined a roseate fantasy—a month, even six weeks of solid research and photographing, then one of the major contributions to the history of California architecture would be his. He even looked with a benevolent eye at Japheth, whom he found standing with some cuttings in one hand and clippers in the other, staring at a rose. He delivered his message with positive friendliness; Japheth winked at him, touched his cap with the clippers, and then, leering, pulled off a rose-branch so that it half split the cane. "It wasn't so in the old country," he whispered. Bingham left unhurriedly. Walking away, he rummaged about in his mind for his fantasy, but he could not find it again.

Half from plan and half because it was the nearest entrance, he ran up the back stairs and into the kitchen.

Glistening copper pots and pans hung on the walls; the old wood stove took up far more room than it needed to by the standards of modern efficiency; there was a hatchet in the box with the kindling; three comfortable, mended kitchen chairs, envy of snobs, sat about the stove; the worn linoleum, black and white checkered, was as clean with scrubbing as a boy's ears; it smelled good in the kitchen, of apples and coffee. Some sort of odd combination of flag-arms, as in a railroad signal, was attached to the wall over the pantry door; even as he was wondering what it was for, one of the flags, the white one, fell out at right angles; obviously a signal for Phoebe. It jiggled up and down; he stepped through the pantry into the dining room, and went with Phoebe into the parlor again.

"Do you approve of my kitchen, Mr. Bingham?"

"I do. Phoebe keeps it in admirable order."

"It's a pleasant place to spend the supper hours in the winter, let me tell you. You must visit us in the winter."

"I should be delighted." He felt constrained to say something more. "Your garden must have been a prize at one time."

"It was."

"A great pity it has fallen into neglect."

"Do you have any ideas for it, Mr. Bingham?" She was full of animation.

"Only the obvious ideas for the circumstances."

"The very thing!" she cried. "It would give you some exercise as we worked on our book. I can see by your figure you don't get enough exercise. Splendid, sir, a splendid addition."

He smiled painfully. "I don't enjoy gardening."

"Nonsense. You need it." She saw that she had gone too far. "Of course, of course," she went on heavily, "there would be no necessity.

Japheth keeps the fuchsias from dying out. Phoebe would work with you in the garden. She likes it. She likes being with you."

Phoebe, having lip-read the gist of the conversation, smiled up at Bingham so sweetly that he, in relief from the old woman, half reached out his hand to her in response; propriety halted him. Phoebe, seeing his broken gesture, stepped beside him and took his hand; all three laughed at his blush.

"Well," said Miss Cudahy, shifting her bulk about, "everything is working out handsomely. Phoebe must show you your room. You must fetch your things and install yourself. We shall take an outing one day soon, Mr. Bingham. Zenobia Dobbs has a house in Greenwood you should see the inside of before you leave here, and I doubt if you went alone that she would be so hospitable to you as I have been."

He did not thank her for her hospitality, as she apparently wanted him to do, because he did not think she had been moved by hospitality to do what she was doing. He said he should like to see the house in Greenwood.

"But where is this town?" he asked. "I don't recognize the name."

"They took to calling it Elk a few years ago," she said. "There are not many like you, Mr. Bingham, who cherish the old things. The world rots and we rot with it."

She tossed some keys to Phoebe, fluttered her hand, and shifted herself back on her chair. Among her pale violet clothes, in that light that cast no shadow, her face seemed nearly ethereal, yet her body was huge.

Upstairs, Phoebe showed him the master bedroom; she kept looking from his face to the mantel or the bedstead or the moulding, pleased yet puzzled by the great impression the room was making on him, trying to see it with his eyes. She showed him the bathroom, Japheth's room, which was a dark cupboard, and her own room facing west, austere this side of barrenness, feminine only in the lace curtains. Then, with sparkling eyes, dancing a little in excitement, taking both his hands in one of hers, she opened the door to the last bedroom. His impression was one of darkness, scent, frills, musty old letters. She threw open the shutters; they were in a boudoir, among a luxury which had made feminine and intimate the stern woodwork, the right-angled room. There was a satin quilt on the low bed; at the sight of it he made a mock-gesture of indolence, and in an instant Phoebe was lying there. She took some pins out of her hair and shook it free; it was brown, fine hair. She laid her head at a certain angle on the pillows, curved one arm up over her head and the other onto her stomach, and turned her body in the fashion of all experience and luxuriation. It was only a moment until she bounced up smiling and clasping his hand, simple and young again.

He heard a clicking in the hall, and Miss Cudahy shouting that she wanted Phoebe. He told her; she put up her hair in a second; on their way down, she flipped the hall flag back up into place. On the landing of the stairs, yielding to what impulse he did not know, he stopped Phoebe just to look at her intently. Her face was cheery and flushed; when she saw his expression, she pressed herself against him, her head bowed onto his shoulder; he held her tightly a moment and kissed the top of her head. Miss Cudahy called again and they went on down.

She looked thunderous.

"Mr. Bingham," she said. "I heard the springs squeak."

He was very angry. "I dare say you did. I pressed the mattress to see what it was like, and Phoebe sat on the bed in the south room."

"Sat on it!" cried Miss Cudahy and motioned to Phoebe to go stand beside her. "Sat on it indeed! She jumped on it."

"Yes, and lay on it," he said, thin-lipped. "It is more luxury than she is used to."

"That was my room, and my mother's before me. I have restored it. I intended that you should look at the architecture and not the décor. I am displeased."

"Indeed. As though the one were not a part of the other."

"Well," she said, and suddenly she smiled and put her arm around Phoebe's legs, stroking her thigh. "One cannot be too careful. What is your opinion of what you saw upstairs?"

"It all but equals the newel in excellence."

"Quite so. Now then, Mr. Bingham," she said affably, "I think we can manage a way of working together. There are problems of course, not insuperable ones, I trust. How soon will you be able to come?"

"Why . . . I am not sure. I would have to arrange for a leave of absence beyond my usual vacation allowance."

"Rather. It will take us months at least, by my plan."

"Oh, I don't . . ."

You have no sentimental ties in Oakland?—No, and Phoebe will be with us. You will be kind to Phoebe, Mr. Bingham? She has suffered from the lack of suitable male acquaintance."

"Why," he stammered, not knowing how to avoid indelicacy, "to be sure, I am fond of Phoebe, I will be kind, there is no problem."

"She means much to me, sir. Perhaps I try, as they say, to relive my youth through her. What does it matter? I mean her to be happy." She pressed her cheek against Phoebe's hip. "Did you ever see finer legs, sir?" Phoebe smoothed, indulgently, the iron-grey hair, smiling at Bingham. "We must handle Phoebe with care, must we not?"

4

On his fourth morning at Miss Cudahy's, he left at dawn to drive up the coast as far as Fort Bragg; the rugged coastline, the sombre landscape illuminated by spring flowers, the old barns patched with moss, the sheep, the small towns, all pleased him greatly, but he found no architectural points of interest to him, nothing he had not seen the like of before. He was not concentrating well, to be sure; he rubbered along, the amateur tourist; he said to himself that he had exhausted the district, but in truth he had left his thoughts disassembled behind. He returned to Stowes Landing not long after lunch, having intended to stay away until dark.

He knocked at the door, which was kept always locked; he had not been entrusted with a key. Finally the old woman herself answered.

"Ho," she said, and pounded her cane on the floor in her pleasure. "I was wanting you. It's too fine a day to waste in old houses. We're going for an outing down to Greenwood. Good. Good. Give me ten minutes in my room and I'll be ready."

"Fifteen," he said. "I want to clean up before going out again."

"Very well," she answered and stalked down the hall towards her room. "That's a fine sun they've got out there. Damn the hedge on a day like this."

There was not a sound upstairs as he washed and changed. There seldom was. He wished he knew whether Phoebe was in her room.

Miss Cudahy clumped back into the hall again and called him down. She was in front of the hall mirror arranging on her head a wide-brimmed, violet hat with a fringe of tiny tassels.

"We're off!" she cried. "Zenobia Dobbs, you must see her house. I haven't been in it for years. So you like my newel, Mr. Bingham."

He exclaimed again that he did. "It's never been photographed." He said what she wanted him to say. "Well, help me down the stairs."

"I did not realize you could go down steps, Miss Cudahy."

"Down I can make it. It's up that breaks my back. You'll have to get Japheth to help you get me up."

She leaned heavily on his shoulder, taking the steps one at a time, and at the bottom she paused to snort like a horse.

"Where is Phoebe?" he asked.

"In the kitchen, I suppose. Where she belongs at any rate."

"She is coming with us?" he asked, just barely polite.

"I had not planned that she should."

"She would enjoy it," he said. "I will fetch her."

"Zenobia and she do not hit it off."

"Then I shall take Phoebe for a walk while you have tea with Mrs. Dobbs."

She did not answer him but started off toward the south side of the house.

Phoebe was not in the kitchen, not anywhere downstairs. He had to open the door to her room to see if she was in it. She was lying crosswise on her bed like a child, her head and bare arms bright in the sunshine that poured through her window. She had taken off her shoes and stockings; her legs were stretched up the side of the wall, one foot rubbing the other. He shook his head to clear it, and told her—he had learned more of her sign-language—to put on her bathing suit and come for a trip. She clapped her hands with joy, leaped up, and pushed him out of her room playfully.

They found Miss Cudahy waving her cane at glowering Japheth and threatening to beat him. Bingham led her to the car.

"Hmph," she snorted as they drove away. "They said he was hopeless but I knew I could handle him. The fools, they decided he needed love and kindness, but he took it for weakness. I've had him for years, and I give him unbuttered bread and a whip. And liquor on Saturday night."

"Miss Cudahy," he said, "have you ever considered having Phoebe taught to speak? I believe there are people who . . ."

"I have considered it, Mr. Bingham, but I shall not have it done. She is happy. At Mrs. Dobbs', you will return for me at five o'clock, and she will show you the house. You might leave Phoebe in the car."

"I would hate to leave Phoebe in the car," he said, and he told himself that only if the house were very attractive would he do it.

Phoebe, having seen their angry heads, leaned forward from the back seat and laid a restraining hand on each of them.

"In the eyes of God, Mr. Bingham, she may be worth ten of us. Meanwhile she does what I tell her to do, and I'd thank you to remember it." He just managed to swallow his anger; as it were in payment she said, "My grandfather, of whom I was telling you yesterday, brought the newel and the two mantels around the Horn on his own ship. They cost him a fortune."

He touched Phoebe's hand with his, and so did Miss Cudahy. They smiled at her and fell silent. There was brilliant sunlight all the way to Elk.

They spent two hours on the beach alone. There was a tunnel through a tall rock island a few yards offshore, through which the ocean drove frothing and soughing; once, the tide coming in, a great wave made a whistling noise in the tunnel. A northbound ship near the horizon spent the two hours going out of sight. They found some crabs in a pool and scared them back into their ledge, and laughed at their anger and clicking. The water was too cold for swimming but they waded in it a little; most of the time they lay on the sand. Bingham thought her legs to be in the lovely hinterland between trim and heavy, and from the way she took off her skirt, from the way she displayed them and drew his head once down into her lap, he knew she wanted him to admire them, to touch them with his fingers. There was scarcely a moment when they were not touching.

He asked her if she wanted to learn to speak. She smiled rather wistfully, and nodded; but she told him she was happy anyway. He told her it was a shame that Miss Cudahy would not do it. She shook her head and put a finger on his lips. He told her there was a school in Oakland where she could learn to speak. She closed her eyes, smiling, till he promised not to continue with the subject, and she kissed the tip of his nose. They were half an hour late for Miss Cudahy. He did not think the Dobbs house worth enough to abandon Phoebe in the car just to see it.

Miss Cudahy did not seem to mind their being late; she seemed mellow. Several times on the way home she motioned for Phoebe's hand, pressed it against her cheek, nipped at her finger with her lips. "You are keeping our bargain, Mr. Bingham," she said. "I have never known Phoebe to be happier. Tomorrow may be a good day for you to commence your photography."

Japheth and he together got her up the front steps; the problem was now to transport her in such a way as to let her think they were only helping her. Japheth did not even try, and she was furious with him. Once she beat Bingham on the neck. "I'm so sorry," she trumpeted. "Mistake, mistake." And she beat Japheth the harder for her error. He spat on the steps as he went back to work in the garden.

At dinner Bingham found it just possible to be civil. Miss Cudahy was wheezing a good deal and did not make much demand upon him; he was able to brood inward upon his own thoughts. They were not even thoughts, just two strong sensations, about which his mind prowled and peered with no result: Miss Cudahy's mistaken blow on his neck and, quite as vivid as that though smaller and softer, the warm light kiss Phoebe had put there as soon as she could, to make up for the blow. He had not been struck in anger since he was a child, nor kissed since then so tenderly. He did not know what to make of such strong experience. He felt neither anger nor grati- tude, felt nothing that deserved so differentiated a name as resent- ment, say, or affection; indeed, so far as he knew he felt nothing except, on the skin and down into the muscles of his neck, the two touches of the two women. Yet, when at the end of the meal, staring at a crumb like a yogi, he did not hear Miss Cudahy ask him a ques- tion and she rapped on her tumbler with her ring, barking out "Mr. Bingham," he started from his chair and glared at her wildly a moment, leaned on the edge of the table and whispered intently "No! No!" "No coffee?" she said, a little taken aback. He subsided, under Phoebe's restraining hand. "Sorry," he mumbled; "I was think- ing of something else. Yes, coffee, please." He had been feeling more than touches on the neck, and with that feudal rap on the glass some of it began turmoiling up and out.

He did not even assist Miss Cudahy from her chair, but bolted into the kitchen where, for the first time, he wiped dishes for Phoebe as she washed. She kept her eyes downcast on her business; even when he patted her arm for attention or physically turned her head about, she did not look at his eyes, but only at his lips, or at his hands stumbling and tripping in their rush like lips stuttering from anger; once, she caught the frustrated things and kissed each palm gently, then turned back to her suds. He stood beside her, the kisses warm in his hands, just staring at her; feeling his chin nearly begin to quiver he bustled back to his job; but his anger was gone, and all he felt now was that Phoebe was altogether delicate and alive and pitiable and needing to be saved. He understood now, without hatred, how Miss Cudahy would want to hold her; but Phoebe must be saved; and more, she must want to be saved.

As she was hanging up the dishcloth, finished, he held her waist with a gentleness she immediately recognized, for she looked back over her shoulder up into his eyes; he kissed her; scarcely moving, she yielded against him. There were tears in their eyes when they drew apart, and at that instant Bingham felt that he might have fetched her coat and hat and driven her off to Oakland without an objection from her. But she must freely desire to leave Miss Cudahy; she must not be swayed from that old woman's will only to become subject to his, though better, will. He sat her by the oven, poured a cup of coffee for each of them, sat in front of her so that their knees touched, and asked her, "Will you come to Oakland with me?" It would have been coy of her, gazing against his earnest gaze, to treat his question playfully, to pretend she didn't take him seriously: the leap of eagerness that brightened her eyes and pressed her hands together meant to him only that she wanted to come to Oakland; yet she did not sign the answer in return. "I can take you with me when I go. I have friends you can stay with till we find a permanent arrangement for you. Don't worry, I will make it a point to see you often." It would have been weak of her, under his insistence, to have begun crying in order to avoid meeting his challenge: yet he saw tears come to her eyes after his last pressing; he would have relented—must she not choose freely?—but that she answered him then: I owe Miss Cudahy so much. "Of course," he answered, "and you can return to her if you want, but you owe it to yourself to go to the school." She needs me, Phoebe pleaded; what would she do without me? And with that he pounded the table; but not too loud, for fear Miss Cudahy would hear him. It would be like a betrayal, Phoebe told him. "You must leave her sooner or later," he responded (No, her head shook), "you owe it to yourself to go now." She buried her face in her hands, but in a heat of compelling he pulled them away and, clutching her wrists hard, said with his lips, "You must come with me." She wilted then, as though he had uttered a magic formula—composed of common words perhaps, but nonetheless magic. She would come if he would get Miss

Cudahy's permission. "But no, but no! You must come of your own free will." Shaking her head, miserable, she sat on his lap and hid her face against his neck, so that all he could do, imagining how that old woman would greet such a proposal, was to hold Phoebe as though she were crying, in need of comforting; yet he was conscious of her warm breathing, of her lips half kissing the soft joining of his shoulder and neck, of her woman's body which his hands were embarrassed how to hold. Old Japheth came in for coffee and at the sight of them muttered "Bitch! Bitch!" In a sort of desperation of confusion, Bingham pushed Phoebe off his lap and, flapping his hands, went up to his room.

But there was no peace for him there at all. To rescue her became, as he writhed on the bed in that handsome, alien room, his obsession and immediate need. His pain was purer and stronger than it could have been had he suspected for a second that there was more causing it than the desire to liberate an oppressed, afflicted person he knew. But as it was, that pain was so great that he had to creep back downstairs again hoping to find Phoebe in the kitchen alone where he could bring matters to a head; for he did not know what he would do if she did not assert herself tonight. The afterwards would work itself out, and if Miss Cudahy should suffer, then she should suffer.

As he reached, silently, the bottom step, he saw through the half-open door to the parlor Phoebe sitting beside Miss Cudahy, who was lolling back in the chaise-longue looking at her from under her eyelids and fondling her arm. For a long time he froze on that step; all he felt for that painful time was the gracefully curving, worn, smooth old wood of the rail in his hand. Quivering with emotions he did not understand and no longer cared about controlling, he went into the room. As he spoke, but not until then, he realized from the suspicion of quiver in his voice that he would not be able to stand up to the old woman.

"Miss Cudahy," he said, as evenly as he could manage, "I thank you for your hospitality, but I am leaving."

"What?" she cried, altogether surprised. "You are just becoming one of us."

"I am not. I am leaving immediately."

"You have not taken your photograph yet."

"No," he said; he had thought he would be adamant. "I am obliged to leave suddenly." He would make no excuse, only get out. But his eye was drawn by the exquisite proportions of the frame

around the window behind the two women. "Perhaps when I come
back up later this summer I shall be able to complete my study."

"*Our* book, Mr. Bingham?"

"Of course, of course, complete our study."

"Perhaps. We shall see." She thrust unhappy Phoebe from the
chair. "I shall get to the bottom of this."

He had packed in five minutes. Phoebe was waiting for him in the
hall, tears in her eyes. He wrote down the name of the motel where
he was going to stay the night and told her to come there first thing
in the morning. She nodded, and looked at him in bewilderment,
longingly.

At the front door he was touching her hands goodbye and telling
her she must come as soon as she could, when Miss Cudahy shouted,
"Send Phoebe to me at once!" He kissed her quickly on the cheek,
and left.

5

He could not remain alone and waking in that alien, ugly motel, but
neither did he want to go near the surge of the sea. He walked
towards the hills through a pleasant pasture, and as he was walking
he heard on the other side of a fence bleating sheep; he went to
the fence to watch them in the light of the high moon. They stared
at him for a moment like citizens in a bus, and when he rattled the
top rail of the fence they stared at him again and shied away; he
played with them off and on for an hour or more, an hour of relief:
their stares were simple and sufficient, they left him alone.

He lay in bed feeling as though he were floating. He put his
hands under his head and gazed at the moon, not thinking so much
as watching thoughts dance through his mind. The moon had
wheeled into the western sky by the time he had fallen asleep.

A rattle at the door awoke him. The moon had set. He sat up and
called, "Who is it?" There was another rattle and a low, amorphous
cry. He opened the door to Phoebe. She grasped both his hands in
hers hard, and threw herself face down on the bed crying, turned
away from him. He closed the windows and built a fire in the stove,
and then for fifteen minutes or so sat on the bed beside her stroking
her hair and arms, shuddering a little with alarm, ready to weep
himself that he could say nothing to her.

At last she turned her face towards him, and gradually her crying subsided. Her mouth, now that he came to watch her face so closely, lost the contours of grief and reassumed its usual expression; hers was somehow softer than most mouths, less revealing of character, more innocent. She ceased to make those hard, inchoate cries that disturbed him. She became Phoebe again. He was astonished in a new way at how tenderly he felt toward her, thinking of what she must be suffering now, partly for his sake.

"Did she scold you?" he asked, and her answer was only the most rueful smile in the world. "What is this?" he cried suddenly and bent down to look at three fresh bruises on the back of Phoebe's leg, just above the knee. "Did she hurt you?" he said to her. She shrugged: what difference did it make? "Pinch?" She shrugged: yes, but it was the least of my pain. "Vicious," he muttered to himself pounding the fist of one hand into the palm of the other, "damned, cruel, vicious old bitch."

Phoebe made him sit beside her and asked him if he would ever come back to the house; he told her no. Her lip quivered; she threw her arms around him as though to hold him forever, and pulled him down beside her. When he could, he freed himself and told her she must go with him. When are you leaving? Tomorrow, he answered, and she turned from him again to cry. He was trembling with anger so hard that Phoebe finally turned over and smiled as best she could. He gave her his handkerchief to use for her tears.

He lay down facing her and put his arm over her waist; their legs were touching. They lay looking at each other peacefully, touching gently. But it seemed to him after a time that something was required of him; the simplest, easiest thing to do would be to kiss her, but just because it was so easy he distrusted it, and besides it would be taking advantage of her as he had sworn to himself not to do; perhaps he should renew his offer to take her to the school in Oakland, assuring her again that he had meant it. But when she saw what he was starting to tell her she stopped him, tenderly but certainly. Her hand, still and yet alive, lay curled against his throat, warm and other and loving, and seemed to him to reproach him for some lack. It was all he could do to support her unflinching gaze; in no way did she actually reproach him, yet he could not respond to that gaze with a smile or in fact with any expression at all; it was not a response her gaze sought, but somehow him himself; an unpitying, devouring, utterly unmalicious gaze; it did not demand, it took. As the uneasy night wore on, lying half embraced on his left side awkwardly, he gradually suffocated with the knowledge that Phoebe had the unopposable rights of one who, in a way he was appalled to imagine, loved.

At the first evidences of dawn he leaped up and dressed, telling her that for the sake of her reputation she must leave the motel immediately. She lay watching his bustle with her steady, innocent, direct gaze. He stood before her urging her to rise. Is this the last time I shall ever see you? He could not bear her directness. "No, no, of course not, it's all settled. How could you say such a thing? You are going with me to Oakland, today, now, as soon as you've packed your bags. We're going to Miss Cudahy's now." He was frenetic and pressed too hard. "I'll be waiting for you in the car outside the hedge at nine o'clock. It's all settled?" She smiled into tears, into the tears, he thought, of joy, and nodded. She pulled him down on top of her and held him so hard and kissed him so ardently that he was alarmed. They left the motel. For a moment, parking outside the hedge, kissing her again, he had the wild notion of driving off with Phoebe then and there, however it might look; but before he had time either to act on the impulse or to reject it, with a cry that startled him she had opened the door of the car and run in.

At nine o'clock she had not emerged from that tunnel in the hedge, nor at quarter past. At nine-thirty he got out of the car and went in the front gate.

At the window of her room on the second floor, Phoebe was standing, wearing her bathrobe, evidently crying. She kept shaking her head. She made a gesture, from her heart to her lips to him, that could have meant only one thing. His heart throbbing in his throat with the pity and the loss, he made the signs "Together, we must go together." If there had been any way for him to get her free from that house he would have used it at that moment; he blamed himself for having let her come back at all; he could scarcely bear to think of her life locked in as it would be and had been. She buried her face in her hands and turned slowly from the window.

He ran to the front door and pounded the knocker; there was no response. He knocked till the great door reverberated; he would have shouted had he not been afraid of alarming the neighbors. Finally there was the sound of a cane and of coughing at the end of the hallway. He trembled; his lips were tense with the recriminations with which he would greet Miss Cudahy. She opened the door, wide, and stood staring at him. "Yes?" Instantly he became aware of his dishevelled appearance. "As you know, my work, it is . . ." "Go get your Kodak, Mr. Bingham," she said, guttural with scorn. She pointed with her cane, holding her arm out full length, the garments trailing. "You may photograph my newel if you're quick about it." His mouth opened, but he did not say anything. "Mind you don't go upstairs," said Miss Cudahy and returned down the hall. He turned, went down the steps, and ran to his car. On his way back in, burdened with his camera and lighting equipment, he glanced furtively up, and was grateful to see that Phoebe had drawn the curtains to her room. He had to run out again for his tripod, because he could not hold the camera steady. There was not another sound in the house as he worked. In fifteen minutes he had finished and left.

ELIZABETH ENRIGHT, *author of* Thimble
Summer, *which won the Newbery Award in 1939,*
appeared last in the O. Henry *with "I Forgot*
Where I Was" in 1946. Her stories have appeared
in Harper's, Harper's Bazaar, Mademoiselle, Cosmopolitan, The Saturday Evening Post, *and a*
collection of them was issued in 1946 under the
title Borrowed Summer. *Born in Chicago, she is*
married, with two children, and lives now in
New York.

THE OPERATOR

FROM HARPER'S MAGAZINE

The strange things you want in this life! . . . When I was nine
or ten years old I wanted a middy blouse more than anything on
earth. I wanted it so badly that I dreamed about it; whined through
my nose for it. But my mother shook all her blond curls in a sort
of vivacious horror: "No, honey! Never! Heavens, shades of Rad-
cliffe girls with chafing dishes and bulging calves all leaping at a
basketball together and having a corking time. Corking! That's the
sort of word that goes with middy blouses. No, Baby. Over my
dead body . . ." And since my mother was the one sun in my sky
(my father had been killed in Belleau Wood) I resigned myself
to the quaint little smocked dresses that she chose for me.

I did not realize at the time that the way I was dressed bore a
relationship to two other things I did not care for: my nickname
and my face, but I tolerated them with the enforced philosophy of
childhood, sensing that the day would surely come when I could
change all three.

Only now, in looking at old photographs can I see that there
was justice in the nickname at least: that I was called "Granny"
not only because my own true name was Grania. The face that I
examine as I might a stranger's seems to predict a weight of age on
its small features, and nothing was done to lessen the effect by the
way I wore my hair, earnestly strained back from my forehead with
a round comb.

I think that my mother unconsciously emphasized the precocious elderly quality of my looks because she was Adair Lovett, the actress, and so young, so young to look at for so long, that the contrast between us must have had a certain humorous originality and she, naturally, was conditioned to audiences. At the time I speak of, 1920 or thereabouts, Mary Pickford wilderness-curls were still the vogue for ingénues, and my mother often wore her hair in this fashion. I used to love to watch her brushing it, and then dipping her comb into the teacup of warm water and curling the tip-ends around her finger till they strutted on her shoulders like little pantalette legs. I was spellbound by all her formidable technique of enhancement, and asked nothing better than to be allowed to watch in the theater dressing room as she put on her make-up: a long, grave ritual starting with her flawless naked face and ending up with the mask of a candy doll.

"Oh, Mama, you look so pretty!"

"Do I, Baby? Well I have to look pretty, after all. It's what pays the darn bills, isn't it? And buys your roller skates and Tootsie Rolls. Now run on home, honey; get to bed. Take her, Mademoiselle."

Her cheek would touch mine, smelling strong of make-up and delicious, like a whole barber shop, and she was gone. Hissing and resisting as Mademoiselle tried to get my arms into my coat sleeves, I would stand at the door of the dressing room, listening to the last bars of the overture; then a great heartbeat interval of silence . . . and all at once a sound as though a door had opened onto the world! It was applause, but at this distance it seemed like a wind from the desert or the sea, huge and thrilling. Then silence again and a tiny voice began to speak, my mother's voice. All the winds and waves were still, and I was proud and jealous and exalted.

"Now, Granny, you *come!*" Mademoiselle would bang my blue beaver hat, also quaint, onto my head, and there was nothing for it but to return to the unreal, unlovable world of reality.

So it came as a bolt from the blue when one day Mademoiselle told my mother that she was leaving immediately to get married. Mademoiselle, that bundle of Gallic twigs! No one had ever considered such a possibility.

"Now what on earth are we going to do!" cried my mother crossly. "Who's going to stay with you at night?"

"Mama, I don't *need* anybody any more."

"Granny baby, don't be so silly. You know I can never get home before eleven-thirty."

"Well, Lutie's here till seven; no, now, Mama, *wait!* Listen. If I get lonesome or anything I can talk to the switchboard lady. She's a very nice lady and she's right downstairs."

"And she doesn't go home till twelve," mused my mother. "Oh, no, honey, I don't think so. . . ."

But I saw that I would soon win my point.

At that time we were living in a second-floor apartment in West 10th Street. The lobby was an asset to the tenants: large, faintly grand, a polished place that smelled strongly of Liquid Veneer and dimly of cats. It was illuminated by paired bracket-lamps, each with one eye blinded by economy, and the melting hues of their Tiffany glass shades reminded me of half-sucked candy. Two staircases—one for the tenants on the east side of the building and one for the tenants on the west—opened out and upward with expansive, old-fashioned gestures; and in each French window stood a twirled iron tripod holding a pot of those plants which somehow cling to life through all: spitting radiators, north light, neglect of janitors. For me the lobby had a soothing elegance; it brought to mind the baronial halls in illustrations by Reginald Birch. I did not see the cracks or feel the drafts. There must have been drafts, for the switchboard stood sheltered in a grotto of burlap screens, and whatever operator worked there wore a sweater on her shoulders.

There, night after night, she sat, in a puddle of Rembrandt light, ministering to the irascible instrument in her charge, and there beside her, perhaps to her secret desperation, I sat, too.

At first there was Miss Delevant, a tall, refined woman in her early fifties who wore silver bangles and Venetian beads, and rattled when she moved even slightly, like a horse in its harness. Indignation was her preferred climate.

"Well, I'm very sorry, but I distinctly under*stood* you to say Stuyvesant," she would tell the mouthpiece. "He did, too, Stuyvesant!" she would hiss at me, her face deeply impressed with outrage. When a caller came to see one of the tenants she would look at him narrowly. "Are you expected?" And somewhere, remotely, there was an implication that she did not believe this possible. "Name, please," was the next question if he was *not* expected, and then the name was appraised silently and repeated as if a little soiled, into the mouthpiece. "A Mr. *Crouch* to see you," she would announce daintily, while Mr. Crouch stood listening to his name recede, flapping his derby nervously against his thigh, until told he might go up. "Oh, no, not that staircase, the *other* one!"

As his footsteps rang out lonely on the stair-treads she would look at me and wink, for I, it seemed, was her one ally. "Crouch," she would repeat, and we would laugh maliciously. Undoubtedly, the poor man could hear us on his way up, and this, I understood tacitly, was part of the plan.

The janitress in those days was a Scandinavian woman named Helga who flapped up and down the basement stairs in dun-colored garments and gray Comfy slippers. Her pale green hair was stuck to her head with big steel pins like croquet wickets that were always falling out onto the floor with a clang. She loved to laugh, and laughed often. Her little eyes would close up, watering, and her wide-open mouth turned down at the corners in a pain of mirth. She and Miss Delevant hated each other.

"Aw, she don't got no red blut, that old mait, she only got winegar in her weins," Helga said; and Miss Delevant said of Helga: "It's so easy for a person to keep themselves clean and dainty. I just don't under*stand* disorder."

Helga, perhaps, was instrumental in getting Miss Delevant dismissed; for one night when I came downstairs I found that there was a new operator, a fat young man named Nigel Eliscue, who talked as though his mouth were full of cake. He was a ballet enthusiast, and we spent many happy evenings discussing Pavlova, of whom I owned thirty-seven photographs, and who I planned to be when I grew up. It was Nigel who, for my benefit, attempted *entrechats* that made the lampshades tingle and brought Helga up from her cozy realm of cats and coffee.

"Cut it out, fella, the plaster's busting down."

Nigel lasted two weeks, and after him came old Mrs. Pohd who handled the switchboard as if it were a loom to weave veils on. And then, after Mrs. Pohd, came Gerald.

I cannot remember his last name though I have tried. Perhaps I never knew it: from the first I called him Gerald. He was young, but younger, and in a different way, than Nigel Eliscue. I do not think that he was more than twenty-two; a handsome boy with dark crisp hair and clear-cut features.

To each of the switchboard operators my mother had given certain directions, disguised as gentle requests, and now she gave them to Gerald, possibly with some misgiving.

"Would you mind if my little girl sits with you a while after the maid goes home? Oh, that's awfully sweet of you, it keeps her from being lonesome. But promise me, won't you, not to let her be a bother, and *promise* me, *please,* that you'll send her up at nine o'clock!"

"I certainly will, Miss Lovett, you can count on me," said Gerald, standing up and staring radiantly at my mother. (He wanted to be an actor, he told me later; was theater mad. "But meantime I have to live, don't I? So that's why I learned this stuff . . . just filling in, honey, just filling in.")

All the other operators had kept these promises faithfully; I never could wheedle more than fifteen extra minutes out of any of them, but Gerald was another story; sometimes he let me stay in the lobby till after eleven. Then he would glance at the prissy little clock in its case on top of the switchboard.

"You better vamoose, Cinderella. And don't leave any glass footgear on the stairs, either, or I'll be in Dutch."

"All right, I won't. Good night, Gerald!"

Upstairs in my bed I would fall into sleep as a stone falls into a well, and often I dreamed of my new friend.

Each evening when Lutie, the maid, was gone I came down the broad east staircase. Halfway down I would pause and lean on the balustrade, staring down at Gerald in his grotto. If he was not busy he would look up, smiling.

"Hello, Melisande."

"Who's that?" I asked suspiciously, the first evening.

"A girl with long hair like yours that looked down from a balcony."

"I thought that was what's-her-name; you know. Juli*ette.*"

"She did, too. Girls are always leaning over balconies and switching their hair around, but I never cared for Juliet."

"I didn't either. Too fat."

"She was?"

"In the opera of her that I saw, she was."

"Fat, huh? Maybe that's why she never appealed to me. Well, come on down. Step into my parlor."

I giggled, went down, and took my place in the little rocker where I had already spent so many evenings. The switchboard lights were very becoming to him; so were the earphones on his head. He looked like Satan as a youth, before his evil had become serious. His hands moved dextrously among the tubes and plugs; I noticed that his fingers were extremely long and supple, with tips that turned back a little, like those of an African or Hindu boy. He spoke to the switchboard as if it were alive: "Quiet now, kid, take it easy, don't get hysterical," or: "Try it in high C, Amelita."

Nearly every night he told me a chapter of his life's history: not his true life history—of that I seldom heard a word—but an imaginary one.

"Did I ever tell you about the time I was practicing veterinary surgery in Bessarabia? No? Honest? Well, it's kind of interesting. The Great Ampere's favorite horse was sick, see. It had horse hives. You've never heard of *horse hives*? They're fierce. They come up all over in ranges like the Appalachians and the horse is in agony; you can't really scratch with a hoof. So . . ."

Naturally he had cured the horse—by giving it injections of turpitude, I think—and had been rewarded handsomely.

"You know what he did for me? He gave me his entire harem. One hundred and ninety-six wives. But to tell you the truth I wasn't too pleased: the youngest one was forty, and all their teeth had been filled with emeralds; when they smiled it was like a lot of Lenox Avenue locals were coming at you. But nobody can refuse a present from the Great Ampere, of course. So I brought them all back with me and turned them over to Cartier's. Got a very nice price for them, too."

"Oh, Gerald, you're so crazy," I protested admiringly. It never mattered to me that his stories were told as if someone else, someone more important, were listening. . . . My mother, at times, gave me the same feeling.

Another of his lives had been spent as organist of the great cathedral of Our Lady of Chevrolet. "See, this is how it goes," he said, demonstrating on the switchboard. "Say you're playing the Fugue by Jules Bache, for instance. This plug here is called the Vox Humana (Judge Howley's line)—and this one here's the Vox Angelica (Mrs. Dunphy's. Can you beat it!)—and *this* one is the Vox Populi. . . . Now, see, you pull this stop out (they're called stops)—and push this one in (Oh, sorry, Mrs. Dunphy, my mistake)—all the time working the pedals, and pretty soon the music begins to build up and get strength, and the organ pipes are standing up there like the Ku Klux Klan, all gold and roaring, and after a while the whole doggone church starts to rattle . . . and you feel as if you're making so much racket that you're drowning out the noise of everything that could ever scare you or hurt you in the world. As if you were murdering those things!"

A quality in the way he spoke made me feel that at that moment we were in shoal water, somewhere just above the truth.

"I bet you really have played the organ, haven't you, Gerald?" I said. "Honestly, now, cross your heart, haven't you?"

"So it's facts we're after now, is it? Everyone's always nosing after facts, and *they* aren't anything. Sure, I have. But it was a one-horse organ in a one-horse church in a one-horse town; and it was the old kind that has to have the air pumped into it by hand; a thing like a pair of bellows. A fat kid used to do it for me, and every now and then he'd get lazy or forget and then the organ would kind of die out loud, w-a-a-a-h, like a mule. . . . So one day, though, who should come to town but Geraldine Farrar . . . you know who she is, don't you?"

"I know *her*. Once I sat on her lap."

I had to tell him all about it before he would go on. This was the currency with which I paid for my entertainment: descriptions of my encounters with the great. "And what's more, Mama has her signed picture right on her bedroom wall!"

"Some day I'm going to sneak some time away from this Medusa and come up and see all these pictures."

"Yes, but now go *on*, Gerald."

"Well, it seems Geraldine is in desperate need of an accompanist (the old one died)—and not only an accompanist, but an instrument to sing *to*. The Steinway at Weaver Brothers Auditorium has had an acute attack of mice in its felts. . . ."

By this turn of events I could see that he had safely steered his craft away from the reef and I was contented that this should be so. Gerald was my first experience of that person who seduces by withholding, whose whole personality, while trimmed with lures of wit and physical beauty, is always kept at a distance. Because of my age I not only accepted but enjoyed this, wishing nothing more; had I been older I might have joined the ranks of women who would inevitably break their ties with him by their need to draw close; who by loving the spell would break the spell.

It did not trouble me that I knew almost nothing about his true life; that he never mentioned his family or any friend. He had told

me that he eked out his income by ushering at a concert hall in the
afternoons, but that was all I knew about his life. It was enough for
me that he was there, made me laugh, and kept me company; and
that he never called me Granny, but wonderful names like Esmeralda, and Melisande.

The other tenants liked him too, and often stopped to chat on
the way in or out. Even Judge Howley, an old throat-clearing, slowly
petrifying magistrate, would pause and make statuesque utterances,
and Miss Geary from the third floor would shift her bundles, or set
them down, and give way to conversation as swimmers give way to
a strong current. In Miss Geary's case it was agreed that after ten
minutes I was to slip up to our apartment, and take down the telephone receiver.

"Get me Syracuse," I would then direct, trying not to laugh.

"Syracuse? Yes sir, right away." Gerald's voice sounded very
businesslike, and in another moment I could hear Miss Geary creak-
ing her big soft self up the stairs to the floor above, and soon, drunk
with conspiracy, I would tiptoe down again.

Helga adored Gerald and often brought him snacks, coffee and
damp fungoid crullers, which he shared with me, and her soiled
scarred cats crept up the stairs to fawn and gargle against his legs.

My mother, who had at first taken a wary view of our relationship,
now reassured herself as she reassured her friends, on the telephone:
"Oh, Granny adores him; he's such a lovable boy. And *responsible*.
Isn't he, Baby?" she would ask, turning to me, and warmly I added
my share to her confidence.

My marks at school took a bracing turn for the better, too. The
first time my report card came home with nothing but A's on it my
mother took me to Schrafft's for a chocolate Luxuro Sundae. She
did not know and I did not tell her that Gerald had been "helping"
me with my homework. "Why strain yourself?" he said magnani-
mously. "I've been through all this stuff in my time, someone might
as well profit by it. You have to help some, though, or they'll smell
a rat. Come on, now, define a participle." He exacted a certain
amount of co-operation from me, and saw to it that I copied, in my
own handwriting, the themes he wrote for me. My English teacher
began to single me out for praise.

Gerald always brought a book with him; for a long time it was
Jean Christophe, I remember, and as I scratched away with my
chewed cedar pencil he would read on, doggedly. From time to time

our studies were interrupted, not unpleasantly, by the staccato demands of the switchboard; by the plate-glass shudder of the vestibule door as the tenants came home, bringing with them a whiff of cold street air. Between these minor events our silence was peaceful: the little clock hurried along its narrow path, the cooling radiator knocked with a metal knuckle.

The one ground-floor apartment that opened onto the lobby was occupied by Mr. and Mrs. Decatur, a gay pair who often went out in the evenings: Mr. Decatur with an opera hat and white scarf; his wife in a brocaded coat.

"Good evening, Gerald; good evening, dear."

Mrs. Decatur's silver slippers blinked across the parquet, and Mr. Decatur stalked at her side with the gait of a Caspian crane. For a few minutes after they had left the whole lobby smelled of Quelques Fleurs.

One night in May they gave a party.

"Killing all their birds with one stone," Gerald surmised, and we gaped with pleasure, as first the caterers and musicians, and then the guests, arrived. Often there were parties in the building, but this was in a different class. "They got the rugs rollt up," Helga said, "and vax on the floor slippery like ice!"

From nine o'clock on, the bell kept ringing and I opened the front door to admit the guests. I soared on a wave of narcissistic pleasure the whole evening. All the men and the fragrant ladies smiled at me, and my greedy ego feasted on praise overheard. "What a charming child!" "So *quaint*. . . ."

It was a warm night. The Decaturs' door was left ajar releasing sounds of gabble and music and popping corks.

At half past ten Mrs. Decatur came into the lobby wearing a dress of rose-colored tulle and walking rather carefully. In one hand she carried a lily-stemmed glass and in the other a plate of *petits fours*.

"Here, children, here's a little party for you, too. Such good quiet little mice. . . . The champagne's for you, Gerald. Don't you go and report us to the mean old blue-noses!"

"Silent unto death!" vowed Gerald, standing up and bowing.

Mrs. Decatur blew us a kiss and returned to her party.

"Sort of like cider," Gerald said, and drank his wine at a gulp, as if he were thirsty. I concentrated on the little cakes, and when Helga came up, sloppy and agog, we gave her some, too.

"It's a real Affair," she said admiringly. "The cars they got, some of them people; and shofers! And listen to that band!"

The orchestra was playing the waltz from *Sari*, and suddenly Gerald leaped to his feet and grabbed Helga around the waist. "Come on, Leonora Hughes, let's show them!" He swept her into his arms and loped gracefully about the lobby carting her with him like a bundle of wash, as her Comfy slippers skidded and the hairpins rang. I jumped up and down in an ecstasy of mirth, stuffing my hair into my mouth, as though laughter must always be kept confined. The switchboard, luxuriously abandoned, buzzed and glared and all the lampshades jingled. What joy! What madness! This was life!

How unfortunate it was that the landlord, Mr. Brainard, should have been invited to the party; that he should have let himself in at the front door just as Gerald had lifted Helga up in his arms and was doing a series of dervish turns to the accompaniment of her maniac shrieks. How unfortunate it was that at the instant of his entrance one of her gray ghastly slippers, the color and texture of lint under a bed, should have flown from her foot in a graceless arc to strike his starched white shirt front.

"*Gerald!!*"

"Oh, my God," said Helga. Gerald set her down, and still unsteady from the turns, they faced him.

"Finish your week out and that's the end," Mr. Brainard said in a still, furious voice. "Now, get the hell over to that switchboard."

"Aw, he yust a kid," protested Helga. "He yust play, like . . ."

"You, too," Mr. Brainard said. "End of the week. You and your cats. I *relied* on you."

Helga gave him a slow northern look, and lifted one shoulder in a shrug. "Ishkabibble. Let somebody else grow mushrooms in your damn cellar," she said; then she retrieved her slipper, took her time about adjusting it to her candid bunioned foot, and left the lobby at a comfortable pace.

Mr. Brainard turned his attention to me: "And you, Grania—that's your name, isn't it? What're you doing down here? What's the matter with your mother, letting you stay up all night like this? With a grown-up man, like this?"

I felt cold, suddenly, and dirty. I wanted to defend my mother, but at the same time I was conscious of a puzzling, treasonous anger toward her, too. I said nothing, and stared at Mr. Brainard's evening

shoes which after a moment walked away and in at the Decaturs'
door.

"Never mind, Esmeralda," Gerald said.

"He's horrid and I hate him!"

"Me, too, the dirty bastard, but never you mind. Look, you better
go up. I'll come with you, shall I? It'll be my last chance to see
those photographs."

"All right."

The north wall of my mother's room was covered with pictures
of her theater friends, all signed with names and endearments in
bold handwriting planned for the public eye.

"Sa-a-y, she's really got the whole stable, hasn't she? Mrs. Fiske!
. . . Gee, and Elsie Janis. Who's this— Oh, William Faversham. . . .
But where's the photo of her best beau?"

"What beau? She's got millions of them but she hasn't any *best*
one."

"Sure she has. I mean the one that brings her home every night.
A big man; good-looking. With a mustache. I see them out in the
vestibule talking and talking."

"I never saw him."

"Honest? Oh, well, it's probably nobody. . . . Look at John
Drew. He's got a profile like a codfish."

But soon Gerald's attention seemed to flag. He wandered aim-
lessly around the room. "I lost my ushering job last week, too,"
he said.

"Oh, no!"

"Yep. It ended in a mess, too. It always ends in a mess. Now this
one has. And I tried. This time I honest to God tried, and still it
ends in a mess. The hell with trying."

"Gerald, I can't *stand* it that you won't be here any more."

"Where will I be, I wonder? I haven't got a bean."

As I myself had not a bean there was nothing I could do to help
him. But his mood changed suddenly and he smiled.

"Forget it, kid. I just blew off some steam. . . . Say, who's that
fellow in the uniform, without a name on him?"

I turned to look. "Oh, that's my father."

"Nice. That's a good portrait job, too. Who did it?"

I leaned toward the picture. "Somebody spelled S-T-E-I-C-H-E-N.
I don't know how you say it."

My father had been a handsome man I could see, now that time had removed him from me. He wore his lieutenant's cap at an angle. His mouth smiled. But suddenly my eye was diverted from the face in the photograph to that which was moving on its surface; I could see Gerald behind me, clearly reflected in the glass, and what was he doing so quietly and quickly? He had half turned away, and with those supple fingers of his was scooping something into his pocket from the dressing table. My memory related to me the fact that there under the light I had just seen my mother's emerald ring and her pearl necklace. Frozen, I stared at the picture and the picture in the picture. I did not turn, and the whole incident took no more than a second.

Gerald came and stood beside me. He put his hand on my shoulder, turning me toward him gently, but my shoulder knew how to slide out from under. Then he picked up a lock of my long hair and twirled it idly in his fingers. I stood patiently tethered, waiting to be released. Above his collar I could see a little pulse, a little pump in the blood, ticking steadily.

"I guess I won't see you again, Melisande."

I said nothing, waiting.

"Miss me?"

"Gerald, listen to the switchboard! You better go!"

"Oh, let it choke itself to death."

"But Mr. Brainard's down there."

"Well, all he can do is fire me and he's fired me. If he thinks I'm going to finish out the week he's crazy."

Remembering his voice it seems to me, now, that it was light and rather nasal. Was it perhaps a touch effeminate? How strange that memory can store impressions until, years later, one is ready to appraise them. And then, of course, there is the possibility that the impressions are not valid; that the emotions have discolored them, for vengeance. . . .

"Maybe I *had* better got out of here," Gerald said. "Can I give you a kiss good-by?"

"I guess so."

Cool lips touched my cheek.

"So long, Melisande."

"So long."

He hesitated, with a flicker of concern.

"You're tired. Go to bed now, won't you, like a good kid?"

"All right."

When he had left I stood where I was, and soon I began to shiver. If I lifted the receiver of the telephone whose voice would answer me but his?

After a while I got into my nightgown but I did not go to bed. Instead I went into the living room to wait for my mother. From the Decaturs' apartment just below came shreds of music and a sprawled sound of laughing.

At last, with terrible relief, I heard the quake of glass in the front door's closing, and in a moment not one, but two pairs of footsteps on the stairs; two pairs on the bare hall floor outside. Then my mother's voice.

"But he's never left the switchboard before twelve——"

"Oh, sweetheart, it's all right. You'll see." This voice, a man's, I had not heard before.

"Leaving her all alone with a boy like that, I never did feel——" The key that had been rattling in the lock performed its task; the door swung open. Beside my mother, holding her against him with his arm, was a tall man with a dark mustache.

"Granny! What! What's wrong, why are you still up?" Terrified, my mother ran to me and put her arms around me.

"I thought I heard a noise," I said.

"Where, honey? Where?"

"I think . . . on the fire escape."

"Ken, go see! Off the bedroom—back there." The tall man dropped his hat on a chair and strode into the bedroom.

"Who's he?" I said.

"His name is Ken, dear. Mr. Kenneth Purdue; he's an awfully nice man, Granny, you're going to just love him. . . . Are you sure you're all right, honey?"

"Yes." The man came back again. He smiled at me.

"Nothing there now, anyway. Maybe it was a cat, Granny. Maybe it was a dream, h-m? . . . I'm glad to meet you, little girl. We're going to be great pals, did you know that?"

"All right," I said.

When I went to bed the sheets were cold; the shivering came back again in grinding spasms.

In the living room I could hear two voices but no words, and from far away the Decaturs' sickening music. All men were thieves.

Later, when they asked me questions, I lied and said that Gerald had never been in our apartment. I repeated my story about a noise on the fire escape; and the guilt of my knowledge lodged under my ribs in an undigested lump. But in the end the summer came, the show closed, and we went to the seashore. In the fall when my mother married again, I was sent to a school in the country, and after a while I was happy enough to be able to tell them the truth; and they were happy enough to be able to leave it alone.

The apartment house still stands in 10th Street. Now and then I pass it and glance into the lobby I once knew so well. Unlike most childhood scenes viewed in maturity it has hardly shrunk at all. But there are changes. The switchboard vanished years ago; in its place a suitable Edwardian Diana bares her bronze breasts and navel to the drafts. The Tiffany glass lampshades have been replaced with plastic ones, and the plants are gone; yet the place retains its luster and decrepit style. Probably it still smells of polish; perhaps of cats. But I am never tempted to investigate.

MARY DEWEES FOWLER *was a native of California until 1947 when she came to New York. In her native state she attended Mills College, married, and lived in Berkeley and San Francisco.* "The impact of these Eastern states," she says, "has made me sit down and write about the Western states, and various experiences there." *At the present time she is doing secretarial work at Vassar College. Her work has appeared in* Perspective, Woman's Day, Everywoman, The Sign, *and* Accent. *She has a married daughter living in Baltimore, Maryland, and a four-year-old-grandson.*

MAN OF DISTINCTION

FROM ACCENT

Father Witherby looked handsome when he had on his good suit, walked with dignity and carried a cane, but sitting in the lumpy over-stuffed chair in his small room he was like any old man. If he thought there was a draft he would wear his flat-looking cap, and this did not enhance his appearance. He had the feeling that his daughter Margaret had given him the coldest room in her apartment. Sometimes he muffled himself up in a tartan scarf left over from better days. The fine old furniture in his room was left over from better days, too. When Margaret said he could have a different room he wouldn't change, and she knew why. He liked the location—exactly halfway down the long hall, where he could keep track of all that went on and not be left out of things. He refused to shut his door, and darted a keen look at anyone who passed. Margaret did not like this, and he knew it. But he didn't care.

His wife Mimi was dead and he was old and money was running out. He was in no position to refuse Margaret's invitation to come live with her and her daughter in their apartment on Webster Street in San Francisco, so he finally accepted. He would have preferred living in the home of his son, John W. Junior, across the Bay in Sausalito, rather than with a couple of business women. John W. had more money than Margaret. But he had three babies, aged two, four and five, also a wife. At Margaret's there was no head of the house since she had divorced that artist chap of hers. Father decided that he would fit in better in a place where he was needed. He could always spend Sunday in Sausalito station and being the guest of honor at one of Geraldine's fine dinners. John's wife was a good cook all right.

Today was Thursday, and he had already begun to think about whether to go this Sunday or not. There was something happening in the house here. He couldn't quite make out what. A continual going and coming past his door. This Madolyn Ross, some friend of Margaret's, seemed to be staying on indefinitely. If he'd realized the apartment was going to be crowded with guests all the time he might have lived with John in spite of the three children. This Madolyn had just drifted in—apparently someone Margaret had picked up in the business world. One of those quick friendships. It seemed to him as if Margaret had been on a kind of wild binge ever since Madolyn had moved into this apartment. (Her nickname was "Mad." Most appropriate.) She was not the kind that Witherbys had ever associated with. In the old days people knew who other people *were* before they invited them into their homes.

Margaret walked down the hall, paused at his door and said, "Are you going over to John's this week, Father?"

Using his shoulders, he turned his whole body toward her.

"Haven't decided. Depends on the weather."

He'd decide when he was good and ready. They seemed overly anxious to promote this trip of his. He searched her face intently as she stood in the doorway smoking a cigarette. "Why do you want to know?"

She shrugged. "I was just asking, that's all." Then she added, "So I'll know how to order."

Father snorted.

"Then you'd better speak to the weather man." His blue eyes stared at her defiantly.

He could hear Madolyn in the living room saying, "Such a darling old character came in Jane's office yesterday. He was *precious*. He doesn't need any more help, he says, because he's going to *carve toys* and sell them."

Then the voice of Louise, calling, "Mother, come here. We're trying to decide on this chair."

Apparently they were still busy with their interior decorating, fixing the flat up modern style. When Margaret went in answer to Louise's call Father shuffled into the kitchen and heated some milk and carried it back to his room. He always felt less depressed if his stomach was at peace.

"Let's take this wonderful canary yellow. Let's not have anything dull or somber in the whole flat!"

He knew what the living room would eventually look like.

With bulldog tenacity Margaret had refused to put Father's furniture in her flat. "It isn't the way I want it to be for Lou*ise*," she protested. "I want everything to be cheerful from now on."

Good-looking solid mahogany furniture left packed up in a storeroom. In this setting what kind of a girl would Louise turn out to be? Queer that Margaret couldn't see what an advantage a family background would be for Louise—even an old-fashioned background —with all the stability and prestige it represented. But no. Fuzzy white rugs, tables so low you had to bend double to lift a book off them, no curtains, drapes with a gaudy design of tropical leaves and flowers that might just as well have been monkeys, and chairs— well—to him they looked like canvas bags to throw trash into. Margaret had put his own easy chair in a corner, with a lamp—but what a lamp. Flexible. Each time he finished reading he left it twisted into some ridiculous shape. "Darn fine lamp," he would say. "Functional."

This visiting woman friend, Madolyn—Father was afraid that Margaret was getting to be pretty suggestible. All her ideas were coming from Madolyn. But Margaret always had been flighty. More McNeil in her than Witherby. Probably why she married that artist, come to think of it. If he had been listened to—— But at that time Margaret's mother had been living, and he had taken a back seat and let them find out for themselves.

Evidently they *were* planning something for Sunday, because Margaret said, "Don't you think wine would be nice, Mad?"

"Wait till we get the rest of it planned, honey."

Honey.

"Where's Grandfather?"

Ah, so they were going to have wine.

"Where would he be but in his room?" Margaret meant that she knew he was listening.

Of course after that there was nothing to do but join them. He wasn't an eavesdropper. (Except that one time that had been a sort of accident, when he happened to hear Madolyn saying behind a closed door, "You've just never stood up to him—not once in your whole life, I bet.") Well, that was that. Just as well he had heard. Better to know where you stand.

"Louise, are you sure you like this color scheme and won't tell me later that you didn't have any say in it? You know how you are."

"Mother, do you think I'm getting fat? I ought to go on my diet again. I'll start next Monday."

Good girl, Louise. Don't let your mother trap you with her tricky questions. Father walked over to his easy chair and started to sit in it.

"No, don't sit there," Louise said, gesturing simultaneously with both hands. "Wait, Grandfather. We're trying to decide whether to upholster that in wine. You help us. The rest of the room is yellow and different shades of green, and white, and of course blond wood."

Blond wood.

One thing about Louise, she treated him as if he were a human being. If only he had more influence around here he could swing her away from all this. There was something about her slim figure and her gentle manners that you could take pride in.

"Do you think wine would be a good color, Grandfather?"

Ah. Louise was trying to sidetrack him, save his feelings, divert his attention. . . .

"I've always thought very highly of a good wine—nothing better than a decent Rhine wine—Riesling, Moselle—or a Burgundy. Depends on what you're eating with it," he said, settling himself in the chair as if no one had asked him not to, and clearing his throat as he opened the newspaper he had brought with him. He peeked around the edge of the paper and gave Louise a knowing look, his eyes large behind his glasses.

"Your grandfather is pulling your leg, dear," said Madolyn.

He cleared his throat again, loudly, and stayed behind the newspaper. He was sick of her dazzling smile. This was what he had come to. A strange young woman called "Mad" could say things *of* him instead of *to* him. Forty years ago she hadn't been born, and he had been the president of a shipping company. People were trying to put him on the shelf, he knew that. He'd be darned if he'd let them do it. He intended to live out his life with dignity. They and their jobs and their high salaries and new-fangled political theories, their hobnobbing with what they called the workers.

All three of these women belonged to clubs of do-gooders—his own daughter to the Business and Professional Women, Madolyn to some kind of a Social Services group and even Louise to the United Office Workers or whatever it was named. In the last three weeks since Madolyn Ross had been staying with Margaret you would think the flat was an international club. Hawaiians sitting in the living room one day, big greasy-haired men. Madolyn had told him they were discussing the music union. Once a Chinese woman came and talked for a long time. A very good way for Margaret to lose the respect of the neighbors, besides being downright foolishness in the first place. Keep this sort of thing downtown. One needn't make *friends* of these people. Help them if you can—and if they need it. "When you going to give a tea for the International Longshoremen?" he had asked.

He moved restlessly in his chair now, making unnecessary noise when he turned the pages of the newspaper. Ten cents used to mean something to him at their age, and here these women were using *wallets* for their folding money, stepping into taxis at the drop of a hat, and acting so important you'd think they were running San Francisco.

I wonder when they'll start considering me an object of charity. As soon as my good clothes wear out and my last bond is cashed, I guess. Who knows how soon that will be? I'm going to keep my membership in the Union League Club if I spend my last ten-dollar bill on it. At least I'll get a good funeral notice. Not much comfort. A few old business men riding along behind the hearse in hired limousines. Old Charlie Jenkins and Hugh Evans . . . (He couldn't think of anybody else.)

Well—(he accepted a glass of limeade with a touch of gin in it that Margaret proffered him) let's get my mind off the subject of being put away. I'm lucky to have a son and daughter. In Margaret's mature face he could see traces of the little girl she had been on the day he had walked along with her up to the schoolyard gate—the day John W. Junior was being born in the St. Francis Hospital. He'd never forget the time John Junior had the mumps. He'd filled the boy's pig-bank with five-dollar gold pieces, and when John W. opened it he just about died. . . .

Madolyn was smiling at him. What now? Better get ready to parry. He took a cigarette from the box on the table at his side and fitted it into a short holder. He couldn't seem to get more than two puffs on a cigarette if it wasn't in a holder. He said, "I could tell you how to fix up this place. Mimi and I used to have one of the finest living rooms in San Francisco. We chose expensive wallpaper—brown and gold it was, the very best—and then we bought good mahogany furniture." There was a short pause. "We thought the world and all of that furniture," he added.

"Vouz avez parfaitement raison . . . gran'père," Madolyn said. "But you know how women are these days."

French.

"When are we going to have dinner, Margaret?" he asked fretfully. "These long drinks take away my appetite. Guess I better not drink it." Although he had already taken two swallows he held the glass out for her to take away.

"Well, put it on the sidetable, for goodness sake," she said, not moving from her chair.

Three days later, Father rose at nine o'clock and spent an hour in his small lavatory, shaving. He stretched the skin of his face with one hand, and shaved with an old-fashioned razor. It was a beautiful April day. Nobody had asked him again about his plans for Sunday. He decided to go ahead with his trip to Sausalito. It was a pleasure to sit after a midday dinner on the glassed-in porch of John's house and enjoy the view of San Francisco Bay. Geraldine was a good-natured woman, and she was raising a fine family for John. They were noisy children, not very well trained, but they were a handsome lot, all boys.

With his military hairbrushes Father vigorously brushed his thick white hair. He knew he was distinguished-looking and took pride in it. His fingers were swollen around the joints, but he stood very straight in his tailormade suit and carried an impressive cane. If you kept up an appearance, people gave you some respect—not much, but some. He saw in the mirror that his skin was pink from the astringent he used, and his hair shining with cleanliness. He had grown stouter these years. Too stout. He had seen men in the club get apoplectic. None of that for him. He wasn't going to let himself get a bit stouter than he already was. He knew that sometimes he spoke loudly and let his face get red. When the occasion warranted. But he hadn't done that for a long time. You couldn't live the good life for so many years and not have to pay for it. Nowadays he was very careful of his health.

"I'm going over to John's for Sunday dinner," he said at breakfast. "I think I forgot to mention it."

"I thought you would if it was a nice day," Margaret said evenly.

He walked out of the house with no goodbyes, stood for a moment at the edge of the sidewalk looking up and down the street as if expecting somebody or something, then went on down to the corner. He had to pass the Congregational church in the middle of the second block, and the doors were still open for latecomers, though the organ was pealing. Father walked past noncommittally. He didn't belong. Never had belonged. Somehow, there had always been plenty to do without *that*. While he waited for the Sausalito bus, he mused on the advantages of being a member of that large, rather noisy church, where so many activities seemed to go on. You had to be geared to that sort of thing. Mimi hadn't been. Neither had he. Though he'd been to church plenty in Indiana as a boy. But back there—that was real. He stopped these thoughts as the bus drew up, belching and snorting.

The bus whizzed across Golden Gate bridge to Sausalito. Even when he'd had his own home, he and Mimi used to come over here for Sunday dinner. He seized the opportunity to tell his seat companion, a young, well-dressed man, about his past life, and to explain why he wasn't in his own car. "Who wants to drive a car over this bridge with all these Sunday drivers? Only a fool would do it."

Will John meet me? he wondered.

Geraldine did, with two children in the back seat and the baby in front. John was playing golf somewhere. Father was glad he didn't have to trundle up the hill road in a taxi.

"I just *thought* you might possibly be on that bus, Father Witherby! How are you? I came down to buy some ice cream."

"John'll be home for dinner, won't he?"

"No—he won't, Father. Isn't that too bad. He's in this golf tournament, and afterwards they're having some kind of doings."

"I said I'd be back early," he remarked, getting in the front seat and settling little Ralphie on his lap.

"*Watch it!*" he said, as Geraldine went swirling around the steep bends in the road.

The two children in the back seat were so quiet that he turned to look at them, and found them blowing bubble-gum.

Later, when Geraldine was putting dinner on the table and John and George started wrangling over a fire engine she spoke to them sternly. Father noticed that they paid no attention. "You ought to make these children obey you, Geraldine. They'll get out of hand," he warned. Their noise, squeaks and shrieks were making him nervous. Too bad John Junior wasn't home to control them.

John Junior, now, knew what he was doing. He was a smart business man, and his property was going up in value. It was only half an acre, but the marine view would always be unobstructed, and they had added on to the house year by year until it was quite an establishment. The country was the place to bring up boys, and commuting to San Francisco was simple. Father felt a great surge of pride in his son. He wiped his forehead with a fine lawn handkerchief smelling of bay rum. "John's done a lot of work in the garden, I see," he commented.

"Wrong, Father Witherby. Give me the credit for that. I did it with my own little hands."

He looked squintingly at the Bay, where a boat race was being held. "When's John going to get himself a sailboat?"

Geraldine gave a weary sigh. "You know perfectly well, Father, we can't afford a sailboat."

"It would be good for these boys as they grow up to learn something about water."

After dinner they sat on the porch. George yelled with excitement and came from the garden dangling a garter snake between two fingers. He began to scare his mother with it, making as if he was going to throw it in her face. Father grasped his little wrist firmly and gave it a quick jerk. The snake went over the porch railing. "Enough of that, young man." George stared at him with indignation.

Time to be getting home, Father thought. Before the busses get crowded. He bent down and patted the sleeping Ralphie's soft cheek. "I think I'll be going along now," he said to Geraldine. She stood up at once and said she would drive him down the hill. "I'll just be a few minutes," she said to the boys. "Watch Ralphie."

She was careful this time, and didn't drive nearly so fast as before. "I guess we're a pretty strenuous family, aren't we?" she said, as the car came alongside the station platform.

"They're a fine bunch of boys. I'm mighty proud of my grandsons, don't make any mistake about it."

She smiled.

"My years are beginning to tell on me. Can't buck things the way I used to."

"Just the same, you're wonderful for your age, Father Witherby," she said, opening the car door for him.

In the bus he admitted to himself that he felt very lonely. Time flows along. Customs change. I'm out of it. Here I am, sitting in this bus . . . and who cares?

The salt air came through the open windows mixed with exhaust fumes. Father was the only one sitting alone, so he talked to himself . . . most everybody I used to know has departed for the next world. Who knows what the next year will do to me. I want to get along better with my grandsons. I'll bring them each some small present when I make my next visit. He brushed a few specks from the sleeve of his coat and finished the trip in a morose silence. From now on he was going to relax and take things easier. He couldn't manage the world. Things were different from the way they used to be and that's all there was to it.

He stopped in at a restaurant on the San Francisco side and had a cup of hot clam juice, sitting at a table with a window that looked over the water. He was afraid to go home too early because they might think he hadn't had a good time at John's. He sniffed the fish smells and low tide, and watched the people for a while. Particularly a gentle old lady and her husband having a cheap shore dinner at the table next to him.

Fifty years ago he had roamed this waterfront, full of excitement and money-making plans, had spent hours in the various shipping offices and walking among the bales and boxes of the cargo sheds. He used to visit the City Pilot's office high up in one of the buildings —(old Cap'n Bill—he couldn't remember his other name—dead now)—and have a couple of whiskies-and-soda, maybe more than a couple. Now who was the City Pilot? He didn't even know. Or care.

Well, let's be practical and hoist these old bones into a bus again and get home where it's warm. Mustn't forget there's two women dying to wait on me hand and foot. If it wasn't for them I'd likely be living alone in a hotel till the end. If I'm a good boy, maybe they'll give me a nice polished granite monument. He left the restaurant.

The sky had a purplish tinge and there was no more sun. It would be good to get in the house again. Louise might be playing some of her records, and he hadn't read the Sunday paper yet. He began to wonder what kind of marriage Louise would make. Hope she'll do better than her mother did, but I doubt it. Already she is eating, thinking, talking her job. What kind of man will take that on? Well —I won't have a word to say. I won't be here. The bus was crowded and he had to stand. No one offered him a seat, and finally he made a joke with the bus-driver. "Haven't any of these people got *homes?*"

He cut the air with his cane as he walked up his own street. When he opened the door he heard voices, a man's among them. They must have friends visiting. There wasn't a thing he could do about it. All he could hope, with Madolyn the social worker in the house, was that the visitors weren't Hottentots. The sounds came from the dining room and he could smell roast lamb. He'd go in and see for himself, and get a serving of dessert, maybe a piece of cake. He stopped in his room, left his hat and cane on the bed and walked down the hall. He could see Louise sitting at the table, but the others were not visible. Then he stood in the doorway.

Glistening with excitement and pleasure, a young man almost as black as coal stood at the head of the table carving a leg of lamb. Father had to fight off a sense of unreality. He put up a hand as if to ward off a blow and then hid the gesture by stroking his upper lip as if the moustache of years ago was still there. Margaret rose from her chair. "Join our party, Father," she said. A funny feeling came over him. He allowed Margaret to propel him to the end of the table, where he sank into a chair. First his eyes focussed on the three women, one after the other, Margaret on his right and Louise and Madolyn on the left, and then he looked directly down the length of the table at the man, who had stopped carving and was standing with a polite waiting look on his face. He wore a yellow silk shirt with rather full sleeves ending in tight cuffs. Father automatically cleared his throat, but found nothing to say. Coming in from outside, he felt the heat in the room oppressive. A weakness, a little trembling that seemed to come from the pit of his stomach, began.

"Well, don't stand around and gape at me," he said harshly. "Open some windows."

"Nobody's standing around, Father," said Margaret. Madolyn and the dark visitor went to open a window.

"You might have waited dinner for me."

"Waited dinner!" said Margaret, off guard.

"Oh, that's right. You thought I wouldn't be here." His blue eyes stared at her.

Madolyn and the guest now stood next to his chair. "Mr. Witherby, I want to present our friend Diessy." Lively eyes flashed in the black face, a hollow showed in the cheek as he smiled. He bowed from the waist, and Father saw a gold-wire loop hanging from his ear. "I am very please to meet you, sir."

To his annoyance Father felt his face get warm. Damn this high blood pressure. He pulled out the cigarette case Louise had given him for his birthday and extracted a cigarette. Diessy whipped out a lighter and clicked on the flame. After he had taken a puff Father said, "Take your seat again Mr. . . . a . . . don't let my sudden appearance interrupt . . . a . . . whatever is going on. I'm only a side show."

Margaret smiled a little sadly and said, "Go on carving, Diessy." Louise went to get a knife, fork and spoon for Father, and brought a napkin which he automatically unfolded and spread across his stomach. When Margaret poured a glass of water for him he drained it at one gulp. Diessy tested the carving knife with his finger and flashed his eyes around the table.

"Nobody pay any attention to me," said Father. "I've had dinner." He gazed at the tight curls on Diessy's head. What was this, anyway? Had Margaret lost her mind? Her own father seated at the foot of the table and this—this—— He put his hand on his water glass and Louise quickly refilled it. There was a bursting feeling in his head. *I'd like to throw this glass clean through the window.* Instead, he knocked it over. His face thickened, then slowly the brick color receded.

"Oh, Grandfather!" Louise started up and dabbed at the wet table-cloth with her napkin.

Madolyn began to smile.

"No harm done," said Margaret calmly, spreading a fresh napkin over the spot and laying the silver back neatly.

"No!" he said in a loud voice. "I said no dinner."

But come what might, he would not go away from this table. No sirree, he would stick it out. It was his business to stay. He noticed they were using his silver. All this for a kinky-haired—— Pretty soon in this house you'd see anything happening, *any*thing. He coughed and pushed his chair back about an inch.

"Don't you have hunger, sir? I have made just right serving for you." Kinky-hair ladled a spoon of mint sauce over two thin slices of lamb and put a small mound of peas on the plate and half a roasted potato, which he slashed in four pieces with the carving knife and then covered with gravy. At the last, he picked up a sprig of parsley with the point of the carving knife and fork held together, and laid it meticulously on the meat. He carried the food to Father's side, holding the plate with a napkin.

"Please eat, Grandfather," Louise pleaded. He saw her flushed, woebegone face. She looked as if she had a fever, poor child. *By God——*

He began to push the food around on his plate.

"Diessy's a friend of ours who's been dropping in Jane's office," said Madolyn. "He's had the worst luck, haven't you, Diessy? He lost the address of the people he was asked to call on when he was in port and someone directed him to us. Tell about some of your adventures, please, Diessy."

"You wish me to? How many years you want me to go back?" Diessy's teeth were like a flash of lightning for a second and then all was dark again. He buttered a roll. "First I remember was on a boat went to pieces and I hung on a log of wood in the water. Mediterranean. Second? I sat on shoulders of a man who ride bareback in the French circus, and he throw me to another man on horse. Back and forth. Back and forth." His teeth flashed once more, and he popped a piece of meat into his mouth.

Margaret and Louise laughed with appreciation. Diessy bowed slightly, and went on. Father ate nervously. His plate was nearly empty, and when Louise passed the rolls his hand closed over two of them at once.

"Later in that circus I ride bicycle on a tightrope. For two years." Diessy made the gesture of holding his hands away from handlebars and wriggled his body. Then he stood up, and grasping the carving knife, said, "But the best time was when I became in the French army for money." He indicated a knife three times as long as the carving knife, and curved.

Remembering his duties he touched the roast with the knife. "But now—shall I make some meat?"

Father's eyes, under his bushy eyebrows, roved restlessly around the table. "First," said Diessy, "I ask *you*, the head of the house."

"No," said Father, proceeding to light a cigarette. "I've had dinner." Margaret took another helping and the dish of peas was passed.

When Margaret passed it to Father he leaned back without touching it, and she had to stretch across the table to hand it to Louise. He cleared his throat. "Tell me, Mr. Deecee, what are you doing *now?*"

"Ah, sir. Taking it easy, maybe not so easy, on a ship."

"What do you do on this ship?"

Diessy raised his right shoulder toward his ear and held out one hand palm upward. "What have you on a ship? Swab deck, carry tray, wash dishes, push crates. Sometimes drink brandy with mate when he want a friend talking to him." He smiled at Father. "Luck is up and down. Once in Martinique I own Hispano."

"Diessy is Senegalese, Father Witherby," said Madolyn.

Since when had she started this "Father Witherby"? That was the last straw. Father stirred his demi-tasse. With a bored sigh he said to Diessy, "You received your education in France?"

"In school all over world. Mostly school of life. But I been in a school some times. In Germany, France, Russia. I learn all three languages." He looked at Father for a minute and then winked. "But not enough of *any*—you think?" He shrugged. "My father say I must be learned man. That is why I not go home—to Senegal. I rather my father think I am learned man, not dishwasher. Father like to be proud of son, *n'est-ce pas?* You have son you are proud of?"

"Yes," said Margaret suddenly. "He has John Junior. John Junior is not exactly a learned man, but——"

Madolyn interrupted.

"Diessy. Tell about your experiences in Turkey—the harem. And Russia. You never finished—remember? Father Witherby came in right in the middle of it." She poured herself another cup of coffee and lit a cigarette. She and Father crossed glances.

Diessy bowed. "I go from one to other thing. Too much jump around. Am taking all attention to me. That not good. First I want to say what I think when you come in this room, Mr. Wederby. I look up. There you are in doorway . . ." He looked at the doorway as if Father were still standing there. "I try to think in that minute what it remind me of. Do you know what?" He waited.

"What?" said Louise.

"There is American ad in the paper. A man holds glass in his hand. The man have fine look—rich. He know what is the good life, you can tell. He is handsome. He is white hair. I think he is in politics. Ad is about what is in glass—but always with the man."

The three women burst out laughing. Even Father laughed.

"I am not making a joke?" asked Diessy, looking worried.

"No—no. You're not making a joke," Madolyn assured him. Margaret made an effort to stop laughing, then began again helplessly. "There you are, Grandfather," said Louise proudly.

Diessy took a sip of coffee, his eyes darting around the white tablecloth. "Cognac?" he said. It was as if he were asking someone to pass the salt.

Father pushed his chair back from the table and crossed one leg over the other. He rolled his cigarette between thumb and forefinger slightly as he smoked, and his blue eyes stared at Diessy with an appraising look. Then he cleared his throat. "Go in the closet in my room, Margaret," he ordered, giving an imperative nod of his head in the direction of the hall, "and bring out that bottle of brandy you'll find there." For a moment Margaret sat still in her chair, her face hot. Then she rose and did as she was bid. Father scratched his head with one finger and raised his eyebrows innocently. "Guess I forgot to say please."

While she was away he opened the glass doors of the dining-room cupboard and brought two small glasses and a box of cigars to the table.

"Now, Diessy, it's our turn," said Madolyn, leaning back. "Go on with your adventures."

Diessy was selecting a cigar. He lifted lustrous eyes full of appreciation to Father, saying, "These damn fine cigars, sir."

"You womenfolk won't mind if we smoke, will you?" said Father as Margaret came into the room with a tall bottle three quarters full.

"Look," Madolyn said to Father. "Aren't you going to give any of us brandy except Diessy?"

"Would you care for some?"

"If I may. How about you, Margaret?" Margaret didn't even answer. "Louise?" Louise gave a slight shake of her head.

Madolyn brought two more glasses to the table. "Come on, Margaret," she urged. "Get in the swim."

"If Mother won't, then I will," said Louise. "A tiny bit."

Diessy passed his glass back and forth under his nose and shut his eyes. "Life is good, n'est-ce pas?" Then he looked at Louise admiringly. "And in the company of such a Beautiful."

Madolyn relaxed in her chair, one arm over the back, a cigarette dangling in her fingers. "Diessy," she prodded.

He looked at Father as if he and Father had some kind of a secret understanding. "They beg a story," he explained. "I try to think of the right one for their ears. I have fear my stories are for after the ladies have leave table."

"Ladies don't leave the table any more, Diessy. Not in this country," said Madolyn. "Do they, Margaret?"

"Not in this house, they don't," Margaret answered. "We never *have*, and I don't think we ever *will*."

"*Comment?*" Diessy looked puzzled.

Father propped his elbow on the table and puffed comfortably on his cigar. "She means that in this country, Mr. Deecee, there is not much difference between women and men. Women are not like they used to be. They are fighting for their rights, and one of their rights is to be like a man."

"I see." Diessy nodded. "Custom is changing."

"Exactly," said Madolyn. "The difference here is between the generations, not between sexes."

"Ah, yes! That has always been. Between older and younger. Respect for older." He raised his brandy glass in a silent toast to Father. "I am glad that America is keeping tradition. In spite of changing other ways."

Father refilled their glasses. He concentrated on keeping his hands from shaking. Easy does it, he said to himself. Louise put her hand over her glass but Madolyn did not. Father remained standing.

"To the ladies!" he said.

Diessy jumped to his feet.

When he sat down again he relit his cigar which had gone out. "Everywhere it is the same," he said in an easy conversational tone. "It is the ladies who make the inspiration. Bring the excitement to the living. Different in each country—yet the same. In Turkey, the harem . . ." He bowed toward Madolyn to show that he was acceding to her request at last. "Couches and silk—silk—— Perfume of rose. Many *bon-bon*, sweet coffee, *ver-y* thick." He held two fingers to measure the small amount one would drink. "These ladies fat. Round white arms, like pillows." He put his hand to his forehead apologetically. "So many ladies all at once—they go to the head."

Father's eyes lighted up with interest. He gave Diessy his undivided attention. So did the others.

"In Russia it was opposite." Diessy glanced around the table at his audience. "Big women. Beautiful in *strong* way. I see in army.

The women stand up straight in uniform." He sat up straighter himself, then pushed back his chair and stood. He ran his hands down over his torso, held his stomach in and stood with his arms hanging down but not touching his sides. "You know how these women do?" He paused, as if to give someone a chance to answer. "No? They take their left breast—so—and throw around under left arm. Then right breast—so—and throw under right arm." He held his arms tight to his sides. "Then take piece of cloth, wind around to keep flat. That way they protect, and *also* have fine figure of soldier." He looked around triumphantly.

Father slapped his leg and guffawed, rocking back and forth, with a red face.

"No, really?" said Margaret.

Diessy walked over to the side of the dining room. He had on black trousers with metal bicycle clips holding them close around his ankles. "In Russia I drink the vodka until nobody is under the table. After four glasses you do this to see if all right." He squatted, folded his arms under his chin and did the familiar Russian dance.

"Bravo!" said Father. "What did you do in France?"

"Ah! Do everything in France!" Diessy pinched his lips together with three fingers, then threw a kiss to the ceiling, rolling his eyes.

Father walked away from the table and struck a pose. He too threw a kiss toward the ceiling and began to sing, in the fashion of Chevalier,

"Ev'ry little breeze
Seems to whisper 'Louise,'
Birds in the trees
Sing 'I love you, Louise.' "

Madolyn got up and placed a hand on Diessy's shoulder. "I will see you tomorrow in Jane's office," she said. "We have a map of the city we want to give you." They walked together into the hall.

"Remember that song?" said Father, following them. He felt Margaret's touch on his arm and shook it off. Diessy turned around at the head of the stairs and bowed. "I am say goodby," he said. "For long time I will have this memory to thank you with. I now go to my bicycle. It is waiting. For a fine roast lamb I thank you every one of you."

"I'll walk downstairs with you," said Father. "I want to see that bicycle."

"That's the spirit, Father Witherby," said Madolyn. "Goodby, Diessy."

When Father stepped outside the front door he gave a bracing motion with his left leg, the way one does in stepping from a cabin onto a rolling deck. He quickly recovered himself and began to examine Diessy's bicycle which was leaning against the side of the house. "Is this the circus bicycle?" he asked with great interest.

"No, sir. The circus bicycle is not right bicycle for streets. This is just any bicycle. Take it on ship—wherever."

"Is that so?"

"It is better to have bicycle. For man of my color." Diessy bent over and put a key in the padlock on the front wheel. "I go anywheres more easy," he explained. Then he laughed. "But for the San Francisco hills not so good. It is not resting me. I am resting *it*, most time." He put his foot on the pedal. "I am glad I meet you, sir. It is my philosophy the father is important. It is the father that makes respectable the whole family. I do not have father."

There was silence. The two men looked at each other. Diessy nudged the pedal and it spun and made a small whirring noise. "I only *say*, so people have respectable opinion of me. Me, I am orphan." Then after a pause he said, "You have money to lend me, sir?"

Father stared, and then said, "No, Mr. Deecee. I never lend money to anybody. That is my philosophy." He leaned forward so he could look right into Diessy's face. "Luck is down, eh?"

Diessy shrugged. "*Eh bien.*" He straddled the bicycle and sat on the seat, balancing himself with one toe on the ground. He looked straight ahead, expressionless, for a moment, then rode off down the street, the back of his yellow shirt billowing out in the wind.

When Father came upstairs the three women were washing dishes. He carried an ash tray into the kitchen. Louise was perched on a stool, polishing glasses, Margaret had her hands in the dishwater, and Madolyn was scraping food off the plates into a white enameled garbage can.

"Wasn't he interesting, Grandfather?" said Louise nervously.

"*Comment?*" Father raised his shaggy eyebrows high. He placed the ash tray filled with cigar ashes on the sink among the dishes, for someone to take care of.

Madolyn raised up, her face pink from bending over the garbage can, and Margaret stopped clattering the dishes and closed her eyes in exasperation.

Father cleared his throat. "He said I was the one who made the womenfolk in this house respectable."

Margaret whirled around and leaned against the sink, resting on her elbows. Her hands dripped water on the floor.

"Re*spec*table! *Well*—!"

Louise widened her eyes. "For goodness sake, don't throw a *fit*, Mother—please."

Father backed away, his right shoulder raised and one hand held palm upward. There was a barely perceptible gleam of triumph in his blue eyes. As he backed through the kitchen door into the hall he had a bit of trouble getting his feet over the lintel and glanced down at it. "*Pardonnez-moi*," he said, then turned and went to his own room and closed the door softly behind him.

DANIEL FUCHS *was born in New York in 1909.
"I was graduated," he writes, "from the College
of the City of New York in 1930, a year after
Leonard Erlich was, and later spent a good deal of
time with him at Yaddo in Saratoga Springs, New
York, that wonderfully helpful writers' colony. I
taught school for seven years, wrote three novels,
went into the Navy during the war, and have done
a lot of movie work. My home, for the past
fifteen years or so, has been in Beverly Hills,
California, and I spend my time now writing short
stories for* The New Yorker. *My wife and I have
two sons, Jake and Tom."*

TWILIGHT IN SOUTHERN CALIFORNIA

FROM THE NEW YORKER

The novelty business was shot to pieces; the whole bottom had
dropped out of the market. Mr. Honti, who manufactured the
gadgets and gewgaws, was going through terrible financial troubles,
dunned and driven on all sides, everything crashing down on his
head, and Morley felt this was no time to run out on him. Morley
Finch was a young physician who had opened a practice in Los
Angeles just two or three years ago. He and his wife had been taken
up by the Hontis, had gone up there to the swimming pool in Coldwater Canyon almost every Saturday, and Morley didn't see how
they could stop going there now. The trouble was Barbara, his wife.
She hated those visits. She said Mr. Honti was unbalanced.

"I'm willing to do anything you want," Barbara said, cool and
trim and beautiful. She was wearing a beige linen jumper, a white
organdie blouse, and white pumps and gloves, and she was ready to
leave—except, of course, she plainly didn't want to.

They were in the office, and the frantic six-lane traffic outside on
Wilshire Boulevard was ripping along as it everlastingly did. "That's
very nice of you," Morley said. He stepped on the scales, weighed
himself, stepped off. Every Saturday, after office hours, Barbara came
to pick him up, and every Saturday there was this little struggle, this

tortured ticktacktoe. Mr. Honti wasn't unbalanced and Barbara knew it. She just couldn't stand him or the rest of them up there. She couldn't stand the noise, the kissing of hands, the way they constantly talked about people making boom-tarra-ra, the way they openly pinched the women. Whenever she went there, the first thing she did was find a place and sit down.

"If I don't want to go, you get mad," Barbara said. "If I say let's go, you say I'm insincere. I don't know what to do."

"Maybe I could think up some excuse," Morley said. "Maybe I could tell them I was called away to the hospital." After all, he was a doctor. But his voice trailed off and he gave it up. He really wanted to go there—because he liked them, or understood them, with all their peculiar ways, or because he felt guilty toward them, or whatever it was. And besides there was no use trying to lie to them. They were so quick, so intelligent. They always knew what was going on in your mind. Mr. Honti hadn't been able to pay his monthly doctor's bill—there had been some trouble at the bank with a check —and if Morley and Barbara failed to appear this afternoon, Honti would think it was because of the bad check, and then he'd get all hurt and humiliated and miserable.

"He gives me a bad check and *I'm* the one that has to feel bad about it," Morley said. "I don't even know why I want to go there."

"Anything you want to do," Barbara said, despondent.

The swimming pool was in a hollow, fringed with poplar trees, just below the house. Mr. Honti was still in town, down in Beverly Hills somewhere, doing business or trying to do business. Morley and Barbara hadn't arrived, and the only one sitting with Mrs. Honti at the pool was a man named Edmond Oleam. Lily Honti was a great coffee drinker. She had an electric percolator out there with her on the lawn, but Oleam wouldn't accept a cup. He had no heart for coffee. He was also in the novelty business, also in distressed financial circumstances, but, in addition, his wife had left him and he had a stiff neck. All these things were more or less connected—the business slump, his wife's leaving him, the stiff neck. When the business started to go slack, his wife moved out. In retaliation, Oleam went on a diet and took a course of bar-bell exercises. That was why he had a stiff neck, from the bar bells. Lily Honti finished her coffee and promptly filled the cup again. "Sad for the children," she said in passing, meaning these separations. There was a child involved, a boy now at a military academy near San Diego.

"Sad for the grownups, too," Oleam said.

He looked at the poplar trees, distracted. The leaves kept dropping into the pool, and in any case poplars weren't suitable for the dry southern California climate. They needed lots of water, became brittle, and were liable to break and go falling down on top of you at any time. If you wanted to pull them out, it would cost you hundreds of dollars. Everything was unsatisfactory, Oleam thought, looking at the trees. Everything turned out badly. And he thought of his wife, only a mile or two away over the hills, living with a Mr. Larry Scorbell in another canyon—Benedict Canyon. Scorbell was not in the novelty business.

"She fell in love," Oleam said gently, wryly. "The fact that he owns three millinery factories had nothing to do with it."

"What should she do—hate him because he is rich?" Lily said. "What is she—a bobby-soxer? Why shouldn't she love him if he has money? Can anybody show me a better reason?"

"You have no ideals," Oleam said.

"This is perfect for you," Lily went on. "You are fat, you are lazy. Maybe this will wake you up."

"Stop," he said.

"Why are you crying—that you have lost her? You know what your life was. You got up late, you lay in bed, you did nothing. When you went to the office, you called her on the phone every minute— did anything come in the mail, was there a telegram, did somebody call up? Anything for an excuse."

"It wasn't for an excuse," Oleam said. "I was anxious. I was hoping for something good to happen."

"Baloney, you were spying on her."

"I was not!" Oleam said. "Nobody understands! You don't know what it is when a business goes sour, when you wait and pray for something to develop."

"Be still," Lily said. Morley and Barbara were approaching, walking down the path from the house. "Now, behave yourself. Watch how you talk—you will frighten her. She is a child. She comes from New Hampshire. How are you, my sweethearts?" Lily said, turning to them, her eyes shining with mischief. "Come—sit down, sit down."

All at once, there was a cloud; everything darkened, there was a strange, muted whoosh of wind, and then they heard an ominous, creeping, tearing patter. Oleam gave a start of fear and jumped up. He thought it was one of the poplars breaking, but it was just a quick rain coming on. "Bring in the cushions!" Lily said, screaming with delight, enjoying the upset. Morley grabbed up an armful, and Oleam wrestled with the big chaise pads. The pads were cumbersome, he couldn't manage them, and suddenly he twisted his stiff neck and felt a stab of pain. "Oh, help me, Dr. Finch," he started to say, calling to Morley. But Oleam didn't say "Dr. Finch." Oleam said "Gladys," which was his wife's name. And now, standing in the shelter of the porch, he realized what he had said, and it was as though he had been punctured. The heart all went out of him and he gave way. He thought of that soft, sun-tanned, warm little body all cuddled up in bed, no longer his, no longer his, now in Benedict Canyon with Larry Scorbell, making boom-tarra-ra there at least two times a day, and he sobbed aloud in deep, hopeless anguish.

The sun came flooding back through the popular trees. The rain was over. "Behold!" Lily said. They put the cushions back and grouped themselves around the pool. It was the kind of rain people find hard to believe when you tell them about it; they were just around the bend or just across the road, they say, and it didn't rain there at all.

At least if there was only a funicular up Coldwater Canyon, Alexander Honti said to himself as he trudged bitterly up the road to his home. They had eaten up the car, Lily and he. The loan company had taken it away, and now the sun beat on his head as though he were back in the desert wilderness, in the time of the Pharaohs again. He had been able to accomplish nothing in town. In days of crisis, the money men became inaccessible, the go-betweens became arrogant and contemptuous, and the secretaries everywhere turned into fierce, haughty virgins. I should commit suicide and get through with it once for all, Honti said to himself—only, what was the use, who would cry? He had no patience; otherwise he would have done it long ago. In a last, desperate effort, he had put all his eggs in one basket. He had signed Tony Brewer, an inventor-designer, laying out eight hundred dollars hard cash in advance. In the novelty business, if you had an ace designer, you could make a beginning, you could do something; the banks at least would *talk* to you. But, no, fate had had to intervene. Brewer had promptly come down with a paralytic stroke; the loudmouths in the trade had diligently passed the good word around; and in no time Honti had been marked lousy again, from Culver City to Burbank, the eight hundred dollars going down the drain along with everything else.

Honti now walked over the rise of ground to the pool. He saw the people assembled there and greeted them lustily, holding up his palm like an Indian on a calendar saluting the morning sun. "My star is risen!" he said, overheated and all wound up, the blood racing in his brain. "Mrs. Maveen has predicted that exactly at three-thirty sharp good news will arrive, my fortunes will change for the better, and everything henceforth will be rosy and serene!" Mrs. Maveen was a professional palm reader who lived in a stucco bungalow on Sunset Boulevard. Honti pretended he was joking, out of reckless despair, out of bravado, but actually he was superstitious and seriously hoped the prophecy would come true. What else was there for him, anyway? "See?" he said, pointing to a line on his palm. "There is the good luck, according to Mrs. Maveen, in the stucco bungalow. This is where it says I must positively get the good news at three-thirty sharp." He paused. He stood gazing at Barbara, forgetting his troubles for the moment. He was always glad to see her. Morley was wearing a pair of swimming trunks, but she hadn't changed, and she looked lovely in that outfit, pure and clean and untouched, with those white pumps and gloves. Honti became softly playful. He beamed at her, treating her like a little child. "Snow-white teeth," he said. "Such deep-blue eyes. So blond. Your face is like a fire. I could warm my hands." He suddenly remembered the check that had bounced. The great big smile ebbed away. He winced. He had promised to straighten everything out at the bank and call Morley right back. He had, of course, done neither. He couldn't face the Doctor now and turned instead to Oleam. "Why did you have to be noble and give Gladys the car?" Honti referred to the settlement Oleam had made at the time of the separation. He could have borrowed Oleam's machine, spared himself the climb up the whole mountain.

"Well, I was in love," Oleam said.

"You have no backbone!" Honti said. "You are a pickpocket. You are less than a pickpocket. You are an oboe!" Honti was putting on his show, as usual, but the truth was he himself didn't know how much of it was kidding. He took off his glasses and placed them on a table. He sat down on the grass, slipped out of his trousers and

went on undressing, preparing himself for a dip in the pool. Maybe
that would cool him off. Maybe a swim would lower his blood pressure and settle him down. He looked up at the sky and scratched
his nose.

"Hobo," Lily said, bland and airy over her coffee cup. "Speak
correct English. 'You are an hobo.' "

"Bassoon!" Honti roared, getting to his feet. "Do not correct me!
I know where I speak. You are a bassoon and he is an oboe. Watch
but your own English!"

"Mr. Alexander Honti is in fine fettle," Oleam said, shy and wistful
in his manner. "When he is onstage, all are forbidden to breathe.
He must monopolize the center of attraction."

"Edmond is right," Lily said. "If business is bad for you, why
must you take it out on him? He has heartaches, too."

"Feed the dog!" Honti bellowed. They had a dog, Fidelio—an
ungainly creature, large and ill-proportioned, with an unfortunate,
sensitive personality. They sometimes forgot about the dog for days
at a stretch, and during their frequent arguments Honti generally
brought the subject up, putting the whole blame on Lily.

"Why do you insist on stirring me up?" he went on, shouting at
her and Oleam both. "Is it a plot? Do you wish me to die of high
blood pressure?" He turned to Barbara and Morley. "He is spineless!"
Honti said, speaking not about the dog but about Oleam. "In Paris,
on the Champs-Elysées, a man kicked him in the behind and he
started running away without even looking back to see who had done
it to him."

"A slander!" Oleam said, disgusted. "How he exaggerates and mis-
represents everything. I did *not* run without looking back."

"Believe me!" Honti said, reaching down and holding Barbara by
the shoulders as she sat there in a cane chair. "I know him. He is
the kind of a man who goes into the public phone booths and sticks
his fingers into the slot—you know, for the coins. He bets on racing
horses and has dealings with bookies. He looks at television——"
Honti checked himself. He took his hands off Barbara and stepped
back. "Do not be alarmed. We are normal people. It is just our way."
He tried to make amends. He beamed broadly again and became
skittish. He bulged his eyes out. He mugged. "It is harmless! Actually, I am very fond of Mr. Oleam. In spite of appearances, I am
really very much like him in disposition. I do not seem like him
because when I am with *him*, I do not have to be like *me*, which

is a *godsend*. Prepare yourself for a shock." He was now barefoot, wearing just his undershorts and one of those flowery tropical shirts. He took off the tropical shirt and stood revealed. There were thick masses of hair on his chest, on his shoulders, all over his arms. "Is it not horrible?" he said with a gleam in his eye. What was so painful was he loved this child, he dearly wanted her esteem, while all the time she disapproved and found him offensive. "Am I not ugly? Like a huge bear in the forest. Would you believe it, once I was a babe in arms and my parents called me Skellbillie? It was my pet name." He turned about and threw himself into the pool. He parted the water with a tremendous smash, disappeared for a moment, then reappeared. He was already turned around, facing them. He stretched his arm out and pointed sternly. "Do not talk about me."

What a deplorable mess I am, Honti said to himself as he flopped about in the water. How ugly it was to be in need, to be obliged always to find some way of disguising your despair. He had only meant to be amusing. He thought now of Morley and the look on his face while he, Honti, was going through his antics. Morley had grinned, had stopped grinning, had glanced constantly at his sweet young wife, nervous and uneasy. Honti remembered the tight, stiff smile on *her* face, the way she had flinched when he put his hands on her shoulders. Why did he always have to act like such a fool in front of her? How could he ever expect her to have any respect for him? He made himself a freak; he raved; he jumped up and down; he was a punchinello, a gargoyle. And what, Honti asked himself as he thrashed through the water—and what would happen Monday morning, the shop opening again and him with no funds for the payroll?

He vowed to reform. From now on, in the child's presence he would always be controlled, dignified. He would conduct himself like any well-adjusted gentleman. He would make agreeable small conversation. "And how is Morley's practice progressing?" he would remark to her. "Very well, I hope? Goodness, what a becoming frock you have on."

Then he heard it. He was in the water and they were all sitting up there, high and dry, but he heard it and they didn't; somebody was ringing the doorbell. Honti looked up at the house. A messenger had arrived. It was the prophecy, Mrs. Maveen's prediction. It had to be! It was a cable, a telegram come to save him, a bonanza!

"Here, boy!" Honti started clambering out of the pool. "Here! Down here we are!"

The others on the lawn looked up, startled. They saw the messenger and were instantly excited, too. After all, it was somewhere around three-thirty, the time that Mrs. Maveen had stipulated. "Oh, swiftly!" Lily called out to the messenger. "Swiftly, swiftly, young man!" Oleam took up the cry, and so did Morley.

"See, you must have faith!" Honti exulted, hopping. "You must believe—— Here, boy!" The messenger came stumbling down the path, all upset and unnerved by the tumult, but when he reached them and they saw the box in his hands, they immediately fell silent. The jubilee was finished.

It wasn't a bonanza. It was a cake—a homemade chocolate layer cake. Mrs. Carneal, the mother-in-law of the inventor-designer, of Tony Brewer, had sent it. Mrs. Carneal, a fine, pious elderly lady, had deeply appreciated Honti's generosity when he hadn't asked for his eight hundred dollars back. Honti couldn't have got it back anyway—the money was already spent—but Mrs. Carneal didn't know that, and she told everybody what a grand, upstanding soul Mr. Honti was. "Thinking of you," the card in the box said. Honti sent the messenger away. For a while, nobody spoke.

" 'Thinking of you'!" Lily said, going back to her percolator and plopping down on the cushions again. "Everything is ducky."

"You pay for your sins," Honti said, standing there, holding the box. He was exhausted, winded.

"His star is risen!" Lily said, trilling. "We shall have good fortune, seven years of milk and honey!"

"*Feed the dog!*" Honti roared at her, his eyes shut tight.

"He is not here," she said. "He is wandering. He is looking for you since early morning, since you went to business."

The dog was remarkably sympathetic, psychic. Whenever Honti was in the dumps, Fidelio seemed to know it and went looking for him, to be near his master, to share his distress, to comfort him. The two had missed connections all day.

Honti put the cake down on a table and rubbed his face with both his hands. "Then drink yourself to death," he said to his wife. "In Berlin, in Prague, in Paris, they chased me like an animal in the fields, and now, finally, in sunny California I am condemned to end my days a bankrupt living with a witch. I am the dog. Fidelio is I. No wonder he is neurotic." Honti was running everything together, feeling sorry for the dog, chastising himself. "He is neglected. It is my fault. I must take care of him. The S.P.C.A. should lock me up. Morley," he said suddenly, thinking of the bad check, almost seeking out the punishment, the mortification. "Morley, I did not call you back about the bank, because, as I knew you would know, I had nothing to say—— *Do not be alarmed!*" he burst out at Barbara, turning on her now in his misery. She sat rigid in the cane chair, big-eyed. "I told you—it is just our way! It means nothing. We are emotional, we overstate everything. . . . Oh, look at her! She sits there dying by inches. Somebody would think—— Oh, goodbye." He plunged into the pool again, putting an end to it. And what would be, he asked himself as he sank into the greenish, opalescent depths—what would be when they finished eating up the house, with the swimming pool and the grounds and the garden? It was like a tune you couldn't get out of your head.

The poplar leaves fluttered listlessly in the slight breeze, showing now their shiny side, now their pale, velvety underside. A humming-bird skidded into, and then out of, a hibiscus blossom the size of a grapefruit. Over it all, the golden sunshine poured down, ever benign, ever patient. "My neck," Oleam said, far away among his private troubles. "It pains."

Lily gazed vacantly at her husband, swimming in the pool. She had her own troubles, and her mind was far away, too. "When the news came that Brewer was stricken, that all was lost, I was on the balcony in the hall," she said, "looking down on Alexander while he stood downstairs by the telephone. Right away, I knew it was a catastrophe; his poor little bald spot turned white."

"Lily," Oleam said, grieving. "Lily, I would like to ask you for an advice. Should I telephone Gladys for an appointment? Should I go over there and have a meeting with them?"

Morley squirmed with discomfort. For the fortieth time, he glanced at Barbara and reproached himself. Why did he have to bring her here? She didn't like these people. She didn't understand how it really was with them. She took everything at its face value and thought they were cynical, corrupt, and materialistic. Barbara often went along with Morley on his calls, waiting alone outside in the car, and when his patients forgot to pay their bills, as they generally did, she was always bitter about it. She said they were deliberately taking advantage of him. She didn't understand how broke they were, how hard-pressed and bedevilled. She didn't understand they were constitutionally bedevilled. She understood nothing. Honti was still chopping and flailing around in the water, and Morley knew he ought to take Barbara home now, quickly, while everything was still quiet, before the explosions started going off again, but he stood rooted to the spot. He couldn't make a move. There was always the difficulty of getting away gracefully. If he and Barbara left too abruptly, it would seem pointed, a reflection on the Hontis, and their feelings would be hurt. So again Morley was torn; again he felt guilty.

"Lily, you do not answer me," Oleam wailed. "Should I go there and discuss the situation—you know, calmly, amicably? Would it be advisable?"

"Why must you interfere and pester?" Lily said, her voice dreamy and lazy. "Leave her alone. It will be good for her, an experience, and you will benefit, too."

"Now," Morley said to himself. "Now."

But just then Oleam rose to his feet and said, "I think I will get a drink of water. Maybe it will make me feel better." He started walking toward the house, his pace altering oddly as he went. The closer he got to the house, the more he seemed to hurry. At the end, he was almost running.

"Barbara," Morley finally said, "I guess we ought to be getting started. I——" He stopped. Honti had climbed out of the pool and was heading directly for Barbara. He grabbed at her hand. She wouldn't let him have it. She shrank back and fidgeted. She didn't know what he was after, and she was, poor thing, frightened by him as he swarmed all over her. He was so big and hairy, the water sluicing off him, and without his glasses he squinted horribly. "Let me," he said. "Oh, just—please!" She gave a shriek and bolted. "Barbara!" Morley called in dismay, but there was no stopping her. Knocking the chair over, she fled for her life, toward the garden in the back.

Honti stared after her. "Has everyone taken leave of their senses?" he asked indignantly. It appeared that he had only wanted to look at her wristwatch. Swimming in the water, thinking of Mrs. Maveen, he had suddenly decided to see how close it actually was to three thirty. "Not that I expect anything from Mrs. Maveen or from anybody else!" Honti said, still dripping water. "I am doomed! Everything goes against me. I have exhausted the whole list of misfortunes. The only thing now is to start all over again from the beginning."

Morley kept swallowing, in pain. It was all so awkward, so garish, and so completely unnecessary. There had been nothing for Barbara to be afraid of. Without his glasses, Honti could barely see; that was why he had had to come up so close, swarming all over her and bringing his nose right up to her hand. "I'll go after her," Morley mumbled. "It's all right. Please just ignore it." He started slowly toward the garden.

Barbara was standing near some oleander bushes. "What did you think he was going to do to you, anyway?" Morley said to her sharply.

"I didn't know what to expect," she blurted out. "How do I know *what* they do? They're depraved! They're degenerate——"

"He only wanted to see the time," Morley said. He told her how it had happened—Honti in the water thinking of Mrs. Maveen, wondering if it was three-thirty, pinning his hopes on palmists and their nutty predictions. "Why did you have to do an awful thing like that?" Morley said. "What's the matter with you? You sat like a mummy. Every time you smiled, you acted as though it was killing you."

"I'm sorry," Barbara said, turning away from him. "I misunderstood. I'll go back and apologize to him." But suddenly she was crying, pressing her face against the pink oleander blossoms, and all the sharpness went out of Morley. In the stillness now, he felt lost and his heart ached—because his wife looked so lovely, because it was true, after all, that Honti was ugly and repellent, and because the sunlight over everything was so clear and brilliant.

Suddenly, he became aware of a commotion going on behind him in the distance. Oleam, at the house, seemed to be shouting furiously, calling something to the Hontis. Now the Hontis themselves went racing up the path, Lily following after her husband, screaming out wildly at him as they ran. Morley was puzzled, even alarmed, but he couldn't leave Barbara crying alone in the garden.

"All right, finish," he said, and told her something was happening at the house, that he wanted to go up there.

"Soon," she said, blubbering. "Just give me a minute—I'll be with you right away."

This is what happened at the pool. Honti was still carrying on, still cursing his luck, when Lily took it into her head to look at her wristwatch. She had one on, too. "If you wanted to know the time," she said, "then why didn't you ask in a civilized way? You are an idiot. You have no taste, and scare innocent people." Somewhere far off, an automobile horn got stuck and started blowing. "It is half past three," Lily said.

Right on the dot, almost before the words were out of her mouth, they heard Oleam shouting "Good news! Good news!" from the terrace, and Honti started to tremble.

"Brewer is on the telephone!" Oleam shouted down to them. "He wants to talk to you!"

"But he is paralyzed!" Lily said. "Don't raise your hopes—you'll only be disappointed!"

"Lubitchka, my dearest," Honti said. There were tears in his eyes, and his voice was husky. He knew she meant well, that she was only trying to save him from himself, from his senseless elations, but he deeply believed in oracles, in signs. It was a lunatic world, and who knew the answers to the riddles or why things happened as they did? Maybe Mrs. Maveen really had an inside line. "Lubitchka, my birdling," Honti said, "is it not strange? Is it not mysterious? Like magic —we didn't even hear the telephone ringing."

"Edmond was standing right by it. He picked it up," Lily said. She tried to explain about Oleam's pestering Gladys and Scorbell for an appointment, but Honti didn't listen. He put on his glasses and started up the path to the house. "Alexander, my watch doesn't even keep good time!" Lily shouted after him. "It was not half past three!"

"A miracle!" he insisted, running and gasping for breath, his eyes still brimming.

He was right and Lily wrong. Brewer was out of the hospital, still partly paralyzed on his left side but ready for work. He had four small children, the two youngest mere infants, and he told Honti to go right ahead—to raise capital, to schedule meetings with the money men. He, Brewer, would be there, willing and able. Honti put the phone back on the rest and prepared to go into action immediately, Saturday afternoon or no Saturday afternoon.

"You will have a downfall!" Lily cried. "You know you—— How you will suffer!"

He turned away from her. Morley and Barbara came into the hall, staring and wondering, but Honti had no time for them, either, and let them wonder. He had to think. In the novelty business, there were levels and levels of importance. Standing at the very top was a certain Mr. Marcellus. This man controlled a good deal of the available investment capital. If he nodded, you functioned. Mr. Marcellus was austere and forbidding by temperament, a czar, his time was

holy, and he could be approached only through go-betweens. Honti
went to work on the phone and dug them up, one after another.
They brushed him off without ceremony. Their time was holy, too.
In the crisis, everyone had become snooty, and nowadays you needed
a go-between to talk to a go-between. Honti wiped the sweat off his
bald spot. The phone in his hand was hot. He thought of Mr. Zeitz
—not a go-between, a relative. Zeitz had entrée on his wife's sister's
side; the sister was married to a Marcellus somewhere. Honti got busy
on the phone again.

"My dear Zeitz," he began, speaking gingerly, because dealing with
relations was ticklish and you had to follow a rigid etiquette. "Can
you do me a great big private favor? I would like to pay you for it,
and, of course, there definitely would be a sizable consideration involved, only it all becomes so complicated. This is something just
between you and I. . . ." Honti went on deftly, sketching out the
situation, but Zeitz, who came from no village himself, smoothly
double-talked right back. Zeitz said he fully appreciated the potential,
but prestigewise it was imperative for him to protect his integrity.
This meant, in plain English, that Zeitz wasn't going to wear out his
welcome with Marcellus by bringing him trash. Honti and Zeitz
understood each other perfectly and finished their conversation.

"Well?" Lily said as Honti hung up. "Nothing doing?"

" 'Thinking of you'!" Honti said savagely. " 'Don't call us, we'll
call you!' You have to eat your heart out before they let you finalize
a dollar——"

He broke off. Oleam was back. He had slipped away during the
excitement, and had gone out to the garage. He had rummaged
around there and had found an old neck brace. He had put it on, for
his stiff neck, for the sake of the impression, and now, in the middle
of everything, he was parading around like a peacock that had lost its
wits. "I have my appointment with Gladys and Mr. Scorbell," Oleam
said, in bliss, almost humming. "I am invited for cocktails, very
stylish. We will discuss matters. We will see what will eventuate."

"Rejoice!" Honti roared. "Our fortunes are made! We shall hold
a fiesta!" He broke off. His eyes went deep, and again he turned tenderly to Lily—his wife, his lifelong friend, his business partner.
"Lubitchka, my angel," he said, "why shouldn't I deal with Mr.
Marcellus direct? Who says I can't call him up myself? After all, I
am somebody, too. I have position. Why not?"

He made his mind up on the instant, grimly set his jaw, and strode

back to the phone. Everyone crept up silently and stood near him as
he dialled the number. He got through to Marcellus's residence.
Honti could hear the phone there ringing. Somebody picked it up—
the butler. Honti squared his shoulders, drew his breath in. Now he
rolled the words out, weighty and important. "This is Mr. Alexander
Honti, of Paris, calling. I wish to speak in person with Mr. Anton
Marcellus—— *Don't hang gup!*" It was useless. Honti heard the click.
He slammed his own phone down on the rest. "May a fire devour
them, Mr. Marcellus and the butler together! May floods engulf
them! May cancers and ulcers fester in their bellies! May their
tongues grow swollen and hang out from their mouths like
beards——" He stopped, transfixed. He had the answer. He knew
exactly where he could get financing. Everything became dead quiet.
In the hush, Oleam suddenly shivered, because Honti was staring
at him so strangely.

"The milliner," Honti said. "Scorbell." That would be his salva-
tion. Why hadn't he thought of it before? Scorbell was rich, owned
factories. Honti would take over Oleam's appointment. Honti would
go there for cocktails.

"No!" Oleam said. Honti silenced him with a bellow. He was
ecstatic, carried away. The hall couldn't hold him, and he swirled
into the living room. He had grovelled, he had fasted and prayed, he
had turned himself inside out, and now, at last, came victory. Honti
trumpeted with joy.

"He is flying, flying!" Lily said. "He will bust!"

He sent her back to the phone, to call up Gladys and pave the way,
so that he would come invited. There was a flurry of movement,
Lily going to the hall and Morley saying it was time to leave. Laughing and happy, the young Doctor started out for the dressing rooms
at the pool, to change back into his clothes. Barbara lingered. Honti
could tell she was remorseful. She knew now how unjust, how cruel,
she had been to him and no doubt wanted to apologize formally,
but he was far too happy to be bothered with trifles.

He saw it all. He couldn't stop talking. He would get his backing,
he would recoup, he would be a power in the industry again. Everyone would smile. He would be popular, universally admired. His visions soared. He would give an enormous party. He would throw a
tent over the garden, hire live musicians, rent dishes from the rental
people, and make all the guests sign the guestbook, so that he would
have tangible evidence when the income-tax officials came to ques-

tion the deductions. Honti even had the menu all worked out—veal, peaches and plums, wild rice, shrimp in aspic, salad. . . . But then some devil got hold of him. Honti couldn't leave well enough alone, and everything came jarring to a halt.

He meant no harm. He did it only out of rapture, out of sheer, bouncing gladness. He pinched Barbara. In an amazing burst of anger, she flared up and cracked him. She cracked him with surprising force, too, in one blow destroying three hundred and fifty dollars' worth of bridgework on his lower jaw.

"Oh, you are disgusting!" she said bitterly, and turned on her heel and walked out of the house, to wait for her husband outside at the car.

Honti was dazed. The first thought that occurred to him was how ludicrous he would look, talking to Scorbell in the millions and no teeth in his mouth. But then Honti forgot about the teeth and a general depression set in. The plans, the happy hopes, the visions all fell away from him. To take their place came a terrible, pitiless clarity. It was the letdown Lily had been predicting. The cycle was completed. He sat down on a chair, sick and dreary.

He had meant to borrow Morley's car for the trip over to Benedict Canyon. Now Honti had no machine, he had no teeth, and he could also see that he wasn't going to get his financing so fast. Scorbell was no dumbbell. A man didn't own three factories by throwing his money around indiscriminately. Honti sat in the gloom of the living room and didn't stir. Black thoughts crowded in his head. He had been feeling so good. Everything had been so wonderful. Why, he asked himself over and over again—why did he have to go and pinch her? He was a pariah. He wasn't fit for human company.

"It is demeaning," Oleam said mournfully, not referring to the pinch—he hadn't even noticed the incident. He was still protesting because Honti was taking away his appointment. Oleam thought it wasn't becoming to bring business matters into a delicate situation like this. It would put the whole affair in a different light. "It is not right," Oleam said sorrowfully, still in the neck brace. "It is cheap. It is vulgar. Scorbell will think we are all adventurers and finaglers."

Morley was driving along Mulholland Drive, on top of the hills, heading for Laurel Canyon, which would take them down to the Crescent Heights section, where they lived. Barbara sat next to him, tight-lipped and flushed. He had never seen her in such a mood and was half afraid to talk to her. She refused to tell him anything. She was just too furious to explain. He racked his brains. It was so tantalizing. He had thought everything was fine and settled. When he left the living room, they were dancing with glee. What in the world could have gone wrong?

"After the way you made me feel!" Barbara said. "After I reproached myself and was even going to go to him and apologize!"

"But what happened?" Morley begged. "If you would only tell me—what did he *do?*"

He stopped short. The car was coasting and came to a stop. The motor had failed. Morley put the brakes on and fiddled with the starter. Then he remembered that the gas line had a slow leak in it. They were out of gas. The car had a number of things the matter with it and needed an overhaul job, but Morley had been putting it off, because he was always so short. There was nothing to do now but start walking to a gas station. Suddenly, Barbara burst into tears.

"All the hours I sat in the car by myself, listening to the dopey radio," she said. She was thinking of the unpaid bills, of the times she had waited alone outside while Morley made his calls.

He frowned. He felt helpless and confused, and didn't know what to say to her. He left her weeping and got out of the car. Sadly, he began the long hike down to the foot of Laurel Canyon, where the nearest gas station was.

Honti was also on Mulholland Drive, but farther to the west, toward Benedict Canyon. He was walking to Scorbell's place—to try there, to keep the appointment. The air was clean. The view extended for miles on either side. The earth lay still and impassive, touched with the solitude of great spaces. Honti felt shrunken in spirit. He was weary. He thought of the few decades that were given to a man, three or four, or five at the most. How swiftly they had gone for him, in what a frenzy. There had hardly been time to stop for anything.

When he was a boy, he used to soak lima beans in water overnight and then plant them in flowerpots. All day long, he would carry the flowerpot from window sill to window sill, to give his plant the benefit of the shifting sun. Honti remembered that home—the warmth there and the peace. He remembered walking with his father along the river in Frankfurt, on a wintry day, holding his father's hand, passing some great cathedral; after all the years, Honti could still see in his mind the clouds etched against the sky that day, like frost on a windowpane. Honti thought of some bricklayers he had seen in Paris, when he and Lily had tried there, when they had thought maybe, maybe in Paris . . . The bricklayers, high up on the scaffolding, had been caught in a sudden shower and covered themselves with their empty plaster troughs, huddling like turtles. These, and perhaps a half dozen others, were the images, the memories, that Honti at the age of fifty had collected to treasure. He loved that moment with the bricklayers, and the light in Paris, and the rivers of France, the Hudson River Valley in this country, and the incredible California sunshine; the tragedy was that they did not love him back. Everywhere he was rejected, everywhere a trespasser. "Forgive me!" Honti suddenly said, pleading quietly but with all his heart and soul. "Forgive me! Forgive me!" Yes, it was his fault. He had trespassed, he had transgressed; he had committed abominations, stretched the truth and kited checks. He must have committed all the sins, for you weren't punished for nothing in this world, and God knew all Honti's lifetime had been a punishment.

He humbly pleaded for forgiveness high on the mountaintop. To his left were the harbors, the beaches, the glinting Pacific Ocean. To the right lay the floor of the San Fernando Valley and, beyond that, the sullen ranges of the San Gabriels.

Avoiding all distractions, ignoring the rabbits and squirrels, ignoring the other dogs as they came out to meet him, ready to fight or frolic, Fidelio was heading back to the house by a series of paths and short cuts. He was hungry. He had been searching all day long. He had been to the barbershop, the restaurants and drugstores, the Turkish bath. He had looked for Honti at the houses of all his friends. Hoping that his master was home, that all was well, he came loping through the thickets and arrived at the clearing. He paused, breathing hard, disappointed. The swimming pool looked abandoned. The lawn was strewn with empty chairs. Fidelio went up to and sniffed an old beach shoe on the tiled edge of the pool, a squiggly wet towel, a torn bathing cap without the strap, the chocolate layer cake. Then he slipped into the bushes and began loping again, resuming his search.

SHIRLEY ANN GRAU *was born in New Orleans in 1929, and was graduated from Newcomb College with an honor degree and Phi Beta Kappa key. She started out to be a schoolteacher, but she abandoned it in favor of writing. Her stories have appeared in such magazines as* Holiday, The New Mexico Quarterly, New World Writing, *and* The New Yorker. *A book of her short stories, titled* The Black Prince *and including "Joshua," will be published shortly by Knopf.*

JOSHUA

FROM THE NEW YORKER

South of New Orleans, down along the stretch that is called the Lower Coast, the land trails off to a narrow strip between river and marsh. Solid ground here is maybe only a couple of hundred feet across, and there is a dirt road that runs along the foot of the green, carefully sodded levee. It once had state highway markers, but people used the white-painted signs for shotgun targets until they were so riddled they crumbled away. The highway commission has never got around to replacing them. Maybe it doesn't even know the signs are gone; highway inspectors hardly ever come down this way. To the east is the expanse of shifting swamp grass, and beyond that is the little, sheltered Bay Cadoux, and farther still, beyond the string of protecting islands, is the Gulf. To the west is the Mississippi, broad and slow and yellow.

At intervals along the road there are towns—scattered collections of rough, unpainted board houses with tin roofs, stores that are like the houses except that they have crooked painted signs, and long, flat, windowless warehouses to store the skins of the muskrats that are taken every year from the marsh. Each building perches on stilts two or three feet high; in the spring the bayous rise. The waters always reach up to the roadbed and sometimes even cover it with a couple of inches of water.

There is no winter to speak of. Sometimes there is a little scum of ice on the pools and backwaters of the bayous and a thin coating over the ruts in the road. But the temperature never stays below freezing more than a day or two, and the little gray film of ice soon disappears under the rain.

For it rains almost constantly from October to March. Not hard; not a storm; there is never any lightning. There is just a steady, cold rain.

The river is high. The trees that grow out on the *batture*—on the land between the river's usual bed and the levee, on the land that all summer has been dry and fertile—are half covered with water.

The inside walls of the houses drip moisture in tiny beads like sweat, and bread turns moldy in a single day. Roofs begin to leak, and the pans put under the leaks have to be emptied twice a day. From the bayous and the swamps to the east come heavy, choking odors of musk and rotting grasses.

It is mostly all colored people here in the lower reaches. Poor people, who live on what they find in the river and the swamps and the Gulf beyond them.

Joshua Samuel Watkin sat at the kitchen table in one of the dozen-odd houses that make up Bon Secour, Good Hope, the farthest of the towns along the dirt highway, which ends there, and the nearest town to the river's mouth.

Joshua Samuel Watkin leaned both elbows on the table and watched the way his mother used her hands when she talked. She swung them from her wrist, limply, while the fingers twisted and poked, way off by themselves.

His small, quick black eyes shifted from her hands to her lips, which were moving rapidly. Joshua stared at them for a moment and then went back to the hands. He had the ability to shut out sounds he did not wish to hear. His mother's flaming, noisy temper he could shut out easily now; it had taken the practice of most of his eleven years.

He glanced at the doorway, where his father was standing. He had just come in. The shoulders of his light-gray jacket were stained black by the rain, and the tan of his cap had turned almost brown. Joshua glanced briefly down at his father's hands. They were empty; he would have dropped the string of fish outside on the porch. Pretty soon, Joshua knew, one of his parents was going to remember those fish and send him outside to clean them for supper. It was a job he had never liked. No reason, really. He would have to squat outside, working carefully, so that most of the mess fell over the side into the yard, where the cats could fight for it.

His father yanked one of the wooden chairs from under the table and sat down on it heavily. He was answering now, Joshua noticed, and his face was beginning to get the straight-down-the-cheek lines of anger. He tilted his chair back against the wall and jammed both hands down deep into his pockets.

From the way things were beginning to look, Josh thought, it might be just as well if he got out for a while. But he'd better stay long enough to see if there was going to be any supper. He still hadn't bothered to listen to them, to either of them; he knew what they were saying. He balanced his spoon across the top of his coffee cup and then tapped it with his finger gently, swinging it. He miscalculated, and the spoon hit the oilcloth with a sharp crack.

His father's chair crashed down, and with an extra rattle one of the rungs came loose. "Christ Almighty," his father said. "Ain't I told you a million times not to do nothing like that?"

"He ain't done nothing," his mother said, and, reaching out her limp black hand, balanced the spoon across the cup again.

Joshua smiled to himself, though his face did not move. It was one sure way to get his mother on his side—just let his father say a word against him. It worked the other way, too; let his mother fuss at him and his father would be sure to take his part. It was as if they couldn't ever be together.

His father let his breath out with a high-pitched hiss.

"He ain't done nothing," his mother repeated. "Just drop his spoon a little."

His father kept on staring at her, his head bent slightly, the dark eyes in his dark face glaring.

"Leastways he ain't just sitting around the house on his tail end, scared to stick his nose outside."

"Woman," his father said, "iffen you ain't the naggingest——"

"Scared." His mother stuck out her underlip. "You just plain scared."

"I ain't scared of nothing a man ain't got cause to be scared of."

"I hear you talking," his mother said. "Only I plain don't see you moving nohow."

"Nagging bitch," his father said, almost gently, under his breath.

His mother's underlip stuck out even farther, and she whistled sharply, derisively, through her teeth.

His father bent forward, slapping a hand down, one on each knee. "Sure I scared!" he shouted in her face. She did not even blink. "Everybody scared!"

Joshua turned his eyes toward the window. All he could see was gray sky. Raining, solid gray sky in all four directions—east over the swamps and west over the river and north to the city and south to the Gulf, where the fishing boats went, and the U-boats were hiding.

His father was saying, "Like Jesse Baxter, you want me to plain get blown to bits."

Joshua did not take his eyes off the square of gray sky, but he was seeing something else. The fishing boats from Bon Secour, three of them, had come on to two U boats, surfaced in the fog and together, exchanging supplies. And one of the ships had lobbed a couple of shots from its deck gun square into Baxter's boat. There wasn't anything but pieces left, and the two other fishing boats hadn't even had time to look for them, they were so busy running. All they'd heard, just for a second or so, was the men around the gun laughing. The two surviving boats had not gone out again. Nobody would take them out.

Joshua had heard the story and he had dreamed about it often enough. He would wake up sweating even in the cold and shaking with fear. He couldn't quite imagine a U-boat, so its outline and shape changed with each dream. But the action was always the same: the gun pointing at him and the laughing.

With a little shudder, Joshua turned his eyes back to his parents. "That been a week and a half," his mother was saying, "and how you think we gonna eat? How you think we gonna eat iffen you don't find a boat?"

"We been eating." His father had his chin pressed down against the rolled collar of his gray wool sweatshirt. "Ain't we been eating?"

His mother snorted. "Why, sure," she said. "You man enough to go sneaking out in the little old back bayous and catch us a couple of fish."

"Fish ain't bad," his father said. "Ask *him* iffen he going hungry."

Joshua felt their eyes focussed on him, and he squirmed.

"Don't go putting words in the boy's mouth," his mother said.

"Just you ask him."

"Ask him iffen there ain't things you got to have money to buy. Ask him iffen he don't got no coat to wear with the cold. Ask him iffen he don't need a new coat." She turned to Joshua. "You tell

him what you want. You tell him what you plain got to have." Her
voice ended in a kind of ragged shriek.

"I get him a coat," his father said.

"When that gonna be? He plain gonna freeze first."

"Ain't no son of mine gonna freeze," his father said.

"You plain scared," his mother taunted. "You just plain scared."

Joshua got to his feet and slipped around the edge of the table
and outside. On the porch he found a square of black canvas and
wrapped it around himself, letting it make a cowl above his head.
It had been used to cover an engine, and it smelled of grease and was
slippery to the touch, but it would keep him dry and very warm.

He noticed the string of fish that his father had brought home.
With the toe of one blue canvas sneaker, he kicked the string down
into the yard. It hit the soggy ground with a little splash. The cats
would be coming around at dark.

He walked down the road, stepping carefully, watching for the
biggest puddles, keeping to the levee side, where the ground was
highest. The rain was falling noisily on his square of tarpaulin.
With the steady, quick, clicking sound of drops all around him,
falling on his head but not touching him, tapping on his shoulders
but not really being there, after a while he wouldn't be sure of his
balance any more, or his direction, there would be such an echo in
his head. He kept blinking to steady himself, but that didn't seem
to do much good. He had heard men say they would rather get
drenched to the skin and maybe get the fever than spend hours under
a tarpaulin with a slow, steady winter rain falling.

The wind blew the rain in swirling eddies—like puffs of smoke,
almost, the drops were so fine. Joshua rubbed the wet from his eyes.
Over the noise of the rain he heard the faint sound of the river
against the levee, a sound that went on day and night, until you got
so used to it you had to make a special effort to hear it. Squinting,
he looked up. The tops of water aspens on the other side of the levee
shuddered under the rain, showing the frightened white underside
of their leaves.

Joshua hunched the tarpaulin higher over his head and walked
faster. Over to the right now he could see the landings where Goose
Bayou swung in close and deep. And there were the boats, moored
and wet under the rain, and empty, just where they'd been for the
last week or more, and, at the far end of one of the landings, the
empty space where Jesse Baxter's boat belonged.

Joshua stopped and stared at the empty space, at the muddy, rain-specked water and Baxter's mooring posts with the ropes still around them but dragging down into the water. Like it was in his dreams, he thought, when, cold and sweating, he saw the shape of a ship in the fog and heard the sound of a deck gun.

He reached the shelter of the overhang of a building and let the tarpaulin drop from his head. He still kept it wrapped around his shoulders, because he was shivering. In the middle of the board platform in front of the building, a yellow dog with black-marked flanks was scratching behind one ear, slowly, limply, and overhead a double-board sign hung upside down at a sharp angle. On one side of it was painted, in white letters, "Bourgeois Store." Years ago, the wind had lifted it and turned it on its hook, and it had jammed that way, with only the blank side showing. Nobody ever seemed to notice. Maybe because nobody ever looked up.

Joshua peeped in through the window. It wasn't much brighter inside the store than out. A single electric-light bulb way up against the ceiling in the center of the room was burning, because the day was so dark. It was a little bulb and almost worn out—you could see the red, glowing coils of wire inside it.

Joshua rubbed his fingers against the glass and stared harder. There were two tables set together lengthwise across the front of the room, and behind them two more. They were covered with clothes in neat little piles, according to size and color. There were wall shelves, too, filled with a clutter of hardware. There were so many things in the room that you couldn't find any single object quickly, even if the thing you were looking for was as big as a man.

Joshua finally located Claude Bourgeois at the side of the room, over by the stove, almost hidden behind small crab nets that were hanging by long cords from the ceiling. There were two men sitting with him. Joshua could have known he would be there; he hardly ever moved from that spot during the winter, his bones ached so. Now that he was old, he'd stopped fighting the rain and the cold; he just let them have their way outside the store. He didn't move outside at all. His wife, Kastka, who was part Indian, rubbed his arms and legs with liniment and kept the fire going full away in the silver-painted potbellied stove.

Joshua opened the door. Just inside, he let his tarpaulin fall in a heap. Claude and the two men with him turned and looked, and

Claude said, "Close that there door quick, boy," and they went back to their talking.

Joshua recognized the two other men: Oscar Lavie and Stanley Phillips. Lavie ran Claude's fishing boat for him now that he was too old to go out, and Phillips was never very far away from Lavie. They always worked together; it had been that way since they were kids.

Joshua walked over to the small glass case that stood against the left wall, the case that was filled with knives. He stood looking down at them, at one in particular, one in the middle of the case. It had a blade at least six inches long, and its handle was of some white stuff, white and iridescent and shining as the inside of an oyster shell that is wet and fresh. Someday, he told himself, when he had money of his own, he would buy that. If just nobody got to it first.

Not that he needed a knife; his father had bought him one a month or less ago, with the money from the last haul the men had made. He remembered how angry his mother had been. "God Almighty," she'd said. "Iffen you ain't plain crazy, you. Buying that there trash when the boy needs a coat."

His father had just winked at him and said, "You don't hear him complaining none."

"Maybe he ain't got no more sense than you," his mother had said, "but he gonna be mighty cold this winter without no coat."

"Woman," his father had said, "ain't you got but one idea in you head?"

Little Henry Bourgeois came and stood alongside of Joshua. He was Claude's son, the son of his old age, the son of the woman who was part Indian. Henry had the round Negro features of his father and the skin color of his mother, a glowing red, deep and far down, so deep that it wasn't so much a skin color as a color under that. It was almost like seeing the blood.

"You heard the news?" Henry asked. His father had a radio in the store, a small one in a square green case. It was the only radio in Bon Secour.

"No," Joshua said.

"They come almost up the river," Henry said. "They sink one of the freighter ships again."

The war and the shooting and the submarines. And just a little way off. Joshua felt his breath catch in the middle of his chest, catch on the lump that was so big and cold that it hurt. And he remembered all his dreams: the fog, and the other ship, and himself in the gray, rain-speckled water, dying, in a million pieces for the fish to chew. His face did not change. He kept on looking at the knife. "That right?" he said.

"Josh," old Claude Bourgeois called to him. "You come over here."

He turned and crossed through the maze of tables and ducked under the hanging skeins of nets.

"Boy," Claude Bourgeois said, "iffen you don't quit leaning on that there glass it gonna crack through, sure as anything."

Joshua looked down at his feet in the blue canvas sneakers, blue stained darker by the water he had been walking through. He wiggled his toes, and they made little bumps on the outside of the canvas.

"You papa home?" Claude Bourgeois asked.

Joshua nodded.

"He wanting to go out fishing?"

"I reckon—it Ma wanting him to go out."

Oscar Lavie shifted in his chair, lifted one bare foot, and hooked it between his cupped hands. "Iffen you want you boat out," he told Claude Bourgeois, "I reckon you plain better take it out yourself."

Claude opened his mouth, and then, thinking better of whatever he was about to say, closed it again.

"I seen that there ship popping up out of the fog," Oscar went on, "and it ain't nobody's fault it ain't blown me up, place of Jesse Baxter."

Stanley Phillips nodded his head slowly. He stuttered badly, and when he talked people hardly ever understood him. So he let others do the talking. But his lack of speech had given him an air of confidence. Sometimes when he stood leaning against the corner of a building, his hands jammed down in his pockets, his slight body arched back and braced for balance, he seemed to own everything he looked at—the streets and the houses and the people. All the women liked him; some of them got a dreamy look in their eyes when he passed. "He don't have to talk, him," they would say. Only last year, Stanley Phillips had married—all proper, in the church over at Petit Bayou—a wife, by far the prettiest colored girl anywhere along the river. And when he'd been out fishing, gone for maybe a couple of days or a week, he'd always head straight home, and when he got within fifty yards of his house, he'd stop and give a long, loud whistle and then walk on slowly, counting his steps, and every fifth step giving another whistle, so his wife would have time to get ready for what was coming.

"Iffen you was in the Army," Claude Bourgeois said softly, "you wouldn't have no chance to say no."

Neither Stanley nor Oscar had bothered to register for the Army. They just disappeared whenever any stranger came around asking questions, which wasn't very often.

"You figure on anything there?" Oscar asked, his eyes resting on the fat, lumpy body of the old man.

"Not me," Claude Bourgeois said hastily. "Not me."

"That real fine of you," Oscar said. "Then I reckon I ain't gonna have to slice up all you fat and feed it to the gators."

"Me?" Claude rolled his eyes around so that they almost disappeared. "I ain't gonna do nothing like that."

"That nice of you," Oscar said.

"Why, man," Claude said, changing the subject quickly, "you plain got to go out eventually."

"That ain't yet," Oscar said, and Stanley nodded. "It ain't worth nothing going out to get blown to pieces."

"How they gonna find you in all that water out there?"

"It ain't worth the chance," Oscar said.

Joshua stared over at the pot of coffee on the stove top, where it always stood to keep warm. Nobody offered him any, so he looked away.

"Why, man"—Claude was holding his hand outspread in front of him—"you can't go on living on bayou fish forever; there other things you got to have money for." He nodded at Joshua. "This here boy need a coat, only his daddy ain't working to give him none."

"Leastways his daddy ain't lying in pieces all over the bottom of the Gulf, with the fishes eating on him," Oscar said. "Leastways, iffen you are so concerned, you plain can give him a coat. Just you give him one on credit now."

"You gonna do that?" Joshua asked.

Claude coughed. "There ain't no cause to do nothing like that," he said. "This here a matter of business, and this ain't good business, any way you looks at it. There all sort of money waiting for his daddy out there, iffen you wasn't too scared to go get it."

Joshua drifted away toward the door. He picked up the tarpaulin, studied it for a minute, then flipped it around himself and went outside. Little Henry Bourgeois followed right behind him. The low gray sky was thickening with the evening. In the branches of a chinaberry tree, a hawk and catbird were fighting. "Where you going?" Henry asked.

Joshua went down the steps and out into the road. The mud was soft and gummy, and stuck to the bottom of his sneakers in heavy cakes. Each step was a sucking sound.

"Damn gumbo mud," he said. He could hear Henry's steps behind him.

They walked about a block, with their heads bent way down, so they really couldn't see where they were going. Henry gave a quick little squishing skip and came abreast of Joshua. "Where you going?" he asked again. "You going there?"

Joshua nodded.

They came to the warehouse. The fur-trading company had put it up maybe ten years ago, when they first discovered all the muskrat around here. There'd been need for extra space then. But things had changed; a couple of hurricanes had drowned out the animals, and they were coming back slowly. It hardly paid for a man to set his traps during the season, since he had to take the skins up to Petit Bayou now to sell them.

But the old warehouse still stood, at the north end of the string of houses. It was a rough building with plain, unpainted wood sides that time and rain and fogs had stained to an almost uniform black. On the far side, behind some low bushes—barberry bushes, with thick thorns and pronged leaves—Joshua had discovered a loose board. It had taken him nearly three hours to work it loose.

The two boys wiggled through the bushes, pried down the board, and slipped inside. They shook themselves like wet puppies and kicked off their shoes. The building was unheated, but somehow it always seemed warm, maybe only because it was dry. The floor boards were double thickness and carefully waterproofed with tar. It was a single room, big and almost empty. There were no windows, and when Henry put the board back in place, the only light came from the thin cracks between the boards. The two boys had been here so often that they knew their way around the room; they did not need to see.

They both walked straight out into the center of the room, until their bare feet felt the familiar rough texture of burlap. There had been a big heap of old bags in the warehouse, and the boys had carefully piled them in a circle, leaving a clear place about four feet across in the middle. When they sat there, the bags were higher than their heads, and kept off drafts and cold. In the corners of the warehouse they had found a few furs—tattered, mangy things, too poor to be sold—and they used these as seats or beds, for sometimes they slept here, too. Their families did not miss them; after all, a boy should be able to look out for himself.

Joshua and Henry settled themselves, and Joshua lit the kerosene lantern he had brought a couple of days before. His mother had stomped and raged for a whole day after she discovered it was missing. Joshua did not even have to lie about it; before she had thought to ask him, his father came home and her anger turned on him, and they argued long and hard, and ended as they always did, by going in their room to make love.

"I done brought something this time," Henry said. He pulled a paper-wrapped package from under his jacket. The greasy stains of food were already smearing the brown paper. "This here is our supper."

They divided the cold fried fish and the bread, and then Joshua put out the lamp—it was hard to get kerosene for it—and they ate in the darkness, with just the sound of rain on the tar-paper roof and the sound of their own chewing and the occasional scurry of a rat or maybe a lizard or a big roach.

"Man," Joshua said slowly. "This is fine, no?"

"Sure," Henry agreed, with his mouth full. "Sure is."

"Look like they gonna be a fog tonight."

"Sure do," Henry said. "It a good night to be right in here. It a fine night to be in here."

Joshua's fingers brushed the surface of one of the moldy-smelling pelts with a faint scratching sound. "You might even could make a coat outa these here, iffen you had enough," he said.

"No," Henry said scornfully.

Joshua did not argue.

They fell asleep then, because it was dark and warm and they weren't hungry any longer. And Joshua dreamed the same dream he dreamed almost every night. There was a thing that he knew was a submarine. Even the way its shape kept changing—from long, like a racing boat, only a hundred times bigger, to narrow and tall, like the picture postcards of the buildings in New Orleans. But it was always fog-colored. At times it slipped back into the fog, and when it came out again, it was a different shape. And he was always there, too, in a boat sometimes, a pirogue or a skiff, hunched down, trying not to be seen, or on foot in the marsh, in knee-high water, crouched down behind some few, almost transparent grasses. Hiding where he knew there was no hiding place.

Joshua shook himself, turned over, bent his other arm and pillowed his head on it, and went back to the dream. From time to time he whimpered.

That night, one of the submarines was destroyed. The patrol boats found it almost a quarter mile inside the pass, heading for the shipping upriver. The heavy, cold, raining night exploded and then exploded again. Joshua woke up and couldn't be sure he wasn't still in his dream, for the waking was like the dream. Alongside him, Henry was whispering, "Sweet Jesus. Sweet Jesus." With fumbling fingers and a quick, sharp scratch of matches, Joshua lit the lantern. The light raced to the roof and stayed there, holding back the darkness. Quickly, afraid, he glanced around the room. He was almost surprised to find it empty.

"What that?" Henry asked. His eyes caught the light and reflected it—bright, flat animal eyes.

Joshua did not answer. His throat was quivering too much. He looked around the empty room again and shook his head slowly.

"What that?" Henry repeated.

Joshua turned up the wick high as it would go. The top of the glass chimney began to cloud with smoke, but he did not lower the flame.

Henry jiggled his elbow persistently. "What that go up out there?" he asked.

"Ain't nothing."

Outside, people were yelling, their voices frightened and sleepy. Their words were muffled and garbled by the walls.

"You reckon maybe we ought to go out and see?" Henry asked.

"I reckon not," Joshua said, and there was a flat note of decision in his voice. "I reckon we best stay right here."

A plane flew by, close overhead. The building shook and the lamp flame wavered.

"I reckon the war come plain close," Joshua said.

"It quiet now," Henry said, and even managed to smile.

Joshua moved his lips but no sound came out. His tongue fluttered around in his mouth.

The shouting outside was stopping. There were now just two voices, calling back and forth to each other, slower and slower, like a clock running down. Finally, they stopped, too.

Henry said, "It smoking some."

Joshua turned the lampwick down. The circle of light around them contracted. He watched it out of the corner of his eye and quickly turned the wick back up again.

"Ain't you better put that out?" Henry said. "We ain't got all that much kerosene."

"We got enough," Joshua said.

"You scared."

"Me?" Joshua said. "Me? No." Even he did not believe this. He tried hard to stay awake, knowing that just as soon as he fell asleep, just as soon as he stepped over that line, the indistinct shape, gray like the fog, would be waiting to kill him.

Suddenly it was broad daylight. The lamp had burned out; its chimney was solid black. Henry pointed to it. Joshua nodded. "You left the lamp burning till it run out of oil," Henry said.

Joshua walked slowly across the room. "Me?" he said. "No."

"I heard you talking in you sleep."

"I don't talk in my sleep, me." Joshua put his shoulder to the loose board and pushed. He felt the cold, damp air in his face. He blinked and looked out at the gray day.

"You was crying," Henry said. "You was crying and saying, 'Don't.' That what you was doing."

Joshua wriggled through the opening without answering.

Henry stuck his head out after him. "You was scared," he shouted.

Joshua kept going steadily. He could feel a trembling behind his knees, and he had to concentrate with all his might to keep his walk straight.

As he went up the splintered wooden steps of his house, he could hear his father singing:

"Mo parle Simon, Simon, Simon,
 Li parle Ramon, Ramon, Ramon,
 Li parle Didine,
 Li tombe dans chagrin."

Sober, his father wouldn't even admit to understanding the down-river version of French. He'd near killed a man once who'd called him a Cajun. Drunk, he would remember that he knew hundreds of Cajun songs.

Joshua opened the door and went inside. His father and Oscar Lavie were in the kitchen, sitting at opposite ends of the table. Stanley Phillips was not around; he wasn't ever one for leaving his wife before afternoon.

In the middle of the green-checked oilcloth table cover were two gallon jugs of light-colored orange wine. One was already half empty. And on the table, too, next to the big wine bottles, was the small, round bottle of white lightning. Just in case they should need it.

They were so busy with their song they did not notice Joshua. He looked at them, wondering where his mother was. Then he went looking for his food. He found some beans on a plate at the back of the stove, and a piece of bread in the wall cupboard. He ate them, standing up in a corner.

Slowly his father swung his head around to him and said, "Look who come in."

Oscar Lavie said, "We celebrating way they blow up everything last night."

"You ma gone rushing out of here like the devils of Hell hanging on her petticoat."

"I ain't done nothing of the kind." His mother popped her head in through the narrow little door that led to the lean-to at the back of the house. "I just went to get some kindling wood, so you crazy fool drunks ain't gonna freeze to death."

Oscar began singing, almost to himself:

"Cher, mo l'aime toi.
Qui, mo l'aime toi.
Vec tou mo coeur
Comme cochon l'aime la bou."

"Ain't I told you to get out?" his father said softly to his mother. "Ain't I told you I sick and tired of looking at you?"

Joshua finished eating silently. Oscar gave a deep sigh. "Us all gonna starve to death," he said. "Us all."

His father poured himself another glass of the wine. Joshua's mother did not move. She stood in the doorway holding the kindling in her arms.

His father's heavy-lidded eyes focussed on Joshua and lifted a little. "What you gonna eat tonight?" his father asked.

The boy turned and put the dish back where he had found it, on the stove. "I don't know, me," he said.

His father began to laugh. He laughed so hard that he had to put his head down on the tabletop, and the table shook, and the wine in the bottle swished back and forth. When he spoke, it was from under his arms. "You hear him, Oscar, man," he said. "He don't know what he going to eat. He don't know."

Oscar did not even smile as he stared off into space. The black of his skin seemed almost blue under the morning light.

"He don't know what he going to eat. I don't know either, me."

Joshua stood watching them.

"I ain't going out today, me, to look for nothing," his father said. "I plain sick of catching a couple of fish or shrimp with a hand net."

"Han Olivier, he got a pig," Lavie said, with a dreamy look on his face.

"Man," Joshua's father said, "Han plain swears he gonna kill anybody what tried to touch his pig, and he been sitting guard on it."

"I seen a dog out front there."

"I just ain't that hungry yet."

Lavie sighed deeply. "It ain't gonna hurt us none not to eat for one day."

"No," his father said, and was silent for so long that Joshua began walking toward the door. He had no clear idea what he would do outside; he only felt he had to leave. His father's head jerked up. "Unless *he* go out."

Joshua stopped short. "Me?" he said.

Oscar looked at him. His eyes faltered, focussed again, and held. "He a fine little boy," he said. "He can go run my lines."

"No," Joshua said.

"He ain't gonna do that," his mother said. She came into the room now and dumped her armload of kindling alongside the stove.

"That kindling plain all wet," Oscar said vaguely, scowling.

"You ain't never found nothing dry in winter," his mother snapped.

"It gonna smoke," Oscar said plaintively.

"No skin off my nose," his mother said.

"Ain't I told you to get out?" his father said.

"You done told me a lot of things," his mother said.

"I tired of hearing you——"

"You ain't sending that little old boy out where you scared to go."

"Ain't scared," Oscar corrected. "Drunk."

"Woman," his father said, "I plain gonna twist you head around till you sees where you been."

He stood up, a little uncertain on his feet, and his chair fell over. His mother turned and ran out. They could see her through the window, scurrying over to the Delattes' house, next door. She was yelling something over her shoulder; they couldn't make out what.

His father looked at Joshua, his eyes travelling up and down every inch of his body. "You going out," he said.

"I ain't," Josh whispered.

"You going out and save you poor old papa some work," his father said. "Or I gonna twist up every bone in you body till you feels just like a shrimp."

Joshua edged his way carefully to the door.

"You know I mean what I done said."

Joshua ducked out the door. Behind him, he heard his father laugh.

Henry was down at the landing, leaning against one of the black tar-coated pilings and teasing a big yellow tomcat with a long piece of rope. Joshua walked past without a word, and righted his father's pirogue and pushed it into the water.

"You going out?" Henry asked, and his voice quivered with interest.

"Reckon so." Josh bent down to tie the lace of one of his sneakers.

"Why you going out?"

"Reckon somebody got to see about getting something to eat."

"Oh," Henry said.

"My papa, he gonna stay drunk today."

"I heard."

"I reckon I could let you come along."

"That O.K. We ain't needing no fish at my house."

"You afraid." Joshua looked at him and lifted his eyebrows. "You plain afraid."

"No-o-o," Henry said, and scowled.

"Why ain't you come along with me, then?"

"I ain't said I ain't coming." Henry tossed the piece of rope away. The cat pounced on it in spitting fury. "I ain't said nothing like that."

"Let's get started, then."

"I tell you what," Henry said. "I gonna go borrow my daddy's shotgun. Maybe we see something worth shooting at. I seen a couple of ducks yesterday or so."

Joshua nodded. It would feel better, having a shotgun with them. Wasn't much good, maybe, but it was something. In his nightmares, he'd wished often enough that he had one with him.

While he waited, he got down in the pirogue and took his place in the stern. Carefully he wrapped the grease-stained black tarpaulin around him. "It cold, all right, man," he said aloud. The yellow tomcat turned his head and watched him. For a minute, Joshua stared into the bright yellow eyes and at the straggling broken tufts of whiskers.

Joshua made the sign of the cross quickly. "If you a evil spirit, you can't touch me now," he said. The cat continued to look at him, its black pupils widening slightly and then contracting. Joshua began to wonder if maybe this wasn't one of his nightmares, if this wasn't all part of something he was dreaming. Maybe when he woke up he'd just be back in his bed, and maybe his mother would be shaking him and telling him to stop yelling and his father would be laughing at him for a coward. He took one of his fingers, cracked and almost blue with the cold, between his teeth. He bit it so hard the tears came to his eyes. But he'd done that before in dreams and still he hadn't waked up. No matter how scared he was, he had to finish it out, right to the end.

He held the lightly moving pirogue in place with his paddle and waited for Henry, impatiently, humming a little tune under his breath—the one he'd heard his father singing:

"Mo parle Simon, Simon, Simon,
Li parle Ramon, Ramon, Ramon . . ."

and told himself that the cold in his stomach was the weather outside.

He noticed something different. He lifted his head, sniffing the air; it had stopped raining. The sky had not cleared or lifted, and the air was still so heavy you could feel it brushing your face. Everything was soaked through; the whole world was floating, drenched, on water. But for a little while there was not the sound of rain.

And he missed that sound. He felt lonesome without it, the way he always did in spring—suspended and floating. For there isn't any real spring here—just a couple of weeks of hesitation and indecision between the rainy winter and the long, dry summer. There are always more fights and knifings then.

Henry came running back, a shotgun in one hand and four or five shells in the other. "I done got it," he said.

"Don't you point that there thing at me," Joshua said, and jerked his head aside.

"Us can go now," Henry said. He laid the gun in the bottom of the boat and then quickly got in the bow and wrapped a narrow blanket around his shoulders and knees. "I feel better with that along, me."

Joshua shrugged. "It don't matter to me."

They paddled out, following the curve of Goose Bayou, grinning to themselves with the fine feel of the pirogue—the tight, delicate, nervous quiver of the wood shell, the feel of walking across the water the way a long-legged fly does.

A couple of hundred yards down Goose Bayou, they turned south, into a smaller bayou, which, for all anybody knew, had no name. It circled on the edge of a thick swamp, which nobody had bothered to name, either, though most people at one time or other had gone exploring in the tangle of old cypress and vines and water aspens and sudden bright hibiscus plants. Way back in the center somewhere, so that people hardly ever saw them, some cats lived—plain house cats gone wild and grown to almost the size of a panther, living up in the tangled branches of the trees, breeding there. Some nights you could hear their screaming—pleasure or maybe pain; you couldn't tell.

Nobody had ever had the courage to go right through the swamp. It wasn't all that big; people simply went around it. Except for one man, and that was an old story, maybe true, maybe not. Anyhow, it had been on to fifty years past. There'd been a white man with yellow hair, the story said, and he'd jumped ship out there in the river. He'd had a long swim in from the channel to the levee, but by the time he climbed up the muddy *batture*, he wasn't as tired as he should have been. Maybe he was hopped up on dope of some sort. Anyhow, when he came walking out of the river, just a little above Bon Secour, his clothes dripping and sticking to his body, his yellow hair all matted and hanging down over his face, there was a girl walking on the levee top. She stopped, watched him stumbling and slipping on the wet, slimy river mud, waved to the people she was with to wait a little, and went down to help him, making her way carefully through the tangle of aspens and hackberries, so that her dress wouldn't get torn.

It was torn clear off her, almost, when they found her half an hour later—those people she'd been walking with. They'd finally got tired waiting for her and gone down to see. They'd have killed him, white man or not, if they'd found him. For nearly two days, the men hunted for him while the women went ahead with the funeral. They trailed him at last to the small stretch of swamp, and then they stopped, because none of them wanted to go in there themselves and they couldn't ever have found him in there, in a stretch about four miles long and maybe a mile wide. They did look in the outer fringes —in the part they knew. They could see that he was heading right straight for the middle of the swamp. Nobody ever saw him again. Maybe he fought his way out, and went on like he intended to, though the way he went crashing around, he didn't seem to know where he was going. Or maybe he kept on living in there; it wouldn't have been hard. He had a knife; he'd killed the girl with it. Or maybe he just died, and the fish and the ants and the little animals cleaned his bones until they were left shining white and the shreds of his hair shining yellow.

Joshua and Henry paddled past the thick swamp and remembered the story, and listened for the screaming of the cats, but since it was daylight, they heard nothing.

"It good to get out, man," Joshua said.

Henry did not answer, but then nobody talked much in the swamps. People got suddenly embarrassed and shy of their words and spoke only in whispers when they said anything at all, because the swamp was like a person listening. The grasses and bushes and trees and water were like a person holding his breath, listening, and ready to laugh at whatever you said.

Joshua and Henry found the trotlines that Oscar Lavie had set out the day before across a little cove that the bayou made in the swampy island. Oscar had tied a red strip of handkerchief to the end of a vine to mark the place. Henry reached up and unknotted the cloth. "Man," he said, "this wet through." He squeezed the rag over the side of the pirogue.

"It been raining," Joshua said. He gave the pirogue a quick shove up among the cypress trees to the one the line was tied to. "Iffen you loose that, we see what all we got." A sudden swinging vine hit his cheek. He jumped slightly, then grinned.

They worked their way back across the little cove, checking each of the seven single lines. The first three were empty, the bait gone.

The next two held only the heads of catfish; the bodies were eaten away. "That plain must have been a gar," Henry said, and Joshua nodded.

They could tell by the drag of the lines that the last two were full. Joshua coaxed the lines slowly to the surface—two catfish with dripping whiskers, and gigs, sharp and pointed and set.

"Watch 'em," Josh said. "They slice you up good."

"You ain't gonna worry about me," Henry said. "You just bring 'em up where I can get at 'em." He picked up the steel-pointed gaff from the bottom of the boat and jabbed it through the whiskered bottom jaw of one of the fish. While Joshua steadied the boat, Henry held the fish until its convulsive movements had all but stopped.

When they had finished, Joshua coiled up the trotline and dropped it in the center of the boat with the fish. "Granddaddies, them, all right," he said.

Henry nodded, breathless from exertion.

Joshua turned the pirogue back out into the bayou and paddled rapidly. Soon they passed the swampy island and were in the salt marshes, miles of grasses rustling lightly and stretching off flat on both sides, with just a few *chênières*—shell ridges with dwarfed, twisted water oaks—scattered on the trembling, shifting surface.

"Man, it cold!" Joshua said. "Sure wish I had me a big old heavy coat."

"Look there," Henry said. From a *chênière* away to the left, four or five shapes pumped heavily up into the air.

"Too far away to do us no good."

"Leastways they still got some duck around."

"That a bunch of pintails," Joshua said.

"How you tell?"

"I just plain know, man. I just plain can tell, that all."

Henry was staring over where the indistinct shapes had faded into the low sky. "It mighty late for them to be around."

Joshua dug his paddle deeper in the water. The pirogue shuddered and shot ahead.

"You can't tell what they are from way over here," Henry said.

"I plain can."

Henry turned his head and studied him. "What the matter with you?"

"I hope to God that that there moccasin chew out you wagging tongue," Joshua said.

Henry jerked around; the pirogue swayed wildly. "Where a moccasin?"

"There." Joshua pointed to a long, dark form that was disappearing among the reeds and the Spanish-fern bushes. "And, man, you plain better stop jumping or you have us in this here water."

"I ain't liked snakes."

"You plain scared," Joshua said softly.

"Maybe we get in shooting range of some ducks," Henry said. Joshua snorted.

Henry said, "Wonder why they all afraid to come out. Ain't nothing out here."

After a moment, Joshua said, "I aim to have a look at where all the trouble was. I aim to keep on going till I can plain see the river." He had been afraid last night; and Henry had seen him. Now there was something he had to prove.

For a while, Henry was quiet. Then he said, "Man, I'm colding stiff. Let's go back."

"Ain't no use to yet," Josh said.

"I'm freezing up."

"Me, too," Josh said. "But there ain't no use to turn back yet."

They moved steadily south, in a twisting line through the narrow waterways, following the pattern of a curve that would bring them to the river, far down where it met the Gulf.

In about an hour, they were there, in a narrow passage of water sheltered by a curve of reeds from the full force of the river but where they could see into the broad stream and across to the faint, low line of grasses on the other side. Here the river was just a yellow-brown pass flowing between banks of sifting mud and reeds and tough, tangled bushes and twisted, dead trees brought down years ago and left far up out of the usual channel by the floodwaters.

The wind was high. The grasses all around bent with a small screaming sound. The water was swift and almost rough. The pirogue shuddered and bounced. They let their bodies move with it, balancing gently. "Watch that old alligator grass there," Henry said as the craft swung over near the tall reeds. "They plain cut you up like a knife."

Joshua turned the pirogue crosswise in the channel. Behind them, a pair of ducks rose, hung for a minute, and then began a quick climb up the strips of wind.

"God Almighty!" Henry said. "There more duck!"

Joshua stood up in the pirogue, following the sweep of their flight. They disappeared almost at once in the low sky. He sat down.

"You reckon we ever gonna get close enough for a shot?" Henry said.

Joshua did not answer. Out of the corner of his eye he had seen something—something blue-colored. And that was one color you did not see down here in the marsh, ever. There were browns and greens and yellows, but never blue—not even the sky in winter. Still, when he had stood up in the pirogue, so that he was taller than the surrounding reeds, and had followed the flight of the ducks, his eyes had passed over a bright blue. He stood up again, balancing himself gently in the moving boat, and let his eyes swing back—carefully, this time.

He found it. Down a way, on the other side of the stretch of reeds, right by the open stream of river. There must be a little shell mound there, he thought, a little solid ground, because bushes grew there, and there was one bare, twisted, dead chinaberry tree. The river was always throwing up little heaps like that and then in a couple of years lifting them away. His eyes found the spot of blue color again. "Look there," he said.

Henry got to his feet slowly, carefully. The wooden shell rocked and then steadied. Henry squinted along the line of the pointing finger. "Sweet Jesus God!" he whispered. "That a man there!"

They were still for a long time. The pirogue drifted over to one side of the channel and nudged gently against the reeds. They took hold of the tops of the grasses, steadying themselves. The water got too rough; they had to sit down quickly.

Joshua found a small channel opening through the grass. He pushed the pirogue through it until there was only a dozen yards or so of low oyster grass ahead of them. The river there was full of driftwood, turning and washing down with the slow force of a truck.

"We plain can't get around the other side," Joshua said.

"Ain't no need to get closer," Henry said.

"I plain wonder who he is."

They could see so clearly now: bright-blue pants and a leather jacket.

They were bent forward, staring. "He got yellow hair," Henry said. The water made a sucking sound against the hull, and he looked down at it with a quick, nervous movement. "Water sound like it talking, times," he said.

"I plain wonder who he is."

"Ain't been here long, that for sure," Henry said. "Ain't puffed up none."

"That right," Joshua said.

"Remember the way it was with the people after the hurricane? And they only out two days?" Henry's voice trailed off to a whisper.

"I remember," Joshua said.

The man had been washed up high into the tough grasses. He was lying face down. He would stay here until the spring floods lifted him away—if there was anything left then.

"He got his hands stuck out up over his head," Henry said. They could not see the hands, but the brown, leather-clad arms were lifted straight ahead and pointing into the tangle of hackberries.

"His fingers is hanging down so the fishes nibble on them," Joshua said, and felt his shoulders twitch.

"I done felt fish nibble on my fingers," Henry said.

"Not when you was dead."

They were quiet again. All around them, the sound of the miles of moving water was like breathing.

Suddenly, Henry remembered. "I bet I know who he is."

"Who?" Joshua did not turn his eyes.

"I bet he off that there submarine that got sunk out in the river."

"Maybe," Joshua said.

"Or maybe he off one of the ships that got sunk."

"It don't make no difference, none."

"It ain't no use to hang around here," Henry said, finally. "What we hanging around here for?"

Joshua did not answer. Henry turned and looked at him. Joshua was rubbing his chin slowly. "He got a mighty nice jacket there," he said.

"Ain't no use hanging around admiring a dead man's clothes, none."

"I might could like that jacket, me," Joshua said.

Henry stared back over his shoulder.

"You think I scared," Joshua said.

"No," Henry said. "I ain't thinking that."

"I ain't scared of going over there and getting that coat that I like," Joshua bragged.

Henry shook his head.

"Him there—he ain't gonna need it no more," Joshua said.

"You ain't gonna do that."

"You think I afraid. I reckon I just gonna do that."

"You plain could get killed going on that river side, with all the driftwood coming down."

"Ain't going on that side," Joshua said. "I gonna climb over from this here side."

"Iffen you ain't drown yourself," Henry said, "you gonna get cut to pieces by sword grass or get bit by one of them snakes we seen a little while ago."

"I ain't afraid," Joshua said.

He handed Henry the paddle. "You steady it now, man," he said. He got to his feet, and the pirogue did not even tremble with his movement. He took a firm grasp on the top of the toughest grasses and jumped over the side. The boat dipped heavily and the yellow, cold water splashed in.

"God Almighty," Henry said. "You like to upset us for sure."

Joshua fought his way through the twenty feet or so of matted oyster grass and waist-high water, until he reached the little shell mound. The water was shallower there; it came only a little above his ankles. He began to move slowly along through the tangle of bushes, working his way across to the river side. A heavy branch snapped away from his shoulders and clipped him in the face. He jerked his head back and clapped his hand to the cut spot.

"What that?" Henry called. "A snake ain't got you?"

"No," Joshua said. "I ain't afraid of no snakes when I sees something I want, me."

He could feel a quivering deep down inside himself. But he said aloud, "That just the cold, just the cold water, boy. I can just think how warm and fine it gonna be with a nice coat, me."

He took his hand away and looked at it. There was blood all over the palm. The branch must have cut his cheek deeply.

"It beginning to rain again," Henry called.

"I ain't afraid of no little rain," Joshua called back.

The ground under his feet must have been covered with moss, for it was slippery walking. He lost his balance once and almost fell. He felt the water splash cold up to his shoulders.

"That a gator got you?" Henry's voice was thin and ragged.

"I ain't afraid of no gators," Joshua called back. He had reached the man now. He bent down and touched the soft brown leather of the jacket. From the feel, he knew that it was buttoned across the chest. He'd have to turn the body over. He tugged at one shoulder, but the arms were caught somehow.

"You come help me," he told Henry, and, getting no answer, he looked around quickly. "Iffen you got any ideas of getting scared and running off, I just gonna peel you hide off."

He spread his legs and braced himself and pulled harder and harder. The body turned over stiffly, with a swish of water. Joshua did not look at the face. He stared at the two buttons, and then his cold fingers fumbled with them. They would not loosen.

"What you doing?" Henry called.

Joshua took out his knife, the one his father had given him, and cut off the buttons. One fell in the water. The other he caught between two fingers and dropped in his own pocket.

"Ain't you near got it?"

Joshua looked up and over at Henry when he pulled the jacket off.

"Come on," Henry said, and waved the paddle in the air.

Joshua, still without looking down, turned and worked his way back, dragging the jacket from one hand, in the water.

By the time they got home, it was almost dark and the rain was falling heavily. All the color had washed out of the country, leaving it gray and streaked and blurry, like the clouds overhead. The marshes off a little way looked just like the lower part of the sky.

Joshua picked up the fish with one hand, and with the other he tossed the jacket over his shoulder.

He could feel the leather pressing cold against his neck. It had a smell, too. He crinkled his nose. A slight smell, one you wouldn't notice unless you were taking particular notice of such things. Faint, but distinct, too—like the way the swamp smelled, because it had so many dead things in it.

There was a cold wind coming up with the night; you could hear its angry murmuring out in the marshes. Wet as he was, and shivering, Joshua stopped for just one moment and turned and looked back the way they had come, down Goose Bayou, across the gray grasses, and he blinked and shook his head, because he couldn't quite see clear. It had gotten that dark.

JOHN GRAVES *was born and grew up in Texas, where he graduated from Rice Institute, Houston. During the war he served as a Marine in the Pacific. After his return he attended graduate school at Columbia and taught English at the University of Texas. His stories have appeared in* The New Yorker, Esquire, Town & Country, *and others. His hobbies are fishing, sailing, and he plans to write a novel. At present he is living in Majorca.*

THE GREEN FLY

FROM TOWN & COUNTRY

In the one-room cottage he had rented at the rear, near the stream and the steep-rising green mountainside, Thomas Hilliard awoke each morning early, sometimes at six with the clean tolling of the bells in the village below, often before. An old man named Celestino brought fruit and rolls and coffee from the kitchen at the main house of the hacienda; and afterward, Hilliard would walk a few minutes along the stream, watching for fish, then would go back to work until noon at his typewriter.

In the thin, high foreign air, undistracted, his mind moved spider-like, weaving and linking with a precision that he had not really expected; the work went well. Though he had half agreed, laughing, when Wright Forsythe had told him that Mexico was a hell of a place to go to finish a dissertation in English literature, it nevertheless went smoothly and fast. Within a few days his existence at the hacienda had shaped itself into a life, a backwater life without conflict or crisis or betrayal, to last only until Wright and Deirdre drove down to join him later and to take him back northeastward, but a life, full enough.

There was the fishing. In the afternoons Hilliard fished, because for a man who prized trout it was beautiful fishing, the best he had known. It flavored that life indispensably, and when old Dr. Elizondo came, it was through the fishing that they met at the start, and the fishing gave their meeting its meaning. In the rich water of the rapids and pools, in the small dammed lake at the stream's end, before it plunged to the valley below and the river, the trout moved thick among broken walls and aqueducts and insignificant stone masses that had had use in the long-gone days. The Mexican families at the hacienda, clumsy with worming gear, took small fish by the basketful, but in the smooth water of the pool-heads the big rainbows lay haughty and selective. It needed a pretty fly on a long, fine leader, deftly cast from downstream, to hook them.

No other Americans came. Hilliard did not miss them. Within the formal limits of his acquaintance with them, he liked the pleasant, prosperous Mexicans vacationing in the other cottages and rooms. In the evenings by the fireplace in the big house they would talk, quietly and with their friendly foreign distantness, to one another and to Hilliard, enduring with grave humor his faulty Spanish and the incomprehensible fact that he spent half of each day flourishing a *caña* over the stream.

They came and went away and one evening in Hilliard's third week a new man appeared at dinner, graying and baldish, alone, with a strong Iberian nose and tawny well-shaped eyes that gazed, afterward in the sitting room, with remote gentleness into the fire while the others around him talked. Then the next day Hilliard, casting into white water where the stream debouched from a jumble of huge weathered building stones into a pool, glanced up to see him watching from the bank. In that moment the line twitched and Hilliard raised his rod tip against the tug of a stout fifteen-incher that thrashed up and down the pool before coming finally exhausted to the net.

"*Bien hecho,*" called the man on the bank.

Smiling, Hilliard wet his hand and held the fish up for a moment for the other to see before he shook the fly from its lip and dropped' it back into the water. For a moment, spent, it hung there and then with a drunken flirt of its body rode the current downward out of sight. Hilliard waded ashore.

"You released him," the man said, in the flat courteous Spanish manner that is neither statement nor question. In the sun he looked older, his face hollow, leathery old-man's wrinkles radiating from the corners of the alert, almost golden eyes. He was dressed to fish, in a tie and a rusty black coat and patched wading boots, and held a long, old-fashioned English fly rod with close-spaced silk windings. Before that battered old-world formality Hilliard, in khakis and glittering American equipment, suddenly felt shabby.

He said, "I let most of them go. What I care about is the fishing."

Nodding, the old man smiled. "They're noble fish. Permit me. I am Juan Elizondo."

Hilliard took the old, slim hand and then, with the ease of strangers who share enthusiasm, they talked for a while. The doctor—he said he was a doctor, and fished little nowadays—asked politely, in measured Castilian, about the personality of the stream and its trout. Of specific spots and lures he said nothing and Hilliard, watching him finally trudge off downstream, the long rod bobbing, comprehended the painstaking pleasure he would find in learning those things for himself.

And from that meeting—because, as the doctor remarked later, no one else at the hacienda was insane enough to possess an *afición* for angling—a mannered, mild comradeship sprang up between them. On the stream they met often to smoke and talk, nearly always of fish, and in the evenings by the fire. They traded flies, the doctor tied his own, European patterns strange to Hilliard, which he whipped together deftly and with care. "*Esta,*" he would say with love, holding up a gaudy tuft of tinsel and peacock herl. "This one. She did much killing on the Gallego. My colleague, Aguirre, used to call her the Green Traitor."

That sufficient basis for friendship widened itself without effort on Hilliard's part. From the voluminous morning gossip of old Celestino he learned that the doctor was Spanish, a Republican *refugiado*; it explained the coolness, the distance apparent between him and the upper-class Mexican guests. Having listened well in good places, Celestino knew also that the doctor had once been a surgeon very noted, Señor, but now, with exile and political discredit, was lucky to have work in the medical office of a tile factory, in Puebla. Devoutly religious, the old servant found pleasure in the fact that the doctor was poor, and that his wife and daughter in Madrid, *franquistas*, did not write him, not a word. . . .

Hilliard said curtly that morning, ashamed to have listened, "All this is none of my business, or the señora's, or yours."

Celestino, making the bed, patted a pillow. "*Pos, quizá,*" he said equably. "Maybe. But the suitcases of this doctor, how barbarous. You should see."

Talking to the doctor himself, Hilliard had other glimpses of a past that had been clearly busy, full of high accomplishment. Vienna-trained, he had traveled through all Europe, and had fished most of it. "The medicine and the sport were companions," he said, smiling. "Sweethearts. With the scalpel, the rod."

That with their association the other guests' coolness toward the doctor came also to envelop him did not disturb Hilliard. He understood it, so well that when the señora, the unworldly patrician widow who owned and operated the hacienda, approached him about it he nearly avoided anger, nearly but not quite. He liked the señora. She stopped him in her office, a tiny room baroque with the sculptured furnishings of Diaz' day—at the hacienda they were all *porfiristas*, forty years out of date—and when he grasped what she was saying he flared at her with a quickness that brought terror to her diffident, velvet-wrinkled face. She was trying, unskillfully, to draw him out about the doctor—no, Señor, he had done nothing, but she felt . . .

Hilliard said, "Then why did you let him come here, Señora?"

Her shy hands writhed against the black silk of her skirt. "Don't mistake me, Señor 'Illiard. He was sent by a friend in the capital. A cousin, but with acquaintances most strange . . ."

Hilliard, opening the office's carved door, said with finality, "Pos. He is more *caballero* than anyone I've seen here. They won't suffer."

"I meant only . . . you're American. You can't know."

"Yes, I can," Hilliard said. He had seen fights between Spaniards in Mexico City cafés and, though they were not his people and it was not his fight, had felt the acrid, hating pain still knife-sharp after a dozen years. As much as one could understand others' hatreds he thought he understood, as he understood also the señora's sequestered fearfulness, but when it touched the doctor it made him somehow furious. "*Con permiso, Señora,*" he said, and as he went through the door she answered with the automatic, "*Pase usted.*"

It aligned Hilliard. The doctor had begun—when, he did not notice—to call him by the familiar *tu*, like a son. They ate together now in the dining room, at a corner table, and he knew, without always being able to say how, a great deal more about the old man.

The Forsythes had been good friends to him. Wright Forsythe, seven years older than Hilliard, was one of the young emergents of the university's faculty, and it had been important that someone like that should have taken keen interest in him—almost as important as that a warm and graceful woman like Deirdre Forsythe had made him welcome always in her home. They were intelligent and balanced each other in a life built around the quiet, unexuberant luxury of inherited money, and they had treated Hilliard as a younger brother.

And yet, he had never thought of them apart from the university and its town, so that into that hypnotically pleasant regularity of work and fishing and friendship with the old doctor, the letter that came finally from the Forsythes, already in Mexico City, arrived as a mild shock, as though he had forgotten them—almost, he had. The letter came on a Wednesday, ten days before the doctor was to leave, and when he had read it Hilliard sent off a wire by the hacienda's rickety telephone, telling them to drive up immediately. At lunch he told the doctor. "I'm content to hear it," the old man said in his courtly Castilian.

"You'll like them," Hilliard said.

"I'm certain. And for a change you'll have some compatriots."

It was somehow an odd thought. "Yes. I will, won't I?"

That Wednesday became entirely remarkable when in the afternoon the doctor, as a sort of climax to his vacation, took his seven-and-three-quarter-pound trout, stalked it laboriously in the spot where he had first seen it weeks before, teased it to his gaudy peacock fly, and played it with a half-century's skill on the delicate old rod before dipping it at last from the water. He quit fishing then, and came almost running up the streamside path to where Hilliard was wading, his reserve shattered by tremendous pleasure. "He is handsome, no?" he demanded, holding the big trout across his palms, its living iridescence not yet dulled. "He is noble?"

"Beautiful," Hilliard agreed, as happy about it as the old man was, for he knew what it meant and would mean to him. When they had weighed it on the doctor's old brass scale, he wanted badly to offer to have it taken to the city, for mounting, but he did not. It was not the kind of thing one could offer the doctor, not conceivably, and when they carried the fish to the big charcoal-pungent kitchen of the hacienda, the fat head cook, Felix, bellowed in unaffected astonishment.

And that night, at dinner, when Felix had brought the trout in on a plank, with ceremony, its smoky pink flesh perfectly baked, and had offered it around at the tables, even the wary Mexican bankers and lawyers smiled to the doctor and raised their glasses in congratulation. He was quietly triumphant. In the trout's honor, Hilliard ordered a bottle of wine and afterward, instead of his usual one, the doctor smoked two thin, dark cigars. "An insanity, to excite oneself

.over the murder of a fish," he said. "But he was big, no? On the plank. I wish your friends had arrived for him."

Hilliard grinned. "They aren't fishermen. The small ones will be good enough."

"People of intelligence," the doctor said. "Common-sense Americans, not like you. *Caray*, what a fish."

Nor were they like Hilliard, the Forsythes. He felt it more strongly than he ever had after lunch the next day, when they emerged from their car into the quiet air of the old courtyard like a robust, alien breeze—handsome, blonde people, congenitally crisp and Northern. It was good to see them. On the long, tiled gallery of the big house, when he had introduced them to the señora and they had seen their rooms, the three of them talked.

"You look healthy," Wright Forsythe said. "Unscholarly as hell."

Hilliard answered, "I've worked. I've gotten a lot done."

"I wouldn't," Deirdre said, gazing from a huge leather chair out across the stone-walled court where a gnarled ahuehuete tree clung to dry life and two brown children scrambled obscurely in the dust. Her small, sandaled feet rested on the veranda's railing; after the decorous Mexican ladies the pose seemed odd to Hilliard, but like everything he had even seen her do it looked also fitting. She sighed, making a face. "Work? Not here. How did you ever find it?"

"Divination," Hilliard said. "And you'd better reserve judgment for a while. For one thing, the plumbing's haunted."

Wright wore a checked gingham shirt and flannels and looked inevitably like a scholar. He grinned, poking with a twig at his pipe bowl which he held three inches before his face because he was not wearing his glasses. "We had a year of Venetian *pensiones*, after the war. What gets me is how you've stood it."

Hilliard said that it had not been a matter of standing anything; there were people and fishing.

"Fishing," Wright said, grimacing. "You wrote about it. I did bring a pole, for trolling if they've got a lake."

"They have," Hilliard said, with a smile because Wright, who knew the nomenclature of everything, had said "pole" with deliberate amateurism, to bait him. Nor did he say anything about the trolling which, being a fly-fisherman, he disliked; he had found long before that the ritual of angling, like most rituals, was not logically defensible. "I know a Spaniard here," he said. "You'll like him."

"I might, if he speaks English."

"He doesn't," Hilliard said. "Or very little. He's a refugee."

Wright lifted an eyebrow humorously. "A kumrad."

Hilliard said, "No. I don't think so. It wouldn't make much difference. He's a doctor."

"Doctor, schmoctor," Wright said idly. "It always makes a difference." He regarded a buzzard, wheeling above the ahuehuete in the domed mountain sky. "Read anything decent in between fish?"

"Not yet, please," his wife said. "It's too nice here. Let's just talk awhile about things that aren't printed on paper."

"As though anything worth talking about," Wright said, smiling, "hadn't been printed on paper."

The doctor smiled warmly in the dining room that night, bowing to Deirdre. His English was labored. "How do you do. It is good."

"It is good, indeed," said Wright in tweeds, with grave irony as to an Indian chieftain.

Hilliard said, "I spoke to Felix. We're all to sit together."

Comprehending, the doctor touched his arm. "With permission," he said in Spanish. "I'd rather . . . you with the friends alone." Nor would he reconsider, making the gentle semicircular gesture with an outward palm which is polite, firm refusal. "You have enough to say," he said. "For knowing one another there is time later."

Wright grinned after him, and glanced at Hilliard. "Exclusive?"

"It's not that. He didn't want to be in the way."

"He's fine, Tom," Deirdre said. "Like someone from a long, long time ago."

"So long ago," Wright said, "that it might not count. He looks like the emperor Vespasian, on a coin. Maybe with a hammer and sickle on the obverse. And let's sit down."

Quite simply it did not work. The chemistry was wrong. After dinner, by the fire, for the first time since Hilliard had met him the doctor seemed awkward, not self-possessed. He sat for a time listening, politely uncomprehending, to their conversation in English, and once he and Wright exchanged a few remarks in French, but it had no warmth. Hilliard knew that it was not going to work, and when finally, earlier than usual, the doctor had gone upstairs, Wright chuckled. "With all respect, I'm afraid your old revolutionary's something of a dud, Tom. Or maybe," they had talked of the doctor's big trout, "he's still dazed from wrestling that seven-pound whale."

Deirdre said, "He's only shy."

Hilliard, flipping a chip of eucalyptus at the fire, did not want to discuss the doctor. He said, "He's not shy; just hard to know, I guess. He's all right."

"*De gustibus*," Wright said.

Hilliard grinned, wryly. He had tried before in his life, and failed, to bring people together when the chemistry was bad. "*De gustibus*," he repeated.

So he did not try to mix them again. On the two afternoons of the following week when Hilliard was not wrangling over his dissertation with Wright, who liked it, or wandering with the warm, unbookish Deirdre around the neighborhood, gossiping about Mexico and the university town they lived in, he went to the stream to fish and the doctor was the same, gentle and friendly and glad to stop fishing and talk awhile on the soft, drooping grasses of the bank. He asked courteously after the Forsythes but avoided them, either going to his room in the evenings early or reading alone in a corner of the great sitting room.

The señora, approving of the Forsythes, grew friendly again. Wright developed mild dyspepsia from the seasoning so that his food had to be cooked separately; and Deirdre tumbled harmlessly from a burro on a trip to the Toltec pyramid around the mountain, where the conquistadors had built a chapel; and Hilliard's work began to take final shape. Then, abruptly, one day it was Saturday. The next day Dr. Elizondo was to leave, to go back to his factory and whatever existence was there.

Hilliard felt relief when Wright, who had wandered along with them to the stream, grew restless and said that he was going to try fishing from the battered canoe in the lake. "Leave a few," Hilliard said as Wright set off.

"I intend," answered Wright over his shoulder, "to wipe your puristical eye. Trolling."

"What says the friend?" the doctor asked, smiling up from a knot in his leader. Hilliard translated, and the old man laughed. He was in a good humor, buoyant, as though the imminence of his departure made the day not worse but better. "Some troll," he said. "Some pull nets like San Pedro, but you and I, we fish with reeds and spider threads. *Pos*, who is crazy?"

They fished together, watching one another cast into the alternating stair-step pools. Unmuddied by recent rain, the stream was clear and full and the fish fed well, with just sufficient caution to compel stealth. They talked much, resting frequently, and before it was at last time to stop they had between them caught and freed nineteen heavy, healthy trout, one within a pound of the doctor's record. Never, the old man said as they walked in the almost-dusk back toward the hacienda, not anywhere had he known fishing like that of this stream.

"Not even on the Gallego?" Hilliard said, slyly because the doctor had always kept special reverence for the Pyrenean rivers.

The doctor grunted humorously. "*Bueno*, not even there. No." It had been an afternoon good enough to make trivial its finality, its quality of farewell.

Nearly among the first cottages, Wright's voice called to them from ahead, and they saw his white shirt luminous against the black-green of the stream's deep glen. His wife stood behind him, and when they approached Hilliard saw that his hand was wrapped in a handkerchief. He said to Hilliard, with a slight wryness of pain, "The trout rodeo's over. I need your friend."

Deirdre held a heavy bass-stringer festooned with small dead trout. She said, "The fish weren't big enough. He decided to catch himself."

"What a comic," Wright said, taking the handkerchief away. Pendant from the flesh web between his thumb and forefinger, one point of its coarse treble hook imbedded above the barb, dangled a heavy red-and-white trolling spoon.

Carefully the doctor leaned his fly rod against a bush, and taking the hand, examined it. He looked up into Wright's face and smiled, touching with his finger a small white scar on the back of his own left hand and another on his cheek, near his eye. To Hilliard in Spanish he said, "The mark of the angler."

"It's nice everybody gets such a boot out of this," Wright said.

"All right," said Deirdre. "Who stuck that in you?"

The doctor had brought from his pocket a pair of long-nosed pliers that Hilliard had seen him use as hook disgorgers with the trout. "To pull it now will relieve him sooner," he said. "This serves as well as any instrument I have."

"Yes," Hilliard said from personal suffering with hooks, and then without hesitation, moving surely, the doctor grasped Wright's wrist in his left hand, seized the hook at its bend, and in one strong pull drew it free.

Wright, who had not expected it, wrenched his hand away and glared furiously at the doctor. He said, "Good Jesus Christ!"

The doctor smiled uncertainly at Hilliard. "Tell him . . . there had to be pain. At the hacienda we will clean it."

Watching Wright, Hilliard said, "Take it easy. You have to pull hooks that way. Or push them through and cut them."

His friend, pale, did not answer. No one spoke as they ascended the hill to the main house, and Wright said nothing until the three of them stood waiting in the courtyard while the doctor went to his room for bandages. Then, whimsically, he looked at Hilliard. "You said he was a bone specialist?"

"I think so," Hilliard said shortly.

"T-bones," Wright said. "He's a pure butcher, that boy."

Silently, Hilliard dismantled his fly rod and when the doctor returned he cleansed the wound of its black, crusted blood, bandaged it, then glanced up at Wright, who had not winced, with a slight quirk of his mouth. "Thus," he said in Spanish.

"Good as new," Wright said. "Barring gangrene."

Hilliard said to the old man's interrogative face, "The friend thanks you."

The doctor nodded politely and for a moment, on the ancient weed-tufted paving stones, they stood awkward, without speaking. There was nothing to say until Wright, twisting to reach his hip with his left hand, brought out a wallet. Hilliard saw suddenly that he was very angry.

His wife said, "Wright."

The doctor looked at the billfold and at the sheaf of money which Wright's finger had brought half into view. Hilliard said sharply, "Put that away."

The corners of Wright's mouth turned downward in stubborn amusement. "I pay my way," he said. "Ask him how much."

Even as Hilliard spoke, he felt the hurt shock in Deirdre's eyes swinging to his face. He knew that it was the end of something. "You bastard," he said clearly to Wright. "You complete bastard."

Staring back, Wright was not grinning now, but after a long moment he lowered his eyes, slipped the wallet into his side pocket, and stood looking away, strumming his thumb against the inside of the fingers of his left hand in an odd gesture Hilliard had seen him use in classrooms. To the doctor finally, who watched with stoic perception, Hilliard spoke quietly: "There was a fault of comprehension. The friend . . ."

"I am sure," the doctor said.

But this time, for once, the courtesy was language only. It was not in his tone, nor in the tawny eyes that turned from Wright Forsythe to Hilliard now, and to the pretty young woman at his side, flicking them. In the eyes was the end of something else: a rebuff of sympathy and of friendship, ancient pride that had stood long years alone and would stand again alone for the years that might remain. There was no anger. The doctor picked up his rod from against the old ahuehuete, then bowed slightly, a bow that held not politeness but condescension.

"With your permission." It was the formal pronoun.

"Pass," Hilliard answered mechanically.

Without glancing again toward him the doctor turned, and the three Americans stood silently watching as he walked away toward his room and the meager packing he had to do, the delicate, long, antiquated rod in his hand waving up and down with the slow rhythm of his old-man's stride.

J. F. POWERS *was first represented in* The O. Henry Awards *in 1944 with* "Lions, Harts, Leaping Does," *which was also the title of his first collection of short stories. A second,* Prince of Darkness, *followed. His work has appeared often in magazines such as* Accent, The Commonweal, The New Yorker. *A recipient of an Iowa-Rockefeller Writers' Fellowship, he is currently at work on a novel which will be published by Doubleday & Co., Inc.*

THE PRESENCE OF GRACE

FROM ACCENT

On a fine Sunday morning in June, Father Fabre opened the announcement book to familiarize himself with the names of the deceased in the parish for whom Masses would be offered in the coming week, and came upon a letter from the chancery office. The letter, dated December, dealt with the Legion of Decency pledge which should have been administered to the people at that time. Evidently Father Fabre was supposed to read it at the nine-thirty and eleven o'clock Masses that morning. He went to look for the pastor.

Father Fabre, ordained not quite a year, had his hands full at Trinity. It wasn't a well-run parish. The pastor was a hard man to interest in a problem. They saw each other at meals. Father Fabre had been inside the pastor's bedroom, the seat of all his inactivity, only once; Miss Burke, the housekeeper, never. The press of things was very great in the pastor's room, statues, candlesticks, cases of sacramental wine, bales of pious literature and outdated collection envelopes, two stray pews and a prie-dieu, the implements and furniture of his calling. There was a large table-model radio in his bed, and he obviously slept and made the bed around it. That was about it.

Father Fabre found the pastor in the dining room. "Little late for this, isn't it?" he said. He held out the letter which had wintered in the pastor's room.

"Don't watch me eat," said the pastor, a greying dormouse. He had had the six-thirty and eight o'clocks, and was breaking his fast —not very well, Father Fabre thought, still trying to see what was in the bowl. Shredded wheat *and* oatmeal? Something he'd made himself? Not necessarily. Miss Burke could make dishes like that.

The pastor shifted into a sidesaddle position, bending one of his narrow shoulders over the bowl, obstructing the curate's view.

Father Fabre considered the letter in his hand. . . . *immoral motion pictures / demoralizing television / indecent plays / vulgar radio programs / pernicious books / vicious papers and periodicals / degrading dance halls / and unwholesome taverns* . . . Was this the mind, the tongue of the Church? "Little late for this, isn't it?"

"No."

"I thought we were supposed to give it a long time ago." On the Sunday within the Octave of the Immaculate Conception, in fact. On that day, Trinity, pledgeless, had been unique among the churches of the diocese—so he'd bragged to friends, curates who were unhappy about the pledge, as he was, and he hadn't really blamed them for what they'd said out of envy, that it had been his duty to repair the omission at his Masses. "Weren't we?"

"No."

"No?"

The dormouse shook his head a half inch. The spoon in his right hand was a precision instrument, scraping up the last of whatever had filled the bowl. Grain.

"I don't feel right about this," Father Fabre said, going away with the letter. He went to the sacristy to vest for the nine-thirty, talking to himself. It *was* a little late for the pledge. No. The Sunday within the Octave *had* been the day for it. No.

The white fiddleback chasuble he was putting on had been spoiled on Christmas. He'd been vesting, as now, when the pastor, writing out a Mass card for a parishioner, had flicked his pen at the floor to get the ink flowing. Father Fabre had called his attention to the ink spots on the chasuble. "S'not ink," he'd said. Asked what it was, he'd said, "S'not ink," and that was all he'd say. For a time, after that, Father Fabre wondered if the pastor's pen could contain some new kind of writing fluid—not ink—and thought perhaps the spots would disappear. The spots, the *s'not ink* spots, were still there. But a recent incident seemed to explain the pastor's odd denials. "Not a ball point, is it?" he'd said to Father Fabre who was about to fill his fountain pen from the big bottle in the office. "No, Father," said

Father Fabre, presenting his pen for inspection. "Takes ink," said the pastor. "*Yes*, Father." The pastor pointed to the big bottle from which Father Fabre customarily filled his pen, and said, "Why don't you try that?" "Say, that's an idea," said Father Fabre, going the pastor one better. "Better go and flush your pen with water first," said the pastor. And the funny part was that Father Fabre had gone and flushed his pen, before filling it from the big bottle that time. "I think you'll like *that*," said the pastor. *That* was *Quink*. The dormouse had the casuist's gift, and more.

He escaped much of man's fate. Instead of arguing his way out of a jam, or confessing himself in error, the pastor simply denied everything. It was simple—as simple as when he, as priest, changed the bread and wine into the body and blood of Christ. But he had no power from his priesthood to deny the undeniable, for instance that he'd spoiled a good chasuble. When he said "S'not ink," nothing was changed. He could really slow you up, though, if you were inclined to disagree with him and to be rational about it.

When the pastor entered the sacristy before the nine-thirty, Father Fabre was ready for him. "Father," he said, "I can't give this pledge in conscience—not as it's given in some parishes. I can't ask the people to rise as a body and raise their right hands, to repeat after me words which many of them either don't understand the full meaning of, or don't mean to abide by. I don't see anything *wrong* with giving it to those who mean to keep it." He'd wrangled against the pledge in the seminary. If it was "not an oath," as some maintained, wasn't it administered by a priest in church, and didn't it cheapen the clergy to participate in such a ceremony, and one which many merely paid lip service to? Didn't the chancery use the word "invite" and wasn't "demand" the word for the way the thing was rammed through in some parishes? Couldn't outsiders, with some justice, call the whole procedure totalitarian? What *did* Rome think of it? Wasn't it a concession to the rather *different* tone in America, a pacifier?

But the pastor had gone, saying, "Just so you give it."

Father Fabre got behind his servers and started them moving toward the altar. He saw the pastor in front of a battery of vigil lights, picking up the burned matches. Parishioners who had used them would be surprised to know that the pastor blew out all the lights after the last Mass. "Fire hazard," he'd said, caught in the act.

Before the eleven o'clock, after resting a few minutes between Masses in his room, he went to the bathroom and called down the laundry chute to Miss Burke in the kitchen. "Don't set a place for me. I'm invited out for dinner." He stood ready at the chute to cut her off but heard only a sigh and something about the pastor having said the same thing. He hadn't expected to get away with it so easily. They were having another critical period, and it was necessary, as before, to stand up to her. "I hope I let you know soon enough," he said. She should be happy, with them both gone. She wouldn't have to cook at all. And he was doing her the honor of pretending that she planned their meals ahead.

"Father!"

"Yes, Miss Burke."

"Is it Mrs. Mathers' you're going to?"

He delayed his reply in the hope that she'd see the impertinence of the question, and when this should have been accomplished, he said, "I hope I let you know in time."

He heard the little door slam at the other end of the chute. Then, as always in time of stress, she was speaking intimately to friendly spirits who, of course, weren't there, and then wailing like the wind. "Sure she was puttin' it around she'd have him over! But we none of us"—by which Father Fabre assumed she meant the Altar and Rosary Society—"thought he'd go *there!* Oh, Lord!"

He'd lost the first fall to the pastor, but he'd thrown Miss Burke.

Going downstairs, he heard the coin machines start up in the pastor's room, the tambourines of the separator, the castanets of the counter. The pastor was getting an early start on the day's collections. He wore a green visor in his room and worked under fluorescent tubes. Sometimes he worked a night shift. It was like a war plant, his room, except that no help was wanted. The pastor lived to himself, in a half-light.

In the hallway downstairs, John, the janitor, sitting in the umbrella chair, was having coffee. The chair had a looking-glass back, and when John turned his head he appeared to have two faces.

"Thought you had the day off," said Father Fabre.

"Always plenty to do around here, Father."

"I suppose." They knew each other well enough now for John not to get off that old one about wanting to spend the day with his family.

"She's really rarin' in there," John said. "I had to come out here." He glanced down at the floor, at the cup of muddy water cooling there, and then fearfully in the direction of the kitchen. This did not impress Father Fabre, however, who believed that the janitor and the housekeeper lived in peace. "Not her responsibility," John said.

Father Fabre, knowing he was being tempted, would not discuss the housekeeper with the janitor. Curates came and went, and even pastors, but the janitor, a subtle Slav, stayed on at Trinity.

"I told her it was none of her business."

"*What* isn't?"

"If you want to go there, that's your business," John said. "I had to come out here." John reached down for his cup, without looking, because his hand knew right where it was. "I don't blame you for being sore at her, Father." ("I'm not," Father Fabre murmured, but John, drinking, smiled into his cup.) "I told her it's your business what you do. 'He's old enough,' I said."

"What's she got against Mrs. Mathers?" Father Fabre asked, wondering if Mrs. Mathers was any match for the housekeeper. A natural leader vs. a mental case. It might be close if the Altar and Rosary Society took sides. But the chances were that Miss Burke would soon be fighting on another front. Impossible for her to wage as many wars as she declared.

"Hell, you know how these old maids are, Father," John was saying. "Just needs a man. *You* can understand that."

Father Fabre, calling it a draw with John, turned away and left.

The other guests at Mrs. Mathers' didn't act like Catholics. Mr. Pint, a small man in his sixties, was surprisingly unfriendly, and his daughter, though rather the opposite, went at Father Fabre the wrong way. It might have been the absence of excess respect in her manner that he found unsettling. But Mrs. Mathers, a large motherly but childless widow with puffy elbows, had baked a cake, and was easy to take.

They were all on the back porch of her second-floor flat, watching Mr. Pint make ice cream.

"Let me taste it, Dad," Velma said.

"I can't be standin' here all day with this cream gettin' soft on me," Mr. Pint said.

Velma pouted. She had on a purple dress which reminded Father Fabre of the purple veils they'd had on the statues in church during Passiontide. Otherwise there was nothing lenten about Velma, he thought.

"If you taste it now," he said, "it'll just take that much longer to harden."

Mr. Pint, who might have agreed with that, said nothing. He dropped a handful of rock salt into the freezer, a wood-and-iron affair that must have been as old as he was, and sank again to his knees. He resumed cranking.

Father Fabre smiled at Mrs. Mathers. Parishioners expected a priest to be nice and jolly, and that was how he meant to be at Mrs. Mathers'. With Mr. Pint setting the tone, it might not be easy. Father Fabre hadn't expected to be the second most important person there. The cake, he believed, had not been baked for him.

"Your good suit," said Mrs. Mathers. She snatched a *Better Homes and Gardens* from a pile of such magazines and slid it under Mr. Pint's knees.

"Sir Walter Reilly," said Velma, looking at Father Fabre to see if he followed her.

He nodded, doubting her intelligence, wondering if she was bright enough to be a nurse. Mrs. Mathers was a registered nurse.

"Aw, come on," Velma said. "Let me taste it, Dad."

Mr. Pint churned up a chunk of ice and batted it down with the heel of his hand. "By Dad!" he breathed, a little god invoking himself.

Mrs. Mathers wisely retired to the kitchen. Velma, after a moment, ingloriously followed.

Father Fabre gazed over the porch railing. With all the apartment buildings backed up together, it was like a crowded harbor, but with no sign of life—a port of plague. Miss Burke, he remembered, had warned him not to go. John, however, had said go. Mr. Pint's shirt had broken out in patches of deeper blue, and his elastic suspenders, of soft canary hue, were stained a little. Pity moved Father Fabre to offer the helping hand, prudence stayed it, then pity rose again. "Let me take it awhile," he said quietly.

But Mr. Pint, out to deny his size and years, needed no help, or lost in his exertions, had not heard.

Father Fabre went inside where he found the women, by contrast, laughing and gay. Velma left off tossing the salad, and Mrs. Mathers' stirring spoon hung expectantly in mid-air. "I'm afraid I wasn't much help out there," he said.

"That's just Dad's way," Mrs. Mathers said. "Come in here a minute, Father, if you want to see something nice."

Mrs. Mathers led him into a little room off the kitchen. She wanted him to see her new day bed. He felt the springs as she had and praised the bed in her terms. He meant it when he said he wished he had one, and sat down on it. Mrs. Mathers left the room, and returned a moment later whispering that she believed in flushing the toilet before she made coffee. That was the quickest way to bring fresh water into the house. Father Fabre, rising from the day bed, regretted that he wouldn't be able to pass this household hint on to Miss Burke.

Then, leaving the room, they met Mr. Pint, all salt and sweat, coming in from the back porch. He came among them as one from years at sea, scornful of soft living, suspicious of the women-folk and young stay-at-home males.

The women followed Mr. Pint, and Father Fabre followed the women, into the dining room.

"You're a sight," said Velma.

"Your good blue shirt," said Mrs. Mathers. She went down the hall after Mr. Pint.

"We're going to eat in a minute," Velma said to Father Fabre. "You want to wash or anything?"

"No, thanks," he said. "I never wash."

He had tried to be funny, but Velma seemed ready to believe him. Mrs. Mathers, looking upset, entered the dining room.

"Should I take off her plate?" Velma asked.

"Leave it on in case she does come," Mrs. Mathers said. "Father, you know Grace."

"No, I don't think so."

"Grace Halloran. She's in the Society."

"Of course." Of course he knew Grace, a maiden lady. He saw her almost daily, a shadow moving around the sanctuary, dusting the altar rail and filling vases with flowers—paid for by herself, the pastor said. Her brother was a big builder of highways. She wasn't the kind to use her means and position, however, to fraternize with the clergy. "Maybe she's just late," he said, rather hoping she wouldn't make it. The present company was difficult enough to assimilate.

Mr. Pint appeared among them again, now wearing a white shirt. Had he brought an extra? Or had Mrs. Mathers given him one which had belonged to her late husband? Father Fabre decided it would be unwise to ask.

They sat down to eat. It was like dining in a convent, with Velma in the role of the nun assigned to him, plying him with food. "Pickles?" He took one and passed the dish to Mr. Pint.

"He can't eat 'em," Velma said.

"That's too bad," said Father Fabre.

Mrs. Mathers, brooding, said: "I can't understand Grace, though heaven knows she can be difficult sometimes."

"If she'd only come," said Velma.

"Yes," said Father Fabre.

"Vel had to work last Sunday and didn't get a chance to meet her," said Mrs. Mathers.

"That's too bad," said Father Fabre.

"Grace was my best friend," Mrs. Mathers said. "In the Society, I mean."

Father Fabre frowned. *Was?*

"I was dying to meet her," said Velma, looking at Father Fabre.

"Very nice person," he said.

"I just can't understand it," declared Mrs. Mathers, without conviction. Then: "It's no surprise to me! You soon find out who your friends are!"

Father Fabre applied his fingers to the fried chicken. "Well," he said. "She doesn't know what she's missing." Grace's plate, however, seemed to reject the statement. "Did she know I was coming?"

"Oh, indeed, she did, Father! That's what makes me so blamed mad!"

Velma went to answer the telephone. "Yoo-hoo! It's for you-hoo!" she called.

"She means you," Mrs. Mathers said to Father Fabre, who wondered how she could have known.

He went to the bedroom, where Mrs. Mathers, never knowing when she'd be called for special duty, had her telephone. When he said "Hello" there was a click and then nothing. "Funny," he said, returning to the table. "Nobody there."

"Vel," Mrs. Mathers asked, "was *that* Grace?"

"She didn't say, Mildred. Wouldn't she say who she was if she was Grace?"

"It was Grace," said Mrs. Mathers quietly. She looked unwell.

There was a rattle of silverware. "Eat your dinner, Mildred," said Mr. Pint, and she did.

After dinner, they retired to the living room. Soon, with Mrs. Mathers and Mr. Pint yawning on the sofa, Velma said, "I met some Catholic priests that were married, once." She had taken the chair near Father Fabre's. They were using the same ash tray.

"Were they Greek or Russian?"

She seemed to think he was joking. "They were with their wives, two of them—I mean they were two couples—but they said the ones that weren't married could have dates with girls if they wanted to."

He nodded. "It's only been observed among us since the eleventh century—celibacy." Velma looked doubtful. "It may be overrated," he added, smiling.

"I never tried it," Velma said.

"Yes, well . . . in some parts of the world, even now, there are married Catholic priests."

"That's what these were," Velma said.

"Maybe they were *Old* Catholics," he said.

"No, they weren't, not at all."

He looked across the room at the couple on the sofa. Mr. Pint appeared to be asleep, but Mrs. Mathers was trying to fight it with a *Good Housekeeping*. "That's a sect," he said, getting back to Velma. "They go by that name. Old Catholics."

"I wouldn't say they were that," she said.

He was ready to drop it.

"I met them in Chicago," she said.

"I understand Old Catholics are strong there," he said. "Comparatively."

There was a lull during which Velma loaded her cigarette case and Father Fabre surveyed the room—the bookcase with no books in it, only plants and bric-a-brac, and the overstuffed furniture rising like bread beneath the slipcovers, which rivaled nature in the tropics for color and variety of growing things, and the upright piano with the mandolin and two photographs on top: one would be the late Mr. Mathers and somewhere in the other, a group picture of graduating nurses, would be the girl he had married, now stout, being now what she had always been becoming. Mrs. Mathers was openly napping now. The room was filled with breathing, hers and Mr. Pint's in unison, and the sun fell upon them all and upon the trembling ferns.

"Mildred says you can't have dates."

Father Fabre looked Velma right in the eye. "That's right." He'd drifted long enough. He'd left the conversation up to her from the beginning, and where had it got him? "I take it you're not a Catholic."

"Oh, no," she said, "but I see all your movies."

"I beg your pardon."

"I liked *The Miracle of the Bells* the best. But they're all swell."
He felt himself drifting again.

"I enjoyed reading *The Cardinal*," she said.
So had he. He wondered if a start could be made there.

Mrs. Mathers, whom he'd thought asleep, said, "Why don't you
tell Father what you told me, Vel?"

"Mildred!" cried Velma.

Father Fabre blushed, thinking Velma must have remarked favor-
ably on his appearance.

"About the church of your choice," said Mrs. Mathers.

"Oh, that. I told Mildred *The Miracle of the Bells* made me want
to be a Catholic."

Mr. Pint came to and mumbled something.

Father Fabre decided to face up to him. "Do you like to go to the
movies, Mr. Pint?"

"No, sir." Mr. Pint was not looking Father Fabre in the eye, but
it was as though he didn't think it necessary—yet.

"Why, Dad," Mrs. Mathers said, "you took me last Sunday
night."

"Not to those kind, I didn't. Why'nt you let me finish? By Dad,
I ain't so old I can't remember what I did a week back."

"Who said anybody was old?" Velma asked.

"Stop showin' off," Mr. Pint said. "I heard who said it."

Mrs. Mathers clucked sadly, too wise to defend herself.

Mr. Pint blinked at her. "You made me go," he said.

Mrs. Mathers saw her chance. "Ho, ho," she laughed. "I'd just like
to see anybody *make* you do anything!"

"You can say that again! Tell him about your office, Dad," Velma
said, but Mr. Pint would not.

From the women, however, Father Fabre learned that Mr. Pint
had asked "them"—his employers, presumably—to build him an
office of glass so that he could sit in it, out of the dirt and noise, and
keep an eye on the men who worked under him.

"Why shouldn't they do it," said Mrs. Mathers, "when he saves
them all the money he does?"

Father Fabre, about to address Mr. Pint directly, rephrased his
question. "He has men under him? I mean—many?"

"Five," said Mrs. Mathers. "Before he came, they had six. He gets
more out of five men than they did out of six."

"Two he brought with him," Velma said. "They've been with Dad for years."

Father Fabre nodded. Mr. Pint, with his entourage, was like a big-time football coach, but what was Mr. Pint's work?

Velma, who had switched on the radio, cried, "Lee!"

Father Fabre watched the women closely. Evidently "Lee" was the announcer and not some entertainer to follow on the program. His sponsor, a used car dealer, whose name and address he gave, dispensed with commercial announcements on Sunday, he said, and presented music suited to the day. They sat quietly listening to *How Are Things in Glocca Morra?* Then to *The Rosary*, one of Mrs. Mathers' favorite pieces, she said. Then to *Cryin' in the Chapel.* Father Fabre wanted to go home.

Lee came on again with the business about no commercials and also threw in the correct time. (Mr. Pint pulled out his watch.) Lee warned motorists to be careful on the highways.

"Don't judge by this. You should hear him on weekdays," Velma said. "Does he ever kid the sponsors!"

"He's a good disc jockey or he wouldn't be on the air," Mrs. Mathers said tartly. "But he's no Arthur Godfrey." It sounded to Father Fabre as though she'd been over this ground with Velma before. "Do you ever get Arthur, Father?"

"Can't say that I do, Mrs. Mathers."

"He might give you some ideas for your sermons."

"My radio isn't working."

"I'll take Lee," Velma said. She rose and went down the hall to the bathroom.

Mrs. Mathers whispered, "Father, did I tell you she wanted to call in for them to play a song for you? *Our Lady of Fatima* or something. She wanted it to come over the air while you were here. A surprise."

"No," he said. "You didn't tell me about that."

"I told her not to do it. I said maybe you wouldn't want it."

"No, I wouldn't." He was grateful to Mrs. Mathers.

Showing a little interest, Mr. Pint inquired uneasily: "What do you think of this disc jockey business?" He got up and turned off the radio.

"I'm afraid I don't know much about it," Father Fabre said, surprised to find himself engaged in conversation with Mr. Pint.

"Sounds kind of fishy to me," said Mr. Pint, sitting down again,

He had opened up some, not much, but some. "You know it's just playing phonograph records?"

"Yes," said Father Fabre and then wondered if he'd said the right thing. Mr. Pint might have wanted to tell him about it. Fearing a lull, he plunged. "Certainly was good ice cream."

"Glad you liked it."

After the long winter, gentle spring, the sap running. . . . "That's a good idea of yours when you make ice cream—bringing an extra shirt, I mean."

There was a bad silence, the worst of the afternoon, crippling every tongue. Even Velma, back with them, was quiet. Mr. Pint was positively stony. Finally, as if seeing no other way, Mrs. Mathers explained:

"Mr. Pint lives here, Father."

"He does?"

"Yes, Father."

"I guess I didn't know."

"I guess I didn't tell you."

"No reason why you should've," he said quickly. "You do have quite a bit of room here." He seemed to be perspiring. "Certainly do get the sun." He never would have thought it. Was there a chance that Mr. Pint, who acted so strangely, was not her lover? He took a good look at Mr. Pint. Was there a chance that he was? In either case, Mrs. Mathers had planned well. Father Fabre, taking out his handkerchief, blew his nose politely and dabbed at his cold, damp neck. He was in very good health and perspired freely. The fat flowery arms of the overstuffed chair held him fast while the hidden mouth devoured him. The trembling ferns frankly desired him. He just never would have thought it.

"You should see my little room at the Y," Velma said. "So dark." She was looking at Father Fabre, but he could think of nothing to say.

Mrs. Mathers sighed. "Vel, you *could* stay here, you know. She could too." Mrs. Mathers appealed to Father Fabre. "The day bed is always ready."

"Oh, well," said Velma.

"So I had this extra bedroom," Mrs. Mathers said, as if coming to the end of a long explanation, "and I thought I might as well have the income from it—what's your opinion, Father?"

"Swell," he said. In the future he ought to listen to Miss Burke and stay away from John, with his rotten talk against her. A very sound person, Miss Burke, voices, visions and all. He ought to develop a retiring nature, too, stick close to the pastor, maybe try to get a job in his war plant. "I hate to rush off," he said, rising.

"Don't tell me it's time for devotions," said Mrs.Mathers.

They went down the street together. "You know, Father," said Mrs. Mathers. "I almost asked them to come along with us."

"You did?" Mrs. Mathers was hard to figure. He'd heard that hospital life made iconoclasts.

"What'd you think of Vel?"

"Who? Oh, fine." He didn't know what he thought of Vel. "What does she do?"

"She's with the telephone company, Father. She thinks she's in line for a supervisor's, but I don't know. The seniority system is the one big thing in her favor. Of course, it wouldn't come right away."

"I suppose not," Father Fabre said. "She seems quite young for that."

"Yes, and they're pretty careful about those jobs."

"What I understand." He was in line for a pastor's himself. They were pretty careful about those jobs too. "What does Mr. Pint do?"

"Didn't I tell you?"

"No," he said bleakly.

Mr. Pint was an engineer. "But he never touches a wrench. He's like an executive."

"Where?"

"At the hospital, Father."

"At City?"

"At Mercy, Father."

Oh, God, he thought, the nuns were going to be in on it too. They walked the next block in silence.

"Who plays the mandolin?" he asked.

"He does."

They walked another block in silence. "I don't want to get TV," she said plaintively. She brightened at the sight of a squirrel.

"Don't care for TV?"

"No, it's not that. I just don't know how long I'll keep my apartment."

Was Mrs. Mathers saying that she'd get out of town, or only that she'd move to another parish? If so, she was a little late. By feasting at their board, he had blessed the union, if any, in the eyes of the parish. What a deal! It was too late for him to condemn the enamored couple, one of whom was out of his jurisdiction anyway (in parting he had shaken Mr. Pint's hand). It was a bad situation, bad in itself and bad because it involved him. Better, though, that they live in sin than marry in haste. That was something, however, that it would take theologians (contemplating the dangers of mixed marriage, the evil of divorce) to see. He knew what the parishioners would think of that.

And the pastor . . .

At the church, at the moment of parting, he said, "You're going to be early for devotions." That was all. To thank her, as he wanted to, for the good dinner would be, in a way, to thank her for compromising him with parish and pastor. It was quite enough that he say nothing to hurt her, and go.

"I've got some things to do around the side altars," Mrs. Mathers said.

He nodded, backing away.

"You suppose Grace'll be inside?" she called after him, just as if all were now well between her and her best friend in the Society.

He had his back to her and kept going, plowed on, nodding though, vigorously nodding like one of the famous yes-horses of Odense. For a moment he entertained the idea that Mrs. Mathers was a mental case, which would explain everything, but it wouldn't do. Mrs. Mathers remained a mystery to him.

In the rectory, he started up the front stairs for his room. Then he went back down, led by sounds to the converts' parlor. There he found a congregation of middle-aged women dressed mostly in navy blues and blacks, unmistakably Altar and Rosary, almost a full consistory, and swarming.

"Could I be of any service to you ladies?"

The swarming let up. "Miss Burke said we should wait in here," someone said.

He hadn't seen who had spoken. "For me?" he said, looking them over. He saw Grace sorrowing in their midst.

"No, Father," said someone else, also hidden from him. "We're here to see the pastor."

"Oh," he said.

"*He* went out on a sick call," said someone else.

"Oh," he said, and escaped.

One minute later he was settling down in the garage, on the bottom rung of a folding ladder, the best seat he could find. He picked up a wrench, got grease on his fingers, and remembered that Mr. Pint never touched a wrench. He wondered where he'd gone wrong, if there was anything he might have done, or might yet do. There was nothing. He attributed his trouble to his belief, probably mistaken, that the chancery had wanted a man at Trinity to compensate for the pastor. Father Fabre had tried to be that man, one who would be accessible to the people. The pastor strenuously avoided people. He was happy with the machines in his room, or on a picnic with himself, topped off perhaps with a visit to the zoo. The assistant was the one to see at Trinity. Naturally there were people who would try to capitalize on his inexperience. The pastor gave him a lot of rope. Some pastors wouldn't let their curates dine out with parishioners—with good reason, it appeared. The pastor was watchful, though, and would rein in the rope on the merest suspicion. Father Fabre was thinking of the young lady of charm and education who had come to him after Mass one Sunday with the idea of starting up a study club at Trinity. He'd told the pastor and the pastor had told him, "It's under study." You might think that would be the end of it. It had been, so far as the young lady was concerned, but that evening at table Father Fabre was asked by the dormouse if he knew about young ladies.

"Know about them?"

"Ummm." The dormouse was feasting on a soda cracker.

"No," said Father Fabre, very wise.

"Well, Father. I had them all in a sodality some years ago." (Ordinarily untalkative to the point of being occult, the pastor spoke now as a man compelled, and Father Fabre attended his every word. The seminary professors had harped on the wisdom of pastors, as against the all-consuming ignorance of curates.) It seemed that the pastor, being so busy, didn't notice how the young ladies showed up for induction during the few years of the sodality's existence at Trinity, but from the day he did, there had been no more of that. (*What?* Father Fabre wondered but did not interrupt.) The pastor was not narrow-minded, he said, and he granted that a young woman might wear a bit of paint on her wedding day. But when sodalists, dedicated to the Blessed Virgin, the Mother of God, Mary Immaculate, presented themselves at the communion rail in low-necked evening gowns, wearing lipstick, stuff in their eyes, and with their hair up in the permanent wave, why then, Gentlemen—the pastor used that word, causing Father Fabre to blink and then to realize he was hearing a speech the pastor must have given at a clergy conference—there was something wrong somewhere and that was why he had suppressed the sodality in his parish.

By God, thought Father Fabre, nodding vigorously, the pastor had a point! Here was something to remember if he ever got a church of his own.

It must have touched the pastor to see his point so well taken by his young curate, for he smiled. "You might say the scales dropped from my eyes," he said.

But by then Father Fabre, gazing at the cracker flake on the pastor's black bosom, had begun to wonder what all this had to do with a study club, and must have shown it.

"A study club's just another name for a sodality," the pastor prompted. "See what I mean?"

Father Fabre did not, not unless the pastor meant that young ladies were apt to belong to either and that, therefore, his curate would do well to steer clear of both. Hear their sins, visit them in sickness and prison, give them the Sacrament. Beyond that, there wasn't much to be done for or about them. In time they would get old and useful. The pastor, for his part, had put them away in the cellar part of his mind to ripen like cheese. But the good ladies of the Altar and Rosary were something else again. Nuns could not have kept the church cleaner, and the good ladies, unlike nuns, didn't labor under the illusion that they were somehow priests, only different, and so weren't always trying to vault the communion rail to the altar.

"You want to be one of these 'youth priests,' Father?"

"I haven't thought much about it."

"Good."

But, as the pastor must have noticed, Father Fabre had wanted to get some "activities" going at Trinity, believing that his apostolate lay in the world, with the people, as the pastor's obviously didn't. Well, he had failed. But he wasn't sorry. Wasn't there enough to do at Trinity, just doing the regular chores? For the poor, the sick and dying, yes, anything. But non-essentials he'd drop, including dining out with parishioners, and major decisions he'd cheerfully hand over to the pastor. (He still thought the man who rented owls to rid you of pigeons might have something, for that was nature's way, no cruel machines or powders. But he'd stop agitating for the owls, for that was another problem for the pastor, to solve or, probably, not to solve.) Of course the parish was indifferently run, but wasn't it a mistake to keep trying to take up *all* the slack? He'd had himself under observation, of late. It seemed to him his outlook was changing, not from a diminution of zeal, not from loss of vision, but from growing older and wiser. At least he hoped so. He was beginning to believe he wasn't the man to compensate for the pastor—not that he'd ask for a transfer. The bishop was a gentle administrator but always seemed to find a place in one of the salt mines for a young man seeking a change. Father Fabre's predecessor in the curate's job at Trinity had been anti-social, which some of the gadabout clergy said could be a grievous fault in a parish priest, but he hadn't asked for a change—it had come to him—and now he was back in the seminary, as a professor with little pocket money, it was true, but enjoying food and handball again. That afternoon, sitting in the garage, Father Fabre envied him.

The pastor handed a wicker basket to Father Fabre, and himself carried a thermos bottle. He showed no surprise at finding his curate waiting for him in the garage and asked no questions. Father Fabre, the moment he saw the basket and bottle, understood that the pastor was returning from a picnic, and that Miss Burke, telling the ladies he'd gone on a sick call, thought it part of her job to create a good impression whenever possible, part of being loyal, the prime requisite. Who but the pastor would have her for a housekeeper?

They walked to the back door at the pastor's pace.

"Some coffee in here for you," the pastor said, jiggling the thermos bottle.

"Thanks," said Father Fabre, but he'd not be having any of that.

"One of the bears died at Como," the pastor said. "One of the babies."

"That's too bad," said Father Fabre. He pushed in the door for the pastor, then stood aside. "Some women to see you in the converts' parlor," he said, as the pastor passed in front of him.

The pastor nodded. Women in the converts' parlor; he would see them.

"I don't know," Father Fabre said. "It may concern me—indirectly." Then, staring down at the kitchen linoleum, he began an account of his afternoon at Mrs. Mathers'. At the worst part—his chagrin on learning of the set-up there—the pastor interrupted. He filled an unwashed cup from the sink with the fluid from the thermos bottle, gave it to Father Fabre to drink, and watched to see that he did. Father Fabre drank Miss Burke's foul coffee to the dregs and chewed up a few grounds. When he started up his account again, the pastor interrupted.

"That's enough," he said.

Father Fabre, for a moment, thought he was in for it. But when he looked into the pastor's eyes, there was nothing in them for him to fear, nor was there fear, nor even fear of fear, bravado. The pastor's eyes were blue, blank and blue.

Father Fabre followed the pastor at a little distance, out of the kitchen, down the hallway. "Will you need me?" he said.

With an almost imperceptible shake of his head, the pastor walked into the converts' parlor, leaving the door ajar as always when dealing with women.

Father Fabre stayed to listen, out of sight of those inside. He soon realized that it had been a mistake to omit all mention of Velma in his account, as he had, thinking her presence at Mrs. Mathers' incidental, her youth likely to sidetrack the pastor, to arouse memories of so-called study clubs and suppressed sodalists. Why, if the pastor was to hear the details, didn't they tell him that Grace had been invited to dinner? Then there would have been five of them. The pastor was sure to get the wrong impression. To hear the ladies tell it, Mr. Pint and Father Fabre were as bad as sailors on leave, kindred evil spirits double-dating a couple of dazzled working girls. The ladies weren't being fair to Father Fabre or, he felt, even to Mr. Pint. He wondered at the pastor's silence. When all was said and done, there was little solidarity among priests—a nest of tables scratching each other.

In the next room, it was the old, old story, right from Scripture, the multitude crying, "Father, this woman was taken in adultery. The law commandeth us to stone such a one. What sayest thou?" The old story with the difference that the pastor had nothing to say. Why didn't he say: She that is without sin among you, let her first cast a stone at her! But there was one close by who could and would speak, who knew what it was to have the mob against him, and who was not afraid. With chapter and verse he'd atomize 'em. *This day thou shouldst be pastor.* Yes, it did look that way, but he'd wait a bit, to give the pastor a chance to redeem himself. He imagined how it would be if he hit them with that text. They, hearing him, would

go out one by one, even the pastor, from that day forward his disciple. And he alone would remain, and the woman. And he, lifting
up himself, would say, Woman, where are they that accused thee?
Hath no one condemned thee? Who would say, No one, master.
Neither will I condemn thee. Go, and sin no more.

"Think he can handle it?"

Whirling, Father Fabre beheld his tempter. "Be gone, John," he
said, and watched the janitor slink away.

Father Fabre, after that, endeavored to think well of the pastor, to
discover the meaning in his silence. Was this forbearance? It seemed
more like paralysis. The bomb was there to be used, but the pastor
couldn't or wouldn't use it. He'd have to do something, though. The
ladies, calmed at first by his silence, sounded restless. Soon they might
regard his silence not as response to a grave problem but as refusal
to hold council with them.

"We don't feel it's any of our business to know *what* you intend
to do, Father, but we would like some assurance that something will
be done. Is that asking too much?"

The pastor said nothing.

"We thought you'd know what to do, Father," said another.
"What would be best for all concerned, Father. Gosh, I don't know
what to think!"

The pastor cleared his throat, touched, possibly, by the last speaker's humility, but he said nothing.

"I wonder if we've made ourselves clear," said the one who had
spoken before the last one. She wasn't speaking to the pastor but
to the multitude. "Maybe that's what comes from trying to describe
everything in the best possible light." (Father Fabre remembered
the raw deal they'd given him.) "Not *all* of us, I'm afraid, believe
that man's there against Mildred's will."

"S'*not* so."

Father Fabre gasped. Oh, no! Not that! But yes, the pastor had
spoken.

"Father, do you mean to say we're lying?"

"*No.*"

Father Fabre shook his head. In all arguments with the pastor
there was a place like the Sargasso Sea, and the ladies had reached
it. It was authority that counted then, as Father Fabre knew, who
had always lacked it. The ladies hadn't taken a vow of obedience,
though, and they might not take "S'not so" for an answer. They

might very well go to the chancery. At the prospect of that, of the fine slandering he'd get there, and realizing only then that he and the pastor were in the same boat, Father Fabre began to consider the position as defined by "S'not so" and "No." The pastor was saying (a) that the situation, as reported by the ladies, was not so, and (b) that the ladies were not lying. He seemed to be contradicting himself, as was frequently the case in disputations with his curate. This was no intramural spat, however. The pastor would have to make sense for a change, to come out on top. *Could* the dormouse be right? And the ladies wrong in what they thought? What if what they thought was just not so? *Honi soit qui mal y pense?*

One said, "I just can't understand Mildred," but Father Fabre thought he could, now. At no time had Mrs. Mathers sounded guilty, and that—her seeming innocence—was what had thrown everything out of kilter. When she said Mr. Pint lived with her, when she said she was thinking of giving up her apartment, she had sounded not guilty but regretful, regretful and flustered, as though she knew that her friends and even her clergy were about to desert her. Mrs. Mathers was a veteran nurse, the human body was her work bench, sex probably a matter of technical concern, as with elderly plumbers who distinguish between the male and female connections. It was quite possible that Mrs. Mathers had thought nothing of letting a room to a member of the opposite sex. She could not have known that what was only an economy measure for her would appear to others as something very different—and so, in fact, it had become for her, in time. Mrs. Mathers and Mr. Pint were best described as victims of their love for each other. It was true love, of that Father Fabre was now certain. He had only to recollect it. If it were the other kind, Mrs. Mathers never would have invited him over—and Grace—to meet Mr. Pint. Mr. Pint, non-Catholic and priest-shy, had never really believed that Mrs. Mathers' friends would understand, and when Grace defaulted, he had become sullen, ready to take on anybody, even a priest, which showed the quality of his regard for Mrs. Mathers, that he meant to marry her willy nilly, in or out of the Church. There must be no delay. All Mrs. Mathers needed now, all she'd ever needed, was a little time—and help. If she could get Mr. Pint to take instructions, they could have a church wedding. Velma, already Catholic in spirit, could be bridesmaid. That was it. The ladies had done their worst—Father Fabre's part in the affair was criminally exaggerated—but the pastor, the angelic dormouse, had not failed to sniff out the benign object of Mrs. Mathers' grand plan. Or what would have been its object. The ladies could easily spoil everything.

One of the ladies got sarcastic. "Would it be too much to ask, then, just what you do mean?"

The pastor said nothing.

Then the one who earlier had succeeded in getting him to clear his throat said, "Father, it's not always easy for us to understand everything you say. Now, Father, I always get a lot out of your sermons—why, some I've heard on television aren't half as good—but I don't kid myself that I can understand *every* word you say. Still waters run deep, I guess, and I haven't got the education I should have. So, Father, would you please tell us what you mean, in words we can all understand?"

It would have surprised Father Fabre if, after all that, the pastor had said nothing.

"*S'not so*," he said.

Father Fabre had to leave then, for devotions.

In the sacristy, he slipped into his cassock, eased the zipper past the spot where it stuck, pawed the hangers for his surplice, found it on the floor. The altar boys had come, but he wasn't in the mood for them, for the deceptive small talk that he seemed to do so well, from ballplayers to St. John Bosco in one leap, using the Socratic method to get them to do their own thinking and then breaking off the conversation when he'd brought out the best in them. It wasn't necessary with the two on hand—twins who were going to be priests anyway, according to them at the age of ten. They had fired the censer too soon, and it would be petering out after the rosary, when it would be needed for benediction. He stood at the door of the sacristy and gazed out into the almost empty church. It was the nice weather that kept people away from devotions, it was said, and it was the bad weather that kept them away in the wintertime. He saw Mrs. Mathers kneeling alone in prayer. The pastor had done well for her, everything considered, but not well enough, Father Fabre feared. He feared a scandal. Great schisms from little squabbles grew. . . .

And great affirmations! He'd expected the pastor to dismiss the ladies in time for devotions, but he hadn't expected them to come, not in such numbers, and he took it as a sign from heaven when they didn't kneel apart from Mrs. Mathers, the woman taken in adultery, or thereabouts; a sign that the pastor had triumphed, as truth must always triumph over error, sooner or later, always: that was heaven's promise to pastors. Life was a dark business for everyone in it, but the way for pastors was ever lit by flares of special grace. Father Fabre, knowing full well that he, in spirit, had been no better than the ladies, thanked God for the little patience he'd had, and asked forgiveness for thinking ill of the pastor, for coveting his authority. He who would have been proud to hurl the ready answer at Mrs. Mathers' persecutors, to stone them back, to lose the ninety-nine sheep and save not the one whose innocence he would have violated publicly then as he had in his heart, in his heart humbled himself with thoughts of his unworthiness, marveled at the great good lesson he'd learned that day from the pastor, that Solomon. But the pastor, he knew, was zealous in matters affecting the common weal, champion of decency in his demesne, and might have a word or two for his curate at table that evening, and for Mrs. Mathers there would certainly be a just poke or two from the blunt sword of his mercy.

Father Fabre, trailing the boys out of the sacristy, gazed upon the peaceful flock, and then beyond, in a dim, dell-like recess of the nave used for baptism, he saw the shepherd carrying a stick and then he heard him opening a few windows.

WILLIAM HENRY SHULTZ *was born in Hanover, Pennsylvania. After attending the University of Virginia and Gettysburg College, he worked for several years in New York for Doubleday, Doran, and then went to the University of Chicago, where he received an M.A. in English in 1942. Since that time he has been living and teaching in New Mexico. His short stories have appeared in* The New Mexico Quarterly, Esquire, The Best Short Stories of 1953, *and other publications. At present he is working on more short stories, on a novel about modern Indian life and character, and on a series of essays on certain aspects of contemporary music.*

THE SHIRTS OFF THEIR BACKS

FROM ESQUIRE

The summer Hugh Manley's wife was out West getting her divorce, Hugh took to going around without a shirt. He wore a shirt to town, naturally; but as soon as he got home he shed it and didn't return to it till he had to. Week ends and holidays he didn't wear a shirt from sunup till sundown, even though his friends dropped in.

Weekday afternoons, as soon as he got back from town, he discarded his shirt, and often his shoes and socks as well, and went at once to the terrace in back of the house to relax in a canvas deck chair. Serena, the colored maid and cook who had stayed on after Terry left for the West, would bring out a tray with cans of beer, an opener, and a stein, and Hugh would settle down until dinner was ready. During those first few weeks of summer he drank alone.

But then, one afternoon while the sun was still hot and the only sounds in the air were those of pots and pans and the neighborhood radios, he heard the voice of Henry Allen, who lived next door, cursing his wife because there was no cold beer in the refrigerator.

Hugh and Terry had not known the Allens very well—they had never played bridge with each other every Friday night, for instance; and there had even been a time when the two wives were scarcely nodding to each other in the supermarket—but Hugh had nevertheless called out to Allen from his chair on the terrace, "Hey, Allen, you want some cold beer?" Allen had replied at once, bawling from the kitchen window, "You're god-damn right I do. You got any?" "Plenty," Hugh had replied; and thus had begun a beautiful friendship.

Allen's wife, soon after this, had left for an extended visit with her relatives in Kentucky, taking with her their only child—a boy of about five; and Allen and Hugh found themselves spending more and more of their time together, largely on Manley's back terrace bolstering up the Beer Trust, as they put it to each other. The late-afternoon sessions frequently extended into the dinner hour—so frequently, as a matter of fact, that it was not long before Serena was cooking dinner for two again.

After several weeks of this, Allen one afternoon brought up the case of Bob Whittier, who lived in the house next beyond Allen's. Hugh and Terry had scarcely even known his name.

"Whittier, the poor old bastard," said Allen, peering moodily into his beer and shaking his head dolefully. "The poor old bastard."

"What about him?" asked Hugh.

"The poor bastard," said Allen again. "His wife's some kind of promoter. Out on the road all the time. Hardly ever sees her."

"What is he, a salesman of some kind?" asked Hugh.

"No, no," said Allen. "Not Bob. His wife. She's the one out on the road. Weeks at a time, poor bastard. She's some kind of promoter."

"What does she promote?"

"God knows, though I think poor Bob has his suspicions sometimes."

"Well, Christ," said Hugh, "in this day and age, with modern detectives and all, I think it should be easy enough for him to find out."

"Don't get me wrong," said Allen. "I don't think it's as bad as that. Or maybe it is. She goes up and down the country organizing chapters of The League for Civic Pride, or whatever it is. She's a great little old organizer."

"My God," said Hugh. "Civic Pride. The poor bastard."

"For weeks on end," said Allen. "Maybe months."

"The poor bastard," said Hugh. "Let's call him up and ask him over for a beer."

"Let me," said Allen. "I know his number."

Whittier came right over, and it wasn't long before he began coming every afternoon, and soon after that Serena had three for dinner every evening. None of them wore any shirts.

The three men had little enough in common to talk about, but they found this unnecessary after a time. They were much of an age—had gone to the same kind of prep school and university, had had similar, unheroic war experiences, and all this was sufficient to make them very congenial companions. Sometimes, when they got drunk enough, they could be very funny together; and reminiscing about how funny they had been was enough to see them through the next several evenings.

Another common bond was the way circumstances were forcing them to take note of the nature and possible home life of a woman down the street who came out on her back porch every evening about dinnertime to call her little boy to table; and they took special pleasure in speculating on the probable character of the woman's husband and the developing neuroticism of the child, none of whom they had ever seen, owing to the high hedges maintained by the people of this block. They were not even sure precisely where she lived, though it could not have been more than five or six houses away; but they had no trouble hearing her. The woman would come out on her back porch, banging the screen door behind her. Then she would begin yelling for her little boy at the top of her lungs. She had a very powerful voice, which could be heard all over the neighborhood and possibly even into the next block or so. Allen took a particular dislike to this voice, holding that it epitomized an extreme distaste for motherhood; she was calling her little boy Russell home to dinner only, he said, because if she didn't, he would soon starve to death and then she would get in trouble with the police. Allen was sure that she beat him regularly, and it was perfectly true that they often heard her threatening the boy, in her fishwife's voice, with fantastically cruel and unusual punishments. They took to calling her Mrs. Russell.

One evening towards the end of summer, as the three men were sitting over their beer, Allen held up his wrist watch and began counting off the minutes.

"You're too early," said Hugh. "They don't eat till six-thirty."

"It's nearly six-thirty now."

He had hardly finished speaking when the screen door of Mrs.

Russell's back porch banged, and Hugh, Allen, and Whittier simultaneously set down their steins and looked up expectantly.

"Russ-ELL!" screamed the woman.

There was no answer. Often there was no answer. More than half the time little Russell was fortunately, or unfortunately, out of earshot.

"RUSS-ell!" she screamed again.

"I'd like to get out my B-B gun and pepper her," said Hugh.

"Why only your B-B gun?" asked Allen.

"When I was in Switzerland," said Whittier, "they told me they used horns to get the cattle down out of the mountains for winter. You can hear them for twenty miles."

"Thank God Mrs. Russell doesn't have cattle," said Hugh.

"Sometimes it even starts avalanches," said Whittier.

"RUSS-ELL!" screamed Mrs. Russell for the eighth or ninth time.

"She's beginning to get hoarse," said Hugh. "She'll have to stop in another hour or so."

"If I were Russell," said Whittier, "I'd change my name. I'd change it to something so long she could only call it once or twice."

"He's a nice-looking little bastard," said Hugh. "I think I saw him riding his bike down the walk the other day."

"There's lots of kids in this block," said Allen. "It could have been anyone, not necessarily Russell. I had a kid here once myself."

"Once?" said Whittier. "What the hell, he's still yours, isn't he?"

"Is he?" said Allen.

"For Christ sake, Allen," said Whittier, "it isn't as if you didn't know where he was."

"A lot of good that does me," said Allen. "For all I know, she may never bring him back again."

"You can make her," said Whittier. "That's what we've got laws for."

"RUSS-ell!" Mrs. Russell's voice was rapidly turning into an unrecognizable croak.

"Here I am, Mummy," Hugh suddenly bawled at the top of his lungs. "Over here, Mummy, getting drunk with the bad mens."

Mrs. Russell did not reply, but they heard the screen door bang.

"That ought to give Russell another hour with his buddies," said Allen. "What do you suppose the little bastard does with his time, anyway?"

"It's enough for Russell if he just stays out of Mrs. Russell's way," said Whittier. "You're getting old, Allen. You forget."

Serena came out on the terrace from the kitchen.

"How soon do you gentlemen want your dinner served, Mr. Hugh?" she asked.

"In a little while, Serena," said Hugh. "As soon as it gets dark, or whenever you're ready. It doesn't make any difference."

Serena went back into the kitchen and Hugh opened three more cans of beer and passed them around.

"Some friend of yours opportunely arriving just in time for dinner," said Whittier, pointing with his can.

Hugh looked up and saw a stranger approaching the foot of the terrace. The stranger came forward uneasily.

Hugh said, "Howdy, chum. You looking for someone?"

The stranger—a stocky, rather unhappy-looking young man, about Hugh's age—tried to smile.

"Pardon me, sir," he began. "I don't know quite how to say this, but——"

"Come up here on the terrace," said Hugh. "We'll hear you better. Also have a beer to ease the throat muscles, while you're at it. Come on up; we won't bite you."

The man stepped up to the terrace and accepted reluctantly the beer Hugh handed him; but after a moment, he put it back on the table.

"I might just as well come right out with it," he said, putting his hands in his pockets and immediately taking them out again. "I just wanted to know if one of you men is the one who just now insulted my wife."

"Insulted your wife," said Hugh, struggling to his feet. "I don't even know your wife."

"He doesn't even know you, if it comes to that," said Allen.

"Oh," said the man. "Excuse me. I'm Francis Sacker, Frank Sacker. I live several houses from you here, and my wife claims that——"

"Excuse *me*," said Hugh, extending his hand to Mr. Sacker. "I better introduce myself, too. I'm your neighbor, Looie Gottschalk. I live several houses up the block from *you*, by some strange coincidence, and I want you to know my friends here. This," he said, pointing to Allen, "is Father Anthony. He's in mufti this evening. And over here, alas, is P. Pierre Robespierre, my attorney. He can't speak a work of English, so I'm sure *he* didn't insult your wife. And as for Father Anthony, he never has anything to do with women, absolutely anything."

Allen and Whittier both rose, with some difficulty. Allen shook hands ceremoniously with Mr. Sacker, who said, "Pleased to meet you, Father, certainly pleased to meet you." Whittier bowed formally.

"Was your wife insulted in English?" inquired Allen deferentially. "If she was, it could not have been our friend P. Pierre Robespierre over here." He uttered the name with relish. "P. Pierre Robespierre doesn't speak a word of English, as our good host has already indicated."

"He speaks a few words, Father," Hugh corrected him, "but they are mostly cuss words and you wouldn't know them."

"Alas, how true," Allen murmured, rolling his eyes. "But won't you sit down, Mr. Hacker? We're just having a short beer before dinner."

"Hackers," observed Hugh, "were what we used to call the guys at my school who were always raising hell. Hacking, we called it. Raising hell all the time. Where'd you go to school, Hacker?"

"Sacker," said Mr. Sacker. "Francis X. Sacker. They call me Frank."

"Sit down for the second time, Mr. Hacker," said Allen. "I insist you have a short beer with us before dinner." He pulled up a canvas chair for Mr. Sacker and gently pushed him into it.

"Serena!" Hugh called. "Another glass. And set another place at dinner. Mr. Hacker has just arrived."

"Really," said Mr. Sacker. "I can drink it out of the can just as well."

"I didn't know no Mr. Hacker was coming for dinner," said Serena, coming out onto the terrace with another stein.

"Don't we have enough for him?" asked Hugh.

"Sure, we have enough, Mr. Hugh," Serena said. "You just didn't tell me there was gonna be anybody else, that's all."

"Hugh?" said Mr. Sacker. "I thought you said your name was Looie."

"Hughie, Looie," said Hugh. "What's the difference? Forget it."

"You'll forget it after Serena's mince pie, Hacker," said Whittier.

"I'm not staying for dinner," said Mr. Sacker. "My wife has dinner almost ready at home. We're just waiting for Russell."

"We had hackers at my school, too," said Whittier. "Every school has them. There were a couple in my form. I believe they were finally expelled, always hacking around with ketchup bottles and so on."

"Sackers," said Mr. Sacker. "My name is Sacker, and my wife——"

"I thought you didn't speak English," said Allen to Mr. Sacker.

"Me?" said Mr. Sacker.

"It's P. Pierre Robespierre who doesn't speak English," said Hugh.

"Hey, what the hell's going on here?" demanded Mr. Sacker, sitting up in his chair. "That guy's been speaking English right along."

"Who, me?" asked Whittier.

"Only some of the time," said Allen. "Only when he wants to."

"Please let Mr. Hacker finish his story," said Hugh.

"What story?" asked Mr. Sacker.

"The one about your wife," said Allen.

"Before you get too far into it, Hacker," said Hugh, "let me help you to another beer."

"I really shouldn't," said Mr. Sacker. "My wife's waiting dinner."

"Get on with the story," Allen demanded.

"There *is* no god-damn story," said Mr. Sacker. "Somebody insulted my wife and she sent me over here to see if one of you men did it."

"How did she know we were here?" asked Allen.

"I have nevair insult ze lady," said Whittier. "Not since I was in ze, how you say, boarding school. No god-damn lady *in* ze boarding school, ha, ha. I am no hackair."

"Say, Hacker," said Allen, "just where did you say you went to school?"

"Me?" said Sacker. "You mean college?"

"I mean school," said Allen, opening another beer.

"I graduated from Punxsutawney High, in Punxsutawney, Pennsylvania, if that's what you mean," said Mr. Sacker.

"By god," said Hugh, "I've always wanted to meet a product of good old Punxsutawney High."

"You have?" said Mr. Sacker. "Why was that?"

"I want to hear more about Mrs. Hacker," said Allen. "Stop interrupting him all the time."

"Sacker," said Mr. Sacker. "Mrs. Sacker thinks you insulted her, sir."

"Father Anthony," exclaimed Hugh, "wouldn't insult a fly!"

"Nevertheless," insisted Mr. Sacker, opening another beer, "somebody shouted something insulting from this vicinity at my wife, and she won't finish cooking dinner until somebody apologizes."

"Hacker," said Allen, "do you mean to sit there and tell us that your wife is deliberately leaving your dinner half-uncooked until you find somebody to apologize to?"

"You've got it backwards," said Mr. Sacker. "What I'm trying to tell you is that she wants me to find somebody to apologize to *her*."

"But your dinner remains half-uncooked either way?" said Whittier.

"That's right," agreed Mr. Sacker unhappily.

"And what about little Russell?" asked Allen.

"I don't know," Mr. Sacker mumbled.

"Serena!" called Hugh. "Another plate for Mr. Hacker."

"I already got one plate on for him. How many plates he gonna eat?"

"Hacker, how many plates you going to eat?"

"I don't think I'd better eat any," said Mr. Sacker. "Thank you very much just the same. Mrs. Sacker has dinner on the stove at home."

"Your stove is cold, Hacker," said Allen. "You said so yourself. You could die from eating that half-uncooked food of yours."

"You better eat with us," said Hugh.

"Let somebody else apologize for your wife," said Whittier.

The screen door on the Sackers' back porch banged again.

"Fran-CIS!" called Mrs. Sacker.

"She must have found Russell," said Allen.

"He's never very far away," said Mr. Sacker. "Sometimes he doesn't answer on purpose."

"I wonder if he'd like a beer with us before dinner," said Hugh. "We could call him up. You have a phone, Hacker?"

"He's too young for beer," said Mr. Sacker, helping himself to another. "And Mrs. Sacker would never approve."

"Will Mrs. Hacker give him his dinner tonight, do you think?" asked Allen. "I'd hate to think of the poor little bastard going without his dinner just because of us. Does she often make him go without dinner?"

"There's no telling what Mrs. Sacker will do," said Mr. Sacker, solemnly. "Women are unpredictable."

"You can say that again," said Allen.

"I think we should bring him over here for dinner," said Hugh. "It will be absolutely no trouble for Serena to put on another plate."

"Who?" asked Mr. Sacker.

"Russell," said Allen. "Growing boys should not go without dinner."

"Stunts their growth," said Whittier. "Worse than tobacco."

"I mean, who's Serena?" asked Mr. Sacker.

"Serena!" Hugh bawled. "Another plate for Master Russell."

"Who's this Master Russell?" demanded Serena, appearing at the back door. "I don't see no Master Russell."

"Is Serena your wife?" asked Mr. Sacker.

"My wife's in Reno," said Hugh.

"That's in Nevada," said Allen. "Over the hills and far away."

"Over the hills and into the trees," said Whittier.

"Over the hills and over the hills and over the hills and over the hills," said Allen. "*My* wife's in my old Kentucky home, or I should say *her* old Kentucky home. Also my son. He's in *his* old Kentucky home."

"You hear from them, Allen?" asked Whittier.

"You hear from *your* wife?" asked Allen.

"All right," said Whittier.

"Dinner'll be ready in just about fifteen minutes," said Serena from the kitchen door, "if Mr. Hugh and the other gentlemen want to wash up."

"Have you put on an extra plate for Master Russell?" asked Hugh.

"I believe in Master Russell when I see him," said Serena.

"I thought your name was Father Anthony," said Mr. Sacker. "He just called you Allen a little while ago. I may have had a beer or so, but I don't think you are really Father Anthony."

"Sometimes my friends call me Father Allen," said Allen.

"For short," said Hugh. "Are you coming with us, Hacker? We're going to convoy Master Russell to dinner."

"Mrs. Sacker will be very angry," said Mr. Sacker.

"I can handle her," said Whittier, flexing his biceps.

"Let's go, then," said Hugh impatiently, kicking at an empty beer can.

"Aren't you going to put on your shirts?" asked Mr. Sacker.

"I never wear shirts," said Whittier. "Even in Grand Central Station."

"Shirts are a snare and a delusion," said Allen. "I am against them."

"Maybe I'd better take off my shirt too," said Mr. Sacker, doing so, "being as I'm going with you."

"Atta-boy, Hacker," said Hugh. "Old Shirtless Hacker, we used to call him back in the old days."

"Old Hirtless Shacker," said Allen.

"Protective coloration," said Sacker, shivering in the evening air.

"You tell 'um, Hacker," said Whittier. "You can tell Hacker's an old hand at this game. You can always tell an old hand. Good old Hacker."

"Punxsutawney High," said Hugh.

"Shirts are for Beau Brummell," said Allen.

"Who?" said Sacker.

"A friend of Allen's," said Whittier.

"He's no friend of mine," said Allen. "God-damn shirt wearer."

"Better load up with a few for the road," said Hugh, picking up two cans of beer and opening them.

"Just where do you gentlemen think you're going now?" demanded Serena from the kitchen door. "Dinner's practically ready."

"Don't you worry," said Allen. "We'll only be gone a few minutes."

"Just long enough to convoy Master Russell," said Hugh. "Don't you fret, don't you cry."

"I ain't frettin' and I ain't cryin'," said Serena. "I know better."

"This may not be as easy as you think," said Mr. Sacker. "Mrs. Sacker is easily aroused."

"Fran CIS!" bellowed Mrs. Sacker from her back porch.

"Coming, coming, coming," muttered Mr. Sacker under his breath.

"You tell her, Hacker," said Allen, putting his arm around Sacker's bare shoulders. "You tell her good, chum. We'll get Master Russell in no time and then to hell with her."

"To hell with her," said Sacker, his eyes shining.

"You and Master Russell can eat here every night," said Hugh expansively. "Bachelors' Hall. Let Mrs. Hacker stew her own juice."

They went around the side of the house and out to the front walk.

"Which house is it?" asked Hugh.

"The one with the red shutters," said Sacker. "The red shutters were Mrs. Sacker's idea."

Whittier marched up to the front door, the rest following close behind, and rang the doorbell.

"Here," said Sacker. "This is my house. I don't have to ring the doorbell at my own house."

"You let me handle this, Hacker," said Whittier.

Hugh set down his two opened cans of beer on the doorsill.

"Mrs. Sacker's not going to like this," said Mr. Sacker.

The door opened.

"Mrs. Hacker?" asked Whittier.

"Sacker," she said. "Francis, who are these men? I've been calling you for half an hour. And where's your shirt?"

"It's over at Mr. Gottschalk's," said Sacker. "I'm going to have dinner over there, so I left my shirt. It will be all right."

"We've come to get Master Russell," said Whittier. "He's going to eat with us too."

"He's nothing of the kind," said Mrs. Sacker. "Russell's eating his dinner out in the kitchen right now. Francis, have you gone out of your head? Who are these people?"

She advanced a step toward her husband and kicked over Hugh's beer.

"You've upset my beer, Mrs. Hacker," said Hugh, stooping to retrieve the cans before the beer drained out, "but I prefer to think you didn't do it deliberately."

"You're drunk, that's what," said Mrs. Sacker, looking suspiciously at her husband. "You step out of the house for five minutes and come back half naked and blind drunk."

"I told you she wouldn't like the idea," said Mr. Sacker. "Martha, my dear, I want you to meet my friend, Father Anthony."

Mrs. Sacker peered at the four of them with deepening hostility. Whittier, who was standing nearest her, stepped forward, raised his arm, and flexed his biceps three or four times in her face.

"You're all blind drunk," she screamed at them. "Francis, come into the house this instant and tell these men to go back home at once."

"They're my friends," said Sacker. "The only friends I've got."

"They're not the only friends you've got," said Mrs. Sacker. "And you seem to be forgetting that you have a wife and family."

Whittier stepped very close to Mrs. Sacker and looked her in the eye from a distance of two inches. Then he flexed his biceps in her face some more. "Hacker may be afraid of you," he said, "but I'm not afraid of you."

"Get away from me," shrieked Mrs. Sacker. "His name is Sacker."

'Sacker, Shmacker, Thwacker, Swacker," said Hugh.

Mrs. Sacker suddenly reached out and caught hold of her husband's arm, jerking him into the safety of the doorway.

"Take your filthy hands off my friend Hacker," said Allen.

"He's my husband, you drunken idiot," she screamed.

"You don't seem to realize that that is Father Anthony," said Hugh, pointing to Allen. "He is going to get you a divorce tomorrow morning."

"I don't *want* a divorce," she said shrilly. "Francis, what is all this?"

Sacker had one arm around Mrs. Sacker, who had not relaxed her grip on his arm, and his head was resting against her shoulder.

"Come, Hacker," said Allen, "that is no way to behave. You know very well you're dining with us."

"You're lying in your teese. Teeth," said Sacker.

"Hacker," said Whittier, "don't try to worm your way out of it."

"I thought we came to get poor little Master Russell," said Allen.

"Well, you can't have him," said Mrs. Sacker. "Or Francis either, for that matter. So you might just as well go back home."

"I promised them, Martha," said Sacker into her shoulder.

"What did you promise them, you drunken idiot?"

"They invited me for supper, Martha," said Sacker.

"Well," said Mrs. Sacker, "you're going to eat your supper right here."

"An un-half-cooked mass of pottage," said Hugh.

"What?" said Mrs. Sacker.

"He means half-uncooked," said Whittier.

"You ought to be ashamed of yourself, feeding him that kind of stuff," Allen told Mrs. Sacker.

"Francis, what in God's name have you been telling these idiots?"

"Hacker," said Hugh sternly, "are you coming along with us peacefully or do we have to tear you from her arms by main force?"

"You have to tear me from her arms by main force," said Sacker into his wife's shoulder. "It's the only way now."

"You drunken fool," snarled Mrs. Sacker. "Two beers and you turn into a drunken fool. You're not going anywhere, you drunken fool."

"They have my place all set, Martha," he said.

"We're having mince pie tonight," Hugh said. "I smelled it on the way through the house."

"I can't remember going through the house at all," said Sacker through several thicknesses of dress material.

"Look at the disgusting way he's nuzzling her," said Whittier. "Like a horse. Our brave Hacker! It makes me sick at my stomach."

"Come on, Hacker," said Allen. "Strike while the iron is hot."

"You have nothing to lose but your chains, Hacker," said Whittier.

"Mince pie tonight, Hacker," said Hugh. "Um yum."

"Then you'd better get back there and start eating it right away," said Mrs. Sacker, "before I call the police."

"You're just the type who *would* rely on police," said Whittier. "But I'm not afraid of you *or* your police."

"On the other hand, Whittier," said Hugh, "it might look very bad if Mrs. Hacker called the police."

"We're going now, Hacker," said Allen. "This is your last chance."

"Make up your mind, Hacker, before it's too late," said Hugh. "Nothing is to be gained by spending here."

"You mean, nothing is to be *lost* by spending here," Allen corrected.

"I know what I mean," said Hugh. "That isn't it."

Mrs. Sacker had been inching her husband through the doorway into the hall. When she saw that the door would clear, she caught hold of it and flung it to, slamming it in their faces. They heard the lock click.

"Christ," said Whittier. "Right in my face."

"A god-damn Messalina," said Hugh.

Allen tried the door. It was locked indeed.

"Poor Hacker," he whispered, leaning against the door.

Hugh viciously kicked one of the now-empty beer cans off the porch onto the sidewalk, where it clattered noisily along for twenty feet and came to rest in the grass.

"No god-damn hair on his chest at all," Allen said sadly, and turned to follow the beer can off the porch.

"Figuratively, no hair," said Hugh. "Literally, you haven't any either."

Allen looked down to examine his chest. There was no hair there.

"It came out long ago," he said. "Worry did it."

They were on the sidewalk now, and Whittier saw the beer can lying in the grass. He kicked it with his foot, and it went rattling across the sidewalk into the street. Hugh and Allen started after it, but Allen got to it first and gave it another kick. Whittier came running up behind them, straight-arming Hugh and butting Allen with his hip, and pursued the can down the street. When he caught up with it, he gave it a powerful kick which lifted it off the pavement and sent it spinning end over end in a long, high arc until it landed once more in the street with a tinny clangor. Then the three of them went haring after it, shouting and pushing at each other like half-grown boys.

MAX STEELE *was born in Greenville, South Carolina, in 1922. While in the AAF he studied at Vanderbilt U. and after serving overseas was graduated from the University of North Carolina. Since 1944 he has published stories in* Harper's Magazine, The Atlantic Monthly, Collier's, Mademoiselle, *and others. In 1947 he was awarded a Saxton Fellowship to work on a novel,* Debby, *which won the Harper's Prize contest in 1950. For the past few years he has lived in Europe and at present is working on a novel in Paris and acting as an advisory editor to* The Paris Review.

THE WANTON TROOPERS

FROM HARPER'S MAGAZINE

The wanton troopers, riding by,
Have shot my fawn and it will die.
             Andrew Marvell

Between the Café Mona and Saint-Germain-des-Prés, in the heart of the Latin Quarter, the Académie André is hidden away in a mossy courtyard behind huge and peeling dark green doors which open onto a tiny crippled street, which itself is almost hidden from the stranger who passes on the big boulevard or on the rue de Rennes.

Here in the Académie, half the students are American, half are French. The Americans for the most part are veterans who report to class as though to work, put in their hours, and at the end of the month draw their subsistence and supply checks. The French are not so regimentalized and industrious. They wander in and out and the only ones who appear regularly and stay the entire day are the young girls who are inscribed here by their bourgeois parents in an effort to keep them out of the existentialist bars and cafés on Saint-Germain.

Sitting in the vestibule, peeling potatoes for her *pot-au-feu* or making innumerable checked aprons for her little grandson who plays all day in the cold courtyard or upstairs where some heat drifts through from the ateliers, Madame Hélène watches these girls with rational, penetrating eyes, just as she watches everything that transpires in the three huge studios of the Académie. She is a short, rather pudgy-looking woman of about fifty, and it is only when one sees her tiptoeing into a still-life class hugging a heavy granite bust of Victor Hugo that one realizes her quiet and powerful strength. There is a rumor that fifteen years ago she dragged a male model, a well-known Olympic athlete, out of the atelier, through the vestibule, and wrestled him across the courtyard before pushing him naked into the street. Madame Hélène herself is always exasperated when asked about the incident. She throws her short arms toward heaven and explains that indeed it did not happen thus. The man was posing in an old studio where the office now is and after an argument about his fees she merely pushed him down the stairs, after which it was an easy matter to kick him into the courtyard, where he was allowed to dress. For certainly she had more respect and sentiment for the dignity of the Académie than to throw such a man into the street. After all, she concludes, is it not she who preserves the decorum of the school? Is it not she who is the guardian of respectability? Is it not she (and then she goes off into a terrible argot which the Americans cannot understand but which the French students explain with wicked delight) who prevents orgies, of such total degradation that even Chicago would be shocked, from taking place in the ateliers and here in the vestibule and there on the stairs? She grows voluble and specific and points to the courtyard and to various shrieking, protesting students while describing the horrible, intense debauchery which she alone, she, Madame Hélène, for twenty-two years has prevented from being enacted here in this sacred Académie where Claude Félix Cambronne studied and painted.

Listening to her without understanding her words, it is impossible to know whether Madame Hélène believes them or whether she merely raves for the entertainment of the French students and the bewilderment of the American. In any case, it is true that she can, without seeming to glance up from her potatoes, detect a flirtation and she often recognizes the delicate tendrils of love long before the persons concerned are aware of their own involvement.

For several months last winter she regarded with attentive, impartial eye the coy behavior of Anna Barkova toward Nebraska Long. Nebraska was actually born in Iowa and his strong Midwestern accent had a slight Swedish lilt which rendered it less painful, even amusing to Madame Hélène. But then Nebraska had early and accidentally rendered himself sweet to that woman by appearing impressed to learn that Claude Félix Cambronne had studied and painted in this very Académie. (At that time Nebraska, seated always mentally at the far end of the table from his august and chauvinistic landlady, was morbidly ashamed of his education, so that he dared not ask deferentially as the Americans usually did, or boldly as the French, just who exactly was this Claude Félix Cambronne.) Later, after Christmas, when Madame Hélène took him upstairs to her one-room living quarter and showed him a little oil study, 12 x 18, that Cambronne had done of her, some thirty years before when she was a young girl with a plain but truly rapturous and innocent visage, he had had the presence to say that it was certainly a nice thing; and then he had had the gallantry to say that he found her face more interesting now. That was, she said, indeed too charming of him. He had gazed closely at the portrait again and when he looked up at her aging face in the slanted light, they both had turned suddenly, unexpectedly red. She had opened the door and apologized for having taken up so much of his two-hour lunch time.

Nebraska had gone quietly down the steps, across the courtyard, and up the narrow street to Saint-Germain where he boarded with an old family of women which had lived there when Saint-Germain was the fashionable *faubourg* described by Proust. Now two wars, a dead husband, and three dead sons and two dead grandsons later, Madame had taken in this young man who wished so much, she explained his presence to visitors, to have the opportunity to live like a Frenchman, if only for a year. At the long mahogany table, where he often remembered the scrubbed-board kitchen table in Iowa and the muslin curtains, they talked lightly of politics, literature, and the ballet. That is to say, they talked of de Gaulle, Gide (Sartre did not yet exist for them), and of Serge Lifar. When Nebraska mentioned Melville or any American writer or artist, Madame la Générale would lift her white eyebrows and demand whom with such a brilliant and icy smile that Nebraska was never sure whether it was his pronunciation or his taste which was being questioned. At such moments, by narrowing his eyes imperceptibly, he could make the candlelight seem to hesitate, and in the gloom at the far end of the table the black velvet choker-band about her neck would blend into the dark draperies behind her and Madame would be sitting with her head apparently severed completely from her body, guillotined by her own elegance.

He sometimes dreaded these lunches but he remained here, he told himself, because he liked his tremendous room with the heavy dark red velvet hangings, the massive walnut furniture reflected in enormous, gilt-framed mirrors, and the lustrous parquet floor which squeaked so much like a well-chain. Here he stayed alone as much as possible and read American magazines and newspapers bought at Brentano's on his book allowance. Each night he ate out, went afterward to the nearest concert, and stopped at the Café Mona to drink a cup of hot milk while listening without speaking to the difficult and often disagreeable Americans who drank there every night. A little after midnight he returned home to wash out his nylon shirt and shorts and once a week his blue jeans.

It was a solitary life but one toward which all during the army he had planned and saved. "The Solitary Swede," they had called him in the army and again in the university, for he was by nature self-sufficient, happier when not having to think about other people.

The fact that his notebook and pads were full of sketches of Anna Barkova did not, therefore, mean that he had been thinking about her that winter. It was simply that he liked her odd assortment of features and found them so easy to reproduce that, left free, his hand was apt to trace automatically the dramatic sweep of her hair caught up in back, her querulous brows and short tilted nose, or her vulnerable, pouting baby mouth with its even row of white baby teeth. In all it was the soft, round face of a pampered baby—except for the eyes which were tremendously large and dark and, even when she laughed, capable of sorrow. It was these startling, haunting eyes that confronted one from every page of Nebraska's sketchbook. Madame Hélène had, of course, become alert when she first, accidentally, saw these sketches, and when Anna heard of them she became immediately fascinated.

When she finally confirmed, by the plain tactic of snatching his notebook from him, that it was true that the bony, balding Midwesterner was using her as a constant model, little Anna approached him each morning after that with a fondness and directness usually put aside for more subtle means by little girls after the age of four. She had absolutely none of the chic and poise one has been taught to expect of young ladies in Paris, and at almost twenty she was still involved in the baby fat that most young people have resolved at ten or twelve.

Even when not interested in attracting anyone's attention her actions were likely to be awkward with the outgrown spontaneity and enthusiasm of a child. During the fall term she had hung like a puppy at the heels of Bernard Lévy and Suzanne as though it never occurred to her that that couple would want sometime to be alone. She never seemed to notice that they were never as overjoyed as she when she had sixty francs with which to buy the three of them coffee. Nebraska could not understand why she should want to buy coffee for a person as physically dirty, uncombed, and rude as Bernard Lévy who shouted continually at the models and at anyone who even accidentally touched him. He never shouted at Anna though and seemed to tolerate her and her extravagant emotions better than anyone else.

When suddenly Anna turned this childish attentiveness on him, Nebraska was abashed, for at thirty he was still shy and wary of women, even the most gentle. He hurried through the vestibule now and took up each day a place between the model and the stove so that Anna could not sit beside him as she had done for several days after snatching his notebook. When he heard her from time to time tiptoeing playfully up behind him and peeping over his shoulder, he held his notebook unintentionally closer to himself.

During the breaks between poses he rushed out into the narrow street where he smoked, and read and reread the stone plaque attached to the building across from the Académie:

Ici Est Tombé
Mort Pour La France
Gaston Raoult
Etudiant   Age 20 ans

At this distance he could not read the engraved date on which the young student had died, and, even though he intended to, he never crossed over to see if the student had fallen, as most of them had according to the plaques scattered all over the city, during the August of the Liberation.

Soon Anna, watched by Madame Hélène, began following him here to the street before the green doors. Becoming bold, apparently in the belief that he had come here to be followed, she playfully asked him for cigarettes (which later he saw her giving to Suzanne

and to the filthy Bernard Lévy). Or she teased him by asking why
he did not chew chewing gum like all Americans. He had told her
it was because he was fifty-two years old and had false teeth. Even
though he had said this to impress upon her the difference in their
ages, this was just the sort of nonsense Anna loved and so each day
she would try to provoke him out of his silence. One day she said,
more seriously: "Do you have a car?"

"Here in Paris?" he asked.

"Anywhere," she said gravely.

"At home," he said.

"A big car?"

"A Plymouth." He was amused by her seriousness on the subject.
"Is that a big car?"

He shrugged his shoulders in the new way. "Medium."

The next day she said: "Do you have a picture of it?"

"What?" he asked.

"Your car, stupid," she said.

"I don't think so." He grinned. "Why?"

She was embarrassed but persisted, now as though it were a joke:
"Search for one."

He had laughed at her but that night he got out his footlocker
and looked through his photographs. There was one of the farm taken
from the silo, one of the clapboard frame house, one of his father
standing awkwardly in his Sunday suit down at the dusty road by
the heat-blistered, peeling mailbox, one taken during the war of his
mother in overalls and his Aunt Hilda in an apron, plucking chickens
for the Saturday market in Watertown, one of himself on the new
tractor, and several of the family and the new tractor, but none of
the car.

"Well then," Anna said when he told her, "you must draw me a
picture of it."

Nebraska's first drawings had been of cars and planes and his
first solution to the problem of foreshortening had been made one
Sunday afternoon sitting by the mailbox trying to draw a car rounding the curve from Watertown. Somewhat ashamed, but secretly
delighted, and more for his own pleasure than for hers, he began
designing ridiculously elongated, low, streamlined automobiles.
When he, as though by chance, let her see the folio which held
them, he was disappointed in her reaction.

"What is it?" she asked as though greatly annoyed by the first one.

"My car."

"Stupid," she said. "Nobody has a car that looks like that." She flipped the pages and looked at the fantastic cars. "No."

"You don't like them."

"No, no, no. I want you to do a real car. Like you have at home." But she would keep these sketches until he did a sensible one.

That evening, using a big sheet of paper, he drew a caricature of a decrepit T-Model bouncing down a bumpy road, the rubbery wheels and axles buckling under it and throwing the driver, in a duster and goggles, a foot off the seat where the springs were crashing through the split cushions. She had laughed when he showed it to her but again she had protested and asked for a picture of his car, the Plymouth, a real picture. In the meantime she would keep the caricature if she might.

The next morning the first truly spring sun was shining, so instead of going to the Académie, Nebraska went down to sketch-in a water color of the little green grocery shop at the corner by Saint-Julien-le-Pauvre. After lunch he went over to the Académie earlier than usual and while taking off his raincoat in the vestibule he could see Anna, Suzanne, and Bernard Lévy sitting on the edge of the model-stand regarding his automobile sketches which were spread out on the floor. Several other French students were standing nearby looking and laughing.

Feeling rather proud that they were amused by his drawings, Nebraska stood at the threshold of the open door ready to enter when he realized they were not laughing at the humor in his designs but rather at Bernard Lévy who was delivering a lecture: ". . . voilà l'art américain."

It was too late for Nebraska to turn back. He entered the studio and walked along the side, back of the model-stand, to his shelf. The laughter ebbed away but Bernard, whether he had seen Nebraska or not, continued his mock lecture. "You will note the texture of the paper. Only the finest Italian paper for such artists. Naturally. And the pencil strokes. You will note that they were made with the finest pencils from Philadelphia. All bought by a government which can purchase anything, produce anything, including art."

Pretending that he did not understand the words—and all the students assumed that the Americans could understand only simple sentences spoken to them slowly and directly—Nebraska took down a set of water colors and some brushes and went quietly through

the still-life room and back out into the courtyard. There his calm-
ness left him and he began shaking all over. He should go back in
and smash the boy in the face and kick the living hell out of him.
Tear up the drawings. Confront Anna with her deceit.

All afternoon he was too furious to work. He walked along the
Seine hating the sight even of it and of the bridges he usually
loved to look at. He would never understand the French. Not if he
lived here forever. Santayana had said that he had not a single
friendship with a Frenchman which he did not feel was marred by
insincerity. Nebraska felt that they were probably sincere at any
given moment but that they were completely the victims of their
varying impulses. They had developed their elaborate rituals of
politeness to hide this weakness. Anyway, one could not accuse
Bernard Lévy of being insincere, polished, politic. He was openly
hostile to the Americans. He never spoke to them. Within their
hearing, though, he accused them of being the new Germans, the
new fascists, the new supermen, the lovers and rebuilders of a
Germany that would again run riot over Europe. Usually, however,
when he glared at them from his corner of the room or at their
work, he was either silent or spoke in argot to the amusement of the
other French. His chief argument against them seemed to be always
that they had the best of supplies, five thousand francs' worth a
month, paid for by their government, while he, though he did not
mention it, often drew with a black crayon on flattened pages of
Le Monde which, unlike the other newspapers, had few photographs
to interfere with his compositions.

"But it's not fair," Nebraska thought. "There's not an American
there who wouldn't give him papers and pencils and brushes if he
weren't too damned proud to accept them." It was true: almost any
one of the veterans was pleased when he could find a tactful way to
let one of the more talented of the French students have supplies
on his bill, if not as an outright gift then in trade for a small
composition.

All of the Americans wanted especially to own at least one of the
journals on which, using a bamboo stick dipped in India ink, Bernard
drew literally hundreds of hollow-eyed, skull faces with gaunt bodies.
Sometimes these strange birdlike figures were naked and their ribs
and hipbones and thighs were depicted with the terrible accuracy
of an anatomical chart. Sometimes they wore hanging, gauzelike
clothes and carried shovels that seemed to be as heavy for them as

railroad ties. Whether clothed or naked, the stooped bodies were charged with hunger and despair and hopelessness. He worked with a maddening intensity and for weeks he would never look at the model, at whom he nevertheless shouted abuse, but would stand in the back of the room working as though he had a hundred years of work to do in one, drawing and redrawing these haunted, nightmare, wraithlike creatures. At other times but with the same furious intensity, he would draw on gray paper quite marvelous gulls in graceful, lyrical flight. As much as Nebraska, at the moment, despised the boy, he would have given without hesitation his next month's supply allowance for one page of one of the decorated newspapers.

"But it's not fair what he says," Nebraska said again. He thought of Benito Marino from New York who had had three excellent shows and whose work was as good as anyone's at the school, including perhaps Bernard's. And Silvers who had even a better eye, yet with not as much taste. But then look at what some of the French students were doing: those who were caught up in the resurgent Lautrec vogue to the extent of actually putting long black gloves on their paintings of the nude models! Even as his fury subsided he knew he could not go back to work at the Académie for a great many days.

Fortunately the next week was warm for early April, bright and without rain. Nebraska finished his water color of the green grocery and the following week had begun another, near Buci, when the weather broke gray and wet and cold as winter. Reluctantly he returned to the Académie which he had not been able to force himself to think about. He arrived during the eleven o'clock break, just as a few of the students were coming across the courtyard. He glanced quickly to see if Anna were among them. He had decided it was not deceit but childishness, perhaps even pride, which had prompted her to show her friends the automobiles. In any case, he would continue as far as possible not to have any serious words with her.

The moment he opened the door, Madame Hélène seized upon him with a false gaiety that made him want to leave. Had she heard about the mock lecture? She, however, was so full of enthusiasm over his appearance (the sun had tanned his bald brow) and over his work outside that he could not discern the direction of her thoughts.

She led him away from the ateliers to the foot of the stairs, still talking volubly and louder than usual. Suddenly she stopped, turned and faced him directly and said in a low voice, almost a whisper: "The little Anna, she should not be alone. Ask her to take a cup of coffee with you. That would be very nice of you."

Again he wanted to escape. Were the two women conspiring to force him out of his solitude?

"You know, of course, about her friends, Suzanne and Bernard?"

"No," he said.

"Bernard killed himself. It has been eight days now, Suzanne has gone back to Grenoble to be with her family. Little Anna is alone and naturally quite sad!" Madame Hélène dug into the square pocket of her black smock and asked: "Do you have money for two coffees?" She pulled out a handkerchief and wiped her nose.

He said without moving that he did and that it would be nice if Madame Hélène would join them but she protested that she must finish dinner and find a way of digging out a twenty-franc piece for the little grandson who had stuck it into the window sill. He would find Anna in the still-life room.

Without taking off his raincoat, Nebraska walked through and put away his water colors and brushes on the shelf from which two weeks before he had taken them. The atelier was empty now and without sound. He walked through to the still-life room. In the center, her back toward him, the plump curve of her cheeks showing beyond the small ears, Anna sat gazing at a squash and two eggs. She turned when she heard his steps and smiled pleasantly when she saw who it was. "Look," she said, holding out her sketch pad. "It's lurid no matter what angle you draw from." They regarded the studies and laughed. He was surprised, after Madame Hélène's speech, to find her so cheerful and apparently unchanged. Certainly she would love a cup of coffee—if he had any money, she didn't. They pretended to fight over who should open the door and once across the courtyard who should open the big green doors to the street. Finally, because she had opened the first, she consented to his opening the second.

In the street she said: "You must let me walk on the outside. Next the street." He explained that in America young ladies walk on the inside toward the buildings.

"America, bah!" she said but in a good humor. "Besides it's silly to have such a rule."

"It's because the Elizabethan houses hung over the street and the person walking on the outside was liable to be hit with refuse thrown from above," he explained. "Then too, because the horses splashed mud."

"And here the man gives the woman his left arm, to have her near his heart and to leave his sword hand free to draw and protect her."

"In any case," he said, "you're on the wrong side."

"Do you mind?" she asked gravely. She was walking on the curbstones like a child, balancing, and stepping down occasionally when she could not maintain her balance. "I don't like for people to get between me and the curb."

No, he didn't mind. He was delighted that the conversation was so trivial. During the coffee and the walk back they did not mention Bernard Lévy and the fact that he had killed himself.

In the weeks that followed, the classes went on as before, and if many of the students knew about the suicide no one mentioned it. On sunny days the Académie was almost empty but in rainy weather or on cold days the ateliers were full again. Now in the spring no one could take the work seriously and even the models seemed restless and more bored than usual. Nebraska no longer tried to avoid Anna, who still followed him about like a shy child following a department-store Santa Claus. Whether from fear of her or of himself he did not know, but he did not want to be alone with her. For that reason he never stood now, during the breaks, at the door of the Académie from which he could see the plaque with the engraved legend of the fallen student. Anna, though, seemed quite satisfied merely to sit next to him and draw from the same model and to tease him when his perspective was off.

They were sitting thus, side by side, one cold morning in late May. The fire was popping in the potbelly stove and rain was dropping heavily on the skylight. The model before them was a handsome lad with strong nose and cheekbones, a Hamlet haircut, and a square beard that outlined his prominent jawbone and chin. It was a good face to draw, easy to catch a likeness of, and excellent for oils. Students had crowded in from the next room where the fat Negro woman they had drawn all winter was stretched out in a comfortable but impossible pose. Everyone was working and there was only the sound of the fire, the rain, and of the charcoal scraping on paper and canvas. Suddenly the model, who had not twitched a muscle, deliberately turned his head.

"*Ich habe keine Uhr,*" he said in a deep German voice. "*Um welche Zeit gehen Sie fort?*"

For a moment the room was silent. Then regaining his pose he asked in good Swiss French what time it was, that he was probably the only Swiss person in the world who did not have at least one watch.

Several people told him the time and the pencils again sounded on the tightly stretched canvases. Nebraska himself was measuring the distance from the model's nose to his bearded chin when he saw out of the corner of his eye Anna lean forward as though with a stomach cramp. He watched her hide her face in her hands to try to conceal that she was shuddering.

"Anna!" he said softly.

She shook her head.

He waited a moment, his fingertips still poised against his canvas. Anna without standing completely up made her way between the stools and easels. When he reached her in the still-life room she was still shaking and the tears in her eyes were held back only by the long lashes.

"What is it?" he asked in English, then in French.

She shook her head from side to side. "*Rien. Rien.* Nothing." She tried to move away.

He pocketed his pencil. "Let's go get some coffee."

She nodded and walked ahead of him to the vestibule where they put on their coats. Madame Hélène seemed to be not at all aware of their presence or departure, but when Nebraska turned to shut the door he caught her bright eyes regarding him, if not with encouragement or approval, then certainly with understanding.

He did not ask Anna again what the matter was. She walked ahead of him, on the curbstones, and when she had to step down into the street she turned and tried to smile. "I am so silly," she said as though talking about her lack of physical balance. But she continued, first in English which suddenly deserted her and then in French: "If I know the person is a German or I know he is going to speak German, then I'm all right and it doesn't bother me. It's when someone speaks it suddenly, when I do not expect it, that is what makes me tremble all over."

"What are you talking about?" He honestly didn't know.

"The model."

Nebraska realized then that the model had asked a question in German. "But he's Swiss!"

Anna shook her head. "It's silly," she said apologetically. "But I can't help it. I had been sitting there so close to him, studying him so carefully. Not even suspecting that he was sitting there thinking in German!"

In the dark little café they sat quietly for a long while, until finally she was no longer trembling and could look at him again without embarrassment. "It always makes me think of the night in 1942 when they were rounding up all the Jews. My father had already been sent away and my mother was working in the hospital. In the middle of the night a neighbor from downstairs who had a key to our door woke my little sister and me. 'Hurry,' she said, 'they are here.' My sister and I climbed out onto a roof through a toilet window and when they went upstairs to get us, the woman's husband helped us climb down into the alley."

Nebraska drew designs in the spilled coffee on the table and asked without looking up: "How old were you?"

She had been nine and her sister five. It was July, but it was a cold night. They had been afraid to be out in the dark streets and they were afraid to go to any of their friends' houses because they had been told not ever to say where they lived or where any of their friends lived if the Germans ever asked. They had run by back streets down to the Seine and all night they had walked along the embankments below the street on which the Nazi patrols were cruising. When the cars passed, they hid under bridges and for a while they had slept under Pont Alexandre III. At dawn they were on the Ile Saint-Louis and there was a man in a white trench coat looking down the steps to the river. They were almost to the top of the steps, intending to ask his help, when he suddenly spoke, evidently to another man, in a *urinoir* set into the quai. He had used almost those same words the model had: "*Um welche Zeit gehen Sie fort?*"

She and her sister had run past him and down the rue Saint-Louis. When they looked back the man was coming toward them, fast. She had not cried and her sister had not but they knew they were caught. Then suddenly an old, old woman with two huge baskets, who must have been watching them, stepped out of a doorway and screamed: "Ah there you are, you lazy idiots. What do you mean hiding from me? Here, take this basket." And as though they were going over to buy some coal they had, the three of them, walked away from the confused German.

"Thirty thousand Jews were caught that week and packed into the Palais de Sport on Grenelle. That was when Bernard and his family were taken."

"Ah, you knew Bernard before the war?"

"He was the only one who was left. Out of all my schoolmates, he was the only one still alive." She spoke quite matter-of-factly. "You knew he killed himself?"

"Someone mentioned it." Nebraska did not look up. "I was sorry to hear."

She was evidently not convinced or concerned. "Nobody cared. Nobody understood him. Not even me or Suzanne. Suzanne least of all."

"Does anybody know why?"

"He had a cake of soap, you know."

With a real effort Nebraska prevented himself from saying: "But he didn't use it." Instead he raised his eyebrows to question.

"His entire family was taken the same night we got away. They were shipped from the Palais de Sport to concentration camps. His two sisters were sent out in one group, Bernard and the rest of his family in another. He and his mother and father were shipped to the same concentration camp. Bernard was working there in the soap factory and he knew the day his parents were killed so he saved a bar of the soap they were in. We tried to make him throw it away but he wouldn't. He kept it with him all the time. He had it in his hand when Suzanne found him dead."

During the long silence, when the only sound was from distant taxi horns, Nebraska absently traced with the coffee a little two-wheeled toy car on the table. Anna twisted her head to see it better. "That's for children!" she complained. "The kind you pedal."

"Yes," he said, still not looking at her. When he did look up she was laughing. "Do you know why I like to walk on the curb?" she asked.

Her moods seemed to him to change as fast as those of a child and certainly her mind darted childlike from subject to subject.

"Before they carried my father away, my little sister and I used sometimes to be very frightened. We were so silly. We didn't know what of, but we would cry. Then he would take us in his arms and the three of us would sit together in a big chair and he would tell us

that someday we would be walking down the street and a great big
car would stop and we would get in and we would travel and travel
and then we would be in America and there would be plenty of everything to eat and plenty of coal to burn to keep warm. So after that
my little sister and I always walked on the curb one behind the other
so we could jump into the car when it stopped."

Nebraska considered for a long time before he spoke and when he
did his heart stopped beating and choked in his throat. "Would you
like to go to America?"

It was a simple question, but from the solemnity of his tone and
the sudden agitation of his entire body, they both knew what he was
asking and the commitment he was making.

For a moment she looked frightened and uncertain whether to
speak or not. Finally, deliberately casual, she asked: "What will you
do there?"

"I'll probably teach art in some small Midwestern college."

"But you don't know anything about art." She was deeply pre-
occupied and did not seem to know what she was saying. If Nebraska
had looked closely he might have recognized that her lips were trying
to say yes, she would like to go to America but that her sad eyes and
querulous brow were asking: "Me? Anna? Grown? Going to America?
Married?" She had had to dream, as a child dreams, too long to grow
up suddenly into a real world where love and food and warmth were
possible. Her face turned furious in the effort to speak but she could
say nothing.

"That's true. I know nothing about art." He was breathing now,
momentarily relieved that she had not answered his proposal immediately and without contemplation. Until this hour he had not admitted, even to himself, how close he felt toward her, and it would
take time to give up entirely all his fears and suspicions of women.
He hoped she would give him a few days before saying definitely
that she would like to go with him to America. He concentrated
studiously on his words: "Perhaps though I can teach them one thing
I've learned here and that's a sensible attitude toward art. And maybe
I can create, even in just one room, a place where one needn't be
embarrassed by talking about painting and by taking it—as, for instance, Bernard did—as a serious part of living. It would have meant
a great deal to me when I was growing up to have had such a place."

"Bernard did take it seriously," Anna said. "He used to sit in here
by the hour reading newspapers. Whenever he found anything about

rebuilding Germany or about what he called fascist-tactics in America, he would put it aside and plan for weeks the faces he was going to draw on it."

"I thought he drew on newspapers because he didn't have money enough for paper."

"Money!" Anna said the word evidently louder than she had intended, for she leaned over and her voice was an intense whisper. "Money. You think that's what produces art. You can't separate money from art, and money from morality, and money from politics. That's what's wrong with all of you Americans. But you can separate morality from politics and art from both. Art in one isolated room, indeed!"

The words, which were obviously Bernard Lévy's, sounded ridiculous in Anna's childish voice, but the reference to the isolated room which Nebraska had mentioned in a moment of sentimentality was her own, and the sarcastic tone was her own, and to these Nebraska listened with his old wariness of women. Then had she been playing with him merely to laugh at him? Defeat froze slowly over his eyes which stared without blinking. "Let her laugh," he thought and seemed surprised when she did not.

The silence which separated them now was deep and for five minutes they sat without speaking, each in his own inalterable world.

Finally, quite abruptly, Anna stood up. "It's dark in here," she said, tightening the raincoat belt and making her waist as small and chic and ladylike as possible. But when she walked across the café it was in the heavy tread of a woman already old and weighing two hundred pounds.

"It's strange to realize," she said outside, "that the war is truly over and that I don't really want to go to America." She was holding her head tilted and rather proudly, as women do when they have defeated themselves. She did not need to call his attention to the fact that she was no longer compelled to walk on the curbstone, and, unless that was what accounted for the slight trace of smile on her face, she herself did not seem to be aware that she had chosen to walk on the inside near the buildings, like a young lady.

Whatever it was about them that Madame Hélène observed as they came through the huge green doors and across the mossy courtyard, she did not say directly. For a moment she sat in the oblique sunlight, sad as a toad, and waited for the heavy doors to click shut against the outside noise.

WALLACE STEGNER, *as boy, as student, and as teacher, has lived widely over the U.S.A., studying, instructing, and writing at such universities as Utah, Iowa, Wisconsin, Harvard, and Stanford. He has published numerous novels and collections of stories, his last book being* Beyond the Hundredth Meridian, *a life of Major Powell, the first man to go down the Colorado River in a boat.*

THE CITY OF THE LIVING

FROM MADEMOISELLE

At a certain moment he looked around him and was overcome by a feeling almost like terror at how strange this all was.

Not even the international familiarity of washbowl and water closet, not even the familiar labels of pill bottles on his table or the familiar carbolic reek of disinfectant could make him quite accept the fact that this was happening to him and his son, and in this place. The darkened room next door was real to him, and this bathroom with its iron shutters open to night and the mosquitoes, but their reality was an imprecise reality of nightmare. It was hard to keep from believing that under the ghostly mosquito net in the next room lay not his son but someone with a strange face, or no face at all; and that in this tiled cell sat not himself but some alien enduring an ordeal by light and silence.

Outside the window, across the tops of the palms whose occasional dry clashing was the only sound he heard, were the unseen minaret from which the muezzin had cried the hour of prayer at the oncoming of dark, the unseen mud houses of Moslems and Copts, the fluted lotus columns, the secret shine of the Nile, the mud flats spreading toward the rims that guarded the Valley of the Kings. Against his windows the ancient dark of Egypt sucked like the vacuum created by wind under a lee wall. It made him conscious of the beating of his heart.

Turning from the outside dark and the soft clash of palms, he listened at the bedroom door, opened it and slipped in. He could not see the face but only the vague shape under the net. Yet he thought he felt the fever through sheet and net and three feet of air, and when he slipped his hand under to touch the boy's forehead he felt how tentative and fearful a gesture that was.

The luminous hands of his watch showed only one thirty-five. More chloromycetin at two. He was tempted to get the thermometer and see if the heavy dosages since noon had brought the fever down at all. But it wouldn't be fair to wake the boy. He needed the sleep— if it *was* sleep.

Back in the bathroom with his eye to the narrowing crack of the door he watched the sickroom gather its darkness. The netted bed retreated, the shiny bathroom was restored to him, with the vacuum of night at its windows. He stepped out onto the narrow iron balcony, and as he did so something crashed and scrambled in the top of a palm on a level with the rail, almost in his face. Fright, and the thought that whatever it was had been crouched there looking in at him, froze him there; and he heard first the pound of his heart, then a small rustling, then silence, then the mosquitoes gathering with a thin whine around his head. Whatever had been among the palm fronds, a rat or monkey or bird, was quiet. And there was no sound from the town either, not even the bark of a dog.

Above him the sky was the rich blue-black he had seen in fine Persian rugs, with the Milky Way a pale cloud across it and many brilliant dry stars. He thought of shepherds watching their flocks by night and Arab astronomers among the cumbersome stone instruments of their observatories, and he looked for lights but saw only a mysterious red glow like the cigar end in the blackness beyond the Nile, where the City of the Dead had extended in the time of ancient Thebes. He had no idea what it might be. It hung there as enigmatic and watchful as himself on the balcony or his stealthy neighbor in the palm top. After a time it faded. Though he looked hard he saw not a glint, not a reflected glimmer of a star from the river sweeping the town's flank.

A fumbling from behind him sent his hand instantly to the light chain above the washbowl, and as he turned the boy came in, blinking and stumbling, holding up his pajamas with one hand, and groped numbly past and dropped on the toilet and was wracked with explosive diarrhea. With a groan he put his elbows on his knees and held his head in his hands; to his father's scared eyes he looked fatally skinny, his arms pipestems too weak for the big man's hands. His face when he lifted it was puffed at the eyes with fever and sleep but wasted to skeleton thinness along the jaws.

The father held his hand against the boy's forehead to help the weak neck. The forehead was very hot, the lips glazed like agate. "Better now?"

The boy bent his head but sat still. In a moment he was wracked again. His stench was almost unbearable. Holding his breath against the smell, the father shook down the thermometer and put it to the agate lips. They opened obediently, even in the midst of a spasm— how touchingly obedient he was in his sickness—and the two sat on, the boy absorbed with his inward war, the father unwilling to say anything that might demand his son's strength for an answer. Sitting on the tub's edge, he removed the thermometer and read it. A hundred two and a half, exactly what it had been since the night before.

He saw the boy's boy foot and skinny leg, the Achilles' tendon standing out from the heel, the long body jackknifed in an agony of cramps, and the feeling that came over him was like the slipping of a knot or the fraying of a rope that had held something secure until then. He looked with horror at the way the disease had wasted his son in barely more than a day, and he drew into his lungs the inhuman, poisonous stench of the sickness. That was the moment when it first occurred to him that the boy could die.

The thermometer rattled in the glass of germicide as he put it back. With an arm around the skinny shoulders he helped the boy back to bed, where he fed chloromycetin capsules one by one into the obedient mouth and after each one offered the water glass to the enameled lips. He smoothed the sheet and turned the pillow. "Now back to sleep," he said.

For a moment he continued to stare fascinated at the wasted face, the closed eyes. He was talking to a nothing, to a silence. The boy had folded back into the bed with a little groan and had moved nothing but his lips since. The act of drawing the sheet up to his chin was so intimately associated in the father's mind with the last act of a deathbed that he ground his teeth. In one fierce grab he caught a mosquito that had got in under the net. Then he tucked in the edges and tiptoed out. Looking back from the door he felt guilt in him like a knife for all the things he might have done and had failed to do. There was a darkness in his mind where this only child had been. Already the memory of him was all but unbearable.

In the harsh light of the bathroom he felt trapped like an animal in a flashlight beam. The sight of his own trapped eyes glittering was an intense, dreamlike plausibility until he realized that he was looking into a mirror. Darkness would have been a relief, but not the darkness outside. He had a fantasy that the light and the unreal solidity of brass and porcelain, himself and the stench of his son's sickness might all be sucked out into the night and lost. It was better to cling to this, to his separateness and identity, for somehow, at some totally unbearable crisis in his dream of personal pain and loss, he had a faith that he might waken and be saved.

In the end he found occupation in the routines of a sickbed vigil. He scrubbed the toilet and dumped disinfectant in it, washed his hands a long time in germicidal water, drove the mosquitoes out of the room with the DDT bomb. But those jobs, treat them as carefully as he might, lasted him no more than twenty minutes. Then he was back again, caught between the light and the darkness, the only wakeful thing in all the dark city of Thebes except for the animal in the palm top and whoever was responsible for the red glow across the river. The thought of the light raised sudden goose flesh on him, as if grave robbers or vampires prowled there.

After a while he got out his brief case and set about bringing his correspondence up to date. That morning he had filled his pen at the hotel desk. At the same time, as if with foresight, he had picked up a new supply of hotel stationery. He had Egyptian stamps folded into a slip of waxed paper in the brief case. He comforted himself with his own efficient work habits, and he cleaned up several things:

A note to the American Express in Rome returning some unused railroad tickets for refund. A letter of recommendation for a junior colleague trying for a Government job. A word to his secretary saying briefly that illness had changed their plans so that it didn't look as if any mail should be sent to Athens at all. Send anything up to December first to Rome.

The three stamped and addressed envelopes gave him such satisfaction that he wished he had fifty to do. He addressed the two picture post cards he found and wished there were more. But if no more cards and no more details to clear up, then a letter or two. With a sheet of stationery before him and his full pen in his hand, his eyes a little scratchy from sleeplessness, he considered whom he should write to. Not instantly, but over a period of seconds or minutes, it occurred to him that there was no one.

Not for the kind of letter he wanted and feared to write. He had no family closer than cousins, strangers he had not seen for years. His wife was worse than a stranger—an enemy—and though he owed her reports on their son's health and a monthly alimony check he owed her no more than that, and from her he could expect nothing at all. Friends? To what golf companion or bridge companion or house-party acquaintance or business associate could he write a letter beginning, as it must, "My son is in the next room very sick, perhaps dying, with typhoid . . ."?

He put his hands palms down on the desk and held them there a moment before he crumpled the sheet on which he had written the date and a confident "Dear . . ." *Dear who? I am sitting in the bathroom of a hotel in Luxor, Egypt, at nearly three in the morning, and I am just beginning to realize that here or anywhere else I am almost completely alone. I have spent my life avoiding entanglements. I breathed a sigh of relief when Ruth left. The only person I have cared about is this boy in the next room, and he is half a stranger. You should hear the machinery creak when we try to talk to each other. And I have to go and bring him into this rotten country where everybody is stuffed to the eyes with germs . . .*

On a new sheet of paper he wrote, lifting his face while he tried to remember the figures, certain statistics on Egyptian public health he had read somewhere.

Trachoma .... *97 per cent*
Bilharziasis .... *96 per cent*
Syphilis .... *26 per cent*
Tuberculosis .... *? per cent*
Cholera?
Typhoid?

It seemed important to have them down. He wished he had clipped the newspaper or World Health report or whatever he had seen them in. For a moment's flash of memory he remembered Giles at the Mahdi Club in Cairo saying to him quietly as they waited for the boy to wipe off their bowls and hand them back, "Wash your hands in carbolic water after we go in. This kid's got a beautiful case of pinkeye." He saw himself quoting Egyptian health statistics to head-wagging men who dropped in to the office or to people who listened to him around grate fires. It's no joke, he heard himself say. Practically every Egyptian you see is one-eyed, and they've all got bilharzia worms. All the filth diseases, of course—cholera and typhoid are endemic. It was typhoid that nearly got Dan, you know, in Luxor.

He listened, hypnotized by the even world-traveled voice, and raised a hand to brush away a mosquito and smelled the germicide, and said to himself that if the hotel doctor and the manager hadn't been decent Dan might be in a fever hospital right now instead of quarantined in this wing. He went back over his remarks, polishing them, and came to the word "nearly" and stopped.

The thing that he wanted to think about or write about as an adventure of the trip, successfully passed, rose up before him suddenly and blanked his whole mind with fear. Controlling himself, forcing the discipline, he picked up papers and one by one put them away in the brief case, refolding the stamps into their waxed paper. Under some odds and ends of folders he found the return envelope of an insurance company. A premium due. With relief, escaping, he opened the checkbook and unscrewed the pen and wrote the check neatly and tore it out. It lay in his hand, a yellow slip like thousands he had written, a bond with the order and security of home. A checkbook wasn't any good here, of course, but in any good international bank on proper identification and after a reasonable delay, it would . . . they had to know who you were, that was all. Just a little of the machinery of security, a passport, letter of credit, the usual identifications, maybe filling out a form or two . . .

Robert Chapman, age forty-two; nationality, American; place of birth, Sacramento, California; residence, San Francisco; education, B.A. University of California, 1931. Married? Divorced. Children? One son, Daniel. Member Bohemian Club of San Francisco, Mill Valley Club, Kiwanis. Property: one-twelfth of a cooperative apartment house on Green Street, week-end cottage Carmel, certain bonds, Oldsmobile hard-top convertible. Income around eighteen thousand annually. Contributions: the usual good causes, Community Fund, Red Cross, Civil Liberties Union, the Sierra Club's conservation program. Insurance program the usual—forty thousand straight life plus annuity plan.

I believe in insurance, he told the smooth-faced, gray-haired man across the desk. Always have. My parents bought my first policy for me when I was ten, and I've added to it according to a careful plan from time to time. I've known too many people who were wiped out for lack of it. I carry a hundred thousand-fifty thousand on my car, plus all the rest except the freak stuff. Personal injury, property damage, collision, fire, theft—they all pay, even if you never have to collect on them. Real property too. My place at Carmel has comprehensive coverage, practically every sort of damage or accident—window breakage, hail, wind, fire, earthquake, falling airplanes. I carry a twenty-five-dollar deductible personal-property floater. It's indispensable, when you're traveling especially. Protects you wherever you are. Same with my health-plan membership. Anywhere in the world I'm protected on my medical and hospital bills.

For that matter, he said, smiling, my physician gave me some good advice before this last trip. He prescribed me a little kit of pills— penicillin tablets, empirin, sulfaguanidine, dramamine against travel sickness, chloromycetin and aureomycin in case we got sick anywhere out of reach of medical care and had a real emergency. I can tell you we were glad of that doctor's advice when we got way up the Nile, in Luxor, and my son Dan, in spite of inoculations and everything, came down with typhoid. . . .

Neatly he folded the check and folded a sheet of stationery around it and the premium notice and put them in the return envelope, halfirritated that they made it so easy. A man didn't mind addressing an envelope.

His face was greasy with sweat. Restlessly he rose and washed in cool water, looked at his shadowed eyes in the mirror, turned away, slipped into the bedroom and eased into the chair by the bedside. The breathings and the spasmodic small twitchings made the boy under the net seem utterly vulnerable somehow. In the dark, his eyes tiredly closed, he sat for an indefinite time seeing red shapes flow and change in the pocket of his lids. Among them, abruptly, coned with light like an operating table, appeared his son, dead, openmouthed, horribly wasted, and he awoke with a shudder and found his shirt clammy and his lungs laboring at the close air. His watch read twenty minutes to four.

To wait until four was impossible. He opened the bathroom door wide to let in light, and brought the capsules and a glass of water. The boy awoke at a touch, his dry lips working, his eyelids struggling open, and lifted his head weakly to swallow the medicine.

"How do you feel now? Better?"

"Hot," the stiff lips said.

"Would you like a damp towel on your eyes?"

"Yes."

The father slipped the thermometer into the boy's mouth and went into the bathroom. The disease-and-disinfectant smell was newly obnoxious to him as he wrung out the towel. When he returned the boy had turned his head and the thermometer had slipped half out of his parted lips. With a swift searching of the emaciated face the father took it and held it to the light. At first the hairline of mercury would not reveal itself, and helpless anger shook him at people who would make an instrument nobody could read. Then he caught the glittering line, twisted carefully. Its end lay at 102°.

Down half a degree? Suspiciously he felt the forehead, but it was wet from the towel. The dry, slippery hands were still hot. But less hot than they had been? Or had the thermometer slipped out long enough to make the reading inaccurate?

Starting to take the temperature again, he stopped, and then he deliberately pulled down and tucked in the net. He did this, he knew, not out of reassured hope but out of cowardice. His heart had leaped so at that half degree of hope that he did not want to find he had been wrong. In a minute or two he was back in the bathroom, sitting at the table before his worthless and undemanding brief case and the little pile of cards and envelopes. He felt exposed to all the eyes of Luxor; once, after the Long Beach earthquake in 1933, he had seen a man shaving in such a bathroom as this, with the whole outside wall peeled away, and he stood there before the mirror at ten o'clock on a Sunday morning, with his suspenders down and the world looking in. It was a ridiculous image. But he did not get up and pull down the shutters and close himself in.

His eyes were full of the pattern of square tile three feet before his eyes. He found that by squinting or widening his eyes he could make the squares begin to dissolve and spin in a vortex of glittering planes and reflections. When he wanted to he took hold again and forced the spinning to stop and the tiles to settle back to order. Then he narrowed his eyes again and watched the spinning recommence.

Some level of mind apart from his intense concentration told him, without heat, that he could hypnotize himself that way, and some other layer still deeper and more cunning smiled at that warning. He held the squares firmly in focus for a minute, stretched them, let them spin, brought them back under the discipline of will and eye, relaxed again and let them spin, enjoying the control he had of them and of himself. It was as if the whole back of his head was a hollow full of bees.

He was facing the blank wall and his neck was stiff. His head ached dully and his eyes were scratchy in the tired light of the bathroom. The muezzin was crying prayer again across the housetops of Thebes, the open shutters gave not on darkness but on gray twilight, and at the end of his reach of vision, against the sky palely lavender, he saw the minaret and the jutting balcony high up, and on the balcony the small black movement. He could distinguish no words in the rise and fall of the muezzin's cry; it was as empty of meaning as a yodel.

Stiffly he stretched and rolled his stiff neck. His left arm was sore from yesterday's reinoculation; the memory of his night's watch was like a memory of delirium. He felt pleased that it had passed, and looked at his watch. Five-thirty. His mind groped. And then the pretense of awakening to sane reality fell away, and he stood in the pale, overtaken electric light sick with shame at the trick he had played upon his own anxiety and responsibility. What if he had missed a time for the pills?

His flesh lay like putty on his bones. In the membranes of his mouth he tasted all the night's odors—the smell of sickness that was like no human or animal odor but virulent, deadly and obscene; the smells of the things one relied on to stay alive, the disinfectant smell and the DDT spray. His arm was a swollen, throbbing ache. He belched and tasted bile, and bent to hold cool water in cupped handfuls against his eyes. When he took a drink from the carafe the chlorine bite of the halazone tablets gagged him. The effort, the steady, unrelieved, incessant effort that it took in this place to stay alive! He looked at his haggard, smudged face in the mirror and he hated Egypt with a kind of ecstasy. Finally, unwillingly, he went through the bedroom door.

Daybreak had not come here. The room was the vaguest gloom, yet when he turned on the light it had somehow the look that closed rooms have in daylight, a dissipated air like that of a room where a drunkard sleeps through the day. Shaking down the thermometer as he stepped across the rug, holding his breath to hear anything from the bed, the father approached and bent across the net. He bent his head lower, listening. "Dan?" he said. Then in a convulsive panic he tore away the net, knowing his son was dead.

The boy slept peacefully, lightly, his breathing even and soft. His forehead was cool to his father's shaking hand. There was no need for the thermometer: the fever was not merely down but gone. In his jubilation the father picked up the little vulture-headed image he had bought for the boy the first day and tossed it to the ceiling and caught it. He moved around the room, retrieved a horsehair fly whisk from the floor and hung it on the dresser post, eased the shutter up a little way for air. The boy slept on.

Outside the hall he heard soft sounds, and going quickly to the door he surprised the hall boy depositing his shined shoes. The white eyes flashed upward in the face of the crouching figure, the bare feet moved respectfully backward a step, the long, belted robe swung like a dancer's.

"*Saeeda*," the soft voice whispered.

"*Saeeda*. Can I have tea?"

"Only tea?"

"Fruit, maybe. Oranges or plantains."

"Yes. How is your son?"

"Better," the father said, and knew that this was why he had opened the door, just for the chance of telling someone. "Much better. The fever is gone."

The floor boy seemed genuinely pleased. After all, Chapman thought, he probably hadn't liked the business of being quarantined and inoculated any better than anybody else. To an Egyptian typhoid normally meant, if not death, several months in a fever hospital and a long, feeble convalescence. This one now was smiling and delighted as he went away on his sliding black feet. He should have a good tip when they left—a pound note at least.

The muezzin was still calling. It seemed an hour since he had begun. Returning to the bathroom, Chapman stood in the French doors looking out at the town. In the gray light the palm tops lay as quiet as something under glass. The yellow paths of the back garden were quiet geometry below him, and he smelled the authentic, wet-mud smell of Egypt. Across wall and roofs was a yellow reach of river, with a narrow mud island lying against the far shore, then a strip of taffy-colored water, then the shore itself and the far lines of palms indicating villages or canals, and clear beyond, binding the edge of the pure sky, the long desert rim that divided habitable Egypt from the wastes.

Over there was the City of the Dead, where the light had been last night and where he had half imagined ghouls and vampires, jackal-headed men with square shoulders, obscene prowling things. It was innocent and clean now, and the river that when they first came had seemed to him a dirty, mud-banked sewer looked different too. It came down grandly, one of the really mighty rivers, pouring not so much out of the heart of the continent as out of all backward time, and in its yellow water it carried the rich silt for delta cotton fields, the bilharzia worms to infect the sweating fellahin at the ditch heads, then sewage and the waste, the fecundity, the feculence. The river was literally Egypt. Lotus and papyrus, ibis and crocodile, there it came. Incomprehensibly, tears jumped to his eyes. He went into the bedroom and got the binoculars and returned to watch.

The blurry yellow haze sharpened into precise lines as he turned the knob. Beyond the mud margins he saw a line of people coming, leading donkeys and camels loaded with something, perhaps produce for the market. He saw them carry burdens from beast to boat. Farther down, a family was bathing in the river, a woman and four children, who ran and splashed each other and launched themselves like sleds on the water. The thought of swimming in that open drain appalled him—and yet why not? Probably it never occurred to them that the river was polluted. And it was a touching and private thing, somehow, to see the brown-skinned family playing and see them so close and unaware and yet not hear their shouting and laughter.

The far bank was fully alive now. Two feluccas were slanting out across the current of the river, and the river seemed not so much to divide as to unite its two shores. Birds flew over it, camels and donkeys and people clustered at the landing places, the feluccas moved, leaning farther in a riffle of wind. All the Nile's creatures, as inexhaustible as the creatures of the sea, began to creep and crawl and fly. Safe, relieved of anxiety, reassured, rescued, Chapman watched them from his little cell of sanitary plumbing, and on his hands as he held the binoculars to his eyes he smelled the persistent odor of antiseptic.

It was ridiculous, but they made him feel alone and timid. He wished his son would awake so they could talk. He could read aloud to him during the time he was getting stronger; the thought occurred to him as an opportunity he must not miss.

"What a damned country!" he said.

Watching the river, he had not noticed the movement at the far corner of the garden below him, but now as he swung the glasses down he saw there one of the ragged, black-robed boys who raked and sprinkled the paths every day. He had taken off his turban and was kneeling, folding it back and forth until it made a little mat beside one of the garden water taps. On this he knelt, and with a reaching haul pulled the robe over his head. He wore nothing else. His ribs were like the ribs of a basket, his shoulder blades moved as he turned on the tap.

Steadying the glasses against the jamb, Chapman watched the brown boy's face, very serious and composed, and as it turned momentarily he thought he saw one milky blind eye. Face, neck, shoulders, arms, chest and belly, and carefully the loins and rectum, the boy washed himself with cupped handfuls of water. He washed his feet one after the other, he bent and let the tap run a moment over his head. On the yellow ground a dark spot of wet grew.

He stood up, and Chapman stepped back, not to be caught watching, but the boy only pulled on his robe again. Then he knelt once more on the rug of his turban and bowed himself in prayer toward the east.

Chapman kept the glasses steadily on him. The intense concentration and stillness of the bent figure bothered him obscurely. He remembered himself staring at the tiled wall and did not like the memory. Moreover, the shame of that evasion was mixed with an irritated, unwilling perception that the boy kneeling in the garden was humble, touching, even dignified.

Dignified? A skinny, one-eyed boy with a horizon no wider than the garden he worked in, with one dirty robe to his back, and for a home a mud hut where the pigeons nested in the living room and the buffalo owned the inner, safest, most desirable room? The image of Egyptian workmen he had seen picking up the dirt-caked hems of their robes and holding them in their teeth for greater freedom of action stood in his mind like stiff sculpture.

And yet the praying boy was not pathetic or repulsive or ridiculous. His every move had been assured, completely natural. His stillness made Chapman want somehow to lay a hand on his bent back.

They have more death than we do, Chapman thought. Whatever he is praying to has more death in it than anything we know.

Maybe it had more life too. Suppose he had sent up a prayer of thanksgiving a little while ago when he found his son out of danger? He had been doing something like praying all night, praying to modern medicine, propitiating science, purifying himself with germicides, placating the germ theory of disease. But suppose he had prayed in thanksgiving, where would he have directed his prayer? Not to God, not to Allah, not to the Nile or any of its creature-gods or the deities of light. To some laboratory technician in a white coat. To the Antibiotic God. For the first time it occurred to him what the word "antibiotic" really meant.

The distant rim was light-struck now. The first of the morning buzzards came from somewhere and planed across the motionless palm tops. It teetered and banked close so that Chapman saw the curve of its head like the vulture-headed image on the boy's bed table: the vulture head of Mut, the Lady of Thebes, the Mother of the World. They eyed each other with a kind of recognition as it passed. It had a look like patience, and its shadow, passing and returning over the garden, brushing the ragged boy and the palms and the balcony where Chapman stood, might have seemed a threat but might also have been a kind of patrolling, almost a reassurance.

IRA WOLFERT has carved himself a distinguished niche in the ranks of American journalists in his eighteen years as a newspaperman in New York and abroad. He was awarded the Pulitzer Prize for his dispatches from Guadalcanal. His first novel, Tucker's People, *was acclaimed by critics as the best portrayal of America's depression years and as the outstanding novel of 1943. His second novel,* An Act of Love, *was a best seller in 1949, while his* Battle of the Solomons *and* American Guerrilla in the Philippines, *factual non-fiction accounts of Asiatic warfare, were selections of the Literary Guild and Book-of-the-Month Club respectively.*

THE INDOMITABLE BLUE

FROM ESQUIRE

When Wes Olmstead was a little boy growing up along the Susquehanna and wearing a tie on his Sunday shirt that knocked against his knees, his grandfather took him visiting to a nearby farm that sported a cock o' the walk, one of the breed called Arkansas Traveller.

The true gamecock always fights to the death, its opponent's or its own. Since it fights with knifelike spurs and each blow is a murderous one and literally dozens of them are exchanged in the wink of an eye, it is seldom that even the winner is good for anything after the affair is settled. The loser, of course, has its head cut off and is thrown to hands that will boil it for soup, and the winner frequently might be better off for the same fate. But there are lucky ones and, if a winner shows the trueness of its breeding, if it stands up to its death without turning tail or showing fear in any other way, it is permitted to live on—provided, that is, it can—and enjoy the company of hens and the peace of the barnyard.

That was what had happened to the Arkansas Traveller Wes Olmstead saw. It had had what is considered a very long career for a fighting chicken, winning in two mains and one hack fight, and then its owner had decided it could not win any more and was letting it live out its crippled years in retirement.

At that time Wes had never even heard of gamecocks. He saw a
runty little thing, weighing about four pounds, with a body that
seemed to be built of rubber bands. Its feathers were a dirty-white in
color and were of scant length and had no pride or sheen. Its comb
was broken and one wing dragged almost to the ground and it had
soured-up wrinkles in its wattles and one sour red eye, the other having turned milky in blindness.

But his grandfather warned Wes against playing in the barnyard.
He said a chicken like that could break a grown man's leg with one
blow of a naked foot, and didn't enjoy anybody coming up to it or
its hens, even to make friends. Keep away, and keep away from his
lady friends, the old man said.

Wes listened solemnly, his blue eyes round and big. But as soon
as his grandfather went into the house to talk business with the
farmer, Wes began edging toward the barn. Grampa Fred never
exaggerated, even for purposes of entertainment. However, Wes'
father, who was Grampa Fred's son, always did and while Wes perhaps would not have gone so far as to test whether that little old bit
of chicken could actually break his leg with one blow of its naked
foot, he was eager to learn, out of loyalty to his father, whether it
was true Grampa Fred never exaggerated or just never had been
caught at it.

Wes was going to study the chicken carefully. Then, if the situation warranted, he would let himself into the yard and shoo the
chicken out of it and chase it up to the house and past the window
where Grampa was talking business, pretending it had got out by itself and he was trying to get it back in. But the lad didn't get a
chance to do any shooing. All he could do was study, for when he
came around the barn and within sight of the poultry yard he saw
a hound dog digging and shoving its way stealthily under the wire
that fenced the chickens in.

The dog looked over its shoulder at Wes. But it didn't run. It let
out a soft, blood-curdling snarl, and Wes stopped short. Shooing an
angry chicken was one thing, but shooing an angry dog was another,
and this was a big dog, a sixty-pound dog, trained down razor fine.
Besides it had a burry coat, even around the head. That meant it was
one of those killer dogs that lived wild in the hills, terrorizing deer
and foxes and livestock and even bears. Wes stood motionless. He
hoped only that the dog would not attack him. After a moment, the
dog seemed satisfied that so meager a squirt as Wes was at the time

could do it no harm. Perhaps it had some memory of playing with children on some farm somewhere in its puppyhood before it had taken to running wild. Anyway, it resumed digging.

Wes watched fearfully, and so did the hens. The boy had no confidence at all in what his grandfather had said. If he had dared to move, he would have run crying for help. But he didn't dare, and the hens didn't either. They huddled together and fluttered their feathers and squawks and drawls dribbled out of their mouths in a suppressed way as if they were afraid loud protests might make the dog more ferocious than it was, and the cock made no sound at all.

It was the cock that tore it for Wes, finally. The little battler, standing higher than the hens with its neck stretched but looking not nearly so burly, had placed himself in front of its womenfolks and kept its head turned so that its one sour red eye might remain fastened unblinkingly on the dog. But its beak opened now and then and its throat worked dryly and soundlessly and it looked so brave there and lorn that it broke Wes' heart. He turned and twitched desperately into the barn, hoping to find a pitchfork or a hoe that he might use to fend the dog off while shouting for Grampa and the farmer.

But he had hardly got into the barn when he was out of it. A terrible sound in the poultry yard had driven into his ears like a fist and had made him gasp and come running. The dog had squeezed itself under the wire fence and had stood a moment, picking out its dinner and gathering itself to spring upon it, and all the hens had wrung their feathers and squawked and screeched at once, making the sound that had brought Wes out of the barn barehanded.

The cock, however, remained silent. It ran forward with long, strong, limber leaps, and the dog lunged for it. They closed like lightning clashing. It was as dazzling as that. The dog was an experienced and successful killer. It lashed out more quickly than a snake, fangs first, body flung sideways to block its victim's escape and bring its own powerfully trampling hind legs into play.

But the chicken was even faster. In the immeasurable instant between the start of the dog's lunge and its completion, the cock— running head-on to—had changed direction, side-stepped and run completely around the dog and come up on its back. At one moment Wes saw it disappearing in the dog's dripping white teeth and at the next he heard the dog's teeth click on empty air with a shattering sound and saw the cock standing on the dog.

The cock seemed only to be standing there. It seemed only to be fluffing itself out and flouncing a bit. But that was because its legs were moving so fast that the human eye could no more see them than it could see buckshot spraying from a gun. Watch the target and you'll see the shot. Wes watched the target and saw it twist and turn, first to the right and then to the left, and snap its hindquarters in a wide, wild fling as one might snap a whip, and he heard time after time the heart-catching sound of teeth clicking on empty air.

There was no other sound. At the start, as the cock had run forward, one of the hens had uttered a queer, drawling, almost envious sigh and then had fallen silent and the others had remained silent. The cock made no sound and only teeth spoke for the dog as it strove to bite the sour-eyed little murderer off its back.

Then the dog howled and rolled over howling to squash the chicken under it. It was sixty pounds against four, but where the dog had gone over howling it came up shrieking. For trying to squash that chicken was like trying to squash a bale of tight-wound barbed wire with one's naked flesh.

Finally, the dog remembered the hole it had made under the fence. It flung itself through it. The chicken, scraped off the dog's back by the fence, rose into the air with an indignant squawk and the dog ran shrieking on its two front legs. It could not run far. Its hindquarters trailed after it like a rag. The cock had broken its back.

The hens paid no attention to the dog's death agony. The danger was over. They moved out of their cluster and began to scratch the ground. The cock moved away from the fence. It walked high on its legs and its milky eye stared blind and bland and its red eye glared and it looked furious enough to speak. Finally it did speak. It let out a crow so ragged and squeaky that it was like a child's imitation of one. It scowled about, as if to say: *Anybody else want to try?* Then, as all roosters everywhere always have done, it began to search the ground for tidbits for the hens and when it found one it picked it up and dropped it and clucked in invitation and the hens came running and shoved him aside and, without a by-your-leave or a thank-you, ate the tidbit while the dog, brought down at last by a broken back, lay shuddering at the end of a bloody froth and waited for death.

"If a man had the strength of a gamecock," Grampa Fred told Wes on the way home, after the dog had been shot, "he could take his fist and with one blow drive it so deep into an oak tree he'd have to split the tree to get it out."

But it wasn't the strength of it that had captured Wes. It was the willingness to stand up against fear of death. There was no use telling him it was due to a lack of imagination, an inability to comprehend death. He had seen how fearful of death the hens had been. They had comprehended death very well and hens do not have any more imagination than roosters.

"It comes to them from all the way back, from the Egyptians," explained Grampa Fred. "Thousands of years ago, the Egyptians took chickens and bred it into them to be killers, and men in every generation since then have kept the strain pure."

The explanation didn't explain a thing, as far as Wes was concerned. How can you breed something "into" a living thing? You could put a bearing into a wheel. You could put a ball into a bearing. You could put steel into a ball. You could put alloys into steel. But you couldn't put anything living into a living thing. Oh, no. To do that you'd have to have the secret of the greatest mystery of all. You'd have to be able to create life.

Whatever the Egyptians had bred "into" the gamecock had had to be there all the time.

It had had to be in all chickens. Breeding had just brought it out and had made it dominant in one where it had remained recessive in others.

To Wes it was a host of wonders. One wonder was what bringing out in itself a willingness to take its death had done for the fighting chicken. It had given a screechy bit of feathered fluff extraordinary strength. It had turned one of the most helpless of creatures—a creature whose place in the scheme of life was to be easy eating—into a remarkable fighting machine.

But an even greater wonder was this: If breeding could bring out such marvelous talents in a chicken, why couldn't the chicken bring it out by itself unaided? It was there, in a Leghorn, for example, in a Plymouth Rock, a Rhode Island Red, a Buff Orpington, in any breed of chicken you could meet in any poultry yard anywhere—there, buried in the living matter, waiting to be brought out and used. Why, at the moment when a killer dog was coming for a Leghorn's throat and the Leghorn was searching in its deepest flesh for its furthest resources—why then should the Leghorn be unable to use what was in its own living matter to save its own life? But the Leghorn was unable, Wes knew. The gamecock could and the Leghorn couldn't. The gamecock brushed aside the instinct for self-preservation and so preserved himself, and the Leghorn embraced the instinct for self-preservation and so failed to preserve himself.

As Wes grew older, the question became more pressing for him. For if it was true of chickens, then it must be true of men. Who knew what resources lay buried in the living matter of living men, waiting only to be brought out and used? If nothing can be put into life but something can be brought out from it, then the whole future of man on earth must lie in him now waiting to make its appearance, as once man himself had lain waiting in the animal that had stirred in the primeval slime to give him birth.

But the answers Wes got to his question about the chickens were only words without meaning. Breeding, he was told, bloodline, pure strain, stock, heredity. Finally, he stopped asking his question. But there was something there, he knew, something vast and knowable that might change the whole fate of man, that might bring man's future into the present.

Others seemed to know it, too. It was thought disgusting and even perverted or at least insensate and inhuman to breed gamecocks, but they bred them. It was illegal to fight chickens in the United States, but they fought them in every state. Children were terrified of the bloodshed, but their fathers brought them to it by easy stages, first buying them bantams who fight but cannot tear the flesh under the feathers, and getting them at last to the real thing.

In every corner of the United States, almost in every county, there were doors that you, a stranger, could knock upon in the middle of the night and show a chicken and find a fight. The rich would fight you for $50,000 on the side, or five cents, whatever you had, and the poor would fight you for whatever they had.

For, rich and poor, they all knew that there was something there, something vast and knowable. But what it was nobody knew. Nobody that Wes ever met, anyway.

Twenty years is an exceedingly long time to keep a memory alive, particularly when there is nothing to renew it, and Wes had nothing. He never saw a cockfight. He hardly ever saw a live chicken, even of the peaceful variety, and it all—the scene itself and the great question and the meaningless answers it had provoked—faded from him and was no more than leaves that had once fallen from a tree long since chopped down and made into boards.

But one Saturday night he was celebrating. He was fresh out of

Prize stories 1955; The O. Henry Awards.
Selected and edited by Paul Engle and
Hansford.Martin. - Garden City, N.Y.: Doubleday & Company, Inc., 1955.
313 p. : 22 cm.

1. Short stories, American.

college then. He had come to Grand Island as a stranger, knowing no one except his own family, which had moved there from New York while he was still at school. Only a few days after his arrival, while he was still wondering what to do with the remaining years of his life and filling in his time with a job in the edge-tool firm in which his father was a partner, he suddenly discovered what he would do with his life. He would be a businessman.

It came to him as love does, in a wave that mounts sweepingly, to crash with a storm of certainty. The firm had made an incautious purchase of a carload of brass sheets and the management could think of nothing better to do with it for the time being than put it away in inventory. It was none of Wes' business. He was very far from being in management, but an idea had come to him nevertheless. If Grand Island Traction could be induced to use tokens instead of cash as fares on its streetcar lines, the brass sheets could be turned into a profit immediately and a nice little sideline would have been opened.

Wes had got no encouragement in his fathers' firm. They were all edge-tool men there, not the least interested in the streetcar business. The young man worked his idea out by himself in his spare time. He learned about short rides and headways and the riding habits in the various neighborhoods serviced by Grand Island Traction. He studied the company's rate history and rode its lines with a stop watch, noting down time lost in collecting fares and making change. When he had convinced himself that Grand Island Traction would make money by selling tokens to be used as fares, he took his idea right to the top, to George Hicking himself, the company's president.

When Wes began his presentation, his legs were shaking under him. But when he finished they were not. Hicking liked the idea. He wanted to try it out on the Bellefair-Davenport Avenue line right away. From Hicking's office, Wes walked on calm legs to Sharp Street and the Chingo Iron Works. They, he had discovered, owned a Drucie & Bollard coiner which could manufacture the tokens from the brass sheets more cheaply than anything his father's firm owned.

It had been very difficult getting in to see George Hicking. But there was no trouble at all in getting to see John Eldred Chingo, the general manager of Chingo Iron Works. John E., as he was called, was a loud, rich, arrogant man, in the prime of his youth at thirty-two, and ordinarily it would have taken Wes ten years to reach the point where the man would have said hello to him. But now Wes was armed with the name of Hicking. He used it cleverly and John E.'s door flew open. Finally the matter was arranged, and on Wes' terms. Chingo Iron Works would manufacture, Grand Island Traction would merchandise, and Wes, through his father's firm, would supply and manage.

Now all that remained was to get started. Perhaps you have seen a sub score a brilliant, unexpected touchdown. If you've watched him run eagerly to line up for the kick for the extra point and get the marvelous, thrilling game going again, you will understand how Wes felt. But there was no place to run. It was Saturday. The negotiations had lasted well into suppertime. He would have to wait to resume the gorgeous game of business until Monday morning.

Those were long hours in between. Wes decided he would waste them celebrating. He had luck. It turned out that John E. also wanted to waste the Saturday night. John E. knew the town and was a figure in its life. The two young businessmen had a grand time. It was a struggle to carry all the liquor they took in, but their success in the struggle was one of the pleasures of the evening.

In the years since he had been paralyzed by terror of a killer dog who had not been able to frighten a chicken, Wes had grown tall and had developed a powerful body. Now there was a radiance in it. He was in love at the moment—with business, with Grand Island, with life itself and all the world that housed it. It was like a sun in him, making his presence vibrant, and wherever they went—the Hotel Plawell, Frank's, The Spa, The Chicago House—there were men who could recognize the radiance in Wes and came up to warm themselves in it. They had known such moments of love themselves. In their tired hearts they were aware they would never know them again, and they went up to John E., whom they knew, and greeted him in order to meet Wes, whom they did not know, looking at Wes as men might look at their own homeland after they have been exiled from it.

It was a sad parade, but for a long time Wes had no idea it was taking place. He was too busy feeling wonderful and drinking drink for drink with John E. There was a boozy, bellowing hubbub everywhere they went. One by one, occasionally in pairs or groups, the hungering faces came steaming out of it to hang for a moment before Wes and yearn at him. But Wes was as blind as any other lover. It never occurred to him that the men were there for any other reason than to ingratiate themselves with an important personage, the general manager of the Chingo Iron Works.

Then, late, when they were in The Chicago House, a heavy-set red-faced man shouldered up to the bar where John E. and Wes were standing. John E. nodded to the man. Wes had not yet drunk so much that he couldn't notice the nod. He turned and waited with a smile to be introduced. But the man had drunk too much. The wires connecting him to his hands and feet seemed to be awash. Messages were getting garbled. Some of them were not getting through at all. He brushed right past John E. without returning the nod and took Wes' hand and began to shake it up and down.

"May I shake your hand?" the man asked.

"All right," replied Wes.

"I'd like to shake your hand," the man said.

"You are shaking it," Wes pointed out.

The man was too intent on looking at Wes' face to realize it. He kept on shaking Wes' hand up and down, and Wes kept on smiling. "I want to congratulate you," the man said at last.

"What for?"

"Because you're young."

"It was nothing at all, really. But, thank you."

A look of pain came into the man's eyes. "You're young, you're young," he cried. "That's a great thing to be," he added tremblingly.

"Always has been," said Wes.

"Always will be," the man agreed.

"Let's have a drink on that."

The man looked embarrassed. "I've had a drink, I imagine."

"Have another," suggested Wes.

The man debated with himself for a moment. "I think I will," he decided finally. "I'm entitled to it. I was young myself once."

"Who wasn't?"

"You weren't," the man said suddenly. His voice turned bitter. "What did you do to deserve that luck?"

"What luck?"

"You're young now. You've never been old."

For a moment he glared at Wes, his face baleful with envy. Then he turned to John E. They were old friends and he greeted John E. cordially, but at the same time he showed his broad, thick back to Wes with aggressive rudeness.

A cloud passed over Wes' deepest self where a moment before only a shining sun had been. *You're young, you're young.* The cry rang on in Wes. Men can't use the word "love" to each other, and that was why the man had said "young," Wes felt. *You're in love, you're in love,* the man had really said, Wes knew, *I was in love myself once.* And then he had said bitterly, *What did you do to deserve the luck of never having fallen out of love?* It had put into Wes the only sadness a lover can know. He had had an intimation of the mortality of his own love. He felt a grim, wringing pity. If love does not last forever for anybody else, perhaps it would not last forever for him either.

The man had gone away. John E., who sipped his whiskey raw from the shot glass, was lifting the glass to his lips for the hundredth time that evening.

"I want to make some money," said Wes suddenly.

"Why?" asked John E.

"Why not? It's not Sunday yet."

John E. thought a moment. He could not see what that had to do with the subject. "Have a drink," he said at last.

"I've got a drink," replied Wes.

"Have another."

"I'd rather make some money."

"Why?"

"Why not? It's not Sunday yet."

John E. stared somberly. They were back where they had started from. "What do you suggest?" he asked.

"I don't know. You know this town. You suggest."

"It's night. It's night, m'boy," said John E.

"I know. I wish it was morning."

Wes' voice was so full of gloom that John E. was touched. "It's morning," he cried. "It's morning, Wes. It's after one."

"I know, but I mean real morning. I mean Monday morning. Can't we make some money somewhere tonight?"

John E. looked thoughtful. "Well, there's the bank around the corner on Brackett Street. You might break in and rob it."

"No, no, no," cried Wes indignantly. "I mean do business. That's what I mean—do business, make money."

"Are you thinking of waking somebody up in the middle of the night and selling him a bill of goods?"

"I wouldn't mind. I wouldn't mind anything as long as it's action, it's productive, it's not just killing time."

"We could go to Mama Mamie's."

"What's there?"

"Crap, poker, roulette, blackjack, faro, anything you like."

Wes put his hand in his pocket. He had only one bill left. He didn't dare look at it. No doubt they'd cash a check for him, he thought eagerly, as they went out into the street.

In addition to the standard gambling-house equipment, Mama Mamie's maintained in its back yard a pit where mains were staged regularly every Saturday night and where those who could not afford to maintain stables of cocks to pit against other stables could bring their individual chickens and match them in hack fights when the night's main had been concluded.

The night's main was over and the hack fights had begun when Wes and John E. arrived. For, of course, the moment he learned of the pit Wes could not be held back. The whole scene of his childhood and all the questions it had provoked in him later came flooding back to him, and charged his mind so turbulently that he didn't want to delay a moment, even to cash a check. But John E. was no cock fancier. He insisted on delaying at the bar long enough to buy a bottle to take downstairs with them. "We'll need it as a chaser for the blood," he explained sourly.

Mama Mamie's, named after Mamie Stumplebock, who was known among the blades as Mamie Stopaclock, partly because of her name but chiefly because of her dour, meaty face, was across the river on the outskirts of Bellefair. It occupied a limestone house with a high stoop. The roulette and crap tables were kept on the parlor floor, and poker and whist and faro and other card games were run in individual gambling rooms on the upper floors. The cockfights were held in a shed that covered the back yard and was led to by an iron spiral staircase going down from the parlor floor.

The pit was covered over on its bare earth with a sawdust that was so dirty it was difficult to distinguish from the dirt under it. The shed was walled around with slabs of roofing tin that had once been painted white but were now scaling and rusty. The spectators bunched themselves on pine boards laid in tiers, reaching back from the pit level almost to the roof. When the two young businessmen arrived, the crowd had formed a dense, hot, rumbling mass around the pit. There was no room to sit. Everybody stood shoulder to shoulder, packed so tight in the places where a better view was offered that they were pressed sidways and, when somebody let out a yell, somebody else was sure to be pushed out of place.

The chickens awaiting their turn to fight were kept in wooden-slat crates in the open space under the stands. There Wes realized how slender are the threads binding together a man's view of what is real in the world and what he only thinks is real, what is happening and what he only thinks is happening. The chickens were making the ordinary peaceful cluckings and drawlings. In that gloomy, rocking air, pressed down with men and roofed over by their noises on the pine planks above, it seemed insane.

Then he saw something that excited him. The Arkansas Traveller, popularly called the blue, is a favorite among the American breeds and it would be hard to find a cockfight that did not feature several. But when Wes saw one in its crate, he was astounded and delighted. It was as runty as the one that had performed so heroically in his childhood. It had the same sourness in its red eyes and wattles. It might have been the same chicken, except that it had two eyes and an unbroken comb and neither of its wings dragged.

Wes was carrying the bottle John E. had bought. He pointed it at the blue. "I like that one," he announced.

"Do you like him for five?" a voice above him asked.

Wes turned. A huge man was lowering his face toward him in-gratiatingly. Wes was six feet tall, but he had to look up to see the man's face. "I like him for any amount you got in mind," Wes said.

"Wait a minute," interrupted John E. "You don't know what he weighs."

"Do you like him for fifty?" the man asked.

"He doesn't even know who he's matched against," protested John E.

"I don't give a damn if he's matched against a locomotive," said Wes.

"Give me a drink," said John E., and took back the bottle.

"A hundred?" the giant asked.

"A hundred," agreed Wes.

"Dollars?" asked the giant.

"What do you think, bees?"

"I think dollars."

Wes put his hand in his pocket. The huge man laughed. "Don't pay me now. Wait till your blue is dead."

The man went away, and John E. looked at Wes sardonically. "Have you got a hundred?" he asked.

Wes took the bill out of his pocket and looked at it. "Oh, sure," he said.

"Count again. That looks like a five to me."

"Well," explained Wes, "the rest of my money is still temporarily in that guy's pocket."

John E. took a long drink out of the bottle and handed it over to Wes. "You'd better hold on to it," he said. "Your creditor is seven feet tall."

Wes took the bottle, and laughed. "If my seven-foot creditor tries to get tough," he said, "I'll sick my chicken on him."

There were three hack fights before the blue Wes had bet on was brought into the pit. At Mama Mamie's, the chickens fought Sol McCall's rules, with a referee in the pit and a handler for each cock and the gaffs on the birds' spurs round from socket to point. No cutting could be done with such gaffs, and no slashing. It was a fight to the death with ice picks.

The handlers wore heavily quilted leather gauntlets. When they released their charges, the cocks were twelve feet apart. They did not have to prod the bird or goad or urge it. They just had to hold on until time was called, and then let go. Letting go was like pulling a trigger. The chickens bounded at each other unhesitatingly.

All the thinking and maneuvering that was done took place in the time it takes a strong, long-legged chicken running at top speed to cover between seventy and eighty inches. The cocks were on each other before a man could draw a deep breath. They clashed breast to breast, necks arched, and rose into the air to bring their legs to bear in an attack called the shuffle. It was an odd name for such an attack. During a shuffle, their legs moved so fast they seemed not to be moving at all. The eye couldn't follow the movements. But something in each chicken seemed to follow them, estimating each movement, predicting its course and measuring its consequences, parrying, feinting, thrusting.

Wes got a clear look at the first of the fights. The chickens ran at each other, leaped, hung in the air for an instant, and then came down. The fight was over. One chicken had come down dead and the other had come down to strut in a circle around it, and flap its wings and crow.

Wes' eyes blinked. They couldn't stop blinking. "By God," he said, "what happened?"

John E. shrugged disdainfully. This was not for him. It was too gamy for his taste.

"You see the whole thing," said Wes. "But you have to think back over it and piece it together to find out what you saw."

"Aah." John E. made a gesture of contempt. "It's just reflex action."

There was a pause between matches to enable the crowd to get its bets down. There were no bookmakers. The spectators bet among themselves, scurrying to watch the chickens weighed and armed and hooded, and then running out from under the stands to get a vantage place around the pit, waving money over their heads or waving their empty hands and crying out the amount of their wagers. Through it all Wes stood lost in the sight he had seen.

He remembered how the chickens had gone for each other. His mind had stopped over that sight a long time, he realized now— now that the fight was over. But while the fight had been taking place, Wes had been living in ordinary time and the fight had rocketed through it in a nearly single blast of speed. But something in him, as in the chickens, had not been living in ordinary time, had kept step with that nearly single blast of speed. During the fight, he had felt like a man standing on a platform and watching a train hurtle by too fast to be anything but a blur of light. But there had been another man in him, he understood now, who had ridden along beside the train, slowing its motion by that act, transforming its motion into another extraordinary kind of time.

For the sight of the chickens going for each other had stopped Wes' mind for a long time. Both chickens had run in the same way —eager, utterly silent, wide-legged, spurring the earth under them in their long, strong, limber leaps, their fierce eyes calculating relentlessly, their necks stretched forward malignantly, their beaks out like faces held for a kiss. What had stopped Wes' mind was that not only were the two cocks acting alike, but each was acting like the blue he had seen destroy a dog and it had seemed to him that they were one thing and had always been one thing, without change, chicken succeeding chicken, breed succeeding breed, land succeeding land, century succeeding century, all without change in any important particular. In the thousands of years since the Egyptians had first started breeding them, there had been billions of gamecocks. But it had struck Wes that somehow, in some unfathomable way, they had all really been only one. It was a very queer notion and it had made him feel very queer.

The chickens, Wes remembered, had been feinting each other on the way in. He could remember having seen the feinting. Then they had leaped, breast to breast, each trying to get above the other, but not too far above.

The leap had had to be calculated precisely. That, no doubt, was what the feinting on the way in had been about. If one could be induced to leap too soon, the other could get under it, and the one on top would have only back feathers to stab while the one underneath would have the heart. But if there was too long a delay in leaping, if the timing was a thousandth or a hundred thousandth of a second off, that would be fatal, too. The chicken that had leaped first could plummet its weight down from above and knock its opponent off its feet. It would be the equivalent of breaking a swordsman's arms before killing him. But the prize both strove for was to jump just high enough to have the enemy's head at the other's feet—where the gaffs were.

There was no way to count how many separate ruses each cock had tried on the way in to get the other to miscalculate the timing and direction and height of its upward leap. But Wes had a sensation of having witnessed hundreds of separate little slippery shifting twists, as numerous as bubbles in a seethe and as uncountable. Yet something in each of the chickens had counted the bubbles and measured and judged them and acted in response to the judgment arrived at, and, when they had leaped, they were equal. They rose to the shuffle simultaneously. Neither had been able to outwit the other.

But the ruses had continued during the rise. That was when the fatal move had been made. One chicken had made a slight turn during the rise, providing an opening. The other had pounced. But it had pounced into a trap. The pounce had brought it too close to the first chicken's wing. Apparently the first chicken had calculated on that, for it was waiting. In mid-air, rising to shuffle, it was waiting, and it brought its wing down on its opponent, depressing its opponent's rise and accelerating its own, and when it passed its opponent's head it drove the gaffs into the brain.

What had happened in a split flash took a long time of careful recollection for Wes to piece together. He looked at John E. John E. was drinking from the bottle. Wes waited until John E. put the bottle down before he asked his question.

"What was that you called it?"

"What do you mean—what was what I called what?" growled John E.

"Reflexes?"

"What else?"

"I don't know what else," Wes said.

"Reflexes," said John E. "That's all it is, only reflexes."

"I've got reflexes, too," said Wes shyly.

"Chickens got no brains," said John E. "Only reflexes."

Chickens were fighting again, but Wes did not see them. Nor did he see the fight after that. Too many men had closed in around and in front of him and he didn't bother to crane over their heads, or shove an opening through their shoulders. It wasn't that the deaths in the pit had disturbed him. Chickens dying were just meat on the table to him. Besides, if all is one and one is all, then one cannot die. Its death cannot have the meaning of death. Nor can its torment have the meaning of torment.

No. He did not look because the fight he had seen was still alive in him. It seemed to him to have an enormous significance. But what that significance was he could not say. It lay just out of reach in his mind. The reflexes in the chickens were the same as in all chickens. They were the same as in a highly trained, skillful fighting man. The same reflexes were buried in him, as in all chickens, as in all men. The same freedom from the instinct for survival lay buried in him. The only difference was that it had been brought out into the consciousness of the gamecock while in him, as in all other chickens and all other men, it had remained smothered in the unconscious, blind, mute flesh.

Freedom from the instinct for survival. It was the future. It was eternal life. For this freedom could not come to a mortal creature unless it also had freedom from death. The gamecock had it. It was aware that all life is one and one life is all and that therefore there can be no death for one until there is death for all. Wes had it, too. All men had it. The difference was that the gamecock had its freedom from fear in its consciousness where it could use it to command its energies, while men had it buried in them, waiting, waiting, waiting for some interminably delayed future in which by some mysterious process it would be brought out.

Suddenly the men in front of Wes stooped forward and remained that way, bowed and breathless. Wes could see the pit. "You blue there," he heard. "Come on, you blue." Far down, below the rows of bowed, breathless shoulders was a bronze-colored Pierce Shuffler and opposite it was the Arkansas Traveller on which Wes had bet the giant man a hundred dollars he did not have.

It was apparent that the first shuffle was over. One of the bronze's eyes was a red blear, and the other was hanging down its cheek on a string. The blinded chicken did not back up. It stood turning its head from side to side, maneuvering to poke a way through the sudden dense darkness that had fallen upon it and striving to discover where the agony within its flesh was coming from.

The Pierce Shuffler's maneuvers were confusing the blue. It stood, watching tensely, trying to make up its mind what nature of attack this could be. Then it became uncertain whether to strut or make an attack of its own. The bronze was not attacking. Therefore the fight was over, and an instinct clamored within the blue to make a victory strut around its fallen foe. But another instinct was clamoring within the blue at the same time, a warning that the fight was not over yet and that it might be fatal to strut.

There was no instinct of death in either bird, and the bronze kept trying to maneuver out of its blindness and the blue Wes had bet on kept shifting tensely from one posture to the other, from the strut position to the attack position and back again, all in flicks and twitches so rapid they were blurred.

"I lose."

The words in Wes' ear were hardly more than a grunt. Wes turned his heaed. The huge man was standing beside him, staring at the pit. He had worked his way through the crowd to get near Wes and make sure his hundred dollars wouldn't escape, but now he saw that he would have to pay. "That dog," he muttered, "that lemon." Suddenly he put his head back and roared at the bronze who had been continuing to try to poke a way through its dead eyes. "The hell with your eyes. Use your legs, you stupid son of a bitch."

It shocked Wes, but he looked away. The chickens had made a move. The blue had begun dreadfully to move forward. It had made up its mind to attack. It came circling.

Then, even more dreadfully, the bronze made up its mind to

attack, too. It was helpless and hopeless. But if one is all and all is one and death has no meaning, helplessness has no meaning either, nor does hopelessness, and stubbornly, with infinite care, the bronze turned to get at the blue, gauging the blue's movements by the slight, feathering sounds it was making. As the bronze turned, it gathered its legs under it stealthily, feinting all the while, now this way, now that way, now with its head, now with its wings and shoulders, now with its feet. Its head swung from side to side. The eye hanging out on a string swished against its cheek. The crowd had become so still that the little swishing sound could be heard.

The blue swung hard. The bronze heard and started to rise, and the blue pulled back. Frantically, the bronze realized it had been outmaneuvered and tried to pull back. The blue had calculated the bronze would do precisely that. When it saw it happening, the blue rose. The bronze was pulling back and the blue had no trouble getting above it. It exploded its buckshot legs against the bronze's head.

A great terror seized Wes. It came from awe. The bronze was down on its side. A nerve in the back of its head had been severed, and it was paralyzed. It couldn't even move away from its own blood. Its tongue had fallen out. The tongue lay in the clotted dirt of the pit, and the bird couldn't even put its own tongue back into its own mouth.

The bronze's handler thought it was dead and came forward, knife ready to cut off its head. Then he saw the bird was not dead, and he withdrew. That was the rule of it.

No animal took its death unless trapped. But the fighting chicken had to. It had to show men that it could be done. The fighting chicken could not be pushed into a fight, or goaded into it, or attacked into it. It had to seek it out. Otherwise men could not be sure that the gamecock, in its normal conscious self, had prevailed over the instinct for self-preservation.

Nor could the cock allow any of its other instincts to divert it from its meaning to men. If it had been kept away from hens until emaciated for one—as it usually is when in training for a fight—and was then given the choice between a hen in rut and a cock, it had to choose the cock. If it was starved for food, and was given a choice between corn and a cock, it had to choose the cock.

Not a bull nor a lion nor any man who surrenders to his own instincts will stand up to something that has taught him by inflicting pain that it is stronger than he is. It will do so in madness, but not in resolution. When retreat is open, the bull, the lion and the man, however unwillingly, must turn tail and retreat. But the gamecock must not. Otherwise it could not show its meaning to men.

It is a spirit in them. The true gamecock guards its spirit as a mother guards her young, at all costs, at the cost of its own life. The mother guards her young because she knows in some inscrutable way that, individual though she herself may be, still in some inscrutable way her children are her only future. So with the gamecock. It had learned in some inscrutable way that its spirit was its future and must be protected as young are protected. And when it demonstrates this so that men who see may know, its owner can know that he himself has a place among the long line of knowers, a line stretching back through the generations for more than three thousand years when men first bent themselves to keep the spirit of the gamecock supreme above the instincts of its flesh.

So the handler withdrew his knife and backed up when he saw that the blinded and paralyzed bronze was still alive. He wanted the owner's place on the line of men stretching back to the time of the Pharaohs.

It made the giant man come out of a despair, and clutch at hope. "Come on, you bronze bum," he bellowed.

The bellow struck Wes like a blow. But he couldn't loosen the terrifying grip of awe in him, and he couldn't take his eyes off the pit. The blue had begun its victory strut. It put one wing down and made a circle around the fallen body of its opponent. The bronze lay with its tongue in its blood, and the blue's wing dragged through the stillness with a scratching, fluttering sound. Its legs dug and scraped and flurried the earth of the pit. Its chest swelled like that of a man in triumph, and, like a man in triumph, it was about to stretch its arms and beat its chest and roar, and glare from its sour little red eyes.

But Wes could look only at the bronze. It wasn't surrendering. There was no death, so there was nothing to surrender to. It was paralyzed, but something in it wasn't. Staring, his eyes stretched with the awe that was like a terror in him, Wes felt he could almost make this something out. It was faint and blurred, but it was there —under the feathers, under the skin, deep, crouched in a jungle of exhausted, wildly bleeding organs and looking calculatingly through the bronze's blind eyes at the blue strutting around it. Suddenly it sprang. Wes could see it. It was the spirit of the cock. It dragged with it the paralyzed flesh in which it crouched, and aimed for the blue's heart.

Oh God, thought Wes, and closed his eyes.

A shout went up, and he opened them. The bronze was dead, spitted on the blue's gaffs. The blue was standing stuck in the bronze's heart, puzzled by its inability to strut. With a swift, bitter gesture, the handler pulled the bronze free and cut its head off and threw the body to the hangers-on who would boil it for soup.

Wes stood stunned. The irony of it had spitted him. The birds had torn themselves to pieces so that men who saw might know the greatness that lay buried in themselves. The one instinct that stood most intractably in the way of man's highest aspirations, that accounted for his meanest meannesses, his greatest greeds, his most destructive selfishnesses, that accounted for his fears, his hates, his lusts, his wars, for everything that stood in the way of his own future on earth, was his instinct for self-preservation. The chicken had destroyed itself to show that the instinct could be conquered.

The huge man was riffling through a roll of bills with one thumb. He was looking among fives and tens and fifties for a hundred. When he found it, he held it out to Wes.

Wes didn't take it. "You'd better keep it," he said.

"Didn't I have a bet with you?" the giant asked.

"You did," said Wes.

"Well, take it. I lost."

"You seem to need the money an awful lot."

It must be, Wes decided tremulously. The chickens had shown this man and he had looked, but he hadn't seen. He had seen nothing. The blue had torn the bronze to pieces for nothing. All the man had seen was himself winning or losing $100.

"That's all right," the huge man said. He still held the bill extended. "Won't be long before I'll get it back. Who do you like for the next one?"

"Put that money in your pocket," said Wes, "or I'll stuff it down your throat."

The giant looked at Wes, puzzled. "What's the matter with you?" he asked, and Wes struck out violently with a wild, roundhouse right.

But there was no room to swing. John E. had been cradling the bottle in his arms. He was jostled as people jumped to hold Wes and to hold the giant. The bottle fell and there was a loud crash, and John E. crashed with it, and another man slipped with a scream through the pine planks into the chicken crates below.

In the tangle, the giant could not be seen. "Where's that big guy?" Wes cried. "Where did he go?" He wanted to kill the man. If man couldn't see the way to his future even when it was tearing itself to pieces to show itself to him, how could anybody ever achieve it? He tried to bull his way forward through the crowd, and someone said, "Throw them in the pit," and a voice cried, "Gentlemen! Gentlemen!" and another cried, "Kick him in the shorthairs."

Mamie Stopaclock was running down the spiral staircase, a sawed-off baseball bat in her hands, and two men with cauliflowered ears ran behind her. "Pay the man his money, and throw the bum out," she shouted and the $100 bill was snatched from somewhere and lifted high to pass over a crowd of heads and stuffed into Wes' pocket while he bulled and thrashed and cried, "Where'd that dog go?"

He couldn't move. There were a dozen hands on him, holding him fast. "He's the enemy," he shouted. "He's the enemy of all human progress."

"You'll make progress," said Mamie Stopaclock, and the hands that had been pinning Wes lifted him and hustled him over the planks and up the spiral stairway and ran him, on legs that touched the floor only every now and then, through the foyer and there they clapped his hat on his head and pushed him through the door.

"Don't come back, you troublemaker," Mamie said, and the door slammed in Wes' face.

"I'll sick my chicken on you!" he shouted through the door.

Then a policeman had hold of his arm and was preventing him from throwing a rock through Mama Mamie's front window.

"Now, sonny," the policeman was saying, "if you don't do that, I won't do anything either.

"If you're quiet, sonny," the policeman was saying, "I can be quiet, too. Otherwise I'll have to make plenty of noise on your head."

Wes let go of the brick, making sure it would fall on the policeman's foot. The policeman hopped up into the air, and Wes walked away.

MAGAZINES CONSULTED*

ACCENT, Box 102, University Station, Urbana, Ill. AMERICAN MAGAZINE, 640 Fifth Avenue, N.Y.C. AMERICAN MERCURY, 11 East 36th St., N.Y.C. ANTIOCH REVIEW, 212 Xenia Ave., Yellow Springs, O. ARGOSY, 205 East 42nd St., N.Y.C. ARIZONA QUARTERLY, University of Arizona, Tuscon, Ariz. ASTOUNDING SCIENCE FICTION, 575 Madison Ave., N.Y.C. ATLANTIC MONTHLY, 8 Arlington St., Boston, Mass. BETTER LIVING, 230 Park Ave., N.Y.C. BLUE BOOK, 230 Park Ave., N.Y.C. CALIFORNIA QUARTERLY, 7070 Hollywood Blvd., Los Angeles, Cal. CAROLINA QUARTERLY, Box 1117, Chapel Hill, N.C. CATHOLIC WORLD, 411 West 59th St., N.Y.C. COL-LIER'S, 640 Fifth Ave., N.Y.C. COMMENTARY, 34 West 33rd St., N.Y.C. COSMOPOLITAN, 57th St. and Eighth Ave., N.Y.C. COUNTRY GENTLEMAN, Independence Square, Philadelphia, Pa. ELLERY QUEEN'S MYSTERY MAGA-ZINE, 570 Lexington Ave., N.Y.C. EPOCH, 252 Goldwin Smith Hall, Cornell University, Ithaca, N.Y. ESQUIRE, 488 Madison Ave., N.Y.C. EVERY-WOMAN'S, 16 East 40th St., N.Y.C. FAMILY CIRCLE, 25 West 45th St., N.Y.C. FANTASY AND SCIENCE FICTION, 2643 Dana St., Berkeley, Cal. GALAXY SCIENCE FICTION, 421 Hudson St., N.Y.C. GEORGIA REVIEW, University of Georgia, Athens, Ga. GOOD HOUSEKEEPING, 57th St. and Eighth Ave., N.Y.C. HARPER'S BAZAAR, 572 Madison Ave., N.Y.C. HARPER'S MAGAZINE, 49 East 33rd St., N.Y.C. HUDSON REVIEW, 439 West St., N.Y.C. HUSK, Cornell College, Mount Vernon, Ia. JEWISH HORIZON, 154 Nassau St., N.Y.C. KENYON REVIEW, Kenyon College, Gambier, O. LADIES' HOME JOURNAL, Independence Square, Philadelphia, Pa. MADEMOISELLE, 575 Madison Ave., N.Y.C. MASSES & MAINSTREAM, 832 Broadway, N.Y.C. MCCALL'S, 230 Park Ave., N.Y.C. NEW MEXICO QUARTERLY, Box 85, University of New Mexico, Albuquerque, N.M. NEW YORKER, 25 West 43rd

*The editors have decided not to consult the various collections of writing now being published in volume form at intervals through the year. *New World Writing, Discovery, Story* (in book form), and others, while desirable publishing ventures, do not seem to fall in the original category of periodicals on which this anthology was founded.

St., N.Y.C. PACIFIC SPECTATOR, Box 1948, Stanford, Cal. PARIS REVIEW, 8 Rue Garancière, Paris, France. PARK EAST, 220 East 42nd St., N.Y.C. PARTISAN REVIEW, 30 West 12th St., N.Y.C. PERSPECTIVE, Washington University Post Office, St. Louis, Mo. PRAIRIE SCHOONER, 12th and R Sts., Lincoln, Neb. QUARTERLY REVIEW OF LITERATURE, Box 287, Bard College, Annandale-on-Hudson, N.Y. QUARTO, 801 Business, Columbia University, N.Y.C. REDBOOK, 230 Park Ave., N.Y.C. THE REPORTER, 220 East 42nd St., N.Y.C. SATURDAY EVENING POST, Independence Square, Philadelphia, Pa. SEWANEE REVIEW, University of the South, Sewanee, Tenn. SOUTHWEST REVIEW, Southern Methodist University, Dallas, Tex. THIS WEEK, 420 Lexington Ave., N.Y.C. TODAY, 638 Deming Pl., Chicago, Ill. TODAY'S WOMAN, 67 West 44th St., N.Y.C. TOWN & COUNTRY, 572 Madison Ave., N.Y.C. UNIVERSITY OF KANSAS CITY REVIEW, University of Kansas City, Kansas City, Mo. VIRGINIA QUARTERLY REVIEW, One West Range, Charlottesville, Va. WEIRD TALES, 9 Rockefeller Plaza, N.Y.C. WESTERN REVIEW, State University of Iowa, Iowa City, Ia. WOMAN'S DAY, 19 West 44th St., N.Y.C. WOMAN'S HOME COMPANION, 640 Fifth Ave., N.Y.C. YALE REVIEW, Box 1729, New Haven, Conn.